He had aged since his last night with Deborah. The strain and insomnia of the last few days had left Kosov wan, tired looking and in a state of anxiety about the meeting.

It was a scheduled appointment, part of the arrangement with Lambert. Occasional get togethers on certain days, at certain times, in certain places. No phone calls. No letters. No contact in between.

He'd tried to time his arrival to the minute and had gone to elaborate lengths to shake off any possible shadow. It was a pathetic charade, he reflected, as he sat down on the bench near the boat lake. Eventually the assignation would be no secret to either side, but he still couldn't shake off the feeling that he was being watched, that invisible eyes were following him everywhere.

He sat waiting nervously, an insignificant, lone figure in a worn suit.

By George Markstein and published by
New English Library:

TRAITOR FOR A CAUSE
ULTIMATE ISSUE
FERRET

FOREWORD

The Anglo-American UKUSA agreement for the
clandestine sharing of secret intelligence between the two
countries was signed in 1947, and is so highly classified that
its contents have never been revealed to the British
Parliament or the United States Congress. It is still in force,
but not even its existence has been officially admitted. Its
exact terms and provisions remain top secret.

FERRET
George Markstein

NEW ENGLISH LIBRARY

I must acknowledge my debts to Captain .... and Captain
...., ferrets who have to be anonymous, and to my editor,
Jacqui Lyons.

First published in Great Britain in 1983 by Hodder &
Stoughton Limited

First NEL Paperback Edition August 1984

NEL Books are published by
New English Library,
Mill Road, Dunton Green,
Sevenoaks, Kent.
Editorial office: 47 Bedford Square, London WC1B 3DP

Printed and bound in Great Britain by
Cox & Wyman Ltd, Reading

0 450 05703 8

They were sitting at a table on the pavement of a Warsaw café. It was a warm summer's day and both of them were in shirt sleeves.

"When did you stop trusting people?" asked Yudkin, gulping the remainder of his glass of vodka. They were drinking Wyborov, a hundred per cent proof, and he'd already had too much.

"I trust you," murmured Zarubin.

"Then," Yudkin hiccuped, "you're either a fool or you're lying. And I know you're not a fool."

He reached over and grasped Zarubin's hand.

"I was only joking, my friend," he excused himself.

"Of course. I know that."

Zarubin disengaged his hand gently, so that Yudkin would not take offence. The important thing was not to annoy him.

Two militiamen strolled past their table.

"Why are you not drinking?" Yudkin suddenly demanded.

"But I am," Zarubin assured him, indicating his glass of vodka. He was still nursing his first drink.

"Please yourself," shrugged Yudkin. "I'm having another." And he poured himself a fifth glass.

"You see what an ugly thing it is, suspicion," he went on. "A friend drinks less than you do, and you start wondering why. Why is he not keeping up with you? Why does he want to stay sober?"

"I don't have a strong head," explained Zarubin. "I have to watch myself. I don't want to get picked up by your police."

Yudkin chuckled amiably. "Lies, lies, and more lies. But

no matter. It proves my point." He burped.

Zarubin was watching the militiamen who had stopped at a car parked by a lamp post. While one was walking round inspecting it, the other was taking down its licence number in his note book. Anywhere else they might just be two police-men writing out a parking ticket, but here it was more likely to lead to a computer check with the secret police, a scrutiny of identity files. This was the People's Republic of Poland, post Solidarity.

"Once you do this kind of work, you're infected," Yudkin was saying, oblivious of the café, the street, the militiamen. "It's like tuberculosis. Even if they say you are cured, you always have to check up."

"I think it's time we split," suggested Zarubin. He hadn't been keen on sitting here in the open, on display to the world.

"Why are you so nervous?"

"I'm thinking of you," replied Zarubin.

"Don't worry about me, my friend. I am above suspicion. It is me who suspects others. That is why I am so useful to you and your colleagues."

His speech had become slightly slurred.

"And you know how appreciative we are," pointed out Zarubin.

"Really?"

"Of course."

"And you would stand by me, if things went wrong?"

"You know that," confirmed Zarubin, uneasily.

"Actually, I believe you." Yudkin nodded to himself. "You. Not your people. Not the agency you work for. Not the President of the United States. They don't care a zloty for Yudkin. I don't think they'd lose a minute's sleep. But, curiously, you I trust."

"Why?"

Yudkin gave a sad little smile. "Perhaps because I am getting drunk. Perhaps I am getting careless." He frowned. "Tell me, why do you do this work? You are a clever man. You could earn much more money in a safe job in a nice office."

Zarubin glanced round to make sure nobody was listening. "And why do you do it?" he asked. "You have privileges, a guaranteed pension, special status. Why do you risk all that, and your life? Why do you pass us information?"

He wanted to add, why are you a traitor, but that would have been foolish. Yudkin tossed down his vodka. "I suppose," he said finally, "because I am infected. Like you."

They paid, and went their separate ways.

The next day Zarubin fulfilled his mission. He killed Yudkin.

It was after midnight, and as the doctor slowly drove down the narrow tree lined lane, he bitterly regretted his decision to take the short cut. He was exhausted and even though the car's headlights were on full beam, it was difficult to make out the twisting, turning track in the surrounding black gloom.

Then he saw him. Standing in the middle of the road a few yards ahead. A man in a yellow track suit, frantically waving his arms.

The doctor braked, sharply. The man ran up to the car, and knocked on his window.

For a moment the doctor hesitated.

A gaunt face with deeply set eyes, high cheek bones, and very short hair stared in at him. He was in his thirties, and was shivering.

"What's the matter?" asked the doctor, rolling down his window. "What's wrong?"

The man pointed in the direction the car was heading. "Lonn Donn." The pronunciation was hard, guttural. "Lonn Donn?" This time it was a question.

"You're a long way from London," replied the doctor. "Has your car broken down?"

The man's eyes were fixed on his mouth, as if he was trying to read his lips.

"Sovietsky Affitsyer," the man said, speaking rapidly. He paused. "Panagitye minye. Jolye nakhoditsya Sovietskoye Pasoltstvo?"

"I'm sorry," apologised the doctor. "I don't understand you."

They stared at each other.

"Do you need help?" asked the doctor.

7

"Lonn Donn."

"Don't you know any English?"

"Lyotchik," said the man, pointing at himself. "Voyn-naplenni. Zek." He repeated it. "Zek." Again he indicated himself. "Sovietsky Affitsyer."

He was shaking with cold, and seemed to be pleading now.

"I don't understand," the doctor muttered with frustration. "Are you Russian?"

He got a blank look.

"Sovietsky?" tried the doctor.

"Da, da," cried the man.

"And you're trying to get to London?"

The man nodded energetically. "Lonn Donn. Da Passolstva."

And he pointed at the empty passenger seat.

"Well, I'm sorry, but I'm not going that far," said the doctor. He saw the bafflement in the man's eyes. "Parlez-vous Français?"

"Nyet." Then he had a thought. He was searching for a word. He found it. "Hilfe," he said, thickly.

Vaguely, the doctor remembered his smattering of German. Help. Help me.

The man was groping for another word.

"Affitsyer," he said, but it wasn't the word he wanted.

"Soviet," he continued. "Offizier."

"You're a Soviet officer?" repeated the doctor incredulously. Here? In the middle of the night? In the depths of Berkshire? In a track suit?

"Sprechen sie Deutsch?" ventured the doctor. But the man shook his head.

"Tell you what," said the doctor, shouting slightly as if that would make him more comprehensible to the man, "I'll take you to the police station. They'll be able to help you."

He leaned forward and opened the passenger door.

"Jump in," he invited.

The man in the track suit got in and closed the door. Then he turned to the doctor with a warm, grateful smile, and held out his right hand.

A little reluctantly, the doctor shook it. The man pressed his hand strongly, firmly.

8

"Tovarich," he said. "Kamerad. Spasibo."

The doctor started up the car, and continued his slow progress along the primitive road, which was only wide enough for one vehicle.

His passenger sat, arms crossed, his eyes straight ahead peering through the fog. The doctor glanced at him briefly. The track suit was British, he could tell that from the manufacturer's embroidered logo, and it was spattered with mud, as were his running shoes.

On his left hand was a deep gash. Something jagged had ripped it recently. The blood was still oozing.

The man noticed his look, and hastily recrossed his arms, as if to conceal his left hand. Then he seemed to realise the pointlessness of the gesture, and smiled, a little awkwardly. There was blood on the right sleeve of the track suit. The cut was still bleeding quite heavily.

"I'm Dr Wynne," the doctor introduced himself. "Maybe you ought to let me have a look at that."

He nodded at the man's hand, but all he got in return was a smile.

"Physician," amplified Wynne. "Medicine. First Aid."

The man shook his head. Maybe he didn't understand. Maybe he didn't want it examined.

Suddenly Wynne became apprehensive. Suppose the man attacked him? Left him lying in the road, and stole the car? Drove off into the night? The doctor's fingers tightened on the steering wheel. He'd been a fool to pick him up. He could feel the man staring at him. It was almost a physical sensation. He turned and saw the man studying him. The dark eyes were hard, the lips tight, and in the dim light, the high cheek bones gave him a sinister, slightly oriental look. But when the man saw Wynne looking at him, he smiled again.

"The police station's quite close," explained the doctor. Actually it was eleven miles further on, but it reassured him to say it. To his surprise the man nodded.

"Spasibo," he said.

Soon they'd reach the main road, Wynne consoled himself. At least it wouldn't be so deserted, even at this time of night.

The man dug into the pocket of his track suit, took out

9

something, then offered it to the doctor.

"What is it?"

The man still held it, nodding to him, smiling. Wynne halted the car and took it with one hand. It was a wrist watch. The front glass was broken, and it had stopped at nine sixteen. It was a Russian watch; the manufacturer's name was in Cyrillic lettering. It was solidly made, but had had a hard blow.

The man pointed at Wynne, at the watch, at himself, and at Wynne again. He said something Wynne didn't understand.

Then he reached out, closed the doctor's fingers over the watch, indicating he wanted him to have it. To keep it.

"I couldn't," protested Wynne, startled, but the man kept his hand pressed closed. His meaning was clear. "From me to you." He was pleading. His eyes were almost beseeching.

Wynne felt embarrassed. This was the man he had suspected. This was the man he had been afraid of.

"Thank you," he said at last, and put the watch in his pocket. The man leant forward and embraced him.

"Really, you had no need to give me anything," said Wynne, shifting the car into gear. The man nodded, and sat back, a slight smile on his face. For the first time, he seemed to relax.

They were approaching the old medieval toll gate, when a dazzling, bright light suddenly blinded them. Wynne, unable to see, slammed on the brakes. If he had been going at speed, it would have been fatal.

Immediately shadowy figures surrounded them. They materialised out of the darkness and jerked open both doors of the car.

"Out!" ordered a voice, and an arm dragged Wynne from the driver's seat. On the other side, the man was being hustled from the car and Wynne watched, astonished, as men bundled him away, his hands behind his back.

Through the mist, he could see they were taking him towards a cluster of cars on the other side of the toll gate, grouped like a road block. One of them, a sleek, green car, had a blue light flashing on its roof.

"What the devil's going on?" Wynne demanded.

"I'm sorry about this," apologised a voice shining a flash-light in his face. "But it's all right," it continued. "Every-thing's under control. Nothing to worry about."

The man in the track suit was already swallowed up in the darkness. There was the sound of car doors being slammed, and one of the cars beyond the toll gate drove off rapidly.

"Who the hell are you? Police?" challenged Wynne. The flashlight in his eyes made it impossible to see anyone properly.

"You were lucky, sir," remarked the voice. "He can be very dangerous."

"Put that damn light out. It's blinding me."

But the light stayed in his eyes.

"He absconded earlier tonight, and we were afraid he'd get clean away," went on the voice smoothly.

"Who are you talking about?"

"Chummy," replied the voice. "The chap who hitched a ride with you. I'm glad we got him in time."

Wynne turned away from the torch to escape the glare.

"Who is he?" he asked.

"Mental patient. Top security. Cunning bugger. Gave us the slip."

"Where from?" pressed Wynne, and when the voice didn't answer, he repeated: "The slip from where?"

In the distance, another of the cars drove off.

"The hospital," answered the voice, a little impatiently, still concealed behind the flashlight.

"Which hospital?" Then he added: "You'd better know that I'm a doctor."

But the man was already walking off into the mist, and all Wynne could see from his back was that he wore civilian clothes.

"Hey!" he shouted. "Where are you taking him?"

More car doors slammed, and the engines started up. The green car was the last to move off; its blue light was no longer flashing.

Then everything was very quiet again, and Wynne was left standing alone beside his car, shaking a little, but that may have been because he was cold.

* * *

11

Between patients, the receptionist came into Dr Wynne's surgery.

"There's a Mr Druce outside," she announced. She liked to run the doctor's consulting hour like an assembly line, and anything that slowed it up was unwelcome.

"Druce?" Wynne frowned. "Do I know him?"

"He's not a patient," said the receptionist. She was hoping for authority to show the intrusive Mr Druce to the door.

"What does he want, then?"

"I don't know, doctor. He says it's to do with your call to the Chief Constable."

Her manner indicated that it would be helpful if the doctor put her in the picture about such things.

"Ah yes." He took off his glasses. "Send him in."

"Right away?" She was about to say something about the patients who were waiting, but instead she just gave an audible sigh. Next time, resolved Wynne, he'd make sure he hired a younger, less bossy receptionist.

Mr Druce was in his thirties, with wavy hair which was just slightly too long. Wynne disliked him on sight.

"Dr Wynne?"

The fleshy lips were smiling.

"Sit down," said Wynne. "You're from the police?"

"Well, not actually the police." Druce made himself comfortable in the chair opposite the doctor's desk. He had on a blazer, a maroon shirt with a white collar, and sported a gold ring on the little finger of his left hand. "I'm from the Home Office. Sort of complaints department, if you know what I mean. You *did* make a complaint, didn't you?"

He regarded Wynne reproachfully.

"I phoned the Chief Constable because I couldn't get any sense out of the local police station. The sergeant said he didn't know anything about it, the inspector said he'd ask the CID, and the CID were apparently all out. They said they'd call back, and they never did, so I finally got in touch with the Chief Constable . . ." The doctor paused. "I'd still like to know what the hell went on."

"I see," said Druce. "Not very wise, is it, picking up hitchhikers in the middle of the night?"

"It's not a crime, you know."

Druce raised a hand languidly. "Of course not. I'm just trying to get the facts straight. You say you picked up this man, who you think was a Russian . . ." He paused. "I don't understand what's bothering you."

"You forget, Mr Druce, I'm a doctor. I know the mental hospitals in this area. Nobody's absconded. I checked. Even with Broadmoor. No top security patient escaped."

Druce shifted in his chair. "Do you mind if I smoke?" he enquired, pulling out a packet of cigarettes.

"I'd prefer you not to," replied Wynne, coldly.

"Sorry." Druce put the packet back in his blazer. "I don't think the local hospitals would necessarily know, would they? I mean he could have come from much further?"

"Did he?"

Druce played with the ring on his little finger. "It's such an odd story, doctor, you must admit. The police know nothing about it. There's no record of such an incident. You can see we're taking it seriously, that's why I'm here, but there isn't a shred of evidence so far."

"You're suggesting I made it up?"

"Of course not, doctor. But without evidence . . ."

"You think I imagined it?"

"Perhaps you . . ." Druce shrugged. "I mean, for instance, these people who you say grabbed you. You can't describe them." The doctor started to say something, but Druce continued: "Yes, I know, you were blinded by a flashlight. You say that one of the cars was green with a blue light on its roof and seemed to be a police vehicle. Dr Wynne, the local police forces don't have any green cars."

Druce paused triumphantly.

"It was after midnight," he resumed, quite gently. "I understand you've been terribly busy lately, getting very little sleep . . ."

Wynne stood up.

"I'm not used to being called a liar, Mr Druce."

"Nobody's suggesting that."

"But you don't believe it happened."

"Well, perhaps you . . . misinterpreted . . ."

"Oh come on."

"Well, doctor, without proof, there's nothing more I can

do, I'm afraid. No harm's been done. I suggest we all forget about it."

Druce smiled, got up and held out his hand. Wynne didn't take it. Instead he said:

"He gave me his watch, you know."

"Watch?"

"As a present. It's broken. But it's a Russian watch, and I still have it."

Druce regarded him stonily. "May I see it?"

"It's at my house."

"Well, never mind," smiled Druce, genially. "Obviously, your hitchhiker had a broken watch. Funny sort of present, but each to their own. They're quite cheap, aren't they, Russian watches?"

"I wouldn't know."

"Don't lose any sleep over this business," Druce advised, turning to leave. "These things happen."

"You say you're Home Office?"

"General dogsbody, you could say." He took a thin wallet from his blazer pocket. "Here." He handed the doctor a card. It had his name, Laurence Druce, and a phone number, with an extension. "Thank you for your time. I hope I haven't held up your patients too much."

Wynne remained behind his desk.

"Mr Druce."

"Yes?"

"He was a Russian. I think he was a Russian officer. Trying to get away. From something. Or somebody."

"Oh, I don't think that's very likely, do you?" said Druce, and smiled.

Then he left, closing the surgery door behind him very quietly, and made his way to the car which was parked round the corner. Although Her Majesty's Government departments used British made vehicles, this was a Mercedes. The section had special privileges.

The girl behind the wheel had rich chestnut hair framing an oval face, and a creamy complexion. Lightly applied make-up accentuated her high cheek bones, sensual lips, and long lashes fringing her green eyes. She looked expensive – even the sheepskin coat she wore was stylishly cut. She

14

switched off the radio when she saw Druce approach.

He got in beside her, and without a word lit a cigarette.

"God, I needed that." He exhaled. "No smoking in there." Then he realised he hadn't offered her one, and held out the pack. "Sorry, Fern."

"How did you get on?" she asked, after he had lit it for her.

"He's an awkward cuss," commented Druce.

She didn't look at him, but kept her eyes on the quiet street. He was conscious of her aromatic, spicy perfume.

"What now? Back to London?"

"I think I'd better let them know."

"Okay," she said, reaching for the radio telephone.

"No," he stopped her. "By landline."

"I'll find a phone booth." She started the car.

They drove in silence, until they came to a sub post office, which shared premises with a local newsagent. She slowed down, but Druce shook his head.

"Not from there. Too public."

He was living up to his reputation of always going by the book. Faithful servant of Lambert and Pearmain. Everything by the manual.

"I don't believe in taking unnecessary chances," he added, as if he'd read her thoughts.

Some distance away, they found a call box by the roadside, and she waited in the car while he dialled London by the special number. He spoke briefly, and when he came out he reported:

"They said leave it to them."

He looked at his watch.

"I know a lovely little pub near here. How about a spot of lunch?"

"No thanks," said Fern. "I'd like to get back to town."

For the rest of the journey, they hardly said a word.

If it had happened in Athens, or Rome, maybe even Paris, instinctively Flexner would have been on full alert. But because this was London it was different. London was still safe. At least, comparatively . . .

So the fact that the caller knew his unlisted number, and had phoned him on his direct line was no reason to be uneasy, he told himself. There could be many explanations as to how the man came to have the number.

And yet . . .

Was he really as secure as he imagined in his air conditioned office on the third floor of the American embassy?

The diplomatic list described Cyrus Flexner as Political Officer, Research and Development, which entitled him to tax free privileges, the use of an official embassy car, the facilities of the PX, and a smart house in St John's Wood which had particularly pleased Nancy, his somewhat gregarious wife. Outwardly, his was a quiet, rather boring life, but, sub rosa, he was the firm's station chief in London.

Of course, that was hardly a secret. The British knew it; Lambert had actually thrown a cocktail party to welcome him. And the Russians, naturally, were well aware of what he did.

But knowing his office private number was another matter.

The line assured him complete independence from the embassy switchboard. It was on the cards that the British had a tap on it; Lambert's people probably couldn't resist it. And Crawford, down the corridor, might have ambitions in that direction; he was NSA, and eavesdropping was their mission. But technically, it was his own sacrosanct link with the outside.

Then, an hour ago, the call had come, and, yet again, Flexner replayed it in his mind.

"Yes?" he had said, after picking up the receiver.

"Mr Flexner?"

"Yes?" He had been wary. He didn't recognise the voice.

"This is Spiridov, Mr Flexner."

"Who?"

"Anatoly Spiridov." He spoke accented English, with an American inflection. "You can look me up."

Trade talk. Professional to professional.

"Yes?" Now Flexner was very cautious.

"We must meet. Immediately. For our mutual benefit."

Damn it, thought Flexner. He wished he'd had the line rigged so he could tape the call.

"I'm not sure I understand."

16

"Please, Mr Flexner. We have no time." The man spoke urgently. "I shall be in the bar of the Holiday Inn, George Street, at noon."

"Now, just one moment," began Flexner, but the man cut him short:

"It is very important. For you too."

Then he hung up.

In registry, he'd checked out the classified file, and looked up what they had on Spiridov. Not much. A journalist with Novosti Press. In London for the last four months. Before that, a year in Washington. Married, and accompanied by his wife. He had 3 Grading – intelligence connections, but that was normal with a Soviet correspondent.

It was all rather minor league.

Now, in his office, Flexner stood behind the net curtain of his window, gazing thoughtfully across Grosvenor Square. Maybe it was the fact that Spiridov appeared to be low on the totem pole that nagged him. Perhaps he was much more important than they had realised. The Flexner mind was at work. Accept nothing at face value.

It was twenty minutes to noon. He went to his desk, and unlocked a drawer. He took out a heavy cherrywood box, and lifted the lid. In it lay a gun, a Colt Government .45, with an engraved barrel inscribed "Dedicated To All Who Served." Carved on the butt was "Vietnam – Laos – Cambodia – Thailand." He checked the magazine, and put the gun in his jacket.

Then, over the intercom, he told his secretary that he was going out for lunch.

Wynne re-read the letter a second time, in case, initially, he had missed something.

But he hadn't:

HOUSE OF COMMONS

Dear Dr Wynne:

I apologise for the delay in writing to you, but I have been very busy in the House, and also needed time to make some enquiries.

I am afraid I cannot throw much light on this matter. I have been in touch with the Home Office, but they tell me they have no information about any incident involving a Russian hitchhiker.

The Chief Constable of your county assures me that he is also unable to help.

Under the circumstances, I do not see what other line I can pursue.

It is sad that you subsequently had a break-in at your house, but I think the fact that the thief only took a Russian watch, and a broken one at that, would probably indicate that the intruder was a youngster and it was just an unfortunate coincidence.

I enclose an extract from Hansard of my latest speech on juvenile delinquency.

As your Member of Parliament, I will always be glad to be of assistance to you, even though, regretfully, my efforts on this occasion did not yield much.

Yours sincerely,

The signature at the bottom of the letter was almost as illegible as Wynne's own handwriting, but imprinted as if it had been rubber stamped. It struck him that the honourable member probably had a secretary who processed his correspondence like sausages.

He tossed the letter aside. It all fitted.

"I wouldn't worry much about the watch, if that's all you lost," the disinterested detective had remarked, following Wynne's report of the burglary. "Can't be worth much, doctor, can it? I mean, Russian, and broken to boot."

"You're lucky," added his colleague, "that's all they took."

It was then that he'd written to his MP, and it had taken seventeen days to get a reply.

From his wallet, Wynne took out the card Druce had given him, then went over to the phone and dialled the number. A London number.

A high pitched whistle pierced his eardrum.

He re-dialled the number. Again the noise made him wince.

He rang the operator, and asked her to get the number for him.

"What trouble are you having?" she enquired, in a professionally supercilious manner, like talking to a child too lazy to do its own chore.

"All I get is a bloody awful whistle," Wynne snapped.

"One moment, please," she said haughtily.

Then she came back to him.

"I'm sorry caller," she informed him. "The number is unobtainable."

"What do you mean, unobtainable?" he demanded, impatiently. "It's the Home Office."

"No, caller, it isn't." She sounded bored. "It's a ceased line."

By the time the taxi pulled up at the Holiday Inn, Anatoly Spiridov was dead.

The driver turned off the meter waiting for him to get out, and when he didn't move he called out: "We're here!"

Still there was no response. Impatiently the driver turned round to look at his passenger.

Spiridov was slumped in a corner of the cab, his face a greenish pallor and his gold rimmed glasses half way down his nose. His mouth gaped and his eyes were wide open, staring blankly.

"Fuck!" swore the driver. He hated people being taken ill in his cab. If they were sick, it not only meant a lot of cleaning up, he also lost fares while he was off the road.

He got out, and opened the door.

"What's the matter, mate?" he enquired, almost belligerently.

It was when he touched Spiridov's arm, and the man fell forward, that he realised the worst.

"Bloody Hell!" cursed the cabby, and ran into the hotel.

Flexner, nursing an orange juice in the bar, saw none of this. All he knew was that Spiridov was late, and his doubts about the wisdom of keeping the assignation were growing. Every time somebody entered the bar he scrutinised him. The place wasn't very busy. A couple sat by the wall, deep in conversation. They'd not even looked up when Flexer had strolled in.

It was all very normal.

He decided to give it another half an hour. If Spiridov hadn't appeared by then, he'd have some lunch, and leave. In the meantime, he'd get himself a *Herald Tribune*; he always felt better equipped sitting in a bar with a newspaper.

As he crossed the lobby, he noticed a policeman standing outside the hotel. In the souvenir shop, he bought the paper, and it was as he was returning to the bar that he heard the sirens. Through the lobby's glass doors, he saw an ambulance pull up. Then a police car stopped outside.

Instead of going back to the bar, Flexner went into the street.

Both doors of the ambulance were already open, and the two attendants were just taking a man out of the parked taxi, and putting him on a stretcher. One policeman was talking to the cab driver, and making notes. The other was examining the inside of the cab.

An ambulance man started to cover the passenger with a red blanket, but Flexner caught a glimpse of the dead man's face. He had seen that face an hour previously, on a photograph attached to Spiridov's file in the registry.

In death, Spiridov looked startled, surprised. His glasses had been removed, and now one of the ambulance men put them on the red blanket.

"Need any help, mate?" volunteered a policeman.

"He's past it," grunted the ambulance man.

"Heart attack?"

The ambulance man shrugged. His colleague bent over Spiridov's mouth, and sniffed.

"Funny smell," he said.

"Better get moving," urged the policeman.

Flexner stood quietly, and watched them carry the stretcher into the ambulance, then slam the door.

"What about my fare?" asked the cabby.

"Your problem, mate," replied the policeman, unfeeling. "You follow us to the station. We'll need particulars."

The ambulance moved off, but it didn't sound its siren. Dead men, reflected Flexner, don't need to rush.

He remembered he hadn't paid for his orange juice, so he

went and left a pound on the bill.

Then he decided he'd better forget about lunch. There were things to be done.

And Dichter, 3,000 miles away, had to be told.

They sat on Hepplewhite chairs, a Queen Anne low table between them. In his day, Allen Dulles had insisted on an old fashioned log fire in his office; Blanchard was only Assistant Director of the Special Division, but period furniture was his quirk. He had outraged the bureaucrats at Langley by filling his office with English antiques.

"Do you use these?" enquired Blanchard, dropping a sweetner into his cup of China tea and offering the small silver pill box.

"I like it as it is," replied John Dichter.

He stuck to coffee. But even that tasted different on this floor. Better than was served in the commissary. Clearly, Special Division rated a private supply.

Blanchard snapped shut his silver box.

"Now then," he said, and paused.

Dichter waited.

"I've read Flexner's report."

Still Dichter stayed silent.

"It's worrying," continued Blanchard unhappily. "I don't like the implications."

For some moments, neither of them spoke. Then, in a low voice, Dichter said, "I think we need a ferret."

"You can't ask Flexner to do that," declared Blanchard sharply. "You can't put him in that position."

"Of course not. He is head of station. He is embassy. He is official." Dichter shook his head. "He can't be compromised. No, that's why I say, we have to send in a ferret."

Blanchard was abstractedly toying with a ball point pen.

"Then again, we could tip off the British about our suspicions . . ."

"And maybe alert the very people we're after?"

Blanchard put the ball point aside. "Well, who do you suggest?"

"Zarubin. I think it's his kind of job."

The word "job" had a particular meaning when Dichter used it. It indicated the peculiar work Clandestine Services did. Especially the section Dichter headed, the existence of which even Congress didn't know.

"You appreciate I'm not very familiar with him." That was a lie, because the Assistant Director had studied Zarubin's file earlier that day. "I'm sure he's good, but don't you think he's got something of a chip on his shoulder?"

"He can be difficult," agreed Dichter.

"Too individualistic, maybe?"

Blanchard tended to the view that a covert agent who played the game by his own rules was a possible candidate for damnation.

"I can handle Mr Zarubin," said Dichter.

The Assistant Director shifted uneasily. He often wondered about Dichter and his section. Like the curious operations he masterminded, he could be deceptive. Even physically. He was a tall man, over six foot three, but his stooped posture belied his height. He was prematurely grey, in a way women found attractive, yet seemed nervous in their presence. He was neither an academic, nor a scientist, but he made a point of sounding diffident. He had compiled three manuals for use inside the service which were so classified that no outsider would ever be allowed to read them.

"All right. But no paper work, you understand? Nothing on the record. Everything sub rosa. Clear?"

"Absolutely," nodded Dichter. "From now, no record."

Blanchard allowed himself a thin smile.

"John, you're a cunning son of a bitch. You had made up your mind already, hadn't you? That's why you want to send Zarubin to London?"

"Well," said Dichter, "it takes one to catch one, doesn't it?"

They lay in the dark, naked, but they were not asleep. Although their bodies were close, and still warm from making love, their thoughts were separate, and apart.

"You're good," remarked Sara, turning to look at him.

It jarred on Zarubin. It made him sound like a mechanic. "You screwed in that light bulb very expertly." It was the first time she'd irritated him.

He grunted. Then came the second discord. She suddenly switched on the bedside light. Afterwards, he wondered if she'd been annoyed he hadn't returned her compliment. Perhaps she'd expected him to comment on her performance.

Sara lay stretched out, a taut, slim body, with assertive breasts, and long shapely legs. Her eyes were closed.

"I'll make us some coffee in a minute," she said.

"That'll be nice."

It was a large, comfortable double bed, and she'd probably shared it with quite a few men. Zarubin noted that as a statement of fact; it was her business.

"I've been thinking," said Sara.

"That's always dangerous."

"About you."

"How boring," joked Zarubin, lightly. This was a subject that had to be changed. "Can't you manage something more exciting."

Her dark eyes, which could promise all kinds of surprises, remained shut.

"I don't know a thing about you, Andy. Do you realise that?" She didn't sound accusing, more puzzled.

"Oh come on, you can see I'm five foot eleven, weigh 156 pounds, at least I did before dinner. I'm handsome, witty, debonair, with brown hair, and no visible scars. What more could you want to know?"

"Be serious, Andy. You haven't even told me what you do."

"First rule, I'm never serious." He reached for a cigarette, and lit it. "Second rule, a man always tried to impress a woman. So if I did anything interesting, you'd have known after the first martini."

"Third rule, only somebody who's got something to hide doesn't give a straight answer," interrupted Sara.

"So, what do you think I have to hide?"

"No idea." She paused. "I notice you're always watching people. The other night, for instance, when we were having a drink at that bar. Every time somebody entered, you looked at them. No, not looked, scrutinised them."

He wondered whether he should deny it. But Sara was too intelligent. She'd know he was lying.

"*You're* being very observant," he said instead. "But actually, most of the time I'm looking at you, and thinking how very attractive you are."

"Thank you." She turned on her side and faced him. "I don't really care a damn, Andy, I was just curious if you were looking for somebody, or trying to avoid them."

He chuckled. "Rule number four, once a woman is curious, she won't let go. How about, a bit of both? Does that satisfy you?"

"Of course not," she smiled. "What about your wife?"

"I'm not married."

She sat up.

"Pity. I'd laid odds."

"Oh."

"Yes, I'd worked out that's why you're so secretive. Not saying where you work, or anything about yourself. That you didn't want your wife to find out – that's what I thought."

"Shows how wrong one can be," said Zarubin.

She got out of bed, and picked up a Chinese silk robe from the chair where it was lying.

"I'll make that coffee," she said, putting it on.

She went into the kitchen, leaving the bedroom door ajar.

Zarubin was the sort of man who avoided lasting relationships, like someone on the run. In his job, he couldn't afford entanglements – one had cost him too much already. He had only known Sara a couple of weeks, and this was the first time she had brought him home. He hadn't seen much of the apartment: when they'd come in, they had kissed in the hallway, and then she had led him into the bedroom.

It was an elegant room. She had spent money, but it didn't tell him much. As he glanced round, it betrayed no confidences. It could have been a bedroom in any smart hotel.

He heard the phone ring and Sara answering it in the hall. After a moment, she entered the bedroom.

"It's for you," she announced, surprise on her face.

"What?" He was so startled, he gaped at her.

"It's a man asking for Mr Zarubin." She shrugged.

"It can't be." He was bewildered.

"Well, you'd better talk to him, he's holding."

She made a point of closing the kitchen door so that she

24

wouldn't overhear the conversation. And when, a few minutes later, he went into the kitchen, she stopped pouring the coffee, and asked:

"Was it for you?"

"Yes," said Zarubin slowly. "A friend."

But he thought it was ironical, calling Dichter a friend.

She put down the coffee pot. "How on earth did he have this number? How did he know you were here?"

I could tell you, reflected Zarubin. I could tell you how it works. Never out of sight, never out of mind. Dichter likes to play these little games. He likes to prove he knows everything. We haven't been alone tonight, Sara.

"I don't know," said Zarubin aloud.

She frowned. "I don't get it. Why did he call you here? Is it an emergency?"

"He's a guy I work with." She handed him his cup. "Something's come up."

"Well, do you mind telling your friend not to make free with my phone number. I don't appreciate it."

"I agree. He's got a nerve."

Actually Dichter had been quite apologetic on the phone.

"Sorry to break in on you, Andy, I know you're still on leave, but we need you back here."

"Christ almighty, couldn't it wait twenty-four hours? How the hell did you find me here?"

"See you tomorrow," was Dichter's only response. Then he rang off.

Quickly, Zarubin had dialled the unlisted number.

"Yes," replied a voice, without preliminaries.

"He's called," said Zarubin softly, then he'd put the receiver down.

Now, he sipped the coffee, and pulled a face.

"Oh, sorry, I forgot to sugar it."

She pushed the bowl across the kitchen table, and he dropped two lumps in his cup.

"Does that mean you have to leave immediately?" she asked. The silk robe had slipped open, but she made no effort to cover her breasts.

"No," said Zarubin, slowly. "Not right away."

*   *   *

The sign spelt it out in black capital letters:

WARNING RESTRICTED AREA!

It is unlawful to enter this area without permission of the installation commander! While on this installation all personnel and the property under their control are subject to search. USE OF DEADLY FORCE AUTHORISED!

The unsmiling guards in their baseball caps and unmarked combat suits waved down the maroon government car in which Dichter had brought Zarubin to the place.

Wryly, Zarubin thought of the way the other side covered up these things. In the Soviet Union, outsiders wouldn't get within ten miles of such an installation. Here, any passing motorist, turning off the highway, could see the sign, the barbed wire, the patrolling sentries with guard dogs, and all the other clues that told him he was on top of something highly sensitive.

The guards scrutinised their ID cards, and one of them spoke into a walkie talkie. The gates opened, and a jeep appeared ahead of the car, to guide it past anonymous buildings, most two storied with barred windows, and along a tarmacked road.

They pulled up in front of one of the buildings as a man in a short sleeved sports shirt and check slacks appeared. He gave them both plastic identity badges to clip on. Despite the man's informal clothes, he looked military, thought Zarubin as he and Dichter followed him down a corridor, and up a flight of stairs.

Several times they passed more of the baseball capped sentinels, who seemed to roam at will, their radios buzzing. And closed circuit cameras monitored them all the way.

Finally, they arrived at a door. "KEEP OUT" proclaimed a sign, "ENTRY ABSOLUTELY PROHIBITED EXCEPT FOR AUTHORISED PERSONNEL."

The man in the sports shirt pressed a button, and a glass eye above the door examined them frigidly. Then there was a buzzing sound, and the door opened.

"Here we are, gentlemen," announced their guide, standing aside to let them enter. It was the first time he had spoken.

They were in a small projection room, like a preview theatre, with six swivel armchairs, all fixed to the floor.

"Make yourself at home," invited the man.

He nodded, and went out.

The armchairs were deep, and comfortable.

Dichter stretched out his long legs. "This won't take long."

"I don't mind," said Zarubin. "It's a nice place for a nap."

Dichter smiled sourly.

"Are you ready?" enquired a disembodied voice.

Dichter had a small console with three push buttons at the side of his armchair. He turned to Zarubin.

"You ready?" he echoed.

He didn't wait for his answer, but pressed one of the buttons. The room darkened, and the screen came alive.

On it was projected a board, like a director's slate. It displayed one word: SECRET. Beneath was a group of letters, and a reference number.

Then the film came on. It was badly shot, and flickered, but the colour was good. It showed a large aircraft, apparently flying over the sea.

"Recognise it?" asked Dichter, in the dark.

"Badger," replied Zarubin. "Tupolev TU-16."

"Badger-F," corrected Dichter. "The electronic reconnaissance version."

On the screen, nothing appeared to be happening. The plane just kept flying. Then the screen went blank and the lights came up.

"What was all that about?" asked Zarubin.

"That was filmed on 27 June 1980, 180 miles north of Tokyo."

"So?"

"It never made it back," elaborated Dichter. "It came down in the sea."

"Why?"

"Two of the crew died," continued Dichter, ignoring the question.

"Only two? What happened to the rest?"

27

Dichter smiled, and pushed one of the buttons.

Again the board appeared, with a different group of letters and numbers. Again it was marked, SECRET.

It was another Russian plane, filmed from above. The photography was much better than in the previous clip, clear and sharp.

"TU-95," observed Zarubin. "Bear."

"Correct," agreed Dichter. He was watching, not the screen but Zarubin.

The huge plane veered slightly but kept on flying. The camera stayed with it, unmoving.

"That bastard sneaked over Charleston last year."

"Charleston, South Carolina?"

"Right. He was interested in the nuclear subs there."

The screen went blank again.

Once more, the lights came on.

"And I suppose he came down somewhere?" suggested Zarubin.

"How did you guess?" Dichter was quite straight faced. "Out in the Atlantic. Most of the crew were killed."

"Most?"

"We're not through," said Dichter.

The next piece of film was more dramatic. It showed another TU-16, but this time the aircraft was manoeuvring wildly, as if it was taking evasive action. The camera obviously had difficulty keeping the plane in frame. Then the film stopped.

"Scotland," commented Dichter laconically. "Near Holy Loch."

"Any survivors?"

"They all got out," said Dichter. "They were lucky."

"When was that?"

"Last month," replied Dichter quietly. "Show isn't over yet."

Zarubin recognised the TU-22 that was the next film clip. The Blinder was flying high, leaving vapour trails from its two turbo jets, and then suddenly there was a flash, and it began to spiral downwards. The film stopped.

"He was snooping over Akrotiri," announced Dichter.

"Where?"

"Southern Cyprus. There's a NATO installation there they're mighty curious about. He didn't find out very much."

"And the crew?"

"We've got a few more, or have you seen enough?" asked Dichter, as if he hadn't heard.

"I think I have the picture," answered Zarubin quietly.

"I thought you would."

"Who took these films?"

"Oh, various people. The Tokyo one was the Navy. The Air Force intercepted the Charleston one, and the Blinder over Cyprus. The RAF did the Holy Loch film. The NATO boys are pretty good. You should see the stuff the Dutch got on a Backfire." He swung round in the armchair to face Zarubin. "It's going on the whole time, Andy. Nobody talks about it. No headlines. High flying spy planes over our heads. But don't kid yourself. The Russians have mapped London from the air, they've targeted Washington and New York from the sky, they probe every day . . ."

"Satellites?"

"Sure, that too. But we don't tell the public about the real intruders. It's better they don't know there are Soviet jets overhead, testing our reaction, probing our radar, trying out our counter measures . . ."

"And getting shot down," interjected Zarubin.

"Ah." Dichter paused. "Maybe it isn't that simple. After all, we send our intruders over there. To do the same."

And he explained the rules of the game. Each side lets the other get away with so much. Some overflights are tolerated. The flying spies are monitored until they leave local air space. But sometimes the intruders get too nosey. They penetrate ultra sensitive zones. They become too confident. And then they pay the price.

"What happens to the airmen? The ones who don't get killed?"

"There you go again," said Dichter. "You keep asking that question."

"And you don't answer it."

"Okay. I'll lay it on the line. The United States is holding thirty-one Soviet spy airmen prisoner. Secret survivors."

He beamed at Zarubin.

"Of course, they don't exist. You appreciate why. They get well treated, but officially they don't exist. And the Soviets have about two dozen of our guys. Neither side will ever admit that it sent its Air Force illegally to invade the air space of the other side."

"I don't believe it."

"Makes perfect sense," sighed Dichter. "The fact that we both have each other's men ensures nothing stupid is done. Nobody gets badly treated. But as far as the record is concerned, they're dead. On training flights, crashes, whatever."

"Where do we keep them?"

Dichter sneezed, and blew his nose. Then he said, "Have you ever realised just how big Nevada is?"

Zarubin was bothered. The way Dichter told the story it sounded so normal.

"Why no exchange?"

Again Dichter sneezed. "God damn, I hope I haven't caught a chill." He dabbed his nose. "Exchange? Nobody wants it. All those next of kin, all the gossip, then the papers getting on to it. Jesus, no. Who needs that? After all, we both want to keep spying on each other." He looked at his watch, and the cold eyes glinted with a hint of mockery. "Wouldn't surprise me, Andy, if one of theirs isn't fifteen miles above Los Angeles right now, and one of ours peeking at Leningrad."

He leaned forward.

"And now I'm going to tell you why you're going to London." He stood up. "Follow me."

As soon as they entered the Vault, the thick steel door closed hermetically behind them. It made no sound, but suddenly Zarubin felt trapped.

This was the firm's inner santum, the repository of many, but not all, the section's secrets. Here rested the papers that could not be copied, circulated, or quoted. To separate a document from its folder, or attempt to remove it, was a federal offence. And the depository's armed guards had standing orders to shoot and kill anyone who attempted to take possession of a paper from the Vault.

No man could be alone within the steel walls, nothing read

without a witness, and visitors were kept constantly under observation by an armed guard, their hands monitored by closed circuit cameras. Note taking was forbidden. Smoking was prohibited, because it triggered various alarm sensors. There was a bullet proof one way mirror on the wall, through which men on the outside watched those inside.

There was only one table and two chairs at either end. Only one file could be read at a time in the air conditioned, well lit subterranean basement.

"You know 'Pinnacle'?" asked Dichter as they sat down at the table. The grey steel box containing the folder they needed already lay on it.

"No."

"It's a special security classification. You don't often hear about it. More secret than 'Ultra' or 'Cosmic'." He indicated the steel box. "'Pinnacle'."

Dichter nodded to the shirt sleeved guard who pulled out a bunch of keys fastened by a chain to his belt, and unlocked the steel box. Then he sat down, and although he didn't say a word, he never took his eyes off them.

Dichter opened the box, and took out a thin black folder. On the cover was a note: "This is A Classified Document: PINNACLE."

"I got you upgraded clearance to see this," remarked Dichter. Zarubin was surprised; he had always thought that working for the section automatically guaranteed the highest security grading, even the classification "Classified".

Dichter opened the folder, then turned a couple of pages. He stopped at one page, read it, hesitated, and turned that over too. Finally he came to the sheet he wanted.

"Read that," he said, pushing the file towards Zarubin.

Stamped on the top and bottom of the paper was "Most Secret." Also impressed in red was the word "NOFOR", the firm's acronym for "No Foreign Eyes."

It appeared to be a translation, an extract from a longer document:

His activities have shown him to be skilled in the technique of clandestine work. His knowledge of our language

31

and culture are an asset lacking in many of their operatives.

He has demonstrated dedication to his assigned tasks, and, when required, a considerable degree of ruthlessness. The man has physical courage, and has displayed, on at least two occasions to our knowledge, his ability to withstand intensive interrogation, and deprivations of an extreme nature (HANOI, GDANSK).

He is an accomplished dissembler, and takes easily to deception. His section uses the ultimate sanction, and his most recent action was Yudkin (WARSAW).

Subject is not concerned with dialectics. He is heterosexual. On the whole, he is a controlled drinker. He is not addicted to narcotics.

THIS MAN IS DANGEROUS.

On the debit side, he has shown infrequent lapses of self discipline. He is highly drawn to female company. He has smoked marijuana (SAIGON, SAN FRANCISCO) His motivation is an enigma.

In our service, he would not be trusted, as he has a tendency to non conformity. However, his organisation appears to have no doubt about his loyalty.

Special Service II believes that it might be profitable to pay closer attention to this subject, and the Directorate concurs.

That was the end of the page. Zarubin was about to turn the sheet when Dichter intervened.

"The rest doesn't concern you."

He reached over and took the file back.

"Well, how do you like the KGB's assessment of you?"

"How did you get it?" asked Zarubin quietly.

"We got it, that's what matters. I thought you ought to know what they think of you."

"I'd like to see the whole thing."

"Oh; it's pretty dull," said Dichter, airily. "That was the important bit. Right on the ball, aren't they?" He looked down at the sheet. ' "Highly drawn to female company.' Like last night, eh?"

Zarubin's eyes narrowed, but Dichter went on:

"You've got to watch that kind of thing, Andy. You don't want to make it easy for them."

"You still haven't told me," said Zarubin, "why you want me to go to London?"

Dichter stood up, and nodded to the guard.

"We're all through."

"Yes sir." He came over, replaced the file in the steel box, and locked it.

The big heavy door swung open silently. Nobody had pressed a button, or pushed a switch in the room. The custodians, wherever they were, had listened and watched, and knew the time had come to let them out.

Dichter took Zarubin to a sound proofed office. As they went in, he switched on a red light over the door, indicating that entry was forbidden for the time being. What was said in here was a secret unto itself.

"You don't want much, do you?" growled Zarubin after Dichter had briefed him. "A Soviet spy pilot gets shot down in the North Sea, and you want me to find out why it's being covered up by the British. Some Russian newsman kills himself in a cab after contacting our embassy, and you think they got to him. You suspect infiltration of the British service, and it's all down to me to sort out."

"Sure," Dichter nodded amiably. "I told the boss. I'm sending in a ferret. You."

"Why me?"

"Because you're the best man for the job. Anyway, you read your KGB profile. They're interested in you. They want to pay you closer attention. I'm sending them the honey pot. The bees will come buzzing, you can depend on it."

Zarubin started to say something, but the man opposite cut him short:

"Blanchard's already approved it."

How many of the firm had sat in front of Dichter like this, wondered Zarubin, being assigned on one way missions. Thinking they were being told everything, and being told nothing. Always being given a reason why they and only they were the right person to go.

But that wasn't the only reason he finally said:

"I'd rather not go to London."

"Why not?" Maybe the grey man's mildness should have warned him.

"It's personal," shrugged Zarubin.

"What does that mean?"

"I said it's personal."

Dichter snorted.

"I'm sorry, but fuck your personal reasons. If it's some involvement you had, London's a big place. Ten million people. Plenty of room for everybody." His voice softened. "You know what they say, if you crash, take up another plane."

Zarubin played a different card.

"How about Flexner? It's his station. How does he feel about it?"

"I don't think he'll like you. I don't think he'll like you at all."

"In that case . . ."

"In that case," put in Dichter, blandly, "you're just the right man. Anyway, you'll be independent. He does his thing, you do yours."

You want me to dig through their shit but make sure they never find out you're responsible for the stink, thought Zarubin bitterly. I'll be the fall guy.

"Lambert will think you're coming to liaise," Dichter was saying. "It's almost the truth."

"Who's he?"

"Our contact with their special intelligence. It has its own set up. Not a nice outfit, but reasonably efficient. I worked with Lambert years ago, when I was in London." Dichter seemed reflective. "I helped to debrief Penkovsky on his UK trips. You didn't know that, did you?"

"No." There was a lot he didn't really know about Dichter. "Can I trust him?"

Dichter smiled. "You know better than that. I don't suppose you trust anybody except your mother."

"My mother's dead," said Zarubin.

Later, he kept thinking about his KGB dossier. Of course they knew about Hanoi, and Gdansk. And, obviously, it was no mystery who had killed Yudkin in Warsaw. The thing that nagged him was trivial. The reference to smoking marijuana in San Francisco. It had actually been at a party in Sausalito. He tried to think back who had been there but all he could remember was that it had taken place in a large house, a kind if artists, commune. They'd be a freaky, arty crowd and everybody had smoked, passing the joint from one to the other.

Yet what he had done there had found its way into the records of the KGB's Special Service II. Somebody who had been there was . . .

Zarubin wished he could have read the rest of the file. He was pretty sure there was more about him in it.

Maybe it was the part that mattered.

And that was why Dichter wouldn't let him see it.

It was a forbidding place of confinement, not much changed since the fourteenth century. Outwardly, the 600 year old fortified castle, isolated on the edge of a moor, miles from the nearest habitation, was a crumbling ruin, historically too insignificant to be a tourist attraction, hardly worth a mention in guide books. Technically, it belonged to the Crown and was in the care of the Department of the Environment.

Worn, narrow steps led up to the tower cell with its bare stone walls, and two small slits that served as windows. Over the centuries, this dank, musty chamber had become the home of many captives. Rebel barons and royal bastards in the middle ages, Catholic conspirators and Spanish spies in Elizabethan days, an American privateer, one of Napoleon's diplomatic couriers, an officer of the Kaiser's army who had come ashore from a U-boat, and, later, an Irish republican assassin.

Now there were a few modern concessions: a fluorescent strip had been fixed to the ceiling, a camp bed, and a light weight tubular chair that wouldn't knock out a man if he was hit with it had been installed. The most incongruous feature was a central heating radiator, with a wall mounted thermostat control.

All the chamber's inmates shared one thing in common: nobody knew they were or had ever been confined there.

The key in the lock of the steel studded door turned, and the Russian in the yellow track suit stopped his interminable pacing. He faced the two men who entered the gloomy cell.

One of them was upright, with an air of authority. He wore a brown check suit, a wool tie, and solid brogues, as befits an English country gentleman. His companion was younger, and had wavy hair.

The man in the check suit nodded to the Russian, not so much a greeting, more an acknowledgment of his existence.

"Ask him," he instructed the young man, "if he is all right, and if there is anything he needs."

The interpreter translated it into fluent Russian.

The reply came fast, angry, hard. When he had finished, the Russian glared at the man in the check suit.

"He says, sir, that he demands to know what is going on," reported the interpreter, his voice flat. "He understands that people on special missions cannot expect conventional treatment, but he insists that he is entitled to certain rights. He says he is well aware that in such cases certain unofficial arrangements apply. He demands that he be treated accordingly, and invokes those arrangements."

"Thank you," nodded the man politely. "Now tell him that since he has made no complaint of ill treatment, I fail to see why he should be dissatisfied."

The Russian listened to the translation then replied rapidly.

"He demands, sir," interpreted the young man, "to be handed back to the military. He says it is outrageous that he is apparently being held by civilians, and he requests to be transferred to military custody and to be dealt with by officers of his own rank."

"Well, you inform him that technically he has no status. I am not interested in what he calls unofficial arrangements. Further, if it's of any joy to him, I may be a civilian but I have a more senior rank than he has. You tell the major that, and make sure he gets my meaning."

"Yes sir."

The man in the check suit stared at his captive unwaveringly while the translator spoke. Then he pulled out a packet of Russian cigarettes.

"I hope they're his brand," remarked the man, offering one while the interpreter passed the message.

The Russian looked surprised. He put the cigarette in his mouth, and the man lit it for him with a black and gold Dunhill lighter.

"Here," he said, putting the packet on the tubular chair. "Tell him he can keep these."

The Russian spoke again.

"He wants to know how much longer he is going to be cooped up in this barbaric dungeon. It is like the Middle Ages. He demands civilised quarters."

"Say to him I agree it isn't the Hotel Rossiya." The man allowed himself a thin smile. "But you can also point out that he brought it on himself. He could hardly expect less than this after his little escapade. However, you can console him. Tell him he won't stay here for ever. There are other plans for him."

There was a pause after the interpreter had translated. Then the Russian asked something.

"He wants to know what exactly those plans are," related the translator.

That amused the man.

"Tell him he must allow us to have our little secrets."

He nodded to the Russian, then they both left.

The Russian sat down on the camp bed. He picked up the packet of cigarettes, and turned it over a couple of times, as if it could yield some information. Then he studied it more closely, and laughed. He laughed out loud.

Suddenly something was very funny.

The detective stayed within sight of him the whole time. He hadn't been given any background about the American with the funny name. All he'd been told was that Andrew Peter Zarubin, American, travelling on a United States passport, was due to arrive at Building 3, London Airport, from Washington, and that he was to be discreetly observed.

They knew the flight he was expected on, and the address to which he would be going, a block of flats in the Edgware Road, near Marble Arch. They were interested in who, if anybody, met him at Heathrow, and any other circumstances that might arouse curiosity. Once Zarubin arrived at the furnished service apartments, Detective Sergeant Infield could sign off. It was left to Infield to conjecture whether the surveillance would continue in a different form.

In the event, it was all very dull. Zarubin got off the plane, queued patiently for half an hour to go through immigration control, picked up his luggage, walked through the green channel, without being stopped by customs, and joined the taxi line. He didn't appear to be expecting anybody to meet him. He didn't glance round as if he was looking out for somebody. He didn't make a phone call. He didn't even go to the gents.

Infield had his own car strategically placed, and kept on the cab's tail all the way into London.

Still nothing happened. At Park West, Zarubin paid off the taxi and carried his luggage into the block. Just to be on the safe side, Infield remained around for another half hour. Then, as per orders, he took off. He had kept his eyes open for any other possible shadow, but hadn't spotted anybody.

He was a good Special Branch officer, and all this went against the book. One was usually told a subject's background, even given a look at his file, and briefed about what exactly one could expect, and should be on alert for. And it was normal routine to know who was taking over the assignment, and where one would hand over to the relief.

Back at Scotland Yard, Infield couldn't resist it. He exceeded his orders, and put a computer check through on Zarubin. For some reason, the reply never filtered back to his desk.

A call to Home Office immigration control also proved negative. All they had on Zarubin was a three months' landing permit, and a London address; the flat at Park West.

"Anything special about him?" asked Infield, trying to sound nonchalant.

"Should there be?" enquired the cold Home Office voice. That was all.

A remarkably unremarkable man, thought Infield, considering his instructions, and the secrecy in which they were wrapped.

He sat down at his desk, and started typing the report. Because of the supposed sensitivity of the subject, Infield was precluded the use of the secretarial pool, and had to type it himself, pecking it out with two fingers. It was destined for PO Box 500, the official pseudonym for MI5. The inter service postal address for the counter espionage service. In which section's tray would it land? The Watchers? Double Agents? Military Liaison? Special Ops?

Even as he typed the surveillance report, he could not understand what was so delicate about it. Strange, he thought as he neared the end, that the Fourth Floor should designate the matter top secret.

They sat at a table by one of the big windows, overlooking the ornamental eighteenth century gardens. It fitted the mould to pick a place like the restaurant in Holland Park, tucked away, out of sight, thought Zarubin when he got the call.

"Now tell me," said Lambert, dabbing his neatly trimmed moustache with a napkin. "How have you settled in?"

Now we're getting to the point of the lunch, decided Zarubin.

"Fine," he replied. "It's a nice place to be, London."

"I suppose so. It's changed you know. You must have noticed, I mean, you've been here before." Lambert punctiliously folded the napkin. "Doesn't it seem different?"

"Everything changes," said Zarubin.

"Of course. Especially people." He looked at Zarubin. "Have you? Since you were last here, I mean?"

"Maybe. Perhaps I'm not the best person to tell."

Lambert gave a humourless smile.

"I suppose we'll have quite a lot to do with each other."

"We will?" Zarubin sounded vague.

"Oh, don't worry about being indiscreet, we've had a long telex about you. You'll have every cooperation." He leaned forward. "Unofficially, of course."

"I appreciate that," said Zarubin, warily.

"An interesting line, video cassettes," went on Lambert smoothly, as if it was one and the same subject. "Have you started your business yet?"

So, you even know the cover job, Zarubin mentally noted.

"I'm sort of getting into my stride. Slowly."

"What kind of cassettes?" asked Lambert.

"Home movies. Kind of . . ."

"Yes," interrupted Lambert. "That's the new fad isn't it? X certificates in the drawing room. Something TV can't compete with. You should do a roaring trade, importing them. Mature motives, they're called, I believe."

"I'll send you a catalogue. When it's printed."

Lambert sniffed and signalled the waiter for the bill. He was going to pay with a credit card, and Zarubin wondered if the service provided one for each member of the section.

As they waited, Lambert said unexpectedly:

"Unusual name, Zarubin."

"Russian. My folks came from Odessa."

"Oh, really? You don't mind my asking?"

"Why should I?"

Lambert leaned closer.

"And I suppose you speak the language fluently?"

"I can get along."

"How very useful. I'm always trying to get our lot to recruit more peole with your kind of background. Unfortunately, they tend to insist nowadays that one has to be of pure British stock, native born parents, and all that sort of thing. They're very fussy."

"Is that so?" said Zarubin, a little curtly. "I guess every service has its own ground rules."

"Precisely." Lambert lowered his voice slightly. "Actually, some of our best traitors can trace their ancestry right back to William the Conqueror. So I don't think it proves much."

The waiter brought the credit slip, and Lambert signed it. He worked out the gratuity to the exact ten per cent.

"I really enjoyed our little chat," he said as they went down the stairs. "And, look here, if there is any way I . . . we can be of assistance don't hesitate. Get in touch. Unofficially, of course."

"Of course," nodded Zarubin. He now understood the reason for the lunch. It wasn't what he could tell them; Lambert wanted him to be aware of what they knew. And they knew plenty.

"I'm being picked up," he announced outside the restaurant. "Can I drop you somewhere."

"Thanks," said Zarubin. "I think I'll take a stroll in the park."

Lambert looked around, annoyed.

"Where the devil is he?" he muttered, and, as if on cue, a car turned into the driveway.

It pulled up in front of them. The driver, a man in a blazer, got out.

"I'm sorry," he apologised, "the traffic . . ."

"That's all right, Druce," said Lambert. "But I have to get going now." He turned to Zarubin. "Are you sure you won't change your mind? It's no bother."

Zarubin shook his head.

"Well, au revoir then."

Zarubin watched the car disappear through the gateway. Interesting, he thought. Their outfit now uses Mercedes.

He didn't go for a walk. He picked up a cab in Holland Park Avenue, and went back to his flat at Marble Arch.

Once indoors, he took off his jacket, and then his shirt. The contraption that was strapped to his body was especially designed to be light weight, but after a time it tended to become uncomfortable. He was glad to take it off.

Then he sat down, and replayed the tape his tiny concealed microphone had recorded.

"I suppose we'll have quite a lot to do with each other," came Lambert's voice. The sound reproduction wasn't high quality, but that wasn't the object of the body wire. It had however recorded everything.

Blanchard, reflected Zarubin, should be pleased. It still intrigued him, though, why he not only wanted a full report of the meeting with Lambert, but an actual tape of their whole conversation.

Momentarily it made him wonder who it was that Blanchard didn't trust, but then he went and had a shower.

He wasn't really dirty, he just felt like having one.

The old traitor led a quiet, peaceful life these days. He was still a distinguished looking man, tall, carrying his seventy odd years well. He had white hair which nowadays he allowed to grow longer than when in the service.

He still lived in the same bachelor flat in Mount Street and, if the weather was nice, first thing in the morning he would often stroll over to the church yard opposite and sit on one of the wooden seats, reading his copy of *The Times*.

Then he would have coffee at Richoux in South Audley Street, always sitting at the marble topped table by the window, watching the Japanese air hostesses who stayed at a nearby hotel, and the Americans who came in for a midday snack.

South Audley Street had a special piquancy for him, because it was here that the section used to own a pied à terre. He still liked looking at the imposing Georgian house. He knew its secrets, and despite the later unpleasantness, still felt drawn to it. He had interrogated a couple of defectors there, and later, when they became suspicious, he'd had his first session with the inquisitors in the same room. But that was long, long ago.

He wondered if the department still had the flat. The windows were curtained, as they always were, and he couldn't detect any activity. Probably they had moved out years ago. It was an expensive piece of real estate, and he knew the department had cut down on luxuries.

He finished his second cup of coffee, got up and paid. He was a gentle, courteous man, and stepped aside to let the waitress pass.

He had a date with a bookseller in Berkeley Square, and he looked forward to the short walk through Mayfair.

He liked walking. Sometimes, in St James's, in Whitehall, in Curzon Street, he'd bump into people who knew him. It was always a delicate moment. Some cut him dead, others greeted him without thinking and then, as realisation dawned, they'd stammer and excuse themselves. But a few greeted him like the old acquaintance he was, and they would chat briefly.

He made a point of never embarrassing them. He didn't like people to feel awkward.

Although they had taken away his knighthood, he had never been prosecuted. Gradually, the publicity died away, and he had kept his silence. Now he lived in pleasant retirement. Some people even overlooked his loss of the title. The caretaker still called him "Sir Leslie", so did the cleaning woman.

And the one thing that nobody could take away from him was his fame as an oriental scholar. He was the finest living expert on Sun Tzu, the world's greatest spymaster, 2,400 years ago.

His definitive biography on the life of Sun Tzu, which he spent most evenings writing, was not only a labour of love but would be his memorial. Sometimes, as he sat studying the master's philosophy, he wondered if they would ever have uncovered his treachery had he followed the ancient teachings more faithfully.

The Divine Skein. That was it. A net comprising many strands all joined to a single cord. Somewhere his mistake had been to shred too many of the strands.

Not that the old traitor had made many mistakes. That's why they hadn't been able to try him. What he would have exposed would have been too costly. Or too embarrassing which, to them, was the same.

In the bookshop, he was treated as a scholar.

"I got your card," he said. "About the book . . ."

"Ah, yes," nodded the manager. "*The Art of War*. Sun Tzu. A nice volume. I'll get it."

The old traitor had acquired all the editions he could. He studied catalogues, wrote to America for copies, and wherever else he happened to discover there was one. It was, after all, the bible.

"Here we are, sir," said the manager, holding out the book. "A new translation," he went on.

"A recent translation," corrected the old traitor.

He bought it, to add to his collection, and briskly walked back to Mount Street.

In his flat he unwrapped the book, and began leafing through it, like a priest browsing through a holy scripture.

Foreknowledge is the reason the enlightened prince and the wise general conquer the enemy whenever they move (he read, and smiled.) It cannot be elicited from spirits, nor from gods, nor by analogy with past events, nor from calculations. It must be obtained from the men who know the enemy situation.

Quite so, thought the old traitor.

He went over to the sideboard, took out a crystal glass and decanter and poured himself a large armagnac. He held the glass up in a silent toast before drinking. A toast to past comrades – and others. As a gesture, it was entirely unself-concious. He might have been in a roomful of friends.

The old traitor was on his own, but not alone.

Later he rang his tailor, and enquired whether his new suit was ready. He was never too old to look smart.

Few people at Heathrow were aware that morning that the Moscow flight's take off had been delayed. The passengers already seated in the Aeroflot jet were simply told, over the plane's PA system, that departure would be held up for "a few minutes". No announcements were made in the airport itself.

Ten minutes after the Aeroflot desk had received the phone call to hold the flight, a Soviet Zim, with diplomatic licence plates, swept into the concourse of the departure building. Two men helped a woman passenger out of the car, and assisted her to passport control. They didn't bother with the ticket check. That had all been taken care of in London.

Nina Spiridov was pale, her lipstick smudged, and her red rimmed eyes glazed. She slumped between her escorts, and if the two men had not supported her, she would have stumbled and fallen.

One of the men, who had rimless glasses, handed three passports to the immigration officer.

"We are diplomats," he said. "Soviet Embassy."

One by one, the immigration officer examined the documents. Then he looked up at the woman. She was leaning against one of the men, a vacant expression on her face.

"This is not a diplomatic passport," pointed out the immigration officer, tapping the woman's document.

The bespectacled man smiled. "No, *we* are diplomats. We are taking this poor lady back home. You can see she is not well. We are looking after her."

He held out his hand for the passports.

"What's the matter with her?" asked the immigration officer.

The Russian shrugged. "She is sick. She needs good care. Please, our passports."

Out of the corner of his eye he saw another official approaching.

"Please," he repeated. "The plane is waiting. We must go." He lowered his voice. "You must understand, she has had a great shock. Her husband has just died."

"I'm sorry," commiserated the immigration officer. Then his colleague took over.

"Mrs Spiridov," he said. "Can I have a word with you?"

He hadn't looked at the passports, but he knew her name.

Nina Spiridov stared at him, uncomprehending. She held on to the arm of her escort.

The bespectacled Russian was getting angry.

"Can you not see she is sick? What is this for?"

"I would like to speak with the lady in private," insisted the official.

"No!" declared the Russian. "She is under our protection. She is with us. You will be sorry for this interference. We have diplomatic status."

The official took a deep breath. Then he said:

"I am not convinced Mrs Spiridov is leaving the United Kingdom of her own free will. Until I am satisfied that she is going with you voluntarily, she cannot board the plane. You gentlemen are of course free to proceed."

For the first time the other Russian spoke. He had a mild, gentle manner, but his words were different.

"Perhaps you don't understand. She is going with us. I warn you about interfering. It will have the gravest consequences." He paused, then asked silkily, "What precisely are you suggesting? That we are kidnapping her? That she is doped? We are not gangsters, you know."

"I have suggested nothing," said the official. He nodded to two policemen who were standing near the barrier. "I would suggest it's in everybody's interests to cooperate." He peered into the woman's blank eyes. "I also want a doctor to examine her. She may not be fit to travel."

"She is fit," snarled the bespectacled Russian. He said something rapidly in his own language to his colleague.

"Please go ahead," intervened the official. "You are at perfect liberty to call your embassy."

The bespectacled man was taken aback. "I did not realise you speak Russian."

"Let's say I understand it," said the official.

The policemen had taken up a strategic position at the back of the Russian party, and one of them was speaking softly into his radio.

It was then that the official was called to the phone. He went to a telephone cubicle in the passport hall, which was out of earshot of the others.

"Is that you, Rogers?" asked Lambert, at the other end.

"Yes sir."

"Let her go."

"Did you say . . ."

"I said let her board the plane," ordered Lambert.

"But the telex . . ."

"Forget the telex. We've changed our minds. Don't detain her."

The official spoke urgently. Time was running out. "I'm convinced she's under the influence of some kind of narcotic. She doesn't even know where she is. We can't just let them drag her on to the plane. I mean, surely . . ."

"Look here, Rogers, I'm sure you're right, but I have my orders. We don't want an incident."

"But her husband . . ."

"She can't help her husband, can she? Not any more. Give her her passport. Wave them goodbye. And do me a full report."

Rogers started to say something, then stopped.

"Do you understand me?" asked Lambert.

"The telex said under no circumstances . . ."

"I'm telling you. Those instructions are superseded. Goodbye."

Slowly Rogers put the phone down. He walked back to the passport area.

"You may board your flight," he said curtly.

The immigration officer looked baffled.

46

"Give them their documents," added Rogers.

"We will make a protest," said the Russian with the glasses triumphantly. "We will demand an apology."

"I'm sure you'll get it," said Rogers, and turned his back.

Zarubin seldom ate a proper breakfast. Several cups of black coffee, the morning paper, and a couple of cigarettes was the way he liked to start his day.

Now, as he stubbed out his ritual second cigarette and downed the remainder of the coffee, he decided that the moment to make contact with the man Dichter had called Theo the Greek couldn't be put off.

"He works for us?" Zarubin had asked before he'd left for London.

"Theo only works for himself. But he's got connections. All over. Get in touch with him," Dichter had instructed. "Use him. He'll be beneficial, especially on the other side."

"What is he?" What seemed more appropriate than who.

"He's a porn king. Retail, wholesale, you name it. He also controls a good slice of Soho. So deal with him. Sell him stuff. He'll give your cover the Good Housekeeping Seal of Approval."

Zarubin knew very well that sexual predilections were of great interest to Moscow, as were the people who supplied them. The names of their clients opened up all kinds of possibilities, especially when those clients were strategically or sensitively exploitable.

"What's my introduction?"

"The material you'll offer him. High grade porn. None of your mild stuff. Lots of close-ups of pussy and cocks. No simulated screwing. The real thing. He'll love it," Dichter had stated.

Zarubin blinked. The way the grey man said it, for one crazy moment, had made him wonder how Dichter got his kicks.

"Great if I get caught by customs taking it into merry old England," Zarubin had muttered.

"Don't worry about that," Dichter had assured him. "We'll ship it in discreetly. Air Force courier flights, diplomatic bags. British customs won't even get a sniff of it."

It was all so pat. Neatly worked out, pre-arranged.

"All this to set me up as a supplier of porno video tapes?"

"But who knows where it'll lead?" suggested Dichter, smiling coldly.

Then he'd handed Zarubin a photograph.

It was usual practice, supplying an agent with a picture of the person with whom a connection was to be made, and Zarubin was always intrigued by these photographs.

In his time, he had been given photos of contacts taken in night clubs, by the swimming pool, in airport lounges, shopping in supermarkets, walking in some park. Once he'd even been given a print of his target making love in the backroom of a Hong Kong brothel. Mostly they were snapshots, and the subject was completely unaware that it had been taken.

The picture of Theo was curiously anonymous. The background was indistinguishable. It could have been a room, a café, an office, and to judge from Theo's expression, if he'd known he was being photographed, he didn't mind. Maybe he'd actually known the person behind the camera.

Although the shot was only of Theo's head and shoulders, it was enough for Zarubin to take an instant dislike to the man. His fat, moon shaped face with its multiple chins looked greasy, and his thick, rubbery lips were set in a smug self satisfied smile. All that was missing was the blonde he'd probably had his arm around and the bottle of champagne in the ice bucket at his elbow. He did not appear to be the sort of person who would endear himself to Zarubin.

The last questions he had asked about Theo concerned the man's background. Where did he come from? What was his nationality?

"Oh," Dichter had replied airily, "he usually travels on a Greek passport."

Dichter's answer had almost tempted Zarubin to ask who had supplied it. Athens? Moscow? Or . . .

But that wouldn't have been wise.

Zarubin rinsed out his coffee cup, put on his raincoat, and with his samples in a Fortnum and Mason shopping bag, left the apartment.

Outside, the grey London drizzle had reduced Edgware Road to a crawling traffic jam. He couldn't even find a taxi until he'd almost reached the Cumberland Hotel at Marble Arch. Then two fierce German women in plastic raincoats beat him to it, and jumped in ahead of him.

Zarubin swore silently. It took a further fifteen minutes and several aborted attempts before, finally, he succeeded in getting another one.

"Nice day for the ducks," remarked the driver amiably, weaving the cab through the snarled up traffic of Oxford Street.

"Guess so," replied Zarubin without conviction.

The cabby kept chatting all the way to Wardour Street and when Zarubin told him to stop in front of a massage parlour he winked knowingly. Maybe he thought he knew why a lone American wanted to be taken to this part of Soho.

"Enjoy yourself," he smiled.

Zarubin grunted, but he gave the man a generous tip. Even if it wasn't meant, Zarubin appreciated somebody going through the motions of being friendly.

The small, shabby office at the rear of the Old Compton Street sex shop which served as his headquarters belied Theo the Greek's life style. The business had bought him a £250,000 mansion near Windsor, a Rolls Royce, three racehorses, two supermarkets, and paid for a son at Harrow.

"I'm only interested in strong stuff," he declared, resting his feet on the battered desk, and biting off the end of a green cigar.

"It's strong stuff," Zarubin assured him.

"And you've got to supply me regularly. I've a lot of customers to keep happy."

"It'll come regular," said Zarubin.

Theo grunted. He liked American freelance dealers. They were unlikely to be cops; the Yard's vice squad didn't have the wardrobe to pose as Yanks. And they showed initiative. He did well out of Yanks. If it wasn't for an airline pilot on the Atlantic run, and a couple of US Navy yeomen, he wouldn't have some of his best imports. God knows how they got it through customs.

"Well," said Theo, "let's see some of it. Only the strong bits."

Zarubin selected five titles from the collection, and for half an hour they sat, watching bits of the tapes on the 21 inch colour television set.

"Not bad," nodded Theo finally. "Lighting is good, camera work's sharp. Not bad."

He could have been a movie buff discussing Hollywood's latest product. Which, in a way, it was.

"How many titles can you let me have?" he enquired, chewing his cigar.

"As many as you need," replied Zarubin. Dichter would organise that. He wondered if a special section spent its time shooting blue movies.

"And the next lot?"

Christ, thought Zarubin, it's only supposed to be a cover. I'm not going into the pornography business.

"I'll see what I can get."

"Okay then." Theo heaved his bulk out of his chair. "I'll pay you in cash."

"Fine!"

Theo studied Zarubin. "You don't haggle much, do you? Haven't even talked about money. What's the matter, aren't you interested?"

"I guess I trust you." He shrugged.

Theo bit violently on his cigar. Then he said: "You got a lot to learn. But I won't sell you short."

"Of course not," smiled Zarubin. "Otherwise I go to the competition."

Theo's mouth curled. "I wouldn't, friend." He dug his hand into his pocket and came out with a wad of money. He counted off ten fifty pound notes. "Here. You don't deliver, and you'll see what happens. So take it. Now you're obligated, see?"

For a moment Zarubin hesitated.

"Okay," he agreed, wondering whether technically the money now belonged to the government.

"When will you bring the first batch?"

"Soon," said Zarubin.

"Supplying me can make you rich," claimed Theo. "You should see my customers. They got money. I got stockbrokers, bank managers, oil men, lawyers." He chuckled at the thought. "If I get nicked, I can take my pick. Three QCs, five solicitors. Respectable, that's the trade now." He paused, then in a conspiratorial tone added:

"I've even got a couple of vicars. There's one in Surrey who I think gives shows."

"Well, I suppose television is pretty dull these days," grinned Zarubin. "From what I've seen over here."

Theo liked that. He laughed.

"What d'you do?" he asked jovially. "I mean when you're not flogging blue video cassettes?"

"Whatever comes along."

"Well, maybe I can put a little business your way, if it works out, eh? I might expand, you never know."

"That sounds interesting."

Theo took him through the shop in front. Silent men were leafing through glossy sex magazines. Rubber appliances stood displayed on shelves. One was a huge rubber penis.

"It's fantasy time here," said Theo. "Just like Disneyland. You get trade discount."

"Thanks," said Zarubin, "I got my own."

In the street, he took a deep breath of fresh air.

Detective Sergeant Infield, loitering by a lamp post across the road, noted the time Zarubin emerged from the porn emporium. Slowly he began to follow him. Box 500 wanted a full report.

He resented the assignment. Dirty pictures were a job for the Obscene Publications Squad, not Special Branch. Somebody seemed to have his wires crossed.

But he consoled himself that nobody would spot him. In his dirty raincoat, he fitted into Soho perfectly.

The phone rang and, half asleep, Zarubin reached for it, knocking over the glass of water beside it, and soaking his slippers and one sock.

"Shit!" he snarled.

As he picked up the receiver he noticed the alarm clock on the bedside table showed 6.40 am. There was at least another half hour before it was due to sound.

"Yeah?"

"Andrew?" boomed Lambert's voice. He sounded bright, like a man who's been up a long time, jogged for a couple of miles in the park, and eaten a hearty breakfast. "Did I wake you?"

"That's okay." Zarubin's tongue felt thick.

"Sorry about that," apologised Lambert cheerfully. "Listen, can you meet me?"

"What now?" He was still trying to clear his head.

"As soon as possible. Can you make it in half an hour?"

"Can't it wait?"

"No. I'll be expecting you. Kensington police station."

"Eh?"

"Kensington police station. Earl's Court Road."

Zarubin sat up in bed. "What the hell for?"

"This isn't a secure line," Lambert rebuked him. "Just hurry up and get here. We've got to work fast."

And he hung up.

So this is liaising, thought Zarubin, wryly.

Lev Kosov was finishing breakfast when they entered the interview room. The remains of a lone egg, a rasher of bacon, one blackened sausage, a piece of fried bread and the soiled plastic cutlery lay on a tin plate. Next to it stood an enamel mug of tea.

It had been a long night for him. His tie had been taken away, and his shirt was crumpled. He needed a shave. His bloodshot eyes regarded them balefully.

"The food is disgusting," he complained, pushing the plate away. "Too greasy. Not fit for a pig."

"I'm sorry about that," said Lambert. "It's from the canteen."

"Who are you?" demanded Kosov.

"May we sit down?" enquired Lambert politely. The room was empty except for the plain wooden table at which they sat. There was no carpet, and the walls were painted a kind of institutional green. The single window was high up, and barred. He indicated Zarubin. "This is my American colleague."

He didn't give any names, but Kosov nodded.

"Of course, you're CIA."

"Actually, I'm not," said Lambert a little stiffly.

"I have nothing to say to you," snapped Kosov. "I demand to be released immediately."

"Quite right," agreed Lambert, and Zarubin raised an eyebrow.

"You have no right to hold me," went on Kosov, watching them warily. "I have official status."

Lambert pushed the tin plate to one side. The congealed leftovers appeared to offend him.

"Strictly speaking, of course, you do not enjoy diplomatic immunity. But I am inclined to agree. You are special."

Kosov blinked. "I will not mince my words. There has been a deliberate provocation. It is . . . what do you say, a set up. You understand?"

"Perfectly."

"The girl was clearly one of your operatives." Kosov glared at them. "I had no idea. To me, she was just a . . . casual acquaintance. I visited her a couple of times, that's all. Suspecting nothing. How could I know you use common prostitutes?"

Even Zarubin had to smile. But Kosov continued indignantly:

"Last night, I dropped in to say hello. I fell asleep. She probably drugged me. When I wake up, I am surrounded by police. They accuse me of rape. They handcuff me. They bring me here." He snorted. "It is an outrage. So clumsy it is laughable. Do you think a judge, a court would believe this ridiculous fabrication for one moment?"

"Probably not," concurred Lambert. He glanced at Zarubin. "What's your guess? What do you think the odds are?"

Zarubin studied the wall.

"I don't think my colleague is a gambling man," observed Lambert airily.

Kosov's expression was grim. He jabbed a stubby forefinger at them.

"I warn you. The consequences will be serious. When my embassy hears . . ."

"When your embassy hears, you'll be in big trouble, Mr Kosov," interrupted Lambert, very gently. "A promising career will be cut short."

Kosov started to say something, then changed his mind.

"People who become careless and allow themselves to be publicly compromised don't have any future in the service, do they?" Lambert's smile was thin. "I think your ministry will make quite an example of you."

Kosov winced. "But I am innocent."

"What does that have to do with it?" asked Lambert impatiently. "You've become an embarrassment, my friend. An unwise indiscretion has blown up in your face."

The Russian swallowed hard. "I will explain that I have been framed. They will know you organised it."

"And they won't forgive you for giving us the opportunity," purred Lambert. "No, my friend, it's a one way ticket home for you. And a job shovelling cow dung on a collective farm, if you're lucky. Unless they bring charges, to set an example."

Kosov swore in Russian. Lambert didn't seem to understand it, but Zarubin's dark eyes flickered momentarily. It was a very dirty word.

"That is if your people ever find out," added Lambert.

Kosov didn't move.

"Perhaps there is no reason why they ever should," he went on, looking at his wrist watch. "It is now seven forty-five. You're not due at your desk at the Trade Mission until nine. Plenty of time to get a shave, smarten yourself up, and carry on as if nothing's happened."

"I do not understand," muttered Kosov, but he was beginning to. So was Zarubin, and he didn't like it.

"Suppose we forget about the whole thing. Pretend it never happened."

Zarubin held his breath. That was why Lambert had wanted him there. To make him a party to this shabby deal. To share the responsibility. And the guilt, if things went wrong.

"There is a price for this, of course," said Kosov.

"Let's say, one good turn deserves another."

"I am no traitor."

"Good heavens, no. No more than I am. We are all patriots. We all do our duty." Lambert made a gesture, embracing the three of them. "But we also have an obligation. To ourselves. The first law is called self preservation, isn't it? Even the most heroic pilot has a parachute."

Kosov was ashen faced. "You are asking me to betray my motherland."

"Nonsense," declared Lambert. "We are offering you the use of the parachute. But the choice is yours."

He paused.

"If you prefer, the Foreign Office will inform your embassy later this morning that you were arrested for alleged rape. We may even graciously agree to hand you over. And you know what will happen then. The embassy will have you on the next plane to Moscow, you'll be stripped of everything, and face disciplinary action. We will be highly cooperative, and provide full details of your association with the lady, perhaps even the odd picture or two."

He smiled encouragingly at Kosov.

"It's up to you."

Remind me never to turn my back on this man. Every minute I'm in his company, I must be on my guard, thought Zarubin.

Kosov pushed back his chair, and stood up. He walked over to the barred window, but it was too high for him to see out. He stood with his back to them, looking at the wall.

At last he turned round. His face was set.

"What is it you want me to do?" he asked.

Flexner re-read the advertisement in *Time* magazine and sighed.

"We are the Central Intelligence Agency. We're looking for very special people. You may be one of them.

"If you are a college graduate, have an interest in overseas affairs, know a foreign language or can learn one, and can make on-the-spot decisions, we may have room for you.

"There are vacancies," it continued, "for overseas case officers, intelligence analysts, scientists and computer specialists."

Trainees started at $22,000 a year.

Over lunch in the embassy commissary, he'd mentioned it to Crawford, the NSA man.

"Langley's putting in want ads now," he'd remarked, expecting incredulity, maybe outrage. Crawford, after all, was a professional.

"Yeah, I saw that," nodded Crawford, digging into his club sandwich.

"That's not the way to find the right talent."

Crawford shrugged. "Why not?"

"Motivation, for one thing."

"Twenty-two thousand bucks isn't bad motivation for a college leaver, I'd say."

Flexner had dropped the subject.

Back in his office he sat gazing at the advertisement and ruminating how things had changed since the old days. Then it had been a fraternity. Mostly the same accents. They wore tweeds. Smoked pipes. People shook hands. You had to be chosen to become part of it.

Now they had people like Zarubin.

Nothing wrong with Zarubin, of course. He couldn't help his name, or that his parents probably got stuck on Ellis Island before they were finally admitted into the United States.

Maybe it was his eyes. Never still. Always shifting. Looking over your shoulder. And his curiously terse manner. Holding things back. On his guard.

I'd never have recruited him, decided Flexner. Not for the special section. Not for covert operations. As a desk bound translator, maybe. A researcher perhaps. But not as a field agent.

Flexner pressed his intercom.

"Miss Walsh, I've got a headache. I think I'll go home."

"Can I get you something?" asked his secretary. "An aspirin maybe? I can slip down to the dispensary . . ."

"No, I'll be all right," said Flexner. "I'll have an early night."

He left the embassy by the rear entrance, where the cars were parked. He was glad he missed the thin line of pickets, loafing at the railings of the Grosvenor Square gardens, opposite the building's front steps. They were a familiar bunch, brandishing home made placards. He couldn't even remember what they were protesting about this week.

Briskly he walked to the Grosvenor House, looked at his watch, and went into one of the hotel's phone booths. The number rang a couple of times before being answered.

"Hello," replied a woman's voice.

"Debbie, it's me," announced Flexner.

"How lovely," she said.

"I got away early."

"Where are you now?"

There was no reason for his hesitation. It was just an inbuilt caution.

"In town," he said, vaguely.

"Would you like to come round?" she asked.

"Just for an hour."

"Fine."

"I won't be long," added Flexner.

"Hurry up."

He stepped out of the phone booth, pleased with himself. He could just fit it in nicely.

It was safe, completely safe, he reassured himself. She thought he worked for an American cosmetics firm. She had no idea where his office was.

And she was very understanding. She understood his position. A married man, who had to snatch his extra mural pleasures as and when he could. He had a difficult wife, so she quite accepted that it could only be the odd hour here and there.

He was very cautious. They never went out together. Being seen with her in public could cause problems. You never knew who you might come across in a restaurant, or bump into in the street. Flexner didn't believe in unnecessary risks.

He passed one of the hotel's shops, and paused, considering whether to buy her a little present. A box of chocolates perhaps. But, almost immediately, he dismissed the idea. She might misinterpret the gesture. It wasn't that kind of relationship, anyway.

In Park Lane, he hailed a cab, and gave her address. He settled back, and, as he took out his wallet, his hand shook a little.

It wasn't like him. Usually he wasn't nervous. Especially not before seeing her.

Zarubin was about to get into the lift when the hall porter came over. He still remembered the good tip he had received from Zarubin when he'd helped him with his luggage into the block.

"Excuse me," said the porter. "You're Mr Rubin?"

"Zarubin."

"A lady's been asking about you."

"Oh?"

"Didn't say who she was. She just wanted to know about you."

"What did she want to know?" asked Zarubin quietly.

"Which flat you're in. If you go out a lot. How many visitors you have, that sort of thing."

"And what did you tell her?"

"Well, I don't know anything, do I?"

"Smart man," said Zarubin, pressing a five pound note into the hall porter's ready palm. It paid to buy loyalty. "What did she look like?"

"Good looker," said the porter. "Blonde. Black raincoat. Nice legs," he added, his beery face leering.

"Did she go up?"

"Wouldn't let her if she'd wanted. Not when you're not here."

"English?"

"Oh, very much so. You don't mind me telling you?"

"I appreciate it." Zarubin's tone indicated future information would be rewarded. "Did she say anything else, leave any message?"

"No, sir. They just drove off."

"They?"

"Somebody was in the car. Never came in."

"What kind of car?"

"Metro," said the porter disdainfully.

"I see." Zarubin was thoughtful as he turned to open the lift gates.

"By the way, sir, the house manager says could you kindly leave your spare set of keys at the desk. In case of emergency. When you're out."

Zarubin shook his head.

"Tell the house manager that I don't leave my key with anybody."

He closed the lift gates, and pressed the button for his floor.

What was it that Dichter had said about being a pot of honey? Maybe the bees had started buzzing.

By force of habit, Kosov never told a cab driver his exact destination. He would name the neighbourhood, and then, when he was near the location, tell the driver to stop, pay him, and watch the cab drive off, before walking the short remaining distance.

It was a pointless exercise, most times, but Kosov was both nervous and pedantic, and this routine reassured him.

So he got out in the Bayswater Road, and walked into Kensington Palace Gardens.

The forty-two seater blue bus with its diplomatic licence plates was standing in the driveway of the embassy. On Saturday mornings it departed promptly at 11 am, and there was still five minutes to go.

The bus was already three quarters full of embassy personnel who, like Kosov, were casually dressed.

As was customary, they were all off to spend the weekend at Hawkhurst, the country estate of the Soviet Embassy in Kent.

Hawkhurst played a very special role in the social life of the Russian diplomatic community in London. Within the walls surrounding the secluded mansion, the former country seat of an English lord, was a corner of the motherland; providing Russian cooking, a library with the newest Soviet books and periodicals, play facilities for the children, chess games, and, most importantly, togetherness.

For the taciturn men charged with the security of the Kremlin's London mission, Hawkhurst was the solution to many problems. It kept the families together in one place, isolated them, prevented undesirable outside contacts, ensured that they did not slip into non-communist habits, or meet dangerous acquaintances.

Attendance at Hawkhurst was voluntary, but those who were never seen there were noted, unless their rank and position gave them special status, or, of course, they were on duty.

Families had their own suites at Hawkhurst, and for the singles there were individual rooms. Although informality was the key note, there were certain firm rules. One of them was that single men and women did not cohabit. The morality at Hawkhurst would have rejoiced the heart of a YMCA supervisor. It was strict to a degree.

Kosov spent most of his weekends at the place. As a man on his own, the country club offered a great deal. Lots to drink. The kind of cuisine he missed. Conversation with his own kind. Even the odd flirtation.

Of course, he knew that he was expected to avail himself of the facilities. Otherwise they'd start wondering what he did on his weekends off.

Kosov got on the bus, and saw a free window seat at the back. He threaded his way through, picked up a ball that rolled towards him and handed it back to its owner, a little girl with pigtails, smiled at a couple of officials he knew vaguely, nodded to one of the wives he had met at a cocktail party, and finally sank into his seat, grateful to relax.

He was a worried man, and this weekend at Hawkhurst would not be an ordinary one. He stared out of the window at the lone bobby on duty outside the embassy. In his sentry box, he had a thick book in which he logged all the car numbers that called at the Soviet offices.

Kosov closed his eyes. He could hear the chatter of the other passengers, a hum of Russian, the children's giggles. But his thoughts were on his own problem.

He had to make a decision that would affect his whole future. He had to make it soon, or it would be too late. And if it was the wrong decision . . .

In his mind, he had gone over it half a dozen times, and was almost certain. Now, the awful doubt began to grow again.

A gross, plain woman in a garishly patterned dress struggled on to the bus, followed by her husband, an official in the consulate's visa section. He looked hot and bothered. She sat down, then began loudly ordering him about. The man took it all meekly. His weekend relaxation was only just beginning. He had lots more of this to come.

A black car pulled up in Kensington Palace Gardens beside the policeman. Kosov watched the officer bend down and chat to the man in the brown suit behind the wheel. They seemed to know each other. They both looked up at the bus.

They must watch it all, thought Kosov. I bet they film this bus leaving every weekend. I bet they shadow the bus, and know everybody on it. I bet they keep tabs on each one of us.

He gave a small sigh. He knew only too well how they operated.

The driver boarded. He was a burly man, and wore an unzipped windcheater and jeans. Apart from being the driver, he was also one of the embassy's security guards. He started the engine, and the bus swung out of the driveway, towards the Kensington High Street exit.

Kosov settled back. He wasn't a gambling man, but he knew what it must feel like to put all your chips on one number.

If he was about to make a mistake . . .

But as the bus crossed Vauxhall Bridge he knew it was too late to talk about ifs.

Because Soviet Embassy personnel were not allowed to travel beyond a twenty-five mile radius of London, except to certain agreed destinations, Hawkhurst being one of them, the bus had to take a set route.

Only junior personnel used it. Senior staff journeyed to the country club in their own cars. But though they may not have rated high on the Foreign Office list, the passengers were key people in the Embassy hierarchy. They were the clerical staff who handled the secret files, did the cypher work, coded the curious messages passing between London and Moscow; they were the ones who knew the names, and the faces, typed the classified memos, and who watched. Watched others. Watched one another.

Like Kosov watched them. He had long learnt that, whether it was the embassy in Millionaires' Row, the consulate on the Bayswater Road, the Aeroflot office in Piccadilly, the trade mission at Highgate, the cultural activities office, Intourist, or the latest symphony orchestra exchange, one never knew just who might be behind the façade.

As the bus drove through the heartland of bourgeois Kent, Kosov wondered if one of them was keeping him under surveillance. The dark haired girl sitting by the hydraulic door, serious looking, who had glanced back at him a couple of times. Who was she? A stenographer? A clerk?

Then there was the man in the turtle neck sweater, chatting to his wife. He'd given Kosov a curious look.

It's nerves, that's all, Kosov decided and stared out of the window. You are behaving like some Dostoyevsky character, he admonished himself, nagged by guilt, fear.

The bus came to a halt. They had arrived.

A six foot high wall surrounded the Hawkhurst estate, and on the main gate there was a sign with a single word: "Private". Automatically, controlled by those out of sight, the gate slowly swung open, and the bus started making its way towards the big, aristocratic mansion.

Behind it, the gate closed, and as it progressed along the driveway, two men stood, watching it. One of them waved, and a few children waved back.

The men smiled, but Kosov knew they were scrutinising every passenger.

One of the men had just arrived in England and was the person Kosov had come to see.

Vladimir Yenko, deputy chief of Special Service II, the counter intelligence division of the KGB, was slightly built, almost sparrowlike, with keen, sharp eyes that darted everywhere. He smiled readily, deceptively. And he missed nothing, whether it was an exchange of looks at the back of a crowded room, the text of a letter lying upside down on somebody else's desk, or a nervous cough to cover up something embarrassing.

"Perhaps we should go for a little stroll," Yenko greeted him, leading the way round the back of the house to the garden.

Kosov followed, trying not to betray his disquiet. Yenko's amiability bothered him. He knew the man's reputation.

"Isn't it pleasant?" smiled Yenko, taking a deep breath as they crossed the grass towards the trees in the distance. "I must say an English summer's day can be delightful, don't you agree?"

"Yes," replied Kosov dully. This was not at all how he had expected it.

They walked slowly, side by side.

"You people here are very lucky to have this place," Yenko

mused. "It was a brilliant idea to buy it. I wonder who in Moscow thought of it. I gather it belonged to some lord or other?"

"I believe so," said Kosov.

"A gem. An absolute gem. And what beautiful flowers."

They reached the fringe of the little wood that was part of the estate.

"Shall we explore?" suggested Yenko.

He didn't wait for Kosov's answer but entered the wood, and suddenly they were in a gloomy, shadowy world, where there was no sunshine.

"So," began Yenko at last, "they're trying to blackmail you."

To Kosov it was a relief. At last they were talking about it.

"As I reported," he almost gabbled, "an absolute provocation. I know what I did was inexcusable, Comrade Yenko. I admit my gross lapse, but how was I to know the extent of their perfidy? Such a provocation! But they have made a mistake, a great mistake. I know my duty. I am a loyal party member, a patriotic servant of the state. I have an oath of honour, so there has been no question of betraying my trust. There was never any question, believe me. That is why, of course, I had to report this matter, regardless of the consequences to myself. Any disciplinary measures . . ."

Yenko stepped on a twig, and it cracked sharply.

"My friend," he intervened gently, "who on earth is talking about disciplinary measures?"

Kosov stopped and stared at him, his face flushed.

"You mean . . ."

"I mean that of course you were at fault to allow yourself to be compromised, but your conduct now is exemplary."

"Thank you Comrade Yenko," he whispered huskily.

"Please," said Yenko, and took him by the arm. "Tell me how often have you been with Deborah?"

It was said casually, carelessly, and Kosov felt a sudden chill of fear. He had never told Yenko her name.

"Only five . . . five or six times," he stuttered.

"Just sex, was it?"

"Nothing else, I assure you. She . . . she is a whore."

"You paid her?"

Kosov squirmed. "Oh, the odd bottle of vodka now and then. That sort of thing."

"But she gave you good value?" Kosov glanced at the man sharply, but Yenko gave no sign of being sarcastic.

"Come my friend," added Yenko jovially, "we are men of the world. Would you recommend little Deborah? Would you say she gives value in bed?"

The ferret like eyes were fixed on him.

"She was all right," murmured Kosov sullenly. Nothing was going the way he'd expected it.

"Now, about these two men who came to see you at the police station . . ."

"Yes."

"Describe them."

"One was English, sort of upper class. Military moustache, correct haircut, well preserved, skilful. 'We are all patriots,' he said. Quite persuasive, Comrade Yenko. A professional."

"Yes," said Yenko, "Lambert knows his job."

"Lambert?" Once again he felt that icy chill. "You know who it was?"

"His name is Lambert," explained Yenko. "One of their special section people. It's the other I want to know about."

"He was younger and better looking, but he had very cold eyes. Rugged, athletic. I got the impression he didn't like Lambert. My guess is he's an American."

"American?"

"I don't know." Kosov shook his head. "He didn't say a word. But he looked American. His shirt, his tie. And I think he understands Russian."

"Indeed!" Suddenly Yenko was very interested. "What makes you say that?"

"Well, I got angry at this English bastard, and I called him a sow's son, in Russian, and I saw the American's reaction. He knew what I was saying. He understood."

Yenko's thin lips puckered into a smile.

"Very interesting. Well observed, Lev Kosov. Full marks."

They were now in the middle of the wood, and their progress was slower. Occasionally they had to duck to avoid the overhanging low branches of trees.

"Shall we go back now?" proposed Yenko.

Kosov was waiting for the most important question but Yenko didn't ask it until they were out of the wood, and walking back across the lawn.

"All this, all this set up, this provocation, this blackmail, and what is it for? What do they want from you?"

Kosov took a deep breath.

"They want a courier."

"Go on."

"They know I go back and forth quite a lot. They want somebody who can travel easily inside our country. Not a foreigner who is limited to certain areas. They want, as they put it, a postman who can pick up something for them, and bring it back with him."

"Pick up what?" asked Yenko softly.

Kosov spread his hands.

"I have no idea. All they said was that when the time came I would be approached. Somebody would give me something. To bring back to London."

They strolled in silence. Yenko brushed away a bee that came buzzing too close.

"They must trust you a lot," he said eventually. "They must really believe they have frightened the life out of you, and that they've scared you into doing their dirty business."

He shook his head.

"It is so clumsy, is it not? It lacks finesse. They'd be taking such an enormous risk. The odds are too great that you'd report it. As you have done."

Abruptly he stopped.

"Or perhaps there is more to it. Perhaps you did not just sleep with this Deborah. Perhaps you told her things. Pillow talk." His eyes narrowed. "Perhaps you are involved deeper than you've told me."

Kosov turned pale. "Would I have come forward . . ."

"Maybe, my friend, you're an exceptionally good actor," said Yenko.

It pleased him to see Kosov lean against a tree for support. The man seemed about to be sick.

Yenko congratulated himself that he had not lost his touch.

*   *   *

She lay in the centre of the floor, and, apart from false eyelashes, she wore nothing.

Her body was still desirable, but the death mask that was her face made some of the men in the room look away. The photographer was taking pictures, but her twisted grimace made him swallow hard.

"No sign of forcible entry," reported the detective sergeant. "Whoever did it, she let in."

Chief Superintendent McIver nodded. He was waiting for the doctor to complete his examination.

She had only been found an hour before, by the West Indian cleaning woman who was now in the kitchen, her hysterics reduced to quiet sobbing.

The doctor straightened up.

"Suffocation," he announced, stripping off his rubber gloves.

McIver grunted.

The doctor nodded to his secretary, who stood in the corner, note book ready.

"The body is still warm," he began dictating, "and her vaginal temperature is eighty-four degrees fahrenheit. The room temperature is sixty-three. Allowing for the usual rise in temperature of asphyxial death, I estimate the time of death was" – he glanced at his watch – "around midnight. In the absence of any strangulation marks or any other cause for the blocking of the air passages, such as I may find in the autopsy later, I attribute death to suffocation caused by covering the nostrils and mouth with something soft enough to have left no mark."

"Like that?" asked McIver, pointing at a green velvet cushion lying nearby.

"Yes," replied the doctor. "That might be it." He cleared his throat and resumed dictating. "There are bruises on the left side of the face, one three inches to the right of the midline of the jaw, consistent to having been caused by a fist."

The secretary was swiftly noting it in copy book shorthand. She was a plain girl, and McIver had met her on other jobs. She always accompanied the doctor to the scenes of murders, taking his notes. She appeared oblivious to the grisly sights she witnessed. She took putrifying flesh, hacked off limbs, and blood soaked corpses in her stride.

The doctor finished his dictation, and began packing up his small leather bag.

"What was she?" he asked conversationally. "A whore?"

"A business lady," answered McIver tactfully.

"And pretty successful, I imagine," observed the doctor, looking round the room.

"Yes. All right if I have her taken to the mortuary?"

The doctor snapped shut the bag. "As far as I'm concerned."

"You'll let me know about the PM," asked McIver.

"Of course. Later today maybe." He turned to the secretary. "All set, Jean?"

"Yes doctor," she confirmed primly. She stepped past the body as if it didn't exist.

"Hope I haven't got a parking ticket," remarked the doctor as they made their exit. It was for McIver's benefit. He'd be expected to straighten it out.

McIver went to the window and looked down into the street. A couple of police cars were parked outside, and a handful of people stared up at the flat. That was all.

He took out a packet of cigarettes, started to light one, and only then remembered it would set a bad example to smoke at the scene of a crime. He put the cigarettes back in his pocket.

Lambert came out of the bedroom with the American. McIver regarded them with distaste.

"What exactly is your interest in this, Mr Lambert?" he asked, coldly. He resented anonymous faces with the authority to trample around his patch.

"She did some work for us, Superintendent," replied Lambert politely.

"You being . . ."

"Special Branch knows all about it," explained Lambert, airily.

"Well, I'd like to know," snapped McIver. "What work did she do?"

"You can always get me here," said Lambert, evading the question and handing him a card. It had an office address off Berkeley Square printed on it and two telephone numbers, but it clarified nothing.

"And you are?" McIver asked the American.

"He's my colleague," replied Lambert.

The mortuary crew lifted Deborah's body on to a stretcher, covered it with a blanket, then carried it out.

"I know you haven't had much time, but have you any ideas, Mr McIver?" enquired Lambert.

"Ideas?"

"Who might have done this."

"Well," began McIver slowly, "I rather think that whoever killed her knew her very well."

"I think you're absolutely right," concurred Lambert.

He glanced at Zarubin. "Wouldn't you agree, Andrew?"

You bastard, thought Zarubin. Is this how you repay her for setting up Kosov? But he didn't say it aloud.

Lambert and Zarubin left the flat together, then they went their separate ways.

As he walked back towards Marble Arch, Zarubin kept thinking how the poor bitch had been a sitting target.

Of course, they all used girls like her. The CIA, the KGB, the Germans, the French, the Israelis. The oldest profession in the world was the oldest weapon in the arsenal.

What was the phrase Lambert had used? "She did some work for us." Yes, indeed, Deborah had fucked men on behalf of Her Majesty's Government. When ordered, she seduced, lured, trapped unwitting victims. She screwed them for the benefit of hidden cameras, set them up for blackmail, compromised them.

He had come across Debbies in all sorts of places. They were the type who picked up embassy personnel at cocktail parties, homed in on diplomats in smart bars, or boring receptions. They found their likely prospects standing in corners holding a glass, their eyes roving.

Curiously, men who knew better were easy marks for the likes of Debbie. There was the station chief in Lisbon. The second attaché in Rome . . .

He wondered why Deborah had worked for the British service. Was it simply because they paid well or that she'd been given no alternative – it was either that or jail. On the other hand, she might just have been a patriotic whore. He smiled wryly at the thought.

Zarubin's guess was that Lambert had got some hold over her. Perhaps she was paying off a debt, she'd been a girl with expensive tastes, after all. The apartment proved that.

But who had killed her and why?

Maybe, Deborah had just fallen victim to the hazards of her profession. She was a freelance, and had private clients. One of them might have done it: the mortality rate among hookers was notoriously high. But Zarubin didn't buy that.

It could be the other side. Moscow Central might well have decided that she had trapped one man too many, that there would be no more Kosovs. Yet, it wasn't Moscow's style to murder call girls. Unless, of course, she was more important than he'd realised. So, it could be the opposition.

Or Lambert's own section. Zarubin had no illusions. If Deborah had outlived her usefulness, become a nuisance, demanded more money, made threats, they might well have got rid of her. Yes, it certainly could have been the British themselves.

Back in his apartment, Zarubin brewed himself a cup of coffee. He sat in the armchair, thoughtfully sipping the hot liquid. There were a lot of candidates on his list.

He had aged since his last night with Deborah. The strain and insomnia of the last few days had left Kosov wan, tired looking and in a state of anxiety about the meeting.

It was a scheduled appointment, part of the arrangement with Lambert. Occasional get togethers on certain days, at certain times, in certain places. No phone calls. No letters. No contact in between.

He had told Yenko about it, of course. But then by the time Yenko had finished with him, he would have told him anything.

"You must go, naturally," Yenko had instructed him. "Nothing must prevent you. If they want you to do something, appear eager. Encourage them to confide in you. Show enthusiasm. And then you report to me what they said to you."

"Of course, comrade. I will immediately get in touch, and tell you everything."

Yenko's reaction had been withering.

"You do not get in touch," he'd said, almost contemptuously. "We get in touch with you."

Practically identical to Lambert's instructions, they have much in common, thought Kosov ruefully.

He'd tried to time his arrival to the minute and had gone to elaborate lengths to shake off any possible shadow. He'd taken a cab to Madame Tussauds waxworks, paid it off, crossed to the other side of Marylebone Road, walked to Great Portland Street, caught an underground back to Baker Street, then walked to Regent's Park.

It was a pathetic charade, he reflected, as he sat down on the bench near the boat lake, feeling the most conspicuous man in Regent's Park. Eventually the assignation would be no secret to either side, he told himself, but he still couldn't shake off the feeling that he was being watched, that invisible eyes were following him everywhere. Perhaps it was just that the sleepless nights were taking their toll.

He sat waiting nervously, an insignificant, lone figure in a worn suit.

A youngish man in a navy blazer came along the path and sat down on the bench. He was close enough to Kosov to betray a certain degree of familiarity, but not so near as to make it obvious to a stranger.

Damn the fellow, thought Kosov, shifting uneasily. If Lambert saw the man sitting there beside him, he might call the whole thing off. And then he'd have to tell Yenko the meeting had aborted, and Yenko might not believe him.

The unpleasant queasy feeling started again in his stomach. Panic was a familiar companion to Kosov these days.

"Mr Lambert can't make it," said the man. "He sends his apologies, and asked me to come along instead."

Kosov felt cold. His mind became confused. He tried to organise his thinking. What should he do? Get up and walk off? Stay silent? React? Betray himself?

"My name is Druce," added the man. "I work with Mr Lambert."

Kosov swallowed hard. "What do you want?" he finally asked. That, at least, didn't implicate him. It was what one asked a perfect stranger who intruded on one. Somebody who bothered you in the park.

"I just came to say hello on our behalf," said Druce. "Today being the day, so to speak. We must keep our appointments, even if we have nothing particular to say. Friends should always keep in touch."

A mad thought suddenly occurred to Kosov. Perhaps he should tell the man that he had confessed to Yenko. Maybe a double confession would bring double absolution. Surely a man isn't a traitor if he betrays both sides. He was sorely tempted.

"Have you heard that your girl friend is dead?" Druce was asking.

Instantly the idea of double betrayal vanished. Instead, wariness took over.

"My girl friend . . ." echoed Kosov.

"Well, your little playmate. The lady you were so indiscreet with." Druce's tone was brutal. "Somebody's murdered her. I thought you might know."

Kosov avoided his eyes. "Why should I care? She was a prostitute. Working for you. She means nothing to me. Why should it concern me if one of your operatives is killed?"

A mother wheeling a pushchair strolled past. She smiled down at her little boy. He was a bonny, pink faced child.

"Operative?" repeated Druce, grinning. "I say, you got that a bit wrong. She was a freelance. She had her own clients. She only worked for us part time." He took out a cigarette packet, and offered it to Kosov. "No? Wise man. You'll live longer." He lit a cigarette for himself.

"Who killed her?" asked Kosov.

"People are trying to find out. I thought maybe you'd have an idea . . . I mean, I could understand you bearing a grudge."

He was almost supercilious, the kind of Englishman who knew God had a British passport. Kosov loathed him.

"I think I should leave," he said, and surprised himself by taking the initiative.

Druce glanced at his watch. "Good idea. No point in dragging it out. Before you go, is there anything we can do for you? Are you having any problems?" He lowered his voice.

"Are they on to you?"

"I hope not," said Kosov. Again, the temptation to tell all.

"Good," nodded Druce. "I hear you might be making a trip to Moscow soon."

"Only for a couple of weeks." The fear was growing.

"We'll keep in touch," Druce assured him coldly. "Now, let's see. Who makes their exit first, you or me?"

"Does it matter?"

"Of course not, but one shouldn't get careless, should one."

He didn't say goodbye. He didn't even nod or wave. He just threw the cigarette away, got up and walked towards the nearest exit.

Kosov stayed behind for a few minutes. He had a lot to think about.

The St John's Wood town house to which Flexner unexpectedly invited Zarubin for a drink was paid for by the Embassy.

It was a stylish residence with a miniature goldfish pond in a small paved garden and surrounded by ornamental railings.

The doors of the double garages were operated by remote control, and the whole property was studded with electronic devices to guard against unwelcome intruders.

The impromptu invitation meant that Zarubin had lost a bet with himself. Privately he had been playing favourable odds against Flexner wanting to make their relationship anything other than strictly non social.

"Nice place you got here," commented Zarubin, easing himself into one of the damask covered armchairs in the living room.

"Yes, it's very pleasant," agreed Flexner. "Lord's is round the corner."

Zarubin raised his eyebrows. "You're a cricket buff?"

"Sure." Flexner gave him his drink. "It's a real gentleman's game."

He didn't disguise the implication that as such it wouldn't interest Zarubin.

It all fits, thought Zarubin. The copies of *Country Life* and

Horse and Hound prominently displayed on the side table, the Royal Wedding plate on its stand, the replicas of English county coats of arms on the coasters.

"You don't play golf either, do you?"

"No sir."

Flexner nodded. It only served to confirm his impression of Zarubin. "Never mind," he sympathised condescendingly. "There's always time."

He put down his glass. "You think Kosov's going to be useful?"

He said it quite casually, not looking at his guest.

"I think they're crazy."

"Why?"

"Christ, he was compromised from the word go."

"They think we may have use for his services too."

"I don't want to know," Zarubin stated firmly. "The less I know the happier I am."

"You heard of VR 66?" asked Flexner, and suddenly the atmosphere in the room tensed.

"Rumours, that's all."

"It's not rumours, it's real. No more theories. It's here," he said, his voice rising. Then he controlled himself. "They've developed a nerve agent that . . . "

He stopped.

"Go on."

"You've been through Fort Detrick. This thing, there's no escape from it. It penetrates. It's ultimate. It lingers. It doesn't even evaporate in the sun, or freeze in extreme cold, like the others." He spoke very precisely. "We have no defence against it, as of now."

Zarubin finished his drink. "And you seriously believe Kosov will bring us back a sample?"

"The British think they have a connection. He just has to pick up pieces of the jigsaw. Some pieces at least. If he is lucky."

"Bullshit!" exclaimed Zarubin. "He'll only lead Central to the connection. You know what I think? We're all being led by the fucking nose."

Flexner avoided his look. He spoke mildly:

"Don't you think you've got it all wrong, that they're

trying to help us? Letting us in on things?"

"Oh, come on! A clumsy frame of some pathetic comrade, so inept, even the guy says so. And why make me part of the act? To impress us how much they trust us? Or to set me up, maybe."

"You're over-reacting," said Flexner airily. "The subtleties of the game are too sophisticated for you."

"Thanks," snapped Zarubin. He decided that the right moment had come. "Is the disposal of Lambert's little Mata Hari another subtlety?"

"What are you talking about?"

"Oh, don't you know?" asked Zarubin, like a dentist drawing a tooth. Flexner glared at him, but Zarubin went on relentlessly. "Okay, here's an update on the subtleties of the game. Debbie, the girl who set up Kosov, is dead."

If Zarubin had punched Flexner in the stomach, he couldn't have looked more sick. The last time he'd seen blood drain from a man's face like that was when Yudkin had seen Zarubin raise his gun.

They stared at each other, neither noticing the woman softly opening the door. She was tall, and slim, with bobbed hair, and sleepy grey eyes.

"Oh I'm sorry, honey," she apologised. "I didn't know you had somebody with you."

Flexner switched on a welcoming smile.

"Come in, darling." He indicated Zarubin. "This is Andrew Zarubin. Andrew, my wife Nancy."

The sleepy eyes regarded Zarubin coolly, almost insolently.

"Nice to meet you, Andrew. Are you one of Cy's colleagues from the office?"

Five points, thought Zarubin. Very diplomatically phrased. "Colleagues from the office." It covered a multitude of sins.

"No," broke in Flexner. He appeared anxious to have his say. "Andrew works on his own."

"You have business over here?" enquired Nancy, not even glancing at her husband, but moving closer to Zarubin.

"I'm setting one up," he replied. He was studying her. She wore a well cut trouser suit, and the creases in her trousers

74

would have passed on a West Point cadet. She was also younger, he guessed, and harder. Much harder.

She was aware of Zarubin assessing her. She returned his appraisal, her eyes meeting his.

"Is your wife over here with you?" she asked, smiling at him provocatively.

"I'm not married."

"Oh? Maybe I ought to find you a nice girl," she suggested and the way she said it gave Zarubin the distinct impression that she was readily available.

If he could have felt sorry for Flexner, he did at that moment.

"Or do you prefer to play the field?"

She didn't give Zarubin the chance to answer but turned to her husband saying:

"I think Andrew should stay to dinner." Then her eyes turned to Zarubin. "You'd like to, wouldn't you?"

"As a matter of fact," interjected Flexner, "he has a lot on tonight. I believe he's already behind schedule, aren't you, Andrew?"

For a wild moment, Zarubin was tempted to accept her invitation, to thrust himself on Flexner for the evening, to sabotage the man.

But instead he said:

"That's right, Mrs Flexner. I'm sorry."

"Nancy," she corrected. "Are you sure I can't persuade you?"

He made a point of looking at his watch. "My God, I had no idea it was so late. Will you excuse me?"

The relief in Flexner's face was undisguised.

She followed them into the hall.

"I was saying to your husband earlier," said Zarubin. "You have a very attractive house. And right on top of Lord's. Very pleasant."

"Thank you," she smiled.

"Do you ever watch the cricket?" He couldn't resist it.

Her eyes widened with astonishment. "Cricket?" she repeated, wrinkling her nose. "Are you kidding?"

"It isn't your spot," said Zarubin.

Flexner's face was blank.

"I'll be in touch," he said curtly. The message was clear. Don't call me. We'll call you. Perhaps.

"Nice meeting you," said Nancy, her eyes targeting straight into Zarubin's. "Hope to see you again soon."

Not if I see you first, he thought.

The old traitor looked forward to collecting his new suit. It was like stepping back into the past, he thought, as he strolled towards Jermyn Street. In St James's, he passed one of the clubs he'd been a member of for four decades, and from which he'd been required to resign. The joke was he didn't actually miss it. That would hurt his former fellow members much more than it had pained him.

And how shocked they would have been if they had known he'd only joined their establishment because Moscow felt it was a good idea.

"You must be part of the scene, belong to the right set, mix with appropriate society, join the correct clubs," he had been advised. And advice from Central was an order.

Sometimes he wondered how his old school had taken it. He hadn't been back to Dean's Yard since it all came into the open, but he suspected that, although they would never admit it, there was a certain quiet pride about his notoriety. They wouldn't have forgiven him a piece of shoddy, mercenary betrayal for a few pennies, but treason on his level, that had a kind of style.

Or perhaps he was just deluding himself, shirking the real image.

Gillard, his tailor, greeted him as the old trusted customer he was, and the mixture of deference and professional attention he received in the shop was always reassuring.

"A pleasant day, Sir Leslie," remarked Gillard, "but the wind's a bit sharp. Don't want any frost, do we?"

The suit was brought out from the workroom, and unveiled with due respect.

He tried it on in the privacy of a curtained booth, and when he emerged Gillard adjusted the jacket and straightened the sleeves.

"Yes," he muttered to himself, inspecting the suit from all angles. "Yes. Very nice."

The old traitor regarded himself in the full length mirror. A distinguished figure. Upright, patrician looking, the picture of respectability. A public servant of the old school.

"How does it feel on you?" asked Gillard, full of professional confidence.

"Quite good."

Gillard stepped back, and looked downwards.

"Falls nicely," he commented.

"What about the shoulder?" Sir Leslie was always conscious of his right shoulder being slightly higher than his left. It was a problem for his tailor.

"That's been taken care of," confirmed Gillard. He touched the jacket. "Perfect."

"That's all right then."

He went back to the cubicle and changed into his Donegal tweed suit again.

"I'll send it round, shall I, sir?" offered Gillard.

"If you would."

Money, of course, was not discussed. The bill would be sent eventually, and Sir Leslie would return a cheque. Money was never a problem for him. Apart from his share of the Deveaux fortune, he had his Civil Service pension. There had been a row about that, with people in Parliament sounding their outrage at a traitor keeping his pension, but, as the government had pointed out, he had never been charged or convicted. There were no legal grounds to take it away from him.

"Planning to go away, Sir Leslie?" enquired Gillard conversationally as he escorted his customer towards the door.

The grey eyes under the bushy eyebrows hardened. Gillard realised his mistake, and added hurriedly:

"We could all do with a break, I think."

"Ah, yes." Sir Leslie was benign again. "A little sunshine would be very welcome."

"We're planning to visit Malta," said Gillard.

"Be careful about the water."

"Oh really?"

"Don't drink it from the tap."

"I didn't know that."

"Yes," said Sir Leslie, "it can be quite dangerous."

The bell rang as Gillard opened the door for him. The firm was proud of these old fashioned touches.

Before returning to his flat in Mount Street, he stopped by the confectionary counter at Fortnum and Mason. He was lucky. They had just had a delivery of champagne truffles, and he bought himself two pounds. It was a gross indulgence, but he loved to eat a couple as he pored over Sun Tzu.

In Bond Street, near the Air France office, he saw the blind beggar with his tray of matches. He was a shabby looking man, his opaque eyes staring sightlessly at the passing crowd. Pinned to his frayed jacket was a row of war medals; the 8th Army star, the South East Asia star, faded mementos of old campaigns.

Few people in Bond Street took much notice of him, and even those who worked in the vicinity were unaware of his presence. He was like an invisible man, spending a few hours on his pitch two or three days a week, and then disappearing into his void.

In his own way, however, he was something of a fixture. Once, years ago, on a Christmas eve, Sir Leslie had slipped him a ten pound note. Nothing was said, and the blind man did not know until later about the extent of the generosity.

Periodically since then, Sir Leslie, if he happened to pass the man, would remember to make an anonymous donation.

Clutching his package of truffles, Sir Leslie nearly broke with the tradition this time. He walked past the ex-serviceman and then, as if reminded by his conscience, retraced his steps, and put some money in the cardboard tray.

An uncertain hand pushed forward a box of matches for the benefactor, but Sir Leslie ignored it and strolled on. He felt good. It was comforting to be charitable.

It was the kind of postcard sold by art galleries, and had been mailed in Oxford. Zarubin's name and the address of his flat were written in green ink. The rest of the space was blank.

On the reverse side was a reproduction of a modern painting, the sort he would never hang on any of his walls. It was a red design on a white background, some sort of geometric figure, abstract, enigmatic, yet sharply defined. Its title, according to the printed caption, was "Metamorphosis", and it was the work of Tom Weinraub. The publishers of the card were the Steinmetz Gallery, of Westbourne Grove, London.

Zarubin stared at it a long time. The handwriting was clear, precise. It gave him no clue, not even about nationality. There was no telltale continental hint about the lettering, no numerals that betrayed themselves. It was an ordinary, commonplace script, and only the green ink was an individual touch. He could see that it had been written with a fountain pen, not a ball point.

The picture meant nothing to him. Nor did the artist. But the title . . .

Metamorphosis. A change of form or character. Transformation. The emergence of a different person. A new shape.

Somebody was playing games with him. Sending him arty postcards of obscure paintings. Maybe the bees were buzzing again?

The Steinmetz Gallery was small, compact, and sandwiched between an antique shop and a pet store, round the corner from Portobello Road. The pet shop nearly waylaid Zarubin. It had a wire haired terrier in the window with whom he struck up an instant relationship. They stared at one another through the glass with infinite longing.

Apart from a young man with a gold earring dangling from his left lobe, there was no one in the gallery. Zarubin got the impression that it was a place that was never very busy.

"Can I interest you in something?" enquired the young man. He wore a floral shirt, and tight fitting jeans.

"Just want to look round," said Zarubin.

"Please. Make yourself at home. I'll be about the place. Just shout."

And with that he disappeared into a back office.

There were only five pictures on show, brightly coloured primitives: a naked woman with three breasts, a man sitting on a tombstone eating a banana, a bridge, and two garish paintings of a circus.

They were all evidently by the same artist, but none had the familiar red dot on the frame, indicating it had been purchased. Zarubin wondered how the gallery survived.

By the door hung a poster, advertising an exhibition of Painters Against The Bomb, at a gallery in Kentish Town. Apart from a table by the wall, and a chair, the place was bare.

The man with the earring emerged from the little back room.

"You like his work?" he asked.

"I don't know it," replied Zarubin truthfully.

"I think he's pretty good. You know, Ron's only been at it a year."

Figures, thought Zarubin looking at the angle of the bridge.

"Used to work on the assembly line at Ford's."

"Remarkable," said Zarubin.

The man went over to the table, and from a drawer he took out a book.

"Here," he said. "You might as well sign the visitors' book. It's nice when somebody drops in."

He sounded almost wistful.

Zarubin signed his name. For a moment he hesitated. Then he added his address.

"We're in the wrong part of town, you see," went on the young man. "If we were in Bond Street, we'd be selling these like hot cakes. Round here, all they're interested in is the flea market."

He didn't even bother to look at Zarubin's entry.

"Do you sell postcards?" asked Zarubin. "Like this?"

He held out the card.

"Ah, Weinraub," said the young man. "Yes, that was one of ours."

"*Was?*"

"One time we reproduced some of the artists who had shows here. But it didn't pay."

"Who is Weinraub?"

"He's big time now," said the young man. "He's a country-man of yours. You're American aren't you?" He smiled cheerfully. "Tell a mile away. Weinraub's from California. San Francisco. Are you from California?"

"No."

The brow furrowed. "Let's see, it's not actually San Francisco. It's a place called . . . that's it, Sausalito. You know it?"

"Yes, I know it." Something was taking shape. Pieces were beginning to fit. "He is highly drawn to female company. He smoked marijuana. San Francisco." The trivial reference in the KGB file. Somebody had been at that party. Somebody who worked for them. Years ago. And now an unsigned postcard . . . An artist from Sausalito . . . A reminder . . .

"Something bothering you?" interrupted the voice.

"I'm sorry," apologised Zarubin. "I was thinking. Something reminded me . . ." He was aware of the man's interested look. "Tell me, is he over here?"

"Weinraub? I wouldn't know. I think he comes over from time to time. When he's got a show, I suppose. Not here any more, of course. It's Mayfair for him now."

"Does he sell?"

"Two thousand a picture."

"Dollars?"

"Pounds."

Zarubin whistled. "Guess I'm in the wrong racket."

"Yes," said the young man, "I think he is over-rated."

"Tell me, is Mr Steinmetz around?"

The young man didn't blink.

"No, why?"

"Well, it's his place, isn't it? I thought maybe he was back there." He pointed to the room in the rear.

"There's no Steinmetz," said the young man coolly.

"Oh?"

"It's a good name though, isn't it? For an art gallery? Steinmetz has the right sound. And a hell of a sight better than Smith or Brown." He was smiling a little. "No, Mr Zarubin, there ain't no Steinmetz."

He slipped in Zarubin's name as if he had known it for ages, and was totally familiar with it.

"Actually, I run the place. Gibson-Greer. Tony Gibson-Greer."

He held out his hand, and Zarubin shook it. It wasn't the grip of a man who wears an earring.

"Well, thanks for letting me look round," said Zarubin.

"Maybe you'll buy something next time."

"Who knows?" said Zarubin.

"I'll put you on our mailing list," called out Gibson-Greer as he left the gallery.

Don't bother, thought Zarubin. I'm already on it.

In the old days, no one returned to his desk at the unmarked grey stone building in Dzerzhinsky Square without a feeling of trepidation. After any lengthy absence who knew what awaited one? Perhaps a new face presiding over one's own office. If not worse . . .

Things were more civilised now, but still Yenko was re-assured when the regular driver met him at Sheremetyevo Airport and showed the same correct respect.

The guards at the entrance to the building, which was two blocks from the Kremlin, saluted him, and by the time he'd walked along the uncarpeted parquet floor to his office, he was pretty relaxed. His stay in London had not produced visible upheavals behind his back. His secretary was the same, and, as he immediately checked on entering his private room, the wax seal on the combination lock of his personal safe was unbroken.

As soon as he was settled in his leather chair behind his old wooden desk, Olga came in. She was a severe looking woman in her fifties, the widow of a KGB warrant officer, highly efficient, and totally loyal. Loyal to the organisation. Yenko knew it, and accepted it.

"You had a pleasant trip?" she asked, handing him a steel box of documents that needed urgent attention.

"There was a great deal to do," he replied. "I had little time to relax."

Even for a man in his position it was important to get the record straight from the start. It would never do for rumours to spread along the green painted corridors that the deputy chief of Special Service II had indulged in frivolous activities while on a classified mission.

"Of course, I know," agreed Olga, solicitiously. "You look tired."

This was a touch of familiarity which Olga was allow-ed. She had worked for the State Committee since the big reorganisation of the service in 1954, rising from a junior file clerk to senior secretary.

She hesitated a moment, then she asked tentatively:

"Did you have a chance to see Peter?"

Yenko smiled. "Of course. He sends you his love. He is well, and they are very satisfied with him."

Peter was her son, a cypher clerk in the military attaché's office at the embassy in London.

"And when I unpack, I have a present from him for you," added Yenko. "For your birthday."

"He never forgets."

Yenko had also bought her something. A Scottish wool cardigan, but he would keep that as a surprise until later.

Olga became formal again. "These need your attention," she said, indicating the box on his desk. She consulted her note pad. "And the general wishes to see you at four."

Yenko nodded. He had already sent back various coded reports, but now he would be able to talk about even more sensitive things behind closed doors.

"The embassy sent my instructions?" he enquired. He had ordered the top secret signal to be radioed ahead of his arrival.

"Of course. She is here."

"Excellent," said Yenko. "Tell them to bring her in."

"Now?" queried Olga, surprised. The man hadn't even had a chance to settle in.

"Now."

Ten minutes later came the knock on the door.

"Come in."

A nurse entered, pushing a wheelchair in which slumped Nina Spiridov. She wore no make up, her hair hung unwashed, lank, and the dress she had on was like a shapeless hospital gown.

"Please . . ." said Yenko.

The nurse positioned the wheelchair on the other side of his desk.

Despite her condition, she appeared to be alert.

"Would you like anything?"

She shook her head.

Yenko spoke gently. "I never had the opportunity to tell you how sorry I was about your husband."

"You killed him," she stated in a flat, monotonous voice.

The nurse did not even glance at her. Yenko inclined his head, sadly.

"No. That is the complete misapprehension. It was a great shock to all of us. Even those who didn't know him."

Her eyes flickered. "What do you want?"

"Nina Spiridova, my sole concern is for your welfare. You were brought back from London so that you could be looked after. Tell me, are they taking good care of you?"

"Why are you interested?" she asked tonelessly. "You can see how I'm being treated."

"Excellent. I am glad you are better. I am told you were in a bad state . . ."

She raised her arm. It was a feeble gesture of contempt.

"Oobitsa!" she rasped.

Yenko blinked. Then he nodded his head. "Yes, I see you still need help. Well, I am sure they will do wonders. Won't you nurse?"

The nurse only nodded.

"The Institute has an excellent recovery rate," continued Yenko, suavely. "And you do wish to recover, do you not, Nina Spiridova? The fact that your husband, well, that he became a problem to himself, that's no reason why you should not lead a useful and pleasant life. Once we are sure that your . . . thinking is on correct lines."

"I am very sorry," she muttered.

"Oh."

"Yes." And suddenly there was a note of defiance in her voice. "I am sorry that he never had the chance to tell the Americans. To warn them. And I curse the one who betrayed him. If I knew who it was . . ."

"Yes?" prompted Yenko. "If you knew?"

"I'd kill him, the way you murdered Anatoly."

The nurse glanced at Yenko anxiously.

"What a pity," he sighed. "I had so hoped that you were not infected by the same germ. As it is . . . well, you don't make it very easy for us, do you?"

For a moment, Nina Spiridov just gazed at him vacantly. Then she whispered urgently:

"Please, one favour." She paused and Yenko could see

from her expression the inner battle she was fighting to maintain her concentration. "What happened to him? His body? Where is Anatoly buried?"

Yenko bared his teeth.

"His corpse was handed over to us by the British authorities." He shrugged. "After that, I am not sure. Perhaps it was burnt. Or, possibly, fed to the pigs."

Nina Spiridov didn't react immediately. Then she slumped back in the wheelchair, her head lolling to one side. But Yenko was no longer interested.

"Remove her," he ordered.

After she had gone, he started reading the contents of the box Olga had put before him. The second folder he opened had two sheets of paper in it. The top one was headed "Zarubin". He glanced at his watch. He decided he'd better deal with that matter before seeing the general.

Compared to Yenko's slightly built figure, General Maximovich was a mountain of a man. His bulk just fitted into chairs, and easing himself into a car was a considerable achievement.

The general's vastness helped to put people who didn't know him off their guard. With his ruddy complexion, his two double chins, and his twinkling eyes, he was typecast for everybody's favourite uncle. He could be expansive, and genial and, if he was really amused, his laughter rumbled, and the furniture shook. He had a habit of thumping the table when he agreed with a statement, and when that happened, his aides relaxed. They could see he was in a good mood.

When he wasn't . . .

Today he was not in uniform. He wore a dark suit, massively cut, like a tent, to enfold his huge girth. Yenko wasn't the only one who often wondered how Maximovich, despite his massive weight, managed to stay so healthy. There were many who would not be dismayed to hear of a heart attack.

When Yenko appeared at four o'clock, as ordered, he knew at once the general was in a bad humour. There was no preliminary greeting, no enquiry about his trip.

"It should never have happened," Maximovich declared.

"I agree, General," said Yenko. He wasn't just fawning, he really shared the opinion. "Spiridov's negative attitude should have been evident to the others. Before I left, I made it crystal clear that we expected things to be tightened up. Life in London appears to have made some of them rather slack."

The general scowled. "Slack! Is that your word for it? Corrupted would be better. Tainted."

He breathed deeply.

"I cannot comprehend how no one noticed what was going on. A man doesn't betray his motherland on the spur of the moment. The cancer gnaws at him. It must have been going through his mind for a long time. Perhaps since he was in America. Yes." He nodded in agreement with himself. "That was a mistake. We should never transfer anyone straight from one overseas post to another. And to allow him to take his wife to England . . ."

"Another mistake," Yenko nodded unhappily.

"It removes our best sanction," went on the general. "If she'd remained here, we'd have had a hold on such a creature. Has she been helpful to you?"

"She is uncooperative," reported Yenko. "She needs re-education."

"Pshaw!" snorted the general. "She should never have been allowed to accompany him. He should never have been trusted. The whole screening machinery needs an overhaul."

His big chair creaked.

"Luckily, of course, Spiridov wasn't able to achieve his object. We cut him off in time." Yenko said it tentatively. He wasn't sure if this was the right moment. "He didn't say anything to the Americans over the phone. And, as you know, it was possible to deal with him before he reached the rendezvous."

Maximovich scowled. "More luck than design. If he had got there, we'd be right in the pig's shit, wouldn't we?"

There were times, thought Yenko, when it was best to stay silent.

"Well, wouldn't we?"

"Yes, General."

"Hmm."

He regarded Yenko gloomily. "The Inspectorate will probably ask a lot of questions."

"I am sure we can provide the answers that will satisfy them," asserted Yenko. The "we" was no accident, but a gentle reminder to the general that, no matter how elevated his status, he too could be dragged down.

The general's office had sound proof windows but, very faintly, the chimes of the Kremlin clock could be heard.

Maximovich reached over, and pushed a wooden cigar chest across to Yenko.

"These have just arrived from Cuba. I recommend them." He lit one with obvious pleasure. "How about you, Yenko?"

It was a peace offering. But Yenko demurred. "Not just now, General."

Maximovich raised a bushy eyebrow. "What's the matter? You doing penance?"

Yenko's mouth was a little dry. "Penance?" he repeated. "What for?"

The general laughed. One of his big, booming laughs. "That, my dear Yenko, is something only you would know." His two chins wobbled with amusement. "Private sins, eh?" He saw Yenko's unsmiling face, and controlled himself. "Never mind, it was only a joke."

He blew out a cloud of aromatic smoke.

"Your section has so little humour."

"If you say so, General."

Yenko sat at attention, his back straight so that it didn't touch the back of the chair, knees together, hands on his lap.

"Yes," mused the general, "I can see it in your face too. No laugh lines. Very revealing. Never mind, we are not here to discuss your sense of humour." He waved the hand holding the thick cigar. "Relax. Don't be so stiff spined."

"Yes, General."

"As soon as you can, prepare your detailed report about what is going on in England. Your interim despatches leave a lot unanswered."

Yenko shifted uneasily. "I had limited channels of communications."

Maximovich exhaled more cigar smoke. "I should have thought embassy facilities were adequate." Then he remembered. "Oh, I see, some things . . ."

" . . . they need not know," Yenko cut in, greatly daring. He knew that would please the fat man. He was right. Maximovich smiled.

"Very well. Now then. What about Major Ulianov. Is he still in that medieval dungeon?"

"At the moment, General."

"And it is clear that this one must not be handed over to the Americans? We do not want him incarcerated in that Nevada hideout. Not this Ulianov. He must be kept out of their hands."

Yenko was watching the man mountain warily. "It won't be easy, General. Not with this secret NATO concord providing for the allies in Europe to transfer all Soviet intruder pilots who have been captured on illegal missions to America for debriefing and indefinite safekeeping. Already there are agencies in Washington wondering what has happened to Major Ulianov. Where he is. Why, the British haven't handed him over. There will be pressure . . . "

"I don't care a she goat's piss," roared Maximovich, his face visibly reddening. He took a deep breath. "And don't lecture me about the NATO concord. It's ancient history. They keep our ferrets. We keep theirs. It suits us. But Ulianov is different. Once he's caged in that desert, he . . ."

The general stopped, still angry. Then he glowered at Yenko, and added ominously, "I hope it's being taken care of."

It was not a moment for argument. "You can rely on it," Yenko assured him. "Your orders are being followed to the letter."

"I hope so," grunted the general. He didn't add, "for your sake," but the meaning was implicit, and Yenko didn't miss it. "We understand each other. Good." He became genial again. "Anything else, Yenko?"

"Yes, General. The Kosov affair."

Maximovich took out his cigar and studied the end of it. It was wet from him chewing it too much. Some of the leaf was coming loose.

"The bloody Cubans are getting lazy," he muttered. "Look at this." He crushed the cigar in a crystal ash tray. He could afford to be reckless. He had plenty more. "What were you saying, Yenko?"

"Kosov."

"Ah, yes. Our loyal little Kosov." He showed his teeth. "Well, what about him? What is the next move?"

"I've already organised it, General." He savoured the moment. "You can leave everything to me."

The Russian in the yellow track suit lay on his camp bed, his eyes closed, but he wasn't asleep.

He was wondering whether he'd been lucky. The others had gone down with the plane. The specially adapted TU-26, 60,000 feet high in British air space, hadn't expected to be hit by the missile from the American jet. Clearly they had penetrated into an ultra sensitive zone. As the Yanks would say, their ELINT spy mission had hit the jackpot, and somebody pushed the red button.

The explosion had blown the 231 foot long Backfire apart, and he still didn't know how he'd managed to bale out. The others never made it, but after an hour in the North Sea, he was picked up by a motor launch, and brought ashore. He was taken to some military hospital, where he was watched day and night by two armed airmen who had sat either side of his bed.

He had no illusions. He realised that, officially, the whole thing had never happened. The Backfire hadn't invaded NATO air space, the Americans hadn't shot it down, he hadn't been captured. So he knew what to expect; they had all been briefed. Every ferret crew knew what awaited it if it was brought down. Oblivion. Captivity, somewhere, in a prison that didn't exist in a place that probably wasn't even on the map.

When the interrogators came, they weren't what he'd anticipated; nor was what happened.

Instead of transferring him to a military base for interrogation, he had been taken out of the system. Some special section had intervened, and they'd brought him to this medieval place for questioning.

He imagined awaiting execution in a death cell couldn't be much different to his existence in this austere turret prison, with its ancient stone walls. He was allowed to shave, for example, in the presence of a guard, but as soon as he'd finished, the razor was taken away from him. At meal times, he was given plastic cutlery and if he put too much pressure on either the knife or the fork, it snapped in two. Every hour an anonymous eye peered at him through an observation slit in the heavy door, and he suspected that, somewhere, was a sensitive microphone which picked up the sounds he made, relaying them to a listening post.

Yet they allowed him to keep his shoe laces, a note pad, pencils, and a pencil sharpener. It was no secret that a determined man could kill himself with a sharpened, pointed pencil, and they, who seemed so alert, must have been aware of it too. Not that it mattered. Despite often feeling pretty depressed, Major Ulianov had no intention of committing suicide. Even in this isolation, things were far too interesting.

He became aware of the noise of feet shuffling outside the cell door, then it was unlocked, and they were back.

Ulianov sat up, and smoothed back his hair. It had grown too long for his taste, and he felt uncomfortably conscious of it. Being a military man, a neat haircut was second nature.

"And how are you today?" asked the man in the tweed suit, via his translator.

"How do you expect?"

The man nodded when he heard the reply.

"Tell him that I understand he wanted to see me, that is why I am here now," he instructed the interpreter.

"That was three days ago," retorted Ulianov bitterly. He didn't wait for the translation, but went on: "Three days is a long time when a man is locked in here."

"I sympathise," said the man, the translator repeating it in Russian. "But these things do take time. I am sorry that I couldn't be here sooner, but I have other duties as well, as I'm sure he appreciates. Anyway, the point is, I've come. What can I do for him?"

Ulianov spoke rapidly for some minutes, and the interpreter made notes on a little pad, so that he wouldn't forget any of it.

"He has a special request, and he sees no reason why you should not be able to grant it," he translated finally. "He says it is his wife's thirtieth birthday next week, and he would like to send her a greeting. He has written her a note, but if it isn't possible to send that to her, perhaps you could obtain some sort of birthday card which he could sign. He wants her to know that he is well, and that he is thinking of her."

"Ah yes," said the man. He gave Ulianov a brief frosty smile.

"Please tell him," he said, "that as much as I would like to help, he must know that what he asks is impossible. I'm sure his people tell every airman that undertakes illicit intrusions into another country's airspace that if they are caught they no longer officially exist. He must also know that it has been agreed unofficially that neither East nor West admits to the existence of such captives, and that they are listed as missing, presumed killed on training flights. So obviously his request would be a breach of conventions."

The major listened intently to the translation. When it ended, he nodded. But then he added something in Russian.

The interpreter glanced at the man in the tweed suit.

"Sir, he points out that somebody already knows about him. The man in the forest who gave him a lift in his car."

"Inform him that the man has been told that the stranger he picked up that night was a lunatic."

Ulianov's mouth twitched when he heard the reply, and he chuckled wryly. Then he spoke briefly.

"He says that he has had enough of this hole," reported the interpreter, "and he hopes you can come up with something better soon."

"Of course," nodded the man. "Assure him that I am working on it. Tell him it's uppermost in my mind."

Before leaving, he threw a packet of cigarettes on the camp bed.

They were Russian cigarettes, the same brand as before.

"Personally," said the man to his translator, as they left, "I can't stand the taste, but I suppose it's a touch of home for the poor bastard."

They slammed the door shut, and a guard double locked it again.

In the cell, Major Ulianov picked up the packet of cigarettes. He couldn't smoke one because he had to wait for the guard to light it for him. But nevertheless he seemed very pleased.

The summons to No 2 Dzerzhinsky Square did not come as a surprise to Kosov.

From the moment he'd arrived back in Moscow, he'd been under surveillance. He knew he was being watched all the time. Not that he'd once seen them, he just knew the watchers were there. He also knew what they were looking for: a contact. Somebody casually approaching him, in the metro, at a bus stop. Someone who might bump into him, perhaps drop something for him to pick up, maybe stand very close behind him in a queue.

But nobody had.

They were waiting for him to do something unusual, too. Like leaving an envelope, a package, a message in a dead letter box which might be a tree trunk, the crack of a wall, the pages of a book.

But he hadn't.

Day and night they'd been watching him, and now Yenko had asked him to call.

It was not a pleasant experience.

"Let's go over things," said Yenko, peering at him curiously across his desk.

Kosov swallowed, but nodded in a manner which he hoped would indicate that he was only too eager to be helpful.

"Before you left London, did they ask you to do anything?"

"Of course not," replied Kosov.

"Why 'of course not'?" enquired Yenko mildly. "I should have thought it very likely that they would give you some sort of little mission, wouldn't you?"

"If they had, I would have reported it, comrade. As soon as I got back."

"Naturally. Nevertheless, I ask you again. Have any arrangements been made? For you to contact them? Or for them to get in touch with you?"

Kosov's hands felt icy cold.

"Believe me . . ." he began, but Yenko cut him short.

"I do. Really I do," Yenko reassured him. "However . . ."

The "however" frightened Kosov.

Yenko didn't time the lengthy silence, but his eyes never left Kosov's ashen face as they sat opposite one another without speaking a word.

Finally, Yenko smiled encouragingly.

"The meeting you had in the park, are you sure you reported everything that was said?"

"Every word," croaked Kosov. He cleared his throat. "Every word," he repeated in a firmer tone.

"I believe you," said Yenko. "Do not look so concerned. I am your friend. But, sometimes, one has to have a talk in case one has missed something. You know how easy it is to miss something."

Kosov was filled with panic. If he agreed, he knew Yenko would jump on it, press him about what could have been overlooked. And if he said nothing, that would be wrong too.

"I . . ." he stuttered.

But nothing happened. Instead, Yenko asked, almost nonchalantly:

"What do you think of Zarubin?"

"Za . . . Zarubin?" Kosov was baffled.

"The American agent," amplified Yenko patiently.

"I don't know anyone called Zarubin."

"No?"

"I swear."

"Really?"

"Truly," cried Kosov. He felt desperate.

"That, strictly speaking, is a lie," purred Yenko. "You met him at the London police station where they held you. The American who understood Russian. You remember, don't you? The American with the English official, Lambert."

Kosov was confused. "I didn't know his name."

"Never mind. The point is, have you seen him since? Talked with him?"

"No! Never!" Kosov almost shouted.

"They did say they'd have a mission for you over here, didn't they? So, did Zarubin give you any instructions?"

"No, no, no!"

"Calm yourself, Lev Kosov. I'm not accusing you of anything."

"I swear to you . . ."

"Do not distress yourself," murmured Yenko soothingly. "You must remember we are dealing with reptiles. This man Zarubin is particularly dangerous. Perhaps, quite innocently, you've been tricked."

Kosov's lips began to tremble. "I beg you, believe me. Everything that has happened I have told you. Everything."

Yenko nodded. "Of course. And I will always bear in mind that you were the one who came to me. You did your duty, so relax."

Kosov had become so nervous that the collar of his shirt was damp with sweat.

Yenko noted it. He's sweating, he probably feels slightly sick, and I bet he's dying to go to the toilet, he thought with contempt.

Then he stood up.

"Thank you for coming, Lev Kosov," he said. "I hope it hasn't been an inconvenience for you."

Kosov stared at him blankly.

"Please consider this matter closed," Yenko continued. "If, by some chance you come across anything suspicious, or somebody makes any kind of, er, approach, you will report to me at once. Otherwise, forget about it."

"You mean that's all?" asked Kosov, completely bewildered.

"I congratulate you, comrade," said Yenko. "Your loyalty to the state is an example to everyone. In fact, all one can expect. You live fully up to my expectations – something one can't say about everyone these days, eh?"

He thought how well he'd chosen his words.

"Thank you, comrade," Kosov smiled nervously, standing up.

They started to walk across the room, towards the door.

"Tell me, do you miss London, my friend?" Yenko asked conversationally.

Kosov shrugged. "It is all right. But a dangerous place."

"Yes, but our Soviet community there is a very close family, isn't it? Didn't you make some good friends? Everybody knows one another, don't they? Diplomats, business people, Intourist, Aeroflot personnel, journalists . . ."

"I kept to myself, as you know."

"Except for the odd indiscretion, hmm?" But Yenko was smiling genially, so Kosov felt easier. "I was just wondering if you ever met Anatoly Spiridov. One of our journalists there. Perhaps one weekend at Hawkhurst?"

Kosov shook his head. "Not that I recall."

It seemed to satisfy Yenko.

"There's no reason why you should have. You didn't move in the same circles. I merely wondered."

He opened the door. In the corridor outside the uniformed KGB guard who had escorted Kosov up from reception stood waiting.

"Well," said Yenko, and for the first time in their relationship he offered his hand, "unless something unexpected comes up, I don't imagine we'll be seeing each other again, do you?" He grasped Kosov's cold hand. "Good luck, my friend," he added, then turned to the impassive guard:

"Show this comrade out, please. He is free to depart."

The guard held out a clip board, and Yenko signed it.

He closed the door and returned to his desk. Although he was thoughtful, his mind was already made up. It had been before the interview.

He unlocked the right hand drawer and took out Kosov's dossier which Olga had collected from the registry earlier. He opened it up and, with the American silver ball point pen he had bought himself in London, he wrote one word on the margin of the first sheet:

"Unreliable."

Then he initialled the entry.

"We must give a party soon," Nancy Flexner suddenly announced.

"What for?" asked her husband, taken aback.

"I'd like to. I can't remember when we last had one."

"There's a drinks do at the English Speaking Union next week. We're invited to that," Flexner said, in an effort to mollify her.

Nancy's contempt was withering. "I said a party. Our own party. Let's have some fun."

"Who are you thinking of inviting?"

She rattled off a list of names. Embassy people. Neighbours. A few English friends. Then she added:

"Oh, and let's have that pal of yours. The fellow you brought over. What's his name? Andrew? The guy with the funny name."

It was said casually. Too casually for Flexner's ears.

"You mean Zarubin."

"Is that it?" said Nancy airily. "Yes, he must come too."

He tried to reassure himself that, of course, no way did she want to have a party just as an excuse to invite Zarubin. But why mention him? What was so special about him? She'd only met him once, for a couple of minutes.

He knew he should have asked her, but there were certain things Flexner ducked.

"I'll think about it," he grunted at last, hoping he sounded dismissive. But it nagged a lot.

The next day, behind his locked office door, Flexner watched one of the videos Zarubin was importing and felt absolutely appalled. Girls sticking their tongues in each other's eager mouths, fondling one another's buttocks, playing with each other's tits. And that was just for starters.

Flexner had nothing against an agent playing a fake role; deception, after all, was time honoured, and part of the game. In the past, he had himself assumed many covers. In Vienna, on one posting early in his career, he had been a freelance journalist. In Stockholm, briefly, an insurance consultant. But he felt quite strongly one should maintain a respectable front. Technically, a cover was assumed not only to disguise one's activities, it was also a key, intended to provide an opening through many interesting doors. One of the things Flexner admired about British intelligence were the covers their people assumed – Reuter correspondents, British Council cultural officials, export managers, authors in tax exile. They had class.

Not like the role Zarubin had taken on – peddling blue movies. Just what kind of doors did he expect to open in his guise as a pornographic film importer?

He switched off the video player, and put the tape in his safe. If he'd been a religious man, he would have said a silent prayer of thanks that Zarubin operated on his own, that he was not part of the official station roster.

Trouble was, ruminated Flexner, the goddamn bastard had a habit of intruding into his daily life, when he least expected it. Like his remark about Debbie. Was he supposed to take it as a threat? A warning? Did it mean he knew? Perhaps it was time somebody dealt with Zarubin before he upset too many apple carts.

He picked up the phone, and asked for Crawford's extension.

"Lunch?" he suggested.

"Okay," agreed Crawford, "meet you downstairs."

They walked out of the embassy, and crossed Grosvenor Square. The sun was shining, and strolling through Mayfair restored Flexner's humour a little.

They didn't discuss where they'd eat. If it wasn't the embassy commissary, it was always the club.

"You battening down the hatches?"

Flexner stared at him.

"Eh?"

"Getting ready for the gum shoes?"

"What are you talking about?"

"Oh," said Crawford. "Maybe you haven't had the TWX yet. They're sending over some security people."

"Over here?"

"Yeah." He shook his head. "If you ask me, somebody wants a free junket to London. The paper pushers have decided it's our turn. Make sure you don't leave any chewing gum wrappers lying around. You'll get ten demerits."

Flexner excused himself when they got to the club.

"Order me the usual," he said. "I just want to wash my hands."

He wasn't gone long, then joined his NSA colleague at their usual table overlooking Green Park.

"You're very quiet," Crawford remarked, taking a mouthful of the American Club's creole soup. It was a very English institution, despite the flag over Piccadilly, and that was one of the reasons Flexner liked it.

"I hate my routine upset," complained Flexner. "I know these security flaps. I saw what it did at the Bonn embassy once."

Crawford shrugged. "What do you expect? They got to find something for them to do. When I was at the Pentagon, they had one admiral for every two ships. In the Air Force, there's one general for every thirty planes. They fall out of closets. It's the same with the bloodhounds." He paused. "There's nothing that's bothering you, is there, Cy?"

"Of course not."

Then, out of the blue, Crawford asked mildly:

"What's your man Zarubin doing these days?"

"He's not my man," retorted Flexner. He realised he had snapped too sharply. "I had no idea you two knew each other."

"Zarubin gets around," smiled Crawford. It destroyed what was left of Flexner's appetite.

The waitress brought him his hamburger and he cut into it.

"Damn," he cursed, "I asked for it rare."

He wished Crawford wasn't looking at him so curiously.

"Where did you meet him?" he asked.

"Oh, I can't remember," replied Crawford carelessly. "Maybe he was seconded to us at one time, I'm not sure."

"The National Security Agency?" Flexner was interested. "I had no idea Zarubin had been NSA."

"Well," said Crawford, "he's a great linguist, isn't he? Speaks Russian like a native."

Flexner realised that Crawford knew a great deal about Zarubin. He wondered what else he knew. Suddenly, he felt slightly sick.

The announcement on *Izvestia*'s sports page of the cancellation of the nineteenth round game of the first division Soviet Soccer League caused bewilderment amongst the fans.

It was a keenly anticipated needle match between two top teams, Minsk's Dynamos and Tashkent's crack Pakhtarov side. Television coverage had been arranged, sports columnists had already written preliminary articles, and special trains had been laid on for the supporters.

Then, without explanation, the whole fixture was called off.

Forty-eight hours later Tass circulated a brief statement

that two passenger airliners, one from Tashkent bound for Minsk and the other on its way from Chelyabinsk, east of the Urals, to Kishinev, the capital of Soviet Moldavia, had collided mid-air and everyone in both planes had been killed. Among them was the Pakhtarov soccer team.

"The reason for the collision is being investigated by a special commission," added Tass curtly.

For sports enthusiasts it was a horrendous blow. The Pakhtarov side were soccer heroes. They had stood a good chance of winning the league.

It took a further four days for Western correspondents to worm out of Soviet officials some more details. Apparently, the two twin engined TU-134 Aeroflot jets had collided near Dnerprodzerzhinsk, and exploded. The passengers and the crew on both planes had died instantly.

To CIA analysts at Langley, it was not surprising that information was so scarce. In a perfect society, nothing goes wrong. Soviet airliners do not have major disasters, and, if they do, there is no need to publicise them.

At the US embassy on Moscow's Tchaikovskovo street, officials knew that domestic Aeroflot crashes would only be announced if foreign nationals were included amongst the victims, and their embassies had to be informed.

Obviously, it was only because a star soccer team had been wiped out and the football season interrupted that an announcement had to be made, however grudgingly.

The total death roll of 173 people was never made public.

It was of course a terrible disaster, but Western intelligence experts did not feel it was of much significance for NATO.

It took a little more time, however, for Langley to find out that one of those killed was Lev Kosov, lately arrived from London.

Kosov hadn't actually been on the plane, but Yenko thought it quite an ingenious idea to include his name in the final tally of casualties.

The inclusion of Kosov's name, buried in the list of dead passengers, not only explained his sudden disappearance, it also took care of any undue curiosity on the part of anyone who was interested in him. That way he just became a victim of bad luck.

So, his widowed mother, in her single room apartment on Khutynskaya Street, Novgorod, was duly notified of his unfortunate demise in the air crash.

But since Kosov had never been a soccer fan, his mother found it difficult to understand what her son was doing flying to a football match.

Theo the Greek was so delighted with the consignment Zarubin delivered that he took him out to a French patisserie around the corner.

"You had no trouble with Customs?" he enquired anxiously.

Dichter had shipped the batch across on an Air Force courier flight, as part of a diplomatic cargo. It had arrived at Mildenhall, and wasn't even X-rayed.

"They didn't have a clue," Zarubin informed him truthfully.

Theo slapped him on the back. "You interest me, my friend," he said after he'd been served with one of the king size cream eclairs for which the establishment was famous. "You have good connections. If you keep me supplied with this quality stuff, we will both do well."

He pointed to the display of pastries.

"Are you sure you won't have one?"

He looked disappointed at Zarubin's refusal. "But I understand. You don't wish to become like me." He sighed, patting the huge belly under his silk shirt. "And I don't blame you," he added with a wink. "You want to keep handsome for the girls, right? This gets in the way."

He waved to the grey haired woman who presided over the shop.

"Madame, one more. They are delicious today."

Zarubin watched him stuff the pastry into his mouth with relish.

"I have checked up on you, my friend," said Theo, mouth full.

"Why?" Zarubin asked pleasantly. "What's there to check up?"

Theo chuckled. "That's good. No, I tell you because I

think we can do a lot of business. Real business. Big, big consignments. So I have to check on you because . . . I say to myself, this American, he comes in from nowhere, he offers to supply me with merchandise, he doesn't haggle, who is he, what is he? Maybe my trouble is I'm too suspicious."

Zarubin lit a cigarette. "And what did you find out?"

"I am satisfied," pronounced Theo. Zarubin smiled. "Do not be offended. I have to protect my business interests. I had an investment in you, remember? If I had to send people, I must know what I'm dealing with . . . where to find you . . ."

"People," repeated Zarubin slowly.

"Forget it. It would only have been necessary if you'd tricked me. I told you what would happen if you didn't deliver, no? I should have known you are honest, my friend."

"Thanks."

Theo burped. "You know, I am crazy to eat cakes in the middle of the afternoon. I shall regret it." He shook his head sadly. "Never mind. This first consignment, it was only, what is it, a try out. I wanted to see what you can produce. I have finished with samples. Now I want big product. Big quantities."

"That won't be so easy."

Theo held up his hand. "Please! I know the business . . ."

"I'll see," said Zarubin vaguely.

Theo beamed. "That's all I wanted to hear. You are an honest man. I know I can rely on you to come up with the goods."

As they walked out into the street, Theo put his arm round Zarubin.

"You are all alone in London, no?"

"Not really," said Zarubin. He wanted to shake the arm off.

"You have no girl friend, no little lady somewhere?" Theo was leering into his face.

"I get along."

"I can arrange it. Whatever you want. Red head. Blonde. White. Black. Chinese. You name it. Very sweet girls. Very friendly. Absolutely free. Just call me."

"Thanks," said Zarubin. "I appreciate it." He edged away from Theo.

"Good. We will be in touch." Theo nodded, very friendly, very genially and walked off.

Zarubin glanced round, but he noticed nothing out of the ordinary. There seemed no reason to think that Theo had put his arm round him to identify him to somebody. Christ, thought Zarubin. Watch it, man. You're becoming paranoid.

The newspaper seller at Cambridge Circus had two placards on display. They both related to the story headlined on the evening paper's front page.

"Soviet Soccer Team Tragedy" announced one placard. The other was more specific. "Many Die In Russian Air Crash."

Zarubin could hear the telephone ringing as he approached his front door, but by the time he'd undone the two locks it had stopped.

He had a small apartment comprising two rooms, kitchen and bathroom. The landlords described it as a "studio" which they must have felt justified the cramped space and minimum of daylight. The only view Zarubin had was a backyard littered with junk.

He was in the kitchen, fixing himself a drink when the telephone began ringing again.

"Hello?" he replied.

"Andrew?" enquired a woman's voice.

He didn't answer immediately. After so many years, he wasn't certain it was her.

"Who is that?" he asked at last.

"It's been a long time," she said.

A longer pause. Then he said:

"Fern!"

"I didn't think you'd come back," she whispered.

"I didn't either." He hesitated. "How are you?"

He sensed some of Fern's old anger. "Do you care?"

"Of course I do." He thought for a moment. "Look, where are you?"

"At home."

"Fern?"

"Yes?"

"I'd like to see you."

"Why?"

"I'd like to, that's all."

She was silent for a while. Then she said:

"All right."

"I'll be right over." He didn't attempt to disguise his eagerness. "Okay? You still at the same place?"

"No," she said sharply.

"Oh."

"Neutral ground. Please. The old café."

He was disappointed. "Oh, all right, Pablo's. When?"

"In an hour's time."

"I'll be there." Then, he added softly: "It's good to hear you."

The past was catching up with him. A part of him wished Fern hadn't called, but the other half of him wanted to see her. Badly.

For months after he'd left her, left England, she'd remained in his thoughts. Then, he'd hardly been able to sleep with another woman without seeing her face, imagining her body. Now he was about to meet up with the reality again.

It would be all right, he told himself. Time would have healed a lot. And she must want to see him, otherwise she'd never have rung.

Like their relationship, the old Italian trattoria had changed. Pablo was gone, and a Pakistani now owned it. The red check table cloths had disappeared, and the tables now had plastic formica tops. In one corner, a space invaders machine was installed. The cash register was brand new, and electronic. It was not a place that invited companionship.

Although Zarubin was ten minutes early, she was already there, sitting at a table near the rear. As he walked towards her, taking in the familiar face, she stared back at him, unsmiling.

"Hello," he said.

"Hello."

She hadn't altered much. She still wore the same light make-up. The same faint touch of mascara. And the same spicy scent he remembered so well.

"Why don't you sit down?" Fern said, with a touch of

asperity. She often sounded impatient when she was nervous.

"You look great," remarked Zarubin, sitting opposite her, and instantly realised he had said the wrong thing.

"I don't." She took a deep breath. "You know this is a mistake. We shouldn't have done this. I'm sorry."

The waitress appeared, and he ordered coffee without taking his eyes off Fern.

"If you knew . . ." he began, but she cut him short, "Don't."

Zarubin persisted. "You have no idea how often I've thought about you."

"Oh, sure," she said. "I was never out of your mind, you son of a bitch."

She said it without heat, but the bitterness was there.

The coffee was set down in front of him. Neither of them paid attention to the waitress.

"Listen, Fern," he muttered, stretching out his hand across the plastic table top to touch hers.

"Don't," she said, moving her hand out of his reach. "It won't work."

"We could try."

"Oh, yes. How convenient that would be. How useful for you. A warm bed you can come home to every night while you're on assignment here. A woman you can screw. And sweet pillow talk giving you the department's latest news. You see, I've learned from you, Andy. You're a good teacher. I know what you're after. And I'll tell you something else." She leaned forward. "You don't mind missing out on the warm bed, or even on the screw, but by Christ, you do mind about missing out on the gossip."

She stopped. She was trembling slightly.

"That's not fair."

"Fair!" she repeated. "Ha! You made the choice." Her lip quivered momentarily, but she controlled it. "You had all the choice in the world, you bastard. But no, you made your decision, and that's okay. That's fine by me. No room for anyone or anything except your damn secrets. Fucking secrets, fucking spying, fucking cloak and dagger. And now all you've got is your double dealing, so don't come crawling to me. You've left it much too late."

She bit her lip, and Zarubin knew she would never cry in front of him.

'So why did you call me?" he asked very quietly. "Why bother?"

"God, I wish I hadn't."

"But you did . . ."

Fern looked away. "I suppose I wanted to tell you to your face what a goddamn heel I think you are."

"Are you . . . are you still with them?" asked Zarubin, quietly.

"The ministry? Yes." Fern always called it the ministry. Never the service, the department, the organisation. Perhaps she was trying to cling to respectability. "Working for my pension," she added, wryly.

"Did you call me because of something to do with *them*?"

"There you go again," she cried, as if she didn't care who heard. "Them. The work. Christ, Andrew, you don't even understand, do you? It's us you should be talking about. Not them. Not the work. Not the shittiness. God, you make me sick. Us, can't you get that into your head?"

"But . . ."

"It's dead," she said, her big eyes reflecting such sorrow that he wished it wasn't. "It wouldn't work. I'm sorry, I should have known."

She was still good looking. The beautifully proportioned features, the lovely green eyes. After such a long time, seeing her again made him want her all the more.

"Fern, don't shut me out. Please. Let's give it a chance. Let's give ourselves a break."

"So we can – resume our special relationship? Well, forget it. Apart from anything else, I'm living with someone – someone who really cares."

He wanted to hit her, and kiss her, and hurt her and hold her, all at the same time. He wanted her to understand, to . . .

"I'd like to see you again, Fern."

Suddenly she looked sad. She shook her head.

"You've sold your soul, Andrew," she told him. "Some people do this work because they're patriots, some just fall into it, some are blackmailed. You? You like it. You actually enjoy the deceit, the suspicions. You love pulling the strings. I'm not so sure you don't even like being manipulated yourself. For you, our relationship meant nothing more than screwing someone who was a listening post."

She said it rather sorrowfully.

"That's not true," he insisted. "Anyway, we're in the same boat. You work for the British, me the Americans, so what's the difference?"

She sighed. "The difference is, Andy, that whatever I do, it's only a job. You, you're a spook through and through."

Then she got up.

He remained at the table, lost in his own thoughts. At that moment Zarubin felt a very lonely man.

Finally, he stood, and walked over to the counter.

"How much?" he asked.

"It's all right," said the man. "The lady paid."

Zarubin drifted into the West End.

He walked aimlessly along Piccadilly, crossing the Circus, then meandered up Shaftesbury Avenue. Being rejected by her had left him feeling empty, desolate. What she'd said hurt.

"Stupid bastard," he admonished himself, but it was only a pretence. It had taken a long time to shut her out and now the wound was raw again.

And perhaps she'd been right on one point. Did this phantom existence of lies and double dealing mean more than sharing his life with another human being? Was he so indoctrinated . . .

A man bumped into him, and his elbow caught Zarubin.

"Pardon," apologised the man. He was sallow faced, and wore a cheap light brown tropical suit.

Zarubin ambled on. He didn't even bother to check that his wallet hadn't been stolen. Being jostled by a pickpocket was something he was almost programmed against. Another part of the training. But this time he didn't care.

He turned into a side street, and found himself in the neon lit Soho jungle. Tinny, canned music blared from all around him, voices offered, "Young girls, Beautiful girls", the frontage of a sleazy cinema invited him inside to see "Hard Porn, Uncensored, Unedited, Swedish".

He kept on walking. He knew he couldn't go on roaming the streets, wallowing in self pity.

The pub he entered was crowded and it made him feel anonymous, faceless, which was what he wanted. Nobody looked at him. Nobody cared a damn.

It was the kind of pub where they have fights. One of the mirrors was splintered from being struck by something or somebody.

The barman had tatooed forearms. A serpent entwined around a naked woman. And on the other arm, a winged dagger with a scroll inscribed: "Who Dares Wins". He was tough, brawny and Zarubin figured he doubled as a bouncer when he wasn't drawing pints.

He ordered a large scotch, and tossed it down. Like so many things he did, Zarubin got drunk methodically. Never by accident. Never that is, except . . .

He ordered another double. He was going at it fast, too fast.

In the mirror, he saw a girl looking at him. She had frizzy, rust coloured hair, and a very white complexion, like a woman using french chalk as face powder. From a distance, her mouth was a scarlet gash but close up it was carelessly applied, badly smudged lipstick. She was wearing a leather bomber jacket over a faded Wings T-shirt.

He downed his drink and then the girl was standing beside him at the bar. He actually felt grateful to her. She was what he needed, somebody who didn't want to know a damn thing, somebody to get him through the night, and she'd picked up those vibrations.

"Hello," he smiled, and was surprised how thick his speech sounded. "Would you like to join me?"

"Sure."

"What'll it be?"

"Same as you."

"Two double scotches on the rocks," he ordered.

She pressed her body closer to his.

He paid for the drinks, and as she picked up her glass, her eyes confirmed everything.

"Cheers," he toasted.

"Bottoms up." Her blue eye shadow arched.

The pub was getting oppressive, or maybe it was the effect of the scotch invading his bloodstream.

"You're not English, are you?"

"So what?"

She flashed a toothy smile. "What, nothing. I prefer Americans. Where are you from, darling?"

"All over."

"I can do it there too, sweetheart."

She giggled. Somewhere at the back of the pub, a glass smashed, voices were raised. Then there was a burst of reassuring laughter. Everyone relaxed.

She pulled a face. "Noisy in here, isn't it?" She sipped some whisky, then looked into his eyes. "What are you doing tonight?"

"First," said Zarubin, "we'll have one more. Then I'm going to come home with you."

She tittered coyly. "I'd better not get too sozzled then. I won't be much good to you if I'm squiffy, will I?"

"You'll do fine, Fern," he muttered, gulping down his whisky.

She frowned. "Fern?"

He blinked, startled. Christ, he'd got drunk quicker than he'd expected.

"Sorry."

"She your wife?"

"Let's go," was all Zarubin said.

On the way to her place Zarubin stopped the cab at an off licence. When he came out, he was carrying a bottle of vodka.

The taxi moved off again.

"Thirty quid okay?" she said.

"Eh?"

"For the whole night, if you like," she offered grandly. "I like you."

He pulled out his wallet and gave her the money. He had two fivers left.

"You'll have a good time," she promised.

He cradled the vodka bottle. "You're a princess," he told her thickly.

"Right."

In her small shabby room overlooking a derelict junk yard,

108

she helped him off with his jacket.

"Come and get comfortable," she said going over to a small sofa.

He sat beside her. The place smelt of dampness and moth balls. A photograph of Burt Reynolds torn from some magazine was taped on the peeling wallpaper above the wash basin.

"What's your name, darling?" she purred.

"Joe," Zarubin replied.

She got up and stripped off her T-shirt. She stood in front of him, nude to the waist. She had small breasts with green circles painted round the nipples. He stared.

"Like it? It's the latest thing. Neat, eh?"

"Got any glasses?" asked Zarubin, opening the bottle of vodka.

She began unfastening her jeans.

"You don't want any more, Joe. Not now."

He smiled.

Now she stood in front of him naked.

"Come on, Joe," she invited, thrusting her pelvis forward.

He took a swig from the bottle, then stood up, and put his hand on her breast.

The odour of dampness and moth balls was nauseating.

He tried to forget the frustrations of the day and concentrate on making her. But whether it was because he'd had too much to drink, he couldn't respond to her, nor could he erase Fern from his thoughts.

Half an hour later it started raining. Rivulets of water trickled down the dirty window panes of her room.

Zarubin, naked, lay on the bed breathing hard. She glanced at him sideways, anxiously.

"What's the matter? Don't you like me?"

He closed his eyes. He felt weak, impotent, and wished she wasn't there. "You're cute," he muttered. He wanted to get away from her, but he was afraid to be on his own. Physically, he needed her body but was also repelled by it.

"You didn't even come, Joe," she complained, an edge of indignation to her voice. "What's wrong with you?"

He kept his eyes closed. "I'm sorry."

"Blokes always climax with me," she said, like a manufacturer insisting on the quality of the merchandise. "Nobody complains."

"I'm not complaining," sighed Zarubin, wearily.

She moved on top of his body, and thrust her breasts into his face. The green ringed nipples loomed in front of him.

"Come on, darling," she cooed. "Let's try again."

Gently, he eased her off and sat up.

"Christ," she snarled. "You're bloody impotent, aren't you? What's your problem, prefer to do it with men?"

He got up and began to dress.

"I think I'd better be going."

She remained on the bed, the smudged red mouth a living scar.

"I think so too," she agreed harshly. "Perhaps you'd better go and see a doctor."

He put on his jacket.

"Go find your bloody Fern," she shouted. "Get her to suck you off."

"So long," said Zarubin quietly.

Outside, the rain had turned into a drizzle. He glanced at his watch and cursed. There were so many dead hours ahead.

And he was sober. That was the worst thing. But even though he was stone cold sober, he was still thinking of Fern.

Nick Prosser was late with his column. He should have delivered it in the morning, but he didn't push his way through the swing doors of the Fleet Street newsroom until after lunch.

Prosser could get away with it. He was a star in his own right. His tousle haired, boyish face stared at three million readers from the masthead of his newspaper column twice a week. "The Reporter They Cannot Buy" was his catch line. It wasn't strictly accurate, for Prosser was always open to offers; but it conveyed the right meaning to his trusting followers. Here was an incorruptible man.

He travelled extensively, filing pungent first person reports from the trouble spots of the globe. In their time, Cambodia, Angola, Uganda, Cyprus, El Salvador, the Lebanon, the Falklands – all received the Prosser treatment.

His speciality was sincerity and he was particularly effective on television. Ruggedly dressed in battle fatigues, microphone in hand, he faced the camera epitomizing the voice of compassion and indignation at the cruelty of man to man.

When there wasn't a war to cover, he concentrated his talents on a gamut of issues ranging from nuclear disarmament, famines, military juntas, police brutality, through to homosexual freedom of expression, extinction of the panda, banning smoking in public, and fox hunting. First hand accounts from a Green Peace ship during its attempts to sabotage a seal cull, and a week with the PLO in a Beirut refugee camp underlined the extent of his convictions.

Big headlines and small stories on such topics as bare breasted lady wrestlers, adulterous vicars, and pot smoking pop stars were the mainstay of the tabloid Nick Prosser wrote for. So his conscience was doubly valuable to the paper, and worth the generous salary they paid him.

He was also, when he felt like it, a very good reporter, with some intriguing contacts. Being radical chic paid Prosser, but he had never quite buried the real newspaperman in him.

After he'd delivered his copy, he took the lift to the paper's library. He made his way between the book shelves and the filing cabinets to where the chief librarian sat filling his pipe.

"Jerry," he smiled ingratiatingly, "I need a bit of help."

Jerry lit his pipe, and merely grunted.

"Deveaux," went on Prosser. "What have you got on him?"

"Sir Leslie?" Jerry looked displeased. "The old spy?"

"That's the one."

"God, there's tons of it, man."

"I want it all," said Prosser.

"When?"

"Now."

"Oh, sod," groaned Jerry not disguising the reluctance with which he got up from his swivel chair.

"I don't suppose you want Philby and Blunt and Blake as well?" he asked sarcastically.

"Just Deveaux."

Jerry snorted. "It's going to take a little time."

"That's okay."

"Sit down over there," he told Prosser, indicating a table. "I'll see what we can do."

He was getting used to Prosser's peculiar enquiries. The other day it had been the old, faded cuttings on Colonel Oleg Penkovsky, executed over twenty years ago by a Soviet firing squad.

Prosser had spent hours tracing Penkovsky's career from the time he was deputy to General Serov, head of the GRU, the Military Directorate of the Red Army, to his final assignment as key man of the super secret Scientific Research Committee. Actually, there was little contemporary coverage of Penkovsky. His journeys to the West, his smuggling of 5,000 secret plans of Soviet missile and electronic weaponry to NATO agents, his contacts with Western intelligence in London hotels, all these things were not written about at the time.

The brief reports of his show trial, when he'd admitted high treason, had not appeared to interest Prosser very much. He'd concentrated on accounts concerning the little that was known about Penkovsky's activities as a spy before, out of the blue, the KGB had arrested him.

Prosser had returned those files without comment, leaving Jerry as baffled as he was now with the request for the Deveaux material.

The paper had one of the most efficient morgues in Fleet Street, and Jerry supervised it with great skill. In ten minutes, thick manilla envelopes began arriving. On the front of each one was a note of the period the contents covered and they were stuffed with clippings, marked "Deveaux".

"What the hell d'you want all this for?" asked Jerry curiously, dropping the last two batches on the table.

"Just digging around," replied Prosser vaguely.

Jerry pressed down the bowl of his pipe with an ink stained thumb.

"I'd like to see what they've got on him in Whitehall. Sodding traitor, and they never even arrested him. I suppose he's living on a bloody pension."

"That's right."

"What a bloody country," muttered Jerry, shuffling off.

112

After three hours, Prosser had looked at most of the cuttings, giving some a cursory glance, reading others with great care, and, now and then, making notes.

Finally, he neatly stacked the envelopes, went over to Jerry's desk, and told him he was through.

"Will you want them again?" asked Jerry.

Prosser shook his head. "No."

Jerry leaned forward. "What's it all about, Nick?"

"You'd be surprised," winked Prosser.

He went across to the picture library, and asked the art people to show him any photos they had of Deveaux.

The file they gave him was surprisingly thin. Hardly any of the photographs in it had been taken while he was, as the *Who's Who* of those years put it, "attached Foreign Office". There was one picture, taken in the forecourt of Buckingham Palace, when he was knighted in 1955.

The rest had been taken when the story finally broke. Shots of Deveaux, blank faced, getting out of a car on the day he was named as having been a Soviet agent in British intelligence, during the weeks of the enquiry, and the Parliamentary debate that followed. The last one Prosser looked at had been taken on the day the Queen stripped him of his knighthood. Ironically, the back of the picture was still tagged "Sir Leslie Deveaux".

Prosser went to see the art editor.

"Any other pictures of him?" he asked.

"It's all in the folder, mate."

"What about the early days?"

The art editor stopped marking up a negative. "What exactly are you after, Nick?"

"I'm not sure," said Prosser. But he was lying.

In Fleet Street, he hailed a cab and gave the address in Fulham. It pulled up in front of a small terraced house and Prosser paid off the driver. He pulled out his keys, and opened the front door.

"I'm home," he called out.

Fern came out into the hall.

"Hi," she said and they kissed.

"I don't feel like going out tonight," he said. "Do you mind if we stay in?"

"Of course not."

They went into the lounge, and he started to fix himself a drink.

"I'll get some ice," offered Fern.

"Thanks." Then he stopped, and looked at her more closely. "You look a bit pale. Anything the matter?"

"No," she smiled. "Everything's just fine."

In the privacy of his office, after working hours, Dichter deciphered the secret code which was for his eyes only.

Normal communication channels had been bypassed. It had never been seen by the embassy radio room, which generally handled the classified traffic between the London station and head office. Instead, it had been transmitted from CINCNELM headquarters in Mayfair and the Navy operator who relayed it had no idea what he was sending.

Zarubin's situation report was terse:

1. CONFIRM INDICATIONS HOSTILE PENETRATION.
2. IDENTITY NOT YET ESTABLISHED.
3. BELIEVE SPIRIDOV TERMINATED PREVENT REVEALING IDENTITY.
4. SUSPECT UKUSA ARRANGEMENT JEOPARDISED.
5. CAUTION KOSOV OPERATION.
6. NO INFORMATION YET CAPTIVE.
7. WAITING BEES TO TASTE HONEY.

Dichter read the decode very carefully. Then he took out his lighter, and watched the flimsy piece of paper flare up, then disintegrate in its flame. The few wispy ashes that remained he swept into an ashtray which he took into the private bathroom adjoining his office and flushed down the toilet.

Nothing on the record. No paper work. Everything sub rosa. That, after all, was what Blanchard had ordained.

Ulianov was fast asleep when they came to get him in the middle of the night. He didn't hear them enter the turret prison or see the light being switched on. He was awoken by

114

someone shaking him, hard.

With difficulty, he opened his eyes, and blinked. The unexpected light made it impossible to see at first, and he buried his head in the pillow.

"Come on, get up," ordered a voice in Russian.

Slowly, he sat up. He didn't know the voice, or recognise the man to whom it belonged.

There were two other men in the cell, anonymous figures, with expressionless faces.

"What is happening?" asked Ulianov, trying to collect his wits. His speech was slightly slurred, and he couldn't focus properly.

"Get your clothes on," commanded the voice. One of the other men was putting his few belongings into a holdall.

Ulianov's movements were slow, ponderous. It was an effort to get off the camp bed, and stand up.

"I'm sick," he protested, weakly.

"You're all right," the voice assured him. "Just hurry up."

"No." Ulianov felt giddy, and he reached out to steady himself. "I am not well." Only much later did it cross his mind that the food he'd been given the previous evening might have been doped.

Then he saw the man in the tweed suit standing in the doorway.

This time he had no interpreter.

"I have good news, Major," he announced in fluent Russian. "You're leaving at last."

Ulianov shook his head, in an effort to clear his muzziness.

"I promised you we'd try to get you away from here as soon as possible," he continued. "That's what you want, isn't it?"

He came nearer.

"You know you can trust me," he said, putting a reassuring hand on Ulianov's shoulder.

The other three men stood silent, watching.

"What time is it?" asked Ulianov. "Where are you taking me?"

"It is night." The second question was left unanswered.

Ulianov shivered.

"I'm cold," he said, hugging himself to keep warm.

"You'll soon feel better. I'm sorry there isn't anything hot to drink, but we all want to be out of here. You most of all, I imagine."

The interrogator led the way. Two of the silent men took Ulianov's arms, and steered him out of the cell, down the narrow steps. They did it very gently, as if they were helping an invalid.

At the bottom of the stairs was a steel door. The interrogator nodded, and the escort who was behind Ulianov suddenly put a blindfold over his eyes. It was done smoothly, expertly.

"Don't be alarmed," said the interrogator. "It's only a formality. You know what regulations are. Mind your step."

Ulianov heard the steel door open. There was no sound of a lock being turned; it seemed to him, despite his sightlessness, that it must be electronically operated. But he wasn't sure. Nothing was sure. He felt so disorientated.

They guided him with great care, along passages, and an interminable corridor. He heard whispering, and another door open. Then, to his delight, he was in the fresh air.

"There," said the interrogator, "that feels good, doesn't it?"

Ulianov wanted to tear the blindfold from his eyes, but the men held his arms firmly. The air was cold, but he breathed it in deeply, thankfully. It was clean, pure after the confined atmosphere of the turret. The influx of oxygen seemed to help clear his head.

"Careful, mind how you go," warned the interrogator as Ulianov mounted a step, and was half guided, half pushed into some kind of vehicle.

"Here, you can sit."

Somebody untied the blindfold, and a door slammed. He was in a type of lorry with all four walls made of steel. There were no windows and the only illumination came from a small shielded light. It was like being shut in a safe.

Except for one of the guards, he was alone.

He heard the engine start, and the armoured car began to move.

He felt less muddled, as if the effects of the drug, if that is what it had been, were wearing off. It struck him for the first

116

time how anonymous the guard looked. Wearing a track suit like himself. Not yellow, but navy.

As far as he could tell from the motion, they were travelling at high speed. Despite the lack of windows, the vehicle was well ventilated.

"I want to know what is happening to me," said Ulianov sitting back on the leather covered seat.

The guard didn't react.

"Where are you taking me?" he yelled.

But the guard just stared at him impassively.

The hall porter at the block of flats gave Zarubin a curious look as he went to the elevator.

"Your laundry's back," he reported, coolly. The good will bought by two tips seemed to have evaporated.

"I'll get it later," Zarubin told him, sliding open the lift door.

He got out on the second floor, and walked down the passageway to his flat. As soon as he inserted his key in the front door, he sensed trouble. The bottom lock was already undone and the top one needed only one turn; normally it required a double twist. Zarubin glanced up and down the corridor. It was empty. From one of the adjoining flats came reggae music. But soft, the radio turned down.

He braced himself, and opened the door.

Two people were in the tiny lounge, a woman and a man. The woman sat in the only armchair, her shapely legs crossed. The man was perched on the edge of the desk.

Zarubin had never seen either of them before, but something about the woman was strangely familiar, as if she fitted some description he had been given. She was blonde, and had unbuttoned her smart, belted black raincoat. She had very blue eyes.

The man was dapper, with a small toothbrush moustache, and wore an off-the-peg, creased suit. Zarubin noticed his navy tie. It had an unusual motif, a pair of shears cutting a book in half.

Vaguely it came back to him. "Good looker," the porter had called her. The blonde who had asked all the questions about him, and driven off in the Metro.

They both stood up when Zarubin entered. While they'd been waiting for him, they had been busy. The wardrobe was standing open, drawers in the dressing table had been pulled out, his suitcases dragged out from under the bed, and examined, books and magazines lay scattered on the floor.

"Mr Zarubin?" asked the blonde, coldly impersonal.

"Who the hell are you?" he demanded, standing in the doorway.

"Come in and shut the door," instructed the blonde. She was used to giving orders.

"The porter let us in," added the dapper man, as if that explained everything. He didn't even bother to make it sound plausible.

"Stay right where you are," said Zarubin. "I'm going to call the police."

"We are the police." From her raincoat she took an ID card with her photograph. "I am Detective Inspector Turner. Vice squad. This is my sergeant."

She made him sound like her personal property.

Vice squad? This blonde? With those legs?

The blue eyes glinted, as if she'd read his thoughts. "That's right," she confirmed icily.

"What are you doing here?"

"We have two warrants, Mr Zarubin. They're both issued under the Obscene Publications Act. One is to search this flat and your belongings. We have already done that while we waited for you. The second one is for your arrest."

Zarubin laughed. "You must be kidding."

"We have reason to believe that you are trafficking and dealing in obscene matter, namely pornographic film cassettes. Pornographic video cassettes come within the act," pointed out the blonde, without a trace of humour.

"Oh come on," smiled Zarubin, "this is a put on. You're not serious."

The blue eyes raked him. "I am taking you into custody, and you will be charged."

"Let's go, Mr Zarubin," added the Sergeant.

Zarubin was no longer smiling. "Okay." He moved to the phone. "I'm going to call somebody."

"No phone call," intervened the blonde.

"Doesn't London's finest caution people any more?"

"Once you are charged," she said, impassively.

Zarubin started to say something, then turned to go into the bedroom.

"Where are you going?" asked the blonde.

"To get my passport."

"I have it here," said the dapper sergeant, producing it from inside his jacket.

"You'll be given every facility at the police station," the blonde assured Zarubin.

"I bet," he said, glancing round the room. "Tell me, did you find what you were looking for?"

"Come along," pressed the blonde, like a school teacher with a naughty pupil.

The sergeant locked the door of the flat, but kept the keys. Zarubin went down in the lift with them, and past the porter, who stared curiously at the trio.

The Metro was parked outside. The sergeant got into the back with him. She drove.

She was a good driver, and Zarubin would have liked to have seen her handle a more powerful car. They didn't speak during the short journey, but once or twice those cold blue eyes studied him in the driving mirror.

Zarubin stared back at her, and she returned his look boldly. As vice cops went, she was certainly something special.

When they arrived at the police station, Zarubin was taken into a bare, white painted interview room and left to stare at the wall while a uniformed constable guarded the door.

After ten minutes, the blonde inspector returned. She had taken off the raincoat, and her tight fitting sweater and skirt accentuated a very good figure. It was the first time Zarubin had ever looked at a cop in that way.

She dismissed the policeman with a gesture, and sat down at the table opposite Zarubin.

"All right," she began, "do you want to tell me about it?"

She was less formal now, and the blue eyes were a little more human.

"Tell you about what?"

"Your little racket. Where you get the stuff. Your contacts."

She was too smart, he thought, to play it that dumb. She must be aware of the background. She must know about him.

"Have you talked to the embassy?" he asked.

"That'll be taken care of, Mr Zarubin. Right now I'd like a statement from you."

"You call the embassy."

She pursed her lips. "Let me give you a bit of advice. Cooperate. Make a statement. Tell us about your connections. How you get the material into the country."

She waited.

"And if I don't?"

"You'll go to jail," she said pleasantly. "You'll get eighteen months if you're lucky. Two, perhaps three years if you're not. Four or five if we can think up enough charges and the judge has indigestion. Then we'll deport you."

Zarubin nodded.

"Well?" she enquired.

She had long sensitive fingers, and she was playing with a small propelling pencil. He tried to imagine her as a police-woman on the beat, but he couldn't. The cocktail bar at the Savoy was more her line.

"You like it?" he asked.

"What?"

"Your job. Smut. Dirty books. Filthy pictures. Bondage. Women and dogs . . ."

"You needn't go into details, Mr Zarubin," she retorted. "Maybe I should ask you the same. Are you so hard up you have to peddle such garbage?"

He shrugged. "Strange job for a woman that's all."

"You know how passé you sound?" she asked contemptuously. "Very old fashioned, Mr Zarubin."

"Okay. Just tell me. Who put the heat on? Who's behind all this?"

"We don't like foreigners coming over here flogging hard core porn to sex shops. We've got enough of it."

"Very commendable, but it doesn't answer my question. Who ordered me to be arrested?"

She stood up.

"Since you don't wish to cooperate . . . " She walked to the door. "If you change your mind, let me know."

120

She opened the door.

"Hey, what happens now?" he asked.

"You'll be formally charged. Tomorrow you'll appear in court."

"When do I go home?"

For the first time she smiled.

"You don't," she said, and closed the door behind her.

The policeman came in and gave Zarubin a cup of tea. It was very strong, and far too sweet. He took one sip and pulled a face.

Then they took him to a cell and locked him up for the night.

He lay on the bunk thinking for a long time. He also considered whether the cool, blonde inspector would really look that good naked.

Zarubin's case was third on the list the following morning. When he stepped into the dock, the magistrate under the big royal coat of arms was busy writing something in a ledger in front of him and didn't even look up. An eye glass on a silk ribbon hung round his neck, and Zarubin wondered if he sometimes peered at the prisoners in the dock through it, like a male Madame Défarge.

"Who's in charge?" asked the clerk testily. He was surrounded by a stack of papers and glowered at Zarubin resentfully.

The blonde stepped forward, and entered the witness box. She was dressed very formally in a grey business suit, and her make-up was more restrained.

"Yes?" enquired the magistrate shortly.

"Andrew Zarubin," the clerk informed him.

"Ah yes," said the magistrate gloomily. He fixed the eye glass in his eye, stared at Zarubin for a moment, and then took it out again.

"Are you giving evidence of arrest?" asked the clerk. The blonde nodded.

Standing there, Zarubin felt like a dummy whose existence was totally immaterial. They were playing out a set game in which everyone had a part except himself.

"Well?" demanded the magistrate.

She took the oath, and for the first time Zarubin learnt that her name was Helen. Detective Inspector Helen Turner.

"I arrested this man on warrant yesterday," she stated crisply. "I am asking for this case to be remanded for seven days."

That was all.

The magistrate stroked his chin.

"Pornography, eh?"

"The charges are before you, sir," said the clerk fussily.

"Yes I see." He nodded. "Very well, then, seven days. What about bail?"

"We oppose bail," said the blonde, never even glancing across at Zarubin.

"Why?" asked the magistrate.

"We are concerned that he may interfere with our enquiries, and also that he might try to leave the country."

She had it all rehearsed, and was word perfect.

The magistrate peered at Zarubin.

"Well now, you have heard the officer. What do you say on the question of bail?"

"I want bail," replied Zarubin. "I'm not going to run away. Quite the opposite."

"Hmm. These are serious charges, you know." He looked at the blonde. "Do you oppose bail very strongly?"

"Yes, sir."

The magistrate rubbed his chin.

"All right, I'll tell you what I will do, Mr Zarubin. You can have bail if you produce two sureties of £10,000 each or one for £20,000 and your passport must be surrendered."

Zarubin opened his mouth, then shut it again. He thought the blonde was smiling faintly.

"There's no way I can raise £20,000 just like that," he protested.

"In that case, you will be remanded in custody until you can," said the magistrate.

"But . . ."

"Remanded seven days. In custody."

The policeman who stood behind him touched his arm, and started to guide Zarubin down the steps below the dock.

"You'll enjoy Brixton," he whispered, sarcastically.

As Zarubin turned, the blonde was already leaving the

court. But his eyes caught another familiar face. In the second row of the public seats sat Lambert. He was staring straight at Zarubin, without showing a sign of recognition.

It was a sour morning for Flexner. Crawford hadn't helped when he'd greeted him cheerfully in the gents saying:

"I hear your boy's landed in the pokey."

"He's not my boy," retorted Flexner curtly.

Zarubin's name wasn't even mentioned; they both knew who they were talking about.

"Well, good luck," Crawford smiled with what Flexner thought was a touch of malice. He seemed to be enjoying the mess.

Then there was the encounter with the legal attaché. Sullivan was an FBI man who liaised with Scotland Yard, and kept tabs on American citizens who got themselves into trouble.

"How are you going to play this?" he enquired, a shade conspiratorially.

"What the hell's it got to do with me?"

Sullivan shrugged. "Well, he's part of your set up, isn't he?"

"No," snapped Flexner.

"I thought . . ."

"You thought wrong. He's got no official status. He's not here officially. He's just an American in London. Got the picture?"

Sullivan appeared puzzled.

"As I understood it . . ." he began, but Flexner cut him short.

"He's got nothing to do with the embassy. He's on his own."

Sullivan looked concerned. "Supposing there's publicity?"

"Why should there be?"

"Well, if it leaks out . . ."

"What?"

"His background. You can see the headlines, can't you? 'CIA man on porn charges.' That's all we need."

No wonder he's done well in the FBI, thought Flexner. He's a persistent bastard who won't let go. Can't even take a goddamn hint. He took a deep breath.

"Greg, I keep telling you, it's not my department. I don't give him orders. We're not involved. Okay?"

The way Flexner was playing dumb began to annoy the FBI man.

"I'm only trying to be helpful, Cyrus. He's a US citizen who's been arrested on a serious charge, and they'll probably ask the FBI for a background check. I want to make sure I don't put my great big foot in it. I'm trying to be helpful, for Chrissake."

Sullivan loathed spooks. He had a good relationship with the undercover people from the DEA. Narcotics were a clean business compared to these characters. These guys never gave you a straight answer.

"Relax," smiled Flexner, "they won't ask for any background." He hoped it sounded reassuring. "They know all about him. He's not a tourist you know."

"Precisely," said Sullivan drily. "But he is a citizen, and entitled to certain consular protection."

"Not Zarubin," said Flexner curtly. "He's not entitled to anything."

"What's that?"

Flexner controlled himself. "Leave him to it. He'll make out."

Sullivan shrugged. "So be it. He's your baby. If I get pressed, I'll let Washington handle it. If he wants any advice, or requests legal help . . ."

"You pigeon hole it."

Sullivan nodded, not like a man who understands, but more like someone who has become aware of a situation it's best to stay out of.

Suddenly, Flexner wondered if he had come on too strong, and blown it. After all, Sullivan had been field agent in charge of the Los Angeles office. He was a toughie.

"I'm sorry not to be very helpful," he apologised, "but I've got to think of the whole picture. I know how my people want it played."

"And how is that?" asked Sullivan very softly.

"Let it take care of itself. Let him be."

Miss Walsh popped her head round the door.

"Would you gentlemen like some coffee?" she enquired.

"No, thanks, I'm just going," replied Sullivan. "Thanks for your time, Cyrus."

But before he left, he asked one more question.

"What's going on?"

"Sorry, Greg. That's not your department." Flexner shrugged. "You know how it is."

"Sure," said Sullivan.

The FBI man looked forward to his lunch date even more now. Rumour had it that the vice squad cop who was in charge of Zarubin's case was a very good looking lady. It might not only turn out to be a very enjoyable meeting, but he might even learn a few things. Things that other people apparently didn't want him to know.

The last time Zarubin had been a prisoner was in Hoa Lo. Then the windowless cell had measured three feet by six with a hardwood bed jutting out from one wall which left hardly enough space to turn. The walls had been covered with fungus, worms crawled around the floor and much of the time Zarubin had spent staring at a two inch drainhole, his only link with the outside world.

His diet had been a bowlful of rice a day, and weak tea. Once he'd thrown the rice at a guard, and had been punished by having his hands shackled to some iron rings attached to the foot of the bed. Next time the guard came, Zarubin spat at the little man in black pyjamas. They'd blindfolded him.

Zarubin had picked up some ugly words in Saigon and he used them effectively. So they gagged him.

After forty-eight hours, the gag and the blindfold were removed and he was made to sit on a small three legged stool. A guard remained with him day and night to make sure he never got off that stool. If he moved, he was beaten; if he fell asleep, he was kicked, and when, after five days, he keeled over unconscious, they threw him on to the cot and left him.

He never knew the name of his interrogator, but soon nicknamed him the Pig. The man was oriental and fat with a double chin, but somehow he didn't look Vietnamese. Zarubin suspected that he was a specialist from North Korea. He wore no rank insignia, only a five pointed red star on his cap. He spoke good English and also tried talking to Zarubin in Russian. Zarubin had played dumb, as if he didn't understand a word.

Zarubin knew he was on the verge of a breakdown when he actually started to welcome visits from the Pig. The total isolation in which they kept him made any human contact an event, even if the human was the Pig. Sometimes, when he felt like it, the Pig would give him the odd bit of news from the outside world. He was also, of course, responsible for ordering the ill treatment and torture, although he himself was never present on these occasions. That way he was able to keep up the pretence of being a civilised person. Not that he fooled Zarubin.

To begin with, Zarubin had tried talking to himself but he soon gave that up because he knew, if he continued, he would crack. So the Pig became very valuable to Zarubin, because at least he meant conversation.

To his surprise, he was released when the Paris Agreement was signed in 1973. The Pig didn't witness Zarubin's departure for Gia Lam airport, and later Zarubin found out that he had been killed during a raid on Hanoi. Zarubin had been lucky because the Pig had intended to have him executed but never got round to signing the order before he was blown to pieces.

Memories of Hoa Lo came flooding back as Zarubin followed the warder along the decaying, Victorian corridors of rundown Brixton prison.

The Assistant Governor, into whose office Zarubin was escorted, was surprisingly young with spectacles and a Manchester University tie.

"Zarubin, Andrew, sir," the warder barked, handing him a clipboard. "Remand."

The Assistant Governor glanced at it, and then nodded.

"Well, Zarubin," he began, "you will be kept in D Wing. Now, you're not a convicted person, so you can wear your own clothes and you can have your food sent in."

The spectacles peered at Zarubin earnestly.

"You're not here to be punished, but simply to be kept under lock and key until your case is heard. You understand that? Good. You can have any books you want, and write letters. Do you have a special diet?"

"No."

"No, sir," corrected the warder, loudly.

The Assistant Governor waved a hand airily.

"That's all right. I take it you don't suffer from any illnesses? Diabetes, that sort of thing?"

Zarubin shook his head.

"Good. I'm afraid we're shockingly overcrowded here," he continued, glancing at a wall chart. "You'll have to share a cell, but you're lucky. There'll only be the two of you. Now, is there anything you want to ask me?"

"Yes," said Zarubin, "I want to call the American embassy."

"Permission granted." He looked at the warder. "Will you see to that?"

"Yes, sir." The warder was beefy, red faced, and sounded reluctant. "One phone call."

"That's all then. If you have any problems, Zarubin, see the Principal Officer, and if he can't help, I'm here."

"Come along," the warder commanded. Now that he was taking over, he seemed a little happier.

After Hoa Lo, no gaol held any terror for Zarubin and there was no similarity between it and Brixton or the Pig and the studious Assistant Governor.

As he was marched along the grey, peeling wing to the telephone, one thing reminded him of Hoa Lo. The smell. It was the same. The odour of human excrement in unemptied buckets.

It wasn't every day that Miss Walsh put through a call to Flexner from an inmate of Brixton prison, so she was sorely tempted to eavesdrop. But she resisted the urge, deciding it wasn't worth the risk. She'd save that for better things.

In his office, her boss didn't waste time on niceties.

"What the hell's going on?" he demanded.

"You know damn well," said Zarubin. He was very controlled.

Flexner was silent.

"Are you there?" asked Zarubin.

"Yeah."

"Start pushing some buttons. Move yourself."

Sassy bastard, thought Flexner. Aloud he told Zarubin, "It's got nothing to do with me, Andrew. You're subject to United Kingdom jurisdiction. If you get yourself in trouble over here, that's tough. As far as this mission is concerned, you've got no status. Sorry pal."

He didn't like Zarubin's laugh. Or the quiet way he said:

"I want out of here, pronto. And listen, Cyrus, I'll get out, I promise, one way or another. It'd just be nice to think my buddy is right there helping me."

Flexner gave an audible sigh.

"I'd like to help. I'll consult the head shed. But I can't promise quick action. Why the hell didn't you keep your nose clean? This could turn awkward. We don't need it. Dichter won't like it."

"Fuck Dichter," retorted Zarubin. "And fuck you."

He slammed down the phone leaving Flexner staring at the dead receiver in his hand.

"Son of a bitch," he muttered, but it gave him little satisfaction.

The clanging of the studded, grey iron door as it was locked behind Zarubin, was ignored by the cell's other inmate. He lay on one of the two bunks and didn't even look up from the Arabic newspaper he was reading.

The cell had one window which was covered with thick, shatter proof glass, and a wire caged bulb in the ceiling provided most of the light. In a corner stood two covered buckets, and above them was a shelf with a couple of books.

Zarubin went over to the vacant bunk and stared back at the dark eyes watching him from above the newspaper. The fingers that held it were well manicured.

"Hello," said Zarubin, as he sat down.

Slowly, the newspaper dropped, revealing the well chiselled, arrogant features of a handsome man with light brown skin and jet black hair. He was smiling slightly.

"Welcome," he said, sitting up.

He was casually but expensively dressed, in a silk shirt, well cut trousers, and suede shoes. On his left wrist he had a gold Rolex, on the right one a thin, gold chain, and around his neck a gold medallion.

128

"I regret I cannot offer you refreshments," he went on, with only the slightest trace of an accent. "However, if you wish to use the bathroom, please go ahead," and he indicated the buckets with a mocking gesture. "English culture at its best."

"You can say that again."

The man raised an eyebrow. "American?" he asked.

"That's right."

"Really?" He reacted. "What are you doing in here?"

"The same as you, I guess. Enjoying the Queen's hospitality." Zarubin removed his jacket and took a deep breath. "Christ!"

"You'll get used to it," said the man. "Tell me, what is your crime?"

Zarubin smiled.

"Ah, please forgive me," apologised the man. "It is none of my business."

"You're right, it isn't."

The man picked up his Arabic newspaper again, but after a moment lowered it.

"I apologise for any discourtesy. Let us start again. My name is Salim." His white teeth flashed.

"Zarubin."

"Excuse me?"

"Z-a-r-u-b-i-n."

"But you *are* an American?"

"Right."

Salim hesitated. Then he enquired, "Tell me, my friend, are you in trouble with Uncle Sam? The CIA maybe?"

"What makes you think that?" Zarubin asked coldly.

Salim spread his hands. "When the British throw Americans in jail, one sometimes wonders if it is not done on orders. Also, they are tidy in this prison. I am political. So it seems likely that they would put another political in here. It just struck me that you might be somebody like that. You would not be the first, believe me. I imagine it's no news to you to know that there are quite a few Americans in Europe the CIA would like to get its claws on? I just thought that perhaps you might be one of them. After all, there are still a few Americans who . . ."

"Who what?"

"Think differently."

And his dark eyes challenged Zarubin boldly.

"What's your problem?" Zarubin demanded.

"Please?"

"Since you're so interested in me, I'd like to know why you're here."

Salim shrugged. "They say I'm a terrorist."

"And are you?"

He smiled. "What is a terrorist, my friend?"

Zarubin didn't answer.

"Exactly," continued Salim. "You are not a Zionist, are you?"

"No."

"Of course not. They would not arrest a Zionist." Suddenly he sounded bitter.

"What makes them think you're a . . . ."

"A freedom fighter?" His eyes were hard. "Who knows? They say I tried to execute a Zionist."

The word "execute" told Zarubin a great deal.

"Did you?"

"My friend, you ask too many questions. Let us simply agree you cannot make an omelet without breaking eggs."

Salim looked pleased at the way he had put it.

"So now you understand why I have a brotherly feeling for anyone who is a victim of the CIA," he added, "and whom the British wish to get rid of."

From outside came the sound of footsteps approaching the cell. There was the rattle of keys, then the door swung open and a warder carried in a tray covered by a white cloth.

"Lunch," he announced unceremoniously, putting the tray down next to Salim. He ignored Zarubin and left, slamming the cell door behind him.

Salim removed the white cloth. It was a good spread. Melon, half a cold chicken, salad, chocolate gateaux, cheese and a jug of orange juice.

"Please," he invited, "join me. It will give me great pleasure. And I assure you you won't be able to eat the garbage they serve you here."

The cutlery was plastic, as was the beaker.

"You have the fork," offered Salim. "I'll make do with the spoon. Please, tuck in."

"You sure?"

"Of course. Here." He tore the leg off the chicken and held it out.

The sight of the food reminded Zarubin how hungry he was.

"Thanks," he said, biting into the chicken.

Salim poured some orange juice.

"I regret we'll have to share the same mug."

Later, when they'd finished the food, Zarubin asked:

"How did you manage that? Special connections?"

Salim smiled his smile. "I have friends outside. They look after me. This . . . " he made a nonchalant gesture " . . . this is only an interlude. Eventually they will deport me, that's all. No problem."

What he said was true, Zarubin knew that.

"Where to?"

Salim wiped his mouth delicately. "That, I'm happy to say, is causing the British a headache. I don't care. I am at home everywhere, Libya, Iraq, Syria. My friends will assure a good welcome, wherever it is. Perhaps better than the reception that awaits you, maybe?"

"Could be."

"You know too much, you think? Maybe you were CIA yourself. Am I right?"

"Thanks for the lunch," said Zarubin.

"I absolutely understand." Salim nodded amiably. "But I wouldn't be surprised if my friends would be delighted to meet you. And maybe . . ." He considered for a moment. "Maybe you would find it useful too."

"You think?"

"Who knows how we may end up helping each other."

"You sure you haven't got the wrong guy?" Zarubin asked, leaning back against the wall.

Salim shook his head. "Oh no. I never make mistakes."

Then he returned to his paper, but the word "execute" kept resounding in Zarubin's ears.

Sullivan had suggested that they meet at the Albert in

Buckingham Gate, because, although it was only three minutes' walk from Scotland Yard, curiously it wasn't a pub much frequented by the police.

He also liked the Victorian décor, such as the gas lamps over the entrance, the ponderous notices announcing it "purveyed" what it termed "celebrated stouts", and provided a "carvery room" for its "valued patrons".

Sullivan had already discovered during his London tour that few establishments in this town regarded their customers as "valued".

He was five minutes early, and ordered a half pint of bitter in the saloon bar. He was an earnest looking man, and the horn rimmed glasses he wore gave him the appearance of being older than his forty years. Standing in the corner of the pub, dressed in his sober black suit and white shirt, he could have been a lawyer or an accountant which, like so many FBI special agents, he also was.

Detective Inspector Turner showed up exactly on time. Her casual clothes, a roll neck sweater, hip hugging corduroy trousers and high heeled boots took Sullivan by surprise. She didn't fit in with his image of a Scotland Yard vice squad officer.

"I'm sorry I can't stay too long," she announced crisply, without preliminary. "I've got to get back in an hour."

"Oh," said Sullivan, and he didn't try to hide his disappointment. "In that case, we'd better go and eat right away."

He left the remainder of his half pint and led the way upstairs to the restaurant. They cut themselves some roast beef off the joint. She was sparing with the Yorkshire pudding, and took only one roast potato.

"Tell me," said Sullivan, after they'd sat down at a table and he'd ordered the wine. "What do I call you? Inspector? Ms? Turner? Helen?"

Her smile was a little chilly. "Whatever you like, Mr Sullivan."

"Greg, please."

She was ice, this blonde.

He poured her some wine, half expecting her to protest that she didn't drink on duty, but instead she said:

"You know, you're the first FBI man I've met."

"Well, you're my first lady vice cop . . ."

"I'm not a lady vice cop," she retorted stiffly. "I'm a police officer."

"Yes, ma'am."

And just for a moment there was a flash of humour in her eyes.

"You still haven't told me what this is all about. I take it we're here on official business."

Sullivan selected his words carefully.

"Let's just say I thought it was time we got better acquainted."

"Any special reason?"

"Well," began Sullivan, "one of my duties as legal attaché at the Embassy is Liaison with British law enforcement agencies. You're a British law enforcement officer, Helen, so here we are."

"Oh," she mocked him, but not unkindly. "We're liaising, are we?"

"Of course."

They didn't have any dessert, only coffee.

"I'm curious," said Sullivan and she interrupted:

"So I'd gathered."

"Seriously," went on Sullivan. "How come you're doing vice?"

"You mean, what's a nice girl like me, etc? Simple. I'm good at the job."

"You *like* it?" he asked, slightly incredulous. "You actually like the work?"

"You *are* a chauvinist, aren't you?" She declined sugar. "Only nice, clean crime for police women, eh?"

"Well, no. Not exactly . . . "

She glanced at her watch. "I can't stay much longer," she warned.

"Tell me about Mr Zarubin," said Sullivan.

"Aah," she nodded. "Of course. What is it you want to know about him?"

"Why was he picked up?"

"Because he's peddling obscene material."

"Come on," chuckled Sullivan. "You know what I mean."

The blue eyes stared at him innocently. "No, I don't

think I do."

"Somebody's behind it, of course. Who gave the orders? Who wanted him inside?"

She sipped the last of her wine.

"Is this official? Your Embassy wasn't very interested in Mr Zarubin. Why the sudden concern?"

Sullivan said his piece smoothly. "He's a United States citizen in trouble in London, that's all."

"I'm not that naive," chided the blonde impatiently. "I'm fully acquainted with Mr Zarubin's background – I don't have to tell you he's a man with a chequered past. Our authorities have a file on him, and he's not exactly an American tourist on a package holiday, is he?"

She stopped abruptly, as if she felt she had said too much.

"Authorities?" repeated Sullivan. Then he nodded. "You mean . . . not the police. Of course. I understand."

"Really?"

"The Yard arrested Zarubin because somebody wanted him, well, out of circulation. Maybe he was getting on someone's nerves. A tactful hint, and you did the rest."

She looked at her watch again, then stood up.

"I'm afraid I really must go," she smiled. "Thanks for the lunch."

He paid and walked downstairs with her.

In Victoria Street he said:

"Thanks for the information. I appreciate it."

She glanced at him sharply.

"But I haven't given you any . . ."

"You'd be surprised," murmured Sullivan. That had been one of his most successful ploys as an agent in the field, telling people after an interview how helpful they'd been. It kept them awake for nights, wondering what they'd let slip.

Sullivan held out his hand. "I hope we'll meet again, Helen."

"Well I . . ." she began doubtfully, but he cut in:

"Next time we'll discuss vice. It could be fun, comparing notes."

She frowned, then shook his hand.

"So long, Greg," she said and walked off rapidly.

For a moment Sullivan stood watching her. He had to

admit that she had a great figure.

Then, as he strolled off in the opposite direction, he wondered how detailed her report of their lunch would be. And to whom she would make it.

Perhaps it was simply nostalgia that occasionally drew Sir Leslie to the Wallace Collection. For the old traitor, Hertford House was not only the home of some fine examples of eighteenth century art, it was also where, in the old days, he had met his contact. It was ideal. There were never many people around, and the galleries were frequently empty.

When he did return to this storehouse of secrets he could never resist pausing in Gallery II where François Lemoyne's painting of Time Revealing Truth still hung.

The Lemoyne canvas had been the assignation point. Here, they would exchange a nod, and then stroll on separately, until they met up sometimes under the Duchess of Parma's gilt chandelier, or in an empty conservatory on the first floor, anywhere in the museum where they could be alone and unobserved.

Lemoyne's picture had always fascinated Sir Leslie. He had never been able to understand why, after he had finished the painting, Lemoyne had killed himself. There was a time when suicide had not been far from his own thoughts. But why had the Frenchman taken his own life? Dissatisfaction with his work? Frustration? The realisation that he could never excel this masterpiece, that he had reached his ultimate?

Central, of course, couldn't have cared less about any of that. The picture was picked as a rendez-vous simply because it hung in an isolated, virtually deserted gallery.

"Sir Leslie Deveaux?" a voice suddenly enquired.

Was history repeating itself, the old man wondered, as he slowly turned.

Nick Prosser had taken trouble with his appearance. Instead of his usual open necked shirt, he had a tie on. The casual levis had been replaced by a grey suit. His shoes were polished.

"Yes?" It was unwelcoming, cold.

"Sorry to waylay you like this, sir."

The "sir" was carefully used. It was meant to indicate I am not hostile, I respect you, I do not regard you as disgraced.

But it didn't impress. "What is it you want?"

"My name's Prosser. Nick Prosser."

If that meant anything to him, the old man didn't indicate it. But then, he'd had a lifetime's experience deceiving.

"I'm . . . well, I'm a journalist," went on Prosser, unabashed. Never give them time to think. If he could keep on talking . . .

"I don't talk to reporters, and I don't give interviews."

"All I need is a little background . . ."

"Talk to my solicitor." Sir Leslie turned to go, then paused. "How did you know I was here?"

Prosser looked boyishly shamefaced.

"Actually, I followed you. From your flat. I do apologise, but your phone is ex-directory."

"Well, as I've just told you, I don't talk to the Press. Don't waste your time."

He began to walk to the exit.

"Sir Leslie . . ."

The old man didn't even look back.

"It's about Alex."

Deveaux stopped. It was a long time since he'd heard the code name.

"Alex?" he repeated. He faced Prosser. "Who is Alex?"

"Oh come on, Sir Leslie . . ."

"Alex is dead," declared the old man in a flat voice.

"You sure?"

Sir Leslie snorted.

"I mean, can one be sure of anything? Even that Colonel Penkovsky is dead?"

The old man stood very still.

"What are you after?" he asked at last.

Prosser took his arm. "I have my car outside. Perhaps we could have a drink."

Deveaux shook his arm free.

"I don't want to talk about anything."

"Not even Room 202?"

There was a moment's silence.

136

"All right," agreed the old man. "Let's have that drink."

He was thinking how apt the title of Lemoyne's painting happened to be.

Prosser took him to a dimly lit wine bar behind Baker Street.

"I really appreciate this, Sir Leslie," he said earnestly, when they'd been served with their drinks. He raised his glass of hock, but the old man waited impassively.

Prosser placed a little tape recorder on the table between them.

"Put that away," growled Deveaux.

Prosser tried to make a joke of it. "I have a lousy memory. Can't remember five words . . ."

"Put it away, or I leave."

Prosser slipped the little machine into his pocket, and brought out a small note book.

"And I don't want that either," Deveaux informed him.

"Sorry," apologised Prosser meekly. He cleared his throat. "You were involved in the Penkovsky case, of course," he began.

"That's all very old history, Mr Prosser. Hardly worth digging up."

"I'm not so sure about that," argued Prosser, a little arrogantly.

The old man remained unruffled.

"Every time Colonel Penkovsky came to London, he was debriefed by an Anglo-American intelligence group. You were part of that special team, weren't you? You and two others."

"Well?"

"The main debriefings took place in Earl's Court, and at Kensington. Your section had their own sessions with him. In Room 202 of the hotel at Marble Arch."

"This is an excellent sherry," remarked Sir Leslie. "May I have another glass?"

They had to wait for the barman with the bow tie to appear. He refilled the schooner from a wooden keg.

"I must get a bottle of this," said the old man. Then, after the waiter had gone, he looked across at Prosser.

"What exactly are you getting at, Mr Prosser?"

"Penkovsky was betrayed. Somebody at this end tipped off Moscow."

"Really?"

"Perhaps it was one of your disciples."

Deveaux chuckled. "What a vivid imagination you have. I hope you realise your talent for fiction."

But Prosser went straight on. "Tell me about the Penkovsky team. It was an Anglo-American effort, wasn't it?"

"You seem to know."

"I think I do. There was a man called Lambert. Stuart Lambert. The CIA man was called John Dichter. And you, of course, were in charge."

"And between us, we turned in Oleg Penkovsky?" The old man seemed amused.

"Well, you've since admitted to being a Soviet contact."

Deveaux's expression hardened. "I was never charged."

"That's another story. No, I'm interested in Lambert. Tell me about him."

"It's a pity to leave such nice sherry," Deveaux said, glancing regretfully at the half full glass. Then he stood up. "But I've got another engagement. You'll have to excuse me."

"Please . . . five minutes."

The old man turned on Prosser with cold, contemptuous anger.

"Go to hell, Mr Prosser. I've got nothing to say to you. Did you really imagine I would have? You shouldn't judge others by your own standards." Despite his controlled manner, the old traitor's mounting fury was evident. "You think it's a game, don't you? 'Spot the Spy?' Guilt by association. Maybe we all went to Cambridge at the same time. Maybe we're all queer. That would just fit, wouldn't it? Well, hard luck. I went to Oxford. That spoils it a bit, doesn't it? And I was bedding ladies when you were still in kindergarten. And the reason I have never been arrested they'll find in the archives one day, after you and I aren't around any more. Sorry."

Prosser let the storm break over him.

"Lambert," he repeated quietly. "Tell me about him."

"Why don't you ask him?" retorted Deveaux. "You've got the cheek." He was flushed. "By God, you've got the nerve of old Harry."

Prosser resorted to the old excuse of the trade.

"Only doing my job." He shrugged. "The way you're doing yours."

The old man stared at him. "Your job? Who the devil are you working for anyway?"

"Can't you guess?" He smiled. "For whoever pays best."

Deveaux turned his back, and stalked out of the wine bar.

Prosser took out a five pound note. The barman with the bow tie went over to the table. He saw the half full sherry glass.

"I thought your friend liked the sherry," he commented, handing Prosser the bill. Sherry was the wine bar's speciality.

"It's all right," Prosser reassured him. "I don't think he was feeling too well. Something must have disagreed with him."

Later, the barman found the other five pound note. The one Deveaux had slipped surreptitiously under his mat.

The old man didn't intend to be beholden to anyone.

Eight miles up in the sky over Scotland, the Bear-D flew its intrusion mission. The electronic radar system housed in the bulged dome beneath its fuselage was busy monitoring and gauging enemy counter measures.

The TU-142, which operated from a Northern Soviet base, would only be probing British air space for a short time. Then it would return once again to the East.

Its orders were specific. As soon as there was the slightest indication of possible physical contact with NATO defenders, it was to break off. Flee. There must be no risk of interception.

Lately, the Dal'nyaya Aviatsiya, USSR's long range strike command, had been emphatic in its instructions to spy missions. For the time being, planes and crews were under no circumstances to be jeopardised.

Whether or not its assignment was complete, the enemy must not be given even the remotest opportunity of getting its hands on any ferret.

For once, Wynne's mind was not on the game. He hung back at the end of the squash court, waiting for Biffin's service to arrive. His play was lacklustre, and his footwork slow. He hit the little black ball without enthusiasm, and when the match ended with him being beaten, he just shrugged.

Biffin, a radiologist at the county hospital, wasn't used to winning so easily. Their weekly squash game was usually a tough event, both men intent on using every ounce of physical energy. Neither had much opportunity for brisk exercise, so their little duel on the squash court was always taken seriously.

"You need some practice, Tom," remarked Biffin in the locker room afterwards. It was said jocularly, but Wynne rounded on his partner, annoyed.

"Look, if you'd prefer to play against someone else, that's fine by me," he snapped.

Biffin was taken aback. They had been friends since graduating from the same medical school, and had a relationship that fitted like an old shoe. It was best, he decided, to ignore the crack.

But Wynne pulled himself together.

"I'm sorry, Phil, don't take any notice. You know I didn't mean that."

He is edgy, thought Biffin.

"Of course," he reassured Wynne, but it brought home how nervous and tense the doctor had been over the past few weeks. He was behaving like a person who needs a good, long holiday. But he realised this wasn't the time to suggest such an idea. It might aggravate him again. People who are very tired don't like being reminded of it. For a radiologist, Biffin was a keen amateur psychologist.

"Phil . . ." began Wynne, not looking at him, as he zipped his racket into its bag.

"Yes."

"You know the sort of person I am, don't you?"

Biffin straightened up from tying his shoe laces.

"What do you mean?"

"We've been friends a long time, right?"

Biffin stared at him, perplexed.

Wynne faced him. "You don't think I'm . . . I'm a bit mad?"

"Crazy as a loon," replied Biffin cheerfully.

"I'm serious," said Wynne, and he wasn't smiling. "You don't think I've gone . . . well, slightly . . . potty?"

"Tom, what on earth are you getting at?" asked Biffin very quietly.

"Well, you don't think I'm the type who'd start imagining things, do you? Like seeing things . . . things that aren't there. People who don't exist."

"Who says you do?"

"You remember me telling you about that business in the wood?"

"Yes." Biffin had been only politely interested in the story. "Did you ever hear anything more?"

"No."

Biffin regarded his friend thoughtfully. Then he said very gently:

"Something's troubling you, isn't it?"

Wynne sat on the bench next to him.

"I know you won't believe it, but I think I'm being watched." He paused.

"Go on."

"That's it. People are following me. I had to go to London the other day. I noticed this man in the buffet car of the train. Three hours later I saw him again in Wimpole Street. And when I caught the train at Paddington, there he was. The same man, standing on the platform."

"Coincidence," said Biffin.

"That's what I said to myself. But there's been another man. Watching me. Sometimes in a car."

"Perhaps, if you are being followed, you should go to the police."

"What, after the run around they gave me? They never even believed what I told them about the Russian. Can you imagine their reaction if I said people are following me?"

Biffin rubbed his nose absentmindedly. "You're a doctor, Tom. Very responsible. Known locally. Come on." He shook his head. "Anyway, who do you think is following you?"

Wynne glanced at him as if to make sure Biffin was taking him seriously.

"The same people who grabbed the man. Who broke into my house and stole the watch. Mr Druce's lot. They're keeping tabs on me."

"You're sure you're not imagining this?" asked Biffin, and immediately knew he had made a mistake.

"There you are!" exclaimed Wynne. "Even you."

He stood up.

"Tom, I believe you," protested Biffin. "I'm just trying to work it out in my mind. But, honestly, I really do believe you."

"Do you?" asked Wynne sadly.

They left together, and as they walked to the car park, Biffin said:

"Have you tried everything? There must be some ministry, some . . ."

"Everything. The police. They don't know. My MP. He's drawn a blank. The Home Office. They don't know anything. They've never heard of Druce. The Ministry of Defence. Zero. The local paper. Not a sausage."

They stopped by Wynne's Triumph. "That's impossible," said Biffin.

"Is it?"

Wynne drove off in his car, but Biffin sat a moment behind the wheel of his MG. He actually found himself waiting to see if there was anybody following the doctor.

But he saw nobody.

Salim departed without ceremony.

"On your feet" ordered the warder, "you're on your way, mate. Get your things together."

"Ah," sighed Salim, like a man whose patience has at last been rewarded. He rolled down the sleeves of his silk shirt, and buttoned the cuffs.

"Hurry up," ordered the warder. "They want you at the airport in two hours."

And he jangled a pair of handcuffs.

Salim turned to Zarubin.

"Typical, my friend. At last I go home, and they want to

chain me. As if I wished to stay in this stinking hole of a country."

"Get a move on."

Salim slipped into his blazer, with its embossed brass buttons.

"I've enjoyed your company," he said to Zarubin, ignoring the warder. "And I am sorry that I could not offer you better hospitality. Perhaps if you come to the Jamahiriya . . ."

"The what?"

"Really, for an American . . ." He smiled. "The land of the revolution. Libya. It would open your eyes. El Fateh will make you welcome. A man of your . . . potential."

The warder stepped forward.

"Hold out your hands," he instructed.

Salim looked at him contemptuously. Then he addressed Zarubin again:

"Please feel free to call on my friends. They will be happy to provide any . . . comforts they can, while you're stuck here. I will tell them. Anything you need."

The warder reached forward and grabbed Salim's right wrist. The handcuff clicked shut on it. The other half of the bracelet the warder attached to his own left wrist.

"Come on," he commanded, jerking Salim's arm impatiently.

"You see, they have no manners," observed Salim, as if the warder was invisible.

"Is that where you'll be?" asked Zarubin. "Libya?"

"One day. Eventually. Who knows where they'll dump me. But it doesn't matter. What is ordained, will happen . . ." He shrugged. "Just as this was. Us meeting."

Salim flashed Zarubin one of his smiles as the warder tugged at his arm.

"Thank you for being so very entertaining."

His dark eyes glittered, but Zarubin couldn't tell if it was mockery.

"Give my undying love to the CIA."

Then the door slammed, and for the first time Zarubin found himself the sole occupant of the cell. On Salim's bunk lay one of his ubiquitous Arab newspapers, like a memento of his presence.

Zarubin lay down on his bunk, and stretched out his legs. But he didn't close his eyes. He didn't want to go to sleep. He was waiting.

The summons to meet the gum shoes was delivered by Miss Walsh when she brought Flexner his coffee.

"Right away? Are you sure?"

"Positive," confirmed Miss Walsh. "If it's convenient."

They'd been in town a couple of days already, but the two visitors from the Office of Security hadn't been seen round the embassy.

In Flexner's opinion that was all wrong. There was a certain protocol in these matters. One of the first calls should have been on him. The firm's visiting firemen always checked in with the station chief.

"Across the road, did you say?" he asked, perturbed.

"The Navy building. Room 42C."

That was another thing he didn't like. The embassy normally provided logistic support. Why go to the Navy?

But the most disturbing thing was that they'd asked to see him. Damn it, he was senior to two snooping bloodhounds. They should come to him.

He half considered telling Miss Walsh to inform them it would have to be another time, today he was busy. Then he reconsidered. They were Office of Security. The last people he wanted to aggravate.

"All right, I won't be long," he said, hoping that his immediate compliance to the summons wouldn't lose him status in Miss Walsh's eyes. He had the distinct impression as he left his office that she was giving him a curious look.

Only as he headed for the main doors did he remember that he hadn't touched his coffee.

Flexner crossed the square and entered the Navy building in North Audley Street. The marine at the desk scrutinised his ID card, and directed him to the elevators.

There were two lifts in the lobby. One stood empty. The other had a queue of people waiting for it to come down to ground level. Flexner went to the empty lift, but another marine stepped in his way.

"Sorry, sir. That's the admiral's elevator."

"But . . ." Then he shut up, and meekly joined the crowd waiting for the other one.

On the fourth floor, he walked down a corridor, looking for 42C. He found it, in the passage that was restricted to people with special security clearance. The sanctum of the Office of Naval Intelligence.

Christ knows why they're hanging out with ONI, he thought, yet again.

A clean cut, scrubbed chief petty officer asked who he wanted, and then took him into the presence.

There were two of them, a thick set swarthy man with broad shoulders, and a Nixon chin. In the middle of the morning, he already looked as if he needed a shave. The other man was thin, tall, with close cropped hair. They stood up when Flexner entered.

"Good morning, sir," said the thick set man. "I'm Bowyer, Office of Security." He indicated the close cropped one. "This is Mr Houghton."

Then, like a well rehearsed double act, they both produced little wallets and flashed their IDs at him.

I'm going to take control of this, decided Flexner. Right from the start.

"You gentlemen should have come to my office. It's much more comfortable," he said, casting a reproving eye round the sparsely furnished, bare room.

"If you don't mind, this is very convenient," said Bowyer. "Please sit down."

Flexner's neck prickled. Something was going on.

They sat opposite him, side by side, and Houghton said:

"Please smoke, if you want to."

He's got a nerve, thought Flexner. A lousy house dick telling me I can smoke.

"Have you come to London for anything particular?" he asked coldly. "I had expected you people to check in. That's the usual form."

"Mr Flexner," began Bowyer. "This is not formal. There will be no record of our conversation."

The hell there won't be. Flexner wondered where the microphone was. But he also knew he was in trouble.

Deep trouble.

"Does the name Elaine Grant mean anything to you?" he continued.

Flexner was baffled. "Who?"

"Elaine Grant."

"Never heard of her," replied Flexner truthfully.

"How about Michelle Fountain?"

This was crazy. "What is this about? Why these questions? Who are these women?"

"Please, Mr Flexner," broke in Houghton soothingly. "I'm sure you appreciate that we're only doing our job. Neither we nor the department is interested in any private matters except in so far as they relate to sensitive areas involving security."

It could have come straight from the phrasing of the company's manual of investigatory procedures.

Bowyer went on:

"How about the name Debbie?"

"Debbie?" repeated Flexner. His throat was dry.

"Yes, Mr Flexner. Our information is it's all one and the same woman. She used all these names."

There was silence in the room. Flexner was trying to think. He could hear, faintly, the chatter of a teleprinter somewhere, and he wished he could shut it out. It and everything else.

"Would you like a glass of water?" offered Bowyer, solicitously.

Flexner shook his head. "I'm not prepared to continue with this unless I'm told what it's about." He was pleased he was so much in control of himself. It sounded just right.

Bowyer nodded.

"That's absolutely fair, Mr Flexner. So I'll put it right on the button. Please bear with me. Normally, extra mural relationships don't concern us. We're all men of the world, aren't we?"

Again, like a double act, both of them gave thin smiles.

"Now, as I advised you, this is absolutely informal. You can speak to us off the cuff. This woman Grant. Well, let's call her Debbie. You've been seeing her, haven't you?"

Flexner sat very upright in his chair.

"Well, Mr Flexner?"

"No."

"Really?" said Bowyer.

"Are you sure you wouldn't like to reconsider that?" suggested Houghton.

"I have said no. And if this continues, I shall demand counsel and a departmental hearing."

"Your rights will be fully protected, sir."

"The lady in question was murdered in her apartment," said Bowyer. "You know that of course."

"How could I?" Flexner's palms felt clammy.

"It was in the papers," replied Bowyer.

"Why should I have noticed it? She didn't mean anything to me."

"Mr Flexner."

"Well?"

"This woman had links with British intelligence."

Flexner clenched his fist. "Damn it, I keep telling you, what the hell has it got to do with me?"

Bowyer held up his hand. "That's fine. Just let me get it straight. You say you didn't know this Debbie or whatever she called herself?"

"Correct."

"So it follows you weren't having a relationship with her?"

"Right."

"And obviously you didn't see her on the night she was killed. You didn't visit her in her apartment?"

Flexner kept himself in check with supreme effort. Don't lose your cool, he kept warning himself. Be cold, hostile, outraged, but don't blow it.

"How could I?"

"So it would be wrong to infer that you were . . . er . . . involved in her death?"

"Gentleman," said Flexner, and he was icy. "I've just about had enough. I'm not answering anything else. But I have one question."

"Certainly."

"Who dragged my name into this?"

The swarthy man looked at his colleague and then he said:

"We got a tip." He hesitated. "You appreciate there's

147

been a murder. It's being investigated. It's got security angles."

"But who linked me with it?"

Bowyer paused again. Then he said, "We're following up certain leads British security have supplied."

He beamed at Flexner, and after that there was no point in saying anything.

In the lift down, he still couldn't completely accept that his world had collapsed. His career was finished. His file would get the fatal entry. That he already knew, but it wasn't until he stepped into the street that the fact it was all over became a reality.

Slowly, like a man who had aged, he went round the back of the embassy to the rear door. Just as he entered the building a car pulled away. There were two men in it. Crawford was driving, and beside him sat Lambert.

They didn't see him, and Flexner went up to his office. Miss Walsh had left for an early lunch, and he was glad she wasn't there.

"All right, jump to it," shouted the red faced warder, jangling his keys. "You're wanted."

"What for?" Zarubin asked.

"Shut up," replied the warder. The sight of Zarubin seemed to annoy him.

He left the cell door open. You're getting careless, noted Zarubin. If I hit you now, I could get down the corridor, and . . .

But that was not the way he wanted to play it.

Somebody had been sick on the floor of D Wing, and a trusty was cleaning up the vomit. He didn't even look up as Zarubin was marched past.

One thing Zarubin did appreciate. There was no likelihood of a rifle butt being rammed into his back. In Hoa Lo, if the guard thought you weren't walking briskly enough, that was routine.

His destination was the Assistant Governor's office, and they went through the same ritual. His name was barked out, surname first, and his status.

"Just stand easy," instructed the Assistant Governor. He

was looking for a piece of paper. He found it under a stack of documents.

"Ah, yes." He glanced up. "Well, you can leave here, Zarubin."

Now he knew why the warder was sulking. Beefy Face had taken a dislike to him, and hated being deprived of a victim to bully.

"How come?" asked Zarubin. He had reckoned it would happen reasonably quickly, the question was how.

"Somebody's put up your bail."

"Who?"

"Stop asking questions," ordered the warder.

"Don't you know your friends?" enquired the Assistant Governor.

"I've got so many I can't keep up with them."

"Sir," snapped the warder.

"Never mind. I'm sure you'll be glad to get out of here."

"Who's stood bail?" repeated Zarubin. "I'd like to know."

But the Assistant Governor was busy writing on the paper, and the warder shouted:

"Come along. Move it."

In the reception office, Zarubin was handed a large manilla envelope which contained his belongings. Wallet. Credit cards. Keys.

"Better count the money," urged Beefy Face heavily. "Don't want any complaints afterwards."

"Fellow, I know you're as honest as everybody in here," muttered Zarubin.

It took the warder a moment. Then his small eyes narrowed. "Don't come back here," he warned. "Just don't come back, 'cos I'd like to have you again."

Zarubin stepped out of the prison gate, and took a deep, grateful breath. The air of Brixton Hill wasn't the purest, but after D Wing it was like nectar. For a moment he stood enjoying his freedom, but it didn't last long.

One of Zarubin's strongest instincts was his sense of impending danger. Intuition had warned him of hazard in all manner of unlikely places and, so far, it had protected him from the ultimate sanction. It had also saved him when he'd executed Yudkin. But for his instinct he would have turned the corner, where the others were waiting.

And here it was again. On Brixton Hill. The inner voice cautioning watch yourself, don't relax, whatever you do, don't relax.

Any moment he'd know. Somebody would come towards him. Hold out a hand. Somebody would . . .

But he was wrong. Nobody came towards him, as he crossed the main road. Nobody approached, and held out a hand. The only thing that didn't fit was the Rolls-Royce. A gleaming, midnight blue, custom built Rolls, parked incongruously a little way from Brixton Prison.

He heard the horn sound, then the door opened, and a man got out.

"Hey! Andy!" called Theo the Greek, beckoning to him. "Come on, jump in, jump in. You don't want to hang around this joint, it's bad for your health."

He got into the car, and sank into the luxurious dove grey leather upholstery.

"You look fine," Theo said, slapping his knee. "Not even beaten up. What are you waiting for, Ziggy?" he asked the uniformed chauffeur. "Let's get out of here." He wrinkled his nose. "Terrible place, this Brixton. Nothing but spades and prisons."

The Rolls was so silent it didn't even purr, but just glided along the drab, suburban street. It was one of the smoothest rides Zarubin had ever experienced.

"Well, my friend, you didn't expect to see old Theo, did you?"

Zarubin glanced out of the rear window.

Theo frowned. "What are you looking for?" Then his face cleared. "To see if we are followed?" He laughed. "My friend, nobody follows Theo. Why should they? I am as straight as the City of London." That amused him even more.

"Guess I owe you," said Zarubin.

"What for?"

"Standing bail for me."

Theo looked shocked.

"You are surprised? Oh, that hurts me. That's terrible. That you should ever have doubted it. I look after my friends.

What else did you think? I have to take care of my pals."

He came closer.

"Also, let us be frank, it is in my interest. We are associates and I don't like to see an associate in jail. It's bad for business. As a matter of fact, I am very surprised they nicked you."

"So am I," agreed Zarubin.

Theo wagged a finger impatiently. "No, you don't understand. I have good arrangements. The law and I respect each other. I am left alone. So why did they pinch you? Huh? Tell me, who was the cop who arrested you? I'd like to know the name of the bastard."

Zarubin leaned back in the comfort of the car. It felt good after the cell. "No bastard, Theo. A very good looking blonde. A woman detective inspector. Helen Turner. Prettiest vice cop I know."

Theo sat thinking as he took out a cigar and bit the end off it. He lit it, still pondering. Finally he said:

"It's very strange. I know all the vice squad. The dirty porn squad. I know the names. Many I know personally." He grinned knowingly. "Many are good friends. But I have never heard of a woman vice inspector. Never Helen Turner."

"Well, that's who she is," said Zarubin, but he was way ahead of the man beside him. He'd had plenty of time to think it out in D Wing.

Theo exhaled a cloud of smoke.

"I think she could be something else," he mused.

"Like what?"

"I think maybe she could be Special Branch." And the shrewd, ruthless eyes stared straight into his. "Don't you think that's a possibility?"

Zarubin stayed cool. "Why?"

"Ah," said Theo. "Why indeed?"

And he laughed again.

"Where are we going?" Zarubin asked.

"To a party," smiled Theo. "A really nice party."

"That sounds great," said Zarubin. He was pleased. It was all going nicely. Very nicely indeed.

An hour later the Rolls cruised up the private driveway of

151

an estate hidden behind a forest of fir trees and which, as far as Zarubin could make out, was somewhere near Datchet. The car pulled up in front of two enormous stone lions, who sat inanimately guarding a magnificent house.

It was a majestic place, a mansion fit for a duke set in its own extensive, rolling grounds. Obviously porn pays, thought Zarubin ruefully.

The party was already in full swing as Theo led the way in.

"Enjoy yourself," he said, waving an expansive hand. "I'm sure you'll find lots of interesting people." And he drifted off.

It was a curious party, twenty or thirty people, smart, attractive, mostly young, chattering, laughing, with Theo strolling among them, beaming benevolently. A white coated barman doled out the drinks, and beyond him french windows opened on to a vast lawn, across which a string of multicoloured fairy lights had been hung.

Zarubin went over to the bar, got himself a large scotch and stood studying the guests. As far as he could see, there didn't appear to be a hostess. At least not one that he could identify. If there was a Mrs Theo she didn't show herself. There was no shortage of women, though. They outnumbered the men, and they were bright eyed, heavily made-up, scantily clad. They wore fixed smiles, and stood clustered about the men, laughing loudly, looking artificial. They seemed strangely alike, like dolls from the same assembly line.

Nubile, sexy, their eye shadow too heavy, their lipstick too bright, their giggles too shrill. They were as unreal as the plastic girls on the pages of the porn magazines Theo's shops sold, and the erotic performers of simulated sex acts in his blue films.

And that, sensed Zarubin, was who they were. Theo's girls. The stable from which he drew the performers for his industry.

"Can I get you another drink?" asked a girl in silk pyjamas.

Zarubin held up his glass. It was still half full. "No thanks, I'm fine."

She smiled enticingly. "Is there anything else I can do for you?"

"Not right now, honey."

He was trying hard to keep himself together. It wasn't easy. He felt disorientated, tired, and slightly dizzy. The music was too loud; it thumped incessantly, amplified by strategically placed loud speakers. Strobes flashed, on off, on off, coloured spotlights, reflected in the mirrors.

"You're nice," said the girl. "Are you a friend of Theo's?"

"Isn't everybody here?"

"Depends." She shrugged. "If you get bored, I'll be around."

She wandered off, her slinky figure sashaying away suggestively.

"You fancy any of them?" asked Theo. He appeared at Zarubin's elbow, surveying the crowd with the pride of ownership. "You tell me, and I fix it. What about Lois, over there?"

She was a tall redhead, with her arm around a stocky man in denims. She was whispering in his ear, all the time her mascara'd eyes roaming round the room.

"Who's she?" asked Zarubin.

"One of my models," said Theo. "Star material. She's got a great future. Want to meet her?"

"I'd like to look around some more."

"Sure, sure. Help yourself. It's free for all."

The girl in the silk pyjamas came over.

"Introduce us, Theo." She pouted at Zarubin. "He's very standoffish. What does he do?"

"Don't you know? He's a spy," said Theo and roared with laughter.

She was disappointed.

"Oh, how boring." She was a little drunk. "You don't look like a spy."

"What does a spy look like?" asked Zarubin. The lights had been turned down, and in the hazy darkness of the room he started to smell a familiar aroma. People were smoking pot.

"Don't you know?" she giggled. "You can't be a very good spy. You haven't got a false beard."

"Sorry," said Zarubin. "I'll try to remember."

She laid a hand on his arm. "Come upstairs."

Theo nodded approvingly.

"Go ahead. It's all yours."

He seemed very eager to pair him off.

"The night's young," said Zarubin. "I need another drink."

The pyjama girl tossed her head. "I told you he's boring."

Zarubin went over to the bar.

"Scotch," he ordered, "and lots of soda."

The noise, the atmosphere were oppressive, they were beginning to make his head ache.

"Well, well, well, fancy meeting you here," said a voice behind him.

He turned.

"Remember me? Tony Gibson-Greer?" asked the young man with a gold earring.

"Sure," said Zarubin.

"Didn't expect to find you here."

"Didn't you?"

Gibson-Greer shook his head, then said: "Still, Theo has such unexpected friends. Good party, isn't it?"

"Interesting." Zarubin took a sip of scotch. "How's the art business?"

Gibson-Greer shrugged. "I survive." He looked over at the crowd. "The girls are gorgeous, aren't they. But the men . . ." He pulled a face.

"How long have you known Theo?"

"Long enough." He stood closer. "Would you like a snort?"

Zarubin played it dumb. "What?"

"Coke. You use it?"

"Not my scene."

"Ah, of course, I forgot." Gibson-Greer looked knowing. "You smoke, of course. No sooner said than done . . ."

He produced a small gold cigarette case. Inside, five ready-made joints lay neatly in a row.

"On the left, top grade black. Very good stuff. The other two are Moroccan."

"Good selection," murmured Zarubin.

"That's praise indeed, coming from you," said Gibson-Greer.

154

He was delivering the message, Zarubin was sure of that. Weinraub. Sausalito. Hash.

Gibson-Greer put one of the reefers in his mouth and lit it. He passed it over to Zarubin.

"Be my guest."

Perhaps this is the admission price, Zarubin thought as he dragged on the joint. The acrid smoke hit the back of his throat, it tasted different, something he hadn't come across before.

"Nice smoke," he remarked.

"There's more where that came from. Any time you want it."

Zarubin passed it back to him, but Gibson-Greer shook his head.

"Listen," he said, "we ought to get together. We got a lot in common." He laughed. "No, chum, I don't mean that. Sex isn't everything in life. No, I mean mutual interests. Common tastes, you might say."

"Really?"

"Sure. Hands across the sea and all that rubbish."

Zarubin screwed up his eyes. They felt heavy, and it took a great effort to open them again. When he did Gibson-Greer loomed slightly out of focus. He was leaning forward.

"Even common friends . . ."

"Who?" But the word came out awkwardly. His tongue was thick. He took another drag of the joint.

From behind a woman's arms embraced Zarubin, and he caught a whiff of an overpowering perfume. She pressed herself close to him. Gibson-Greer receded but she held on to him.

"Darling," whispered the tall redhead, turning Zarubin round to face her, "give me a kiss."

She pressed her lips hard on his, all the while holding his body close to hers.

"I'm your door prize," Lois told him, stroking the inside of his thigh, "you lucky man."

He stared at her stupidly. The joint was burning his fingers.

"Are you good at fucking?" she asked, with a provocative smile. "Of course you are. And I'm the best screw in town. Let's go."

She took his hand, and began to half drag, half steer him through the crowd. He had an impression of people staring at him. Gibson-Greer, a mocking smile on his thin lips. The girl in the silk pyjamas. The stocky man in denims. And Theo. Theo, smiling broadly.

"Now, don't be coy," chided Lois, playfully.

He held on to her hand. The room was starting to spin, and the noise seemed to be growing louder and louder.

He stumbled, and for a moment, the world turned upside down, the ceiling was below him, the floor on top. Then all was darkness.

It was Philby himself who answered the door of the apartment to Yenko. He was wearing a quilted dressing gown, and old, scuffed leather slippers.

"Come in, come in," he invited, standing aside to let him enter. "Warm yourself."

He was aged yet again, thought Yenko. The worn face was even more lined, odd strands of grey hair hung untidily. But he wasn't drunk. That was good.

"Thank you, General," said Yenko, taking off his fur hat and the thick gloves. Anyone looking less like a general than Philby would be hard to find, he reflected, hanging up his coat on the stand in the hall. But major general he was, and Yenko believed in giving a man his dignity.

Philby led the way into the study, lined with bookshelves, and dominated by a huge old desk, piled high with manuscripts, and volumes. Newspapers were everywhere, on the floor, stacked on a chair, old copies of the London *Times*, the *Guardian*, the *Washington Post*, the *Spectator*, the *New Statesman*.

"Sit down, if you can find room," said Philby, hastily removing a Sotheby's catalogue from one of the armchairs. "The mess gets worse every day. I'm sorry. I must clear up some of this junk."

"Don't worry about it, General," murmured Yenko. By unspoken agreement, they both used English, although Philby could now converse in Russian quite fluently. He sat in the armchair. The springs had gone, and he sank lower than he expected.

"Excuse the get up," apologised Philby. "Felt a bit under the weather." Then he gave a little twisted smile. "Just too bloody lazy, really."

They're so alike this breed, decided Yenko. Philby, Blunt, Deveaux, and the others of their kind. Self deprecating, self mocking, the phoney Noel Coward style. Yes, the dressing gown at three in the afternoon fits.

"You must be tired after the trip," he remarked.

"Well, it *is* a god forsaken hole, isn't it?" Philby snapped his fingers. "God, I'm a rotten host. Do forgive me." If he apologises once more, I'll spew, thought Yenko. But Philby carried on: "Would you like a spot of something to warm you up?"

"Perhaps a little tea?"

"You sure you wouldn't prefer something a little stronger?" offered Philby.

I'm not going to give you the excuse, General, thought Yenko. You only want to justify a blinder in the middle of the afternoon. Aloud he said:

"I don't think so. But if you want to go ahead . . ."

"No," said Philby curtly. "Not if you are happy. I'll get the girl to make some." He shuffled over to the old fashioned bell rope and tugged it. "Talking of trips, how was London?" he asked shifting some magazines aside, and sitting opposite Yenko.

"Harrods is almost the same, not quite, but almost. You'd like it, though. Lots of Arabs."

There was a knock on the door and the maid entered. She and the two bedroomed flat, with study, dining room, kitchen, and separate bathroom were visible proof of the privileges enjoyed by the rank of major general in special intelligence.

"Ah, yes, Harrods," Philby mused, after he'd ordered the tea. "I think it went down hill when they got rid of the armchairs in the banking hall. I sometimes met my contact there." He smiled. "Very infra dig, spying at Harrods."

He took a cigarette holder from his dressing gown pocket, and stuck an English cigarette in it. He used a Dunhill to light it.

"You know what I really miss? Sounds ridiculous, but it's

the Strand. For some crazy reason, I'd give a lot just to walk down the Strand."

Yenko regarded him quizzically. "Really?"

"Yes, stupid isn't it?"

The maid brought in the tea. She was a pudding faced country girl, and her appointment to the Philby ménage had been directly approved by General Maximovich. She looked far too dumb to be what she was, his personal eyes and ears.

Philby dismissed her with a wave, and spooned sugar into the glasses of lemon tea.

"Anyway, my friend, you haven't come to discuss my whims. Let's get down to business. What an awful dump that place is," he said, stirring his tea. "And to have to travel three days to get to it." He shuddered. "You'll forgive me, but your bloody country is just too big."

"I'm sorry," said Yenko. "But we do appreciate the efforts you put in. How were they?"

"Frankly, what do you expect?" asked Philby, pulling a handkerchief from his dressing gown sleeve and blowing his nose. "Poor bastards, stuck in the wilds, cooped up in a secret community, dead as far as the world knows, how do you think they'd be?"

Yenko set down his glass.

"I must remind you that they violated our territory. They came to spy, they invaded our skies, they ferreted into our air space, they are spy pilots, and they are lucky to be alive."

"Lucky?" Philby shook his head.

"General, don't forget the same is being done to our crews," pointed out Yenko. "If they come down, they too disappear. Nothing is said, nothing is admitted. They too end up in a secret place, hidden away, thousands of miles from anywhere. It is, shall we say, a mutual understanding."

Philby blew out some cigarette smoke, and tapped his holder on a crystal ash tray. Yenko's eyes never left him.

"Well, anyway, I did my usual chore." Philby pursed his lips. "I visited the place, and chatted with a few. You know, the friendly touch. Suggested that maybe they could make life easier for themselves. Like making themselves useful to us . . ."

"And?"

Philby shrugged. "It takes time, my friend. Maybe I sowed a few seeds, maybe I didn't. Not everybody is quisling material."

"We have plenty of time, General. And they're not going anywhere. I'm sure your work will bear fruit eventually."

"It's not a job I particularly like, suborning people."

"But you're very good at it," smiled Yenko. "I look forward to reading your report. So, I'm sure, does Chairman Andropov."

His smile, outwardly so sympathetic, hid Yenko's contempt. He was bored with Philby's regular whining after his periodic missions to the establishment near Oimyakton, where they incarcerated the Western ferret airmen. There, hidden away in the vastness, the captured aeronauts were beyond rescue, and beyond escape. Lost men who had permanently disappeared in a void.

Of course, it was a gruelling trip to this desolate hole in north east Siberia. The Yakut republic was a territory four times the size of Texas, and boasted the most uncomfortable continental climate in the world. In winter, it was the coldest inhabited place in the Soviet Union. In summer, the temperature soared to 104 degrees Fahrenheit plus.

But Philby, felt Yenko, had a nerve to complain. He made the journeys in VIP style, as befits an officer of general rank, and his little homilies to the captives were delivered in the comfort of the camp cinema, or in the mess hall. It was luxurious treason, and only a very small repayment of the debt he owed for the generosity with which he was treated.

However Yenko kept these thoughts to himself, and stood up.

"I'm sorry to leave now, but so much piled up during my absence." Then a thought struck him. "Have our little captive hawks ever realised what a distinguished visitor they have periodically?"

"In Soviet uniform, I look like a friendly avuncular type, my friend. Anyway, who cares? I've burnt my boats." Momentarily, he sounded bitter and Yenko made a mental note.

"The motherland appreciates it, General," he said.

After Yenko had gone, Philby went to the cabinet on which the old framed, autographed picture of Brezhnev stood. He opened the cupboard door. The scotch was running low, and the new supply via the Embassy in London wasn't due until next week. The doctor had warned him about gin, but had forgotten to mention vodka. And vodka there was plenty of, without the need of diplomatic bags.

Philby took the bottle and a glass over to one of the armchairs. He scowled at the new signed photo of Andropov.

He was going to get drunk, he decided, very drunk.

Yenko did not immediately return to his office. Instead he made his way to the Hotel Rossiya.

The tap on the door of room 282 was gentle, even tentative. Almost as tentative as Yenko himself when the door opened after a moment's interval.

"Mr Achmet?" he ventured politely, in English.

"Yes," replied Salim, cautiously.

"Forgive the intrusion. I'm Major Yenko. From the ministry."

For an instant Salim hesitated, then stood aside to let Yenko enter.

He had been unpacking and some of his clothes were still lying on the bed. Opposite, the television was switched on and showed a lot of svelte girl gymnasts somersaulting across a mat. Salim went over and switched the set off.

"Oh, please," Yenko smiled, "it doesn't worry me at all. I like looking at pretty women. Don't inconvenience yourself on my account."

"Major Yenko, did you say?" repeated Salim.

"Yes. From the ministry."

"What can I do for you, Major Yenko?"

"No, no. I am here to see what I can do for *you*. How is the room? The service? To your liking?"

"I am very comfortable."

"Good," beamed Yenko. "That's what we want you to be. We want you to enjoy your sojourn in Moscow."

The word threw Salim. "Sojourn?"

"Your . . . stay. An extended visit, perhaps?"

"It depends," replied Salim.

"Of course," nodded Yenko. "You're not short of friends here."

"Colleagues," corrected Salim.

"*And* friends. Your compatriots of course. On every level. Official and unofficial." Uninvited, Yenko went and sat on a chair by the window. "You won't be lonely, I promise you. And I want you to count me among your friends here. Look to me as the key that will open all doors."

Salim glanced at him sharply.

"We pride ourselves that this is home from home for all freedom fighters," continued Yenko. "And I guarantee that the air you breathe here is free from Zionists."

"I never doubted it," murmured Salim.

Yenko nodded approvingly.

"Do carry on with your unpacking," he said, waving a hand airily. "I travel a great deal and I'm never happy until I've put my things away."

But Salim did not move. Instead he enquired:

"Would you like some tea?"

Yenko was amused. "Ah, your faith in our room service is touching. I love my motherland dearly, but I regret to say that room service is not one of our talents. If you take my advice, you will always place your order an hour before you need it, and I don't intend to be here that long."

"That applies in other countries too, Major."

"London, for example?"

"I hope you never stay in the last establishment where I was forced to reside," said Salim. "It was called Brixton."

Yenko stood up.

"I'll leave you to settle yourself in peace. You must be tired and I'm sure your friends will be eager to make contact." He paused, then said in a very gentle voice, "Of course, you appreciate that your presence here is unofficial. The ministry is very anxious about that. We welcome you with open arms and rest assured we will assist in every way. We have even granted your Palestinian friends diplomatic recognition. But we know nothing of the plans you might be making, you understand?"

"Naturally," agreed Salim, silkily.

"Enjoy yourself."

On his way to the door, Yenko placed a visiting card on top of the television.

"That number reaches me. Day and night."

"Major . . ." said Salim.

Yenko turned.

"A question."

"Yes, my friend?"

"How does a stranger like me find company in Moscow?"

"You call that number."

"Ah."

"Or . . ."

Salim waited.

"She finds you." And he shut the door gently.

Back in his office, Yenko asked Olga to get him the Yudkin file. He filled in the chit she would need to get access to the archives, and signed it.

Olga hesitated.

"Yes?" said Yenko. "Anything wrong?"

"This will take me some time, comrade."

"Why?"

"It'll be in the expired section. It's a closed file."

"The Yudkin matter has never expired," stated Yenko firmly.

"But Captain Yudkin is dead . . ." pointed out Olga. She had a good memory.

"The case isn't," snapped Yenko.

"I'll tell them to hurry up with it," she said.

She closed the door softly. Clearly Yenko had things on his mind.

After she left, he went down two floors to see Orlov, in Planning and Analysis.

"Tell me, do you remember the Yudkin business?" he asked.

"How could I forget?" replied Orlov. He had been in the field at the time, in Warsaw.

"Whatever happened to Dobrinski?"

Dobrinski was the Polish liaison man with whom they had dealt.

"He's inside," said Orlov taking off his glasses. He did a lot of reading, and his eyesight was bad. That was why they had moved him from operations and put him behind a desk.

"What?"

"Yes. He got ten years."

Yenko was interested. "Really? What for?"

"Deviationism," said Orlov. "You know the Poles. As unreliable as hell, when was this?"

"During the Solidarity business. He was working at the ministry during the day, and helping the trouble makers at night."

"Ah." Yenko seemed pleased.

"That doesn't surprise you?" asked Orlov.

"No, my friend. It fits. It all fits. I often wondered who'd betrayed Yudkin. Now it becomes clear doesn't it? A man like Dobrinski."

"Do you think it was Dobrinski who tipped them off?"

Yenko nodded.

"Then . . ." began Orlov, and paused. "He was responsible for . . ."

"The Americans killing Yudkin. Of course."

"Who was the man they sent? I remember the row. The general wanted his blood."

"He still does," said Yenko softly.

Orlov took out a red check handkerchief and started polishing his glasses.

"Pity that we never identified him," he sighed.

"But we have," said Yenko.

Orlov was surprised. "Really? I never knew." He put the glasses back on his nose. "They don't tell us anything down here. We plan, we analyse and half the time we're kept in the dark by other sections."

"Not really," smiled Yenko. Orlov and his crowd always blamed the other directorates for their own shortcomings. It was the law of survival.

"Anyway," said Orlov, "who is he? I realise he's one of their special section people, of course. But who?"

"Zarubin," said Yenko. "He's in London right now. Playing a very dirty little game."

"Still in the same department?"

"Of course."

Orlov's chair creaked. He reached over to a little tin, and popped a peppermint in his mouth. He had bad breath, and was very conscious of it.

"Well, I'm glad you've cleared that one up," he said. "It's rankled. I felt very bad about it. Yudkin was a good man. A brave man."

"It's not cleared up," Yenko corrected him. "Not yet."

"But I thought . . ."

Yenko stood up. It was time to go. He only wanted to know if Dobrinski was still around.

"It won't be cleared up," he said, "until Mr Zarubin has been dealt with."

"The orders will have to come from high," pointed out Orlov. "They are getting very sensitive these days. Terminations are no longer as fashionable as they were. Unless the top says so . . ."

"It has. Don't worry, Mikhail, it has received the seal of official approval. Tovarich Zarubin is a dead man. He just doesn't know it yet."

Yenko was in a good mood when he left. A guard with the blue shoulder boards and collar tabs of the uniformed KGB snapped to attention as he passed him in the corridor. Yenko smiled at him which astonished the man.

It was nice to pull strings, thought Yenko. He enjoyed manipulating his little shadowy world. Above all, he would relish pulling the string that broke Zarubin's neck.

From the *Daily Telegraph*:

The body found last night on Hampstead Heath has been identified as that of an American diplomat attached to the US Embassy in London.

Police say that Mr Cyrus Flexner, forty-nine, was found behind a bush with a gunshot wound. A Colt .45 pistol, believed to have belonged to the dead man, was lying nearby.

Scotland Yard do not suspect foul play.

Mr Flexner, who was a political officer on the staff of the embassy, lived in St John's Wood with his wife.

According to an Embassy spokesman, Mr Flexner had no personal problems, but may have been worried about his health.

There will be no inquest since the dead man had diplomatic privilege.

*　　*　　*

Bright sunlight falling on his face aroused Zarubin. Despite his eyes being closed, the strong glare penetrated his eyelids and he turned his head away to avoid it.

Gradually he surfaced from his deep sleep and opened his eyes. It was day, and through the big window sunshine flooded the room.

He was lying naked in a bed so enormous that when he stretched his legs his toes didn't even reach the end.

Slowly he became aware of the soft, regular ticking of a small clock on the mantelpiece. He craned his neck, to see the time. It was just after ten-fifteen. He raised his arm to check his own watch, but his left wrist was bare. He sat up and saw that it had been put on the bedside table together with his wallet and his keys. Next to them lay a passport. An American passport.

He picked it up and opened it. Inside it had his photograph, but not his name. It was a passport for Charles Warren Grange, born 17 July 1942, in St Paul, Minnesota, with a physical description that matched Zarubin's and the occupation given as journalist. All wrong, but if it was a forgery, it was a beautiful job. The visa pages bore an immigration officer's landing stamp, an endorsement granting him leave to stay in the United Kingdom for six months, dated the previous day, and there was also a Swiss police endorsement. Apparently he had permission of residence in Geneva. They all looked authentic, like the rest of the passport.

"How d'you do, Mr Grange," said Zarubin.

He got up, his feet sinking into the luxuriously piled carpet. It was an elegant bedroom, period furniture, wooden panelling, stylish as befits an aristocratic English country mansion. Theo's mansion.

His clothes were neatly laid out. They'd been beautifully pressed and his shirt was freshly laundered. He wandered over to the dressing table, and studied himself in the mirror.

He saw a man who looked as if he'd had a rough night, and he had a foul taste in his mouth. He badly needed a shave, and there were shadows under his slightly bloodshot eyes.

He walked over to the window. The bedroom was on the first floor overlooking the vast lawn, with a nice view of the grounds, and the fir trees in the distance. The fairy lights that had been strung across the lawn for the party had been taken down.

Zarubin only had a hazy recollection of the party. Blurred faces. And the joint. It wasn't hash, that was for sure. He had known it from the first puff, and he thought the way he hadn't let on was a creditable performance. He looked forward to paying back that son of a bitch Gibson-Greer. And he wasn't the only one. There were a few scores to settle.

Then again, maybe it was all working out just right.

He shook his head, not to clear it, but to see if it hurt. It didn't make him dizzy, but he still felt weak.

A door was ajar, and beyond it the bathroom. Fresh towels hung over a heated rail, and shaving tackle had been laid out next to a face cloth and a cellophane wrapped tablet of soap. There was even a tube of toothpaste and a new toothbrush still in their cartons. Zarubin began running the bath.

Half an hour later, refreshed, shaved, dressed in clean clothes, he felt ready to face – well, he would see. He looked at himself in the mirror again. The morning-after grottiness was wearing off.

He slipped on his wrist watch, put his wallet, keys, and the passport in his pocket. His mouth was still dry, and he longed for a cup of coffee. He had a sardonic notion of ringing a bell to summon the butler, and asking Jeeves to bring him breakfast on a silver tray. Theo must have a butler, to go with this mansion and the Rolls.

But he couldn't find a bell. Christ, he wished he had that coffee. Strong, black, hot.

He looked round the room again, to make sure he hadn't missed anything. It was all very anonymous, so genteel. In the bright sunshine nothing looked sinister.

He went over to the oak panelled door. It's time to play games decided Zarubin, opening it.

He found himself looking down a long, carpeted corridor. Slowly he began walking along it, past a suit of armour, and two oil paintings of Tudor gentlemen in their finery. Not Weinraub's work he thought wryly.

The silence of the big house was becoming oppressive. No sound came from anywhere; it was almost as if he had a mansion to himself.

The corridor led on to a landing, below which was the hall. But Zarubin started to go up the stairs. On the second floor was another corridor, with more suits of armour, and two doors. He cautiously opened one of them. It was another bedroom, not unlike the one he had left. It was empty, and a damask coverlet was over the bed.

Zarubin closed the door, quite deliberately slamming it hard, so that the sound reverberated through the whole house. He stood in the corridor, very still, waiting. The noise must have been heard all over. If anybody was around . . .

But nobody appeared.

He tried the second door. It was locked. He knocked, loudly. Nothing. He bent down, squinting through the key hole, and saw a piano. An empty music room? Theo and Chopin didn't go together, but perhaps a Bechstein was required furnishing for a ducal mansion.

Zarubin went down the stairs, to the hall.

"Hey there. Anybody about?" he called.

Somewhere, a grandfather clock chimed Big Ben chords, but that was all.

"I'm down here," shouted Zarubin, but he knew it was unnecessary. Every move he made was being watched, he realised that. Just because he couldn't spot the hidden eyes, the concealed cameras, didn't mean they weren't there. Maybe it amused them to play hide and seek.

"This is getting boring, Theo," he yelled at the ceiling.

He crossed the hall to some double doors on the left, which he thought must be the dining room. But when he opened them, he was in a big, clublike room with an unlit coal fire in the massive grate, leather armchairs, and walls lined with bookshelves. There was a cabinet style television set, and an enormous globe of the world. The floor was covered by a red Persian carpet.

It was the kind of room in which retired country gentlemen dozed in front of the fire, *The Times* on their lap, and a balloon glass of armagnac at their elbow.

Zarubin went over to the bookshelves. The volumes were richly bound in leather with embossed, decorated spines, and looked like they had never been read. They were all sets.

Trollope's novels. The plays of Shakespeare. Hardy. Thackeray. Dickens.

Zarubin walked on, then stopped. He went back to the shelf. He tried to take one of the volumes off, but it didn't move. They weren't books at all. They were trappings, dummies, phoneys. He felt, with the tips of his fingers, along the spines of the books, the edges of the shelving. The whole case was a fake.

"That's enough," said a voice. "Turn around, and keep your hands where I can see them."

Ziggy, the chauffeur, was standing at the door, pointing a gun at him. A Walther PK.

"Oh, there you are," drawled Zarubin. "About time too. Bring me a cup of coffee, will you? Strong, black."

"Let's go," said Ziggy indicating with the gun that Zarubin should lead the way.

He stood aside, leaving a safe distance between himself and Zarubin, then closed the library doors.

"Straight ahead," he ordered, motioning with the gun.

They walked the length of the passageway, then Ziggy said, "In there."

Theo stood in front of a glass aquarium with a welcoming smile. The room was furnished as an office, with a big desk, some telephones, and two armchairs.

"Come in, come in," he invited. Then he saw the gun in Ziggy's hand. "Oh, put that stupid thing away," he scolded. "He gets so nervous when anybody touches the safe," he explained to Zarubin with a wink. "Also, he loves pulling out the gun. He's like a small boy with it. Doesn't get many opportunities. Go on, Ziggy, bring us some coffee."

Ziggy departed.

"Make yourself comfortable," said Theo, sitting down behind the desk, and waving an expansive hand at one of the armchairs. "You look much better this morning. I was quite worried. You went out like a light."

"Yes, strange wasn't it?"

"The kid said it must have been too strong for you."

"The kid?"

"Yes, you know. Tony."

"Sure," nodded Zarubin. "I know Tony. What I don't

know is . . . what the hell's going on." He pulled out the passport. "Like this? Who's Mr Grange?"

"Things might get too hot for you," smiled Theo. "One way or another. You never know. It's all part of the service, my friend. The cops take your passport. I give you another one. You might have to leave the country in a hurry, right? You might feel it's wise to have a little vacation, maybe. You've got to be able to get out. So, a new passport. I look after my people. Theo is a good friend. I stick with my associates." A shadow crossed his face. "You don't like the name Grange? You prefer something else. All right. It will cost me more money, but you shall have it. Give me the name. No problem."

One of the phones buzzed gently. Theo picked it up.

"Yeah?" He looked across at Zarubin. "You want biscuits with your coffee? No, he doesn't want biscuits."

He hung up again.

"Seems to me," said Zarubin, "you've gone to a lot of trouble. Like doping me."

Theo roared with laughter.

"I like it," he gasped. "Oh, I like it a lot. Here's this tough guy who passes out, so he says he was doped. Great." He chuckled jovially. "You are very funny."

"But you did," insisted Zarubin quietly. "Why?"

Ziggy came in carrying a silver tray with two cups, a Georgian coffee pot, and a silver milk jug on it.

"Hot milk," announced Ziggy proudly, placing the tray on the desk.

"It's okay, we'll do it ourselves," said Theo, dismissing him. He started pouring. "White?"

"Black," said Zarubin.

"Like your heart," smiled Theo. He put four lumps of sugar in his own cup, stirred it, and took a sip. "I've a present for you," he said, bending down behind his desk and holding up a brown leather attaché case. "Here, take it."

Zarubin stood up and took the case.

"It has a combination lock," went on Theo. "You can set it yourself, then nobody can open it. Any combination you like. 007 maybe." And again he laughed loudly.

Zarubin opened it. Inside were four glossy eight by ten

photographs. Very explicit photographs.

They showed Zarubin in the bed upstairs, naked. And so were the girls. One was the girl in the silk pyjamas, except she had no pyjamas on. The way she and Zarubin were intertwined left no need for a caption. The second was of Lois, with Zarubin on top of her. The last two were both the girls in bed with him, sharing him between them. The way the pictures were posed, the girls were doing all the work. Zarubin just lay there.

"So what," he said, tossing the photos back into the case.

"You look like you're enjoying yourself," purred Theo.

"I was out cold."

"The camera does not lie, isn't that right?"

"Okay," shrugged Zarubin. "So I screwed them and they fucked me. Who the hell cares."

"Absolutely," agreed Theo. He helped himself to one of his cigars from a wooden box on the desk. He bit it hard, and lit it. "It's a good set, isn't it? Sharp focus. Well exposed. A professional job. You make a good model, Andy. A great triple act, you and the girls. These will please my customers."

"What customers?"

"Collectors. Very special connoisseurs. They specialise in interesting people getting involved in interesting situations."

Zarubin drank a little coffee. "What garbage is all this, Theo?"

"They pay well for pictures of this kind."

"Who?" repeated Zarubin.

"My underwriters." He laughed. "In my business one needs insurance." He paused.

"Life insurance?" asked Zarubin softly.

Theo ignored him. "Let me put it this way. There are rumours. I don't believe them of course. But there are those who rate my friend Zarubin, my supplier of such good merchandise, a bad risk. I guess it's nonsense, but I am a sucker for insurance policies."

"You can't insure against some risks, Theo."

"You're so right," agreed the fat man. "It is all unnecessary. But I insure everything. Even my goldfish. The only goldfish covered for sudden death."

170

There wasn't even a flicker of a smile on Zarubin's face.

"Ah, yes. I suppose you're right. I talk nonsense. So, let's forget about it. Tear up those stupid pictures." He raised his cup of coffee like a toast. "I have the negatives, so everything is fine. Like the passport. I know the name it's in. You cross me, and I tip off Interpol about Mr Grange and the phoney passport he's using. Nobody need ever know, but I'm insured, just in case. Comprehensive cover. All risks, eh?"

Zarubin shrugged, and shut the lid of the case. "Nice leather."

"The best," said Theo. "Italian made. Cost me £150. Nothing is too good for my friends."

Then he offered Zarubin the use of his Rolls-Royce back to town.

"Ziggy will drive you wherever you want to go."

"Have gun, will travel?"

"Very funny. I have told him, so he won't try that again. He'll drive you wherever you say."

"Thanks," said Zarubin. "It's going to do my credit rating the world of good when the doorman sees me arrive in a Rolls."

Theo went down to the car with him to see him off.

"I hope you enjoyed yourself," he said.

"Give my regards to the door prize."

"Ah yes," smiled Theo, "I think she likes you. Maybe next time . . ."

Ziggy stood, holding open the passenger door of the Rolls-Royce.

Zarubin put down the attaché case. "Excuse me," he said, then he hit Ziggy with a left hook to the jaw. Ziggy slid gently to the ground.

"I don't like guys who pull a gun on me," said Zarubin.

Theo stood open mouthed.

"You'd better call me a cab, Theo. I don't think your boy feels up to the trip."

He smiled benignly at Theo, but the Greek caught the look in his eye, and despite the sun, he felt a little chilly.

Two hours later, Zarubin sat in his flat, admiring the attaché case in front of him and sighed. It was sad to have to ruin such a nice case, but as it turned out it was worth it.

With a sharp blade, he cut round the suede lining of the lid. Cunningly inserted under the leather was a tiny, slim, very sophisticated bug. Zarubin extracted it. Under certain circumstances, it was the type of device that would pinpoint a person's whereabouts, like a homing beacon.

The pity of it was that the case was damaged beyond repair. Zarubin wondered if he'd be able to claim it on expenses. Then he flushed the bug down the toilet.

"Now what would you like to see?" asked Galina, Salim's officially assigned Intourist guide, when she first introduced herself in the lobby of the Rossiya. "Perhaps we should start with Red Square and the Kremlin. Or would you prefer a museum? The Red Army Museum in Kommuny Square, maybe? Whatever takes your fancy."

She was a charmer, and Salim was deeply grateful to Yenko, although his name was never mentioned.

"I think," said Salim, as he unashamedly undressed her with his eyes, "I would like to see more of you."

"There's plenty of time for that," smiled Galina, not the least taken aback, and Salim thought what good taste Yenko had, and how cleverly he had picked the girl.

They had a car at their disposal, and Galina chatted, pointing out the city's landmarks, and joking about some of the Muscovites.

"Look at that man, have you ever seen anyone so pompous and self important? I bet he's a deputy assistant nothing."

She must feel very secure in her job, thought Salim, if she can afford to make fun of the bureaucrats.

They had been speaking English. She was very fluent, with a slight American accent. But now she surprised him.

"Do you mind if we talk a little in French?" she asked.

"Why?"

"I don't have much chance to practise it."

"How do you know I can speak French?"

Her big eyes twinkled. "Of course you do. London. Paris. You're a man about Europe."

Yenko had given her a run down on him, evidently.

So they spoke in French for a while.

Now and then, he gave her a sideways look. She was petite, and very attractive. Not at all the prototype of the buxom Russian. She must be hand picked. What was the name these girls had? Swallows? She was a KGB swallow.

Salim liked women, and this one was most entertaining. He wondered how he'd feel if he had to kill her. It was something he often thought about when he met someone he liked. He'd do it of course, if necessary, but it would not be a pleasure. Salim was much too cultured to enjoy destroying anything beautiful.

"You haven't heard a word I was saying," pouted Galina.

"I'm sorry," he apologised, "I was just thinking."

"Most men don't think of other things when they're with me," she said reproachfully, and with a touch of bruised professional pride.

Salim decided to make amends. "I was thinking how much I'm enjoying myself. Will I see you again?"

The smile came back. "But of course. I am assigned to make your stay here in Moscow as memorable and pleasurable as possible."

"Good."

It was she who suggested the Baku restaurant in Gorky Street, and he noted how well she organised it. They were expected, and the attention they got was impressive.

She seemed to read his thoughts.

"You're a very important man," she confided. "I am under orders to make sure you get VIP treatment."

"Everyone is very generous," said Salim diffidently.

She translated the menu of Azerbaijani cuisine which included twenty-three various pilaffs, let him pick the dishes, then ordered them in Russian. The waiter brought bottles of mineral water.

"Wouldn't you like some wine?" offered Salim.

She shook her head. "This is much better for me."

Part of the briefing again. No alcohol. Salim is strict in these matters. Stick to soft drinks. Don't embarrass him.

The goelubtsy Salim was served was the best he'd ever tasted and when they were ready to go, they just rose, the waiter bowing. There was no bill.

"I must pay . . . " protested Salim, but Galina cut him short.

173

"It's all taken care of," she said.

They were indeed being very hospitable, he reflected. The hotel was taken care of. The restaurant paid. A car laid on. And Galina.

Salim, like a good general, planned his moves ahead. But there were some technical problems. At the Rossiya, guests collected their keys on their floor, at the desk of the formidable, unsmiling woman who presided over each corridor, and observed all comings and goings. It would not be easy with a girl at his side.

"Well, now . . ." said Salim, a little awkwardly, when they entered the marble floored entrance hall.

"Come along," said Galina with a wink. She had taken charge.

They took the elevator to his floor. The dragon in charge of the corridor gave him his key, and then, to his surprise, actually produced a slight smile.

Salim unlocked the door of 282, and held it open for Galina. He switched on the light.

"It's a nice room," remarked Galina, securing the lock from the inside. Then she went over to Salim, put her arms round his neck and said: "I hate being disturbed, don't you?"

TOP SECRET
NOT FOR THE FILE
TO: MR BLANCHARD
FROM: JOHN DICHTER

As you know, I am not satisfied about the circumstances surrounding the death of the London Station Chief.

I have known Flexner for many years, and his record speaks for itself. I do not believe, contrary to what the British authorities say, that his death was self inflicted.

I am aware that the Office of Security has been investigating the possibility, based on information from UK organs, that Flexner may have been involved in the murder of a London call girl with whom, it is alleged, he maintained a covert liason. Even if such a relationship existed, I do not accept and have seen no evidence to support the homicide allegation.

Furthermore, Flexner, in my belief, was not an individual who would consider self destruction as a solution to his problems and it seems completely uncharacteristic that an informal interrogation by OS agents would drive him to commit suicide.

I consider it significant that the allegation against Flexner originated through Whitehall. Flexner has, for some time now, been sending us signals concerning his fear that security within the UKUSA intelligence community has been compromised. He also, as you know, indicated his belief that the death of the would be informant Spiridov, and its timing, confirmed the gravest security penetration.

The implications clearly point towards a British connection.

In view of the above, I would advise the utmost caution in treating the death of Flexner as suicide, and recommend that the matter not be considered closed.

May I suggest that personnel records should reflect that Flexner gave his life for his country.

Dichter first drafted the memo in pencil, and when he had finished, he re-read it very carefully.

Then he crossed out the last paragraph. It wouldn't do for Blanchard to think he was sentimental, even if the records were classified.

He was about to buzz for his secretary, but then he hesitated. Maybe this was something he should type himself.

Zarubin arrived late at the Grosvenor chapel and slipped into one of the rear pews, unnoticed by the small congregation gathered to commemorate the passing of Cyrus Flexner.

They were smart, dignified mourners, noted Zarubin as he sat down. Nancy Flexner, suitably dressed in black, was in the front, acknowledging the occasional sympathetic look with a quiet nod. Her eyes weren't red. She hadn't been weeping.

But Miss Walsh had. Clutching a handkerchief, she looked ready to break down, sobbing.

"Let us pray," intoned the clergyman, and there was a respectful rustle, and then silence.

Requiem for a spook, reflected Zarubin wryly. Now I've seen it all.

His eyes wandered round the plain little chapel. Yes, he decided, Cy Flexner definitely would have approved. He found himself wondering how a suicide qualified for such a formal send off. But then, what would a heathen such as he know about such things? In a way, he felt sorry for Flexner. The poor bastard deserved better than being so shit scared he'd been desperate enough to put a bullet through his own brain. Anybody deserved better than that.

Then he spotted them, on the other side, slightly in front of him.

Lambert in a dark suit, his head bowed. Even from the back, he looked distinguished. Next to him the guy who had driven the Mercedes. Zarubin tried to remember his name. Ah, yes. Druce.

Beside them, dressed in a sombre, black suit and looking very pale was Fern.

Fern! What on earth was she doing here? Was it just protocol to have all hands on parade, you and you and you? Or had she known Flexner? After all she was one of them. Perhaps she'd had to talk with him, maybe even meet him as part of her job working for them. The ministry. The department.

Also sitting in the same pew was another man, broad shouldered, hunched like a toad, his hair thinning on top, elderly. A man Zarubin did not know, but who he could almost smell was one of them.

In the rear, by themselves, were the two gum shoes. Bowyer and Houghton, side by side, like faceless twins.

So here you all are, Zarubin mused. The principal members of the cast. Or most of them. Going through the motions.

His eyes returned to Fern. Did she see me arrive, he wondered. Did she notice me slipping in late? He could only glimpse her profile – the profile of the face he remembered so well.

The valediction was torture.

"A lost friend . . . his passing will be mourned . . . God keep my servant . . . "

Zarubin got up and quietly walked out. He'd had enough.

Outside, in South Audley Street, he could hear that they were singing. It was pretty loud, considering how few of them there were.

Beside the chapel was a little cul de sac, where the cars were parked. Three embassy limousines, with diplomatic plates. A couple black and anonymous. But no Mercedes. Obviously, Lambert and his sidekick saved it for other occasions. But not funerals.

A taxi pulled up, and a tousle haired, casually dressed man got out and paid the driver. He noticed Zarubin and walked over to him.

"Excuse me," he said, "are you with this . . . ?"

"Why?"

"Did you know him?"

"Who?"

"Cyrus Flexner."

"Why?"

"Press," replied the man. "Nick Prosser. I hear he was a CIA big shot. I'm always interested in CIA people."

"Is that so, Mr Prosser?"

Prosser smiled. "You're an American, aren't you? From the Embassy? Here to pay your last respects?"

"Maybe," said Zarubin. "You might just make it, if you hurry," he added.

"Thanks," said Prosser coldly, going into the church.

That'll please Dichter, thought Zarubin ruefully. Now the newshounds have got a CIA angle, they'll drag it out and out.

Then the doors opened, and although there was organ music coming from within the church, the service was over.

Almost the first people to emerge were Crawford with Greg Sullivan, the FBI man. They went straight to their car, and drove off.

Then the English contingent drifted out. Fern was first, deep in conversation with the reporter. He was more than just talking to her. From the way he walked beside her, Zarubin could see that they were friends. The way they looked at one another, perhaps this was him. The man she was living with. Zarubin's expression hardened. Had she walked straight past simply because she hadn't seen him? Perhaps she'd decided she didn't want to be seen with him in public. Or was it something quite different? That she didn't want to introduce the tousle haired son of a bitch.

"Oh hello," said Lambert, "were you inside?"

Druce and the thick set man were beside him.

"You know I was," replied Zarubin.

"This is Zarubin, sir," said Lambert, turning to the thick set man.

"Really?" remarked the man. His tone wasn't friendly.

"Mr Pearmain knows all about you," went on Lambert coldly. "Incidentally, I'm glad you got bail. Make sure you turn up in court, won't you?"

Zarubin felt like punching him.

"Keep out of trouble," cautioned Lambert, nodding and walking away.

On the other side of the road Zarubin saw Fern and the reporter getting into a cab. His eyes followed it until . . .

"Mr Zarubin," interrupted a low, husky voice. "I'm so glad you could come."

Black suited her. It made Nancy Flexner look sexy, or maybe it was the way the close fitting dress hugged her figure. Flexner must have had something to attract this woman, he reflected. She could have had her pick. But he just said:

"It was a terrible shock. Unfortunately, I wasn't around, otherwise . . ."

"Of course, I quite understand," she smiled gently. The challenging eyes were mocking.

"If there's anything I can do . . ."

"But there is," she told him.

"Well, please . . ."

"Are you busy right now?"

"Not especially. Nothing that can't keep."

"We can't talk here. Why don't you come back and have a cup of coffee at the house. If you don't mind the mess."

You've just seen your husband get his spiritual send off, and you talk about a cup of coffee?

"Sure," agreed Zarubin. "If it's all right . . ."

178

Miss Walsh came across. She was dabbing her eyes, and now that he saw her close up, the tip of her nose was red.

"Oh, Nancy . . ." she sobbed. "Wasn't it beautiful? So very moving." She blew her nose. "And you're being so brave. I don't know how you manage. Is there anything you need? Shall I take you home? Or maybe you want to be on your own . . ."

"You're very kind," smiled Nancy, "but I'll be fine."

"Is anybody looking after you?" sniffed Miss Walsh anxiously.

"Don't worry, Mildred, I'm well taken care of."

"Just remember, if you need a friend, give me a call," said Miss Walsh, placing a comforting hand on Nancy Flexner's arm.

Nancy looked grateful.

"That's very kind of you," she said.

Miss Walsh just nodded, and with eyes brimming, she darted away before the flood began.

"She was very loyal," commented Nancy. "I think she'll miss Cy."

The blue doors of the chapel were being locked. All the mourners had dispersed.

"I guess it's all over," sighed Nancy. "Come on, let's go."

In the cab, on the way back to the house, she didn't pose as the grief stricken widow, overwhelmed by tragedy. She didn't pretend. No play acting. That was a point in her favour. Maybe the black dress was the only concession. Or did she already have it in her cupboard for cocktail parties?

"You really want coffee?" she asked, when they were inside. "How about something stronger?"

"Whatever you say."

She came into the living room, wheeling a trolley with an ice bucket on it and two glasses.

"You open the champagne, while I change," she instructed him, and left again.

The cork made the plop that reminded him of a shot from a silencer. He poured the champagne expertly, so that he didn't spill any. It was good. Vintage. Expensive. He wondered if Flexner had had a stock of it, or whether she had bought the bottle for a special occasion. Like . . .

Like now?

She entered, but if he expected her to be wearing some slinky negligé, step two in the big seduction scene, he was wrong. She had put on a sweater and slacks.

She took a glass, and raised it.

"Cheers," she said.

They drank, and she sat down on the couch next to him, and lit a cigarette.

"Shocked?" she asked, slightly sarcastically.

"Why should I be shocked?"

"I can guess what you're thinking. The merry widow. Can't wait to see hubby buried six feet down. No tears, no regrets. What a lousy bitch."

"Wrong. That wasn't what I was thinking at all."

"No?" she raised an eyebrow. "Surprise me."

"Well," began Zarubin, "I'm thinking she's a pretty smart lady. Good looking, sexy, and I bet damn good in bed." She smiled at that. "She knows it too. But that's not why she asked me here. She is trying to find out things. She wants to see what I know."

"You flatter yourself, Mr Zarubin," she said coolly. "I'll tell you why I invited you here."

He waited.

She took a deep drag on her cigarette.

"You see, Cy didn't kill himself. He was murdered. I think you can find out who did it."

Still he said nothing.

"I want you to find out. I don't want the bastard who killed him to get away with it. And I . . . well, you won't understand. I knew he was screwing that bitch." She laughed mirthlessly. "Stupid, isn't it? Cyrus Flexner, the cloak and dagger expert, who couldn't even fool his wife about his sordid little affair. But he didn't kill her. I know Cy. No way would he kill anyone. And he didn't shoot himself either."

Zarubin sipped his champagne.

"You knew about Debbie and him?"

"I knew there was somebody. I think he met her at some cocktail party the British gave. Some NATO freebie."

"Who told you?"

"Those two goons Washington sent. They couldn't wait to drip the poison. They got it from the British. Name, details, the lot. And I know something else."

Zarubin waited.

"I know who you are," she said quietly, "and what you are."

"Tell me."

"An executioner."

Zarubin felt in his pocket. "Hell, I'm out of cigarettes."

"Have one of mine," she offered. Her face came very close to his as she leaned over and placed one between his lips. She lit the cigarette with her lighter.

"I think," said Zarubin, picking his words carefully, "you got the wrong guy."

"I think not."

"Well, I don't buy it. Even supposing you are right that somebody killed him. Who? Why?"

"Cy was on to something. He suspected somebody. They wanted to shut him up. Before he got too close."

"Who wanted it?"

"The British."

Zarubin finished his champagne.

"How do you know?"

"We *were* married."

He snorted. "And he confided in you, of course."

"Some things."

"I don't believe it."

"And you don't believe he was murdered either?"

"I don't understand you," Zarubin replied. "Why do you care? The way things were between you two, there wasn't much love lost. You didn't even hide it. What makes you the avenging angel suddenly?"

She raised her hand, and momentarily he thought she was going to hit him. But she controlled herself.

"You are something, you know that?" she said tightly. "You don't understand, do you? That two people can drift apart, but when one of them gets murdered, the other still cares."

"Very touching," sniffed Zarubin. "Almost convincing."

"You bastard," she spat.

And he couldn't believe what he saw. There were tears in her eyes. This hard bitch.

"I'm sorry," apologised Zarubin. Maybe it was true. Maybe she had cared. Once. "Okay," he nodded. "I'll see what I can do."

She stubbed her cigarette out in the ash tray, then put her arms round his neck, and kissed him full on the mouth, pressing her body against his.

Gently Zarubin pushed her away.

"You got it all wrong," he said. "I don't need a down payment."

Somewhere in this concrete fortress might lie the clue, thought Prosser, who was not unfamiliar with the Public Records Office at Kew. Here he sometimes played the game, digging up what Whitehall wanted left buried. It was a game in which all the rules were bent one way, against the player. No document was made available until it was thirty years old. Some documents were never made available if the powers that be designated them too sensitive.

He showed his reader's ticket to the man at the desk, signed the register, then passed through the electronic security check. He went up the stairs to the first floor, and along the wide corridor that led to the Langdale Room.

The smell was different, but otherwise the place could be a mausoleum. A temple of dead secrets.

Prosser collected the bleeper which assigned him a seat number and would summon him when the hidden archives disgorged the requested secret. Then he began his search.

Ministry of Defence. Directorate of Air Intelligence. Intelligence from Enemy Radio Communications. Directorate of Military Operations and Intelligence. Private Papers of the Secretary of State. The titles of the bound volumes cataloguing classified documents, gave little away. But they were the keys to the locked memories of the past.

Prosser went across to the shelves holding the red bound Foreign Office indexes. He knew what he was looking for; whether he'd find it was another matter.

He wanted to track down the names. To see if they were

linked with the treasons of the past. Not that such a link would be obvious, of course, but as a specialist he might uncover a telltale, all revealing pointer. And maybe somewhere, with luck, there might be a document, a copy of a memo, something in the files that confirmed what he suspected.

That a name, a couple of names could be the common denominator.

There was no hope of seeing the Penkovsky file, that they'd never release. But Penkovsky wasn't the only joint operation that had been betrayed. There was another project in which British intelligence and the Americans had combined: Operation Gold. The secret communications tunnel between West and East Berlin, built to enable the West to tap Russian and East German telephones. A brilliant concept, except for one thing.

The KGB knew all about it.

Prosser spent a long time checking the cryptic entries in the Foreign Office logs. They gave hints of intrigues and conspiracies, secret missions and undercover operations, surveillance and monitoring, suspicion and double dealing. But they stayed hints, just terse two and three word catalogue entries, never explicit.

And then he found the name. Group class 54009. Piece number 158006233A. Name: Deveaux.

The subject entry consisted of two words: "Special Report".

Prosser was not an emotional man, but he felt excited as he jotted down the details (in pencil of course, since ink was forbidden in this sanctum). He couldn't believe his luck. It must have slipped through. In this huge bureaucracy, this one single document must somehow have been recorded, and committed to the archives. He straightened his back, stiff from poring over the logs, went over to the computer, sat down, and slowly, very carefully tapped out his own reader's card number, the document reference, then the code to summon up the file.

Sometimes it could take as long as half an hour for a file to arrive, and he tried to calm his excitement. He glanced at his watch, decided he might as well go to the cafeteria for a cup of tea when . . .

His bleeper buzzed.

The speed of it surprised Prosser. Somehow the secret of decades should take longer to surface. He went over to the collection counter.

"You buzzed me."

The man with the horn rimmed glasses and a plastic badge pinned to his shirt said, "Ah yes." He handed Prosser a slip. "Sorry." He smiled.

The slip of paper was headed "Document Not Produced". And under the heading "Reason", somebody had written:

"Retained in Department of Origin."

Of course.

But Prosser tried. "What exactly does that mean?"

"It means," explained the man in horn rimmed glasses, "that they don't want to let it out."

"But it's over thirty years. The law says documents over thirty years . . ."

The man was sympathetic. "I know, it's a nuisance when you've come all the way out here. But there are some things they want to keep quiet."

Yes, thought Prosser, how damn right you are.

"In America," argued Prosser rather foolishly, "there is a Freedom of Information Act . . ."

"This isn't America," pointed out the man amiably.

On the way down, Prosser remembered something he had once heard during a drinking session at El Vino's. That no matter what file you ask for at the Public Records Office, your card is marked.

"It's the computer, you see," his pal had said. "They've got a very shrewd system. The computer demands the identity of the people who want to know too much."

Perhaps, after all, the guy hadn't been drunk.

Hazlebury was a picturesque Sussex hamlet which boasted a pair of well preserved sixteenth century stocks on the village green, a small pub called, for a reason lost in antiquity, The Moor's Head, three cottages with thatched roofs, and a score of houses occupied mainly by London commuters of utmost respectability. It was also where Pearmain lived.

184

Most of the residents knew each other vaguely, but took considerable care not to become too intimately involved. The wives chatted, and the husbands were on nodding terms. Soberly dressed, carrying briefcases, making the same journey to the same offices, they'd briefly meet on the eight-five or eight-sixteen to Victoria every day.

In Hazlebury houses didn't have numbers, they had names. Pearmain's mock Tudor residence was called Les Sylphides, which was carved in Gothic lettering on the front gate.

To the neighbours he was something in the Civil Service. The Inland Revenue was the general consensus, and Pearmain didn't enlighten them. In the quiet life of Hazlebury, Mrs Pearmain was much more important. She usually carried off a prize at the annual church fête for her home made marmalade and jam.

The inhabitants of Hazlebury would have been astonished if they'd known that any reference to the dull Mr Pearmain was prohibited by a D-notice, and that to reveal what he did and where he worked was a breach of the Official Secrets Act. They would have been even more surprised if they'd realised that he was the head of ISAD, the Intelligence Special Activities Division, a directorate so sub rosa that even its acronym was classified top secret.

The only tangible hint that Pearmain did something unusual was that his phone number remained unlisted. Also, the phone itself was a little different, and had been connected by Post Office engineers sent down from London, instead of coming from the local exchange. The instrument's virtue was that, at a touch of a button, the conversation became scrambled, and Pearmain talked on a secure line.

Lambert half expected the summons which came late that Friday afternoon.

"If you've got nothing better to do tomorrow, why don't you come down to the country for a drink at my place," said Pearmain, almost casually, as if the thought had suddenly struck him. "The weather looks nice, and we could sit in the garden. How does that strike you?"

"I think I'd like that."

"Good. Shall we say about eleven?"

"I'll be there."

It was a call to a summit meeting and Lambert knew there would be nothing social about it. Just as Hitler always chose to invade neutral countries at weekends because it caught the democracies napping, so Pearmain liked to start his week with important decisions having already been made.

And he liked to talk about really delicate matters in the tranquillity of his Sussex house. There were those who said it was a little game. They regarded Les Sylphides not as his country retreat, where he forgot the cares of office, but as the centre of the spider's web. If a hint leaked out of what had been discussed, Pearmain knew where to point the finger.

Lambert was greeted by Pearmain wearing his weekend uniform; an old sports jacket with leather patches at the elbows, and shapeless grey flannels. He offered Lambert a glass of sherry, and after some inconsequential small talk, said:

"Come and have a look at my roses."

Affairs of state were about to be discussed.

Pearmain led the way into the garden, pausing at the rose bushes.

"What do you think of these?" he asked, pointing to some yellow roses. "Superb, aren't they? I wouldn't mind entering them for the Chelsea Flower Show."

He was genuinely proud of them, but he didn't wait for Lambert's reaction. "Let's sit over there," he suggested, going towards two deckchairs.

He settled back and closed his eyes.

"I want to sound you out about something," he began, not opening his eyes. "It's this bloody American. Zarubin. Frankly, I'm worried. You sure he is what he's supposed to be?"

"I'm sorry," said Lambert. "I'm not sure I quite understand . . ."

The eyes stayed closed. "Well, look at it this way. Kosov. Dead. The girl. Dead. Their station head. Dead. And you know who keeps intruding all the time? Zarubin. He is, as his American masters would say, bad news, don't you think?" He brushed an insect from his face. "It makes me uneasy. And I don't like the look of him, I don't mind telling you.

Something about his eyes. Not a man I'd like to go hunting tigers with."

Lambert considered his reply carefully. "Of course, I take your point absolutely." One did not disagree too fervently with Pearmain. "But I think you can dismiss Kosov's death. It was an accident, I'm sure. They wouldn't kill one of their best soccer teams just to get rid of him. There're easier ways." He smiled gently; look who he was telling. "As for the girl, well, tarts lead risky lives, and Flexner was in trouble with his own people. So, if you're saying Zarubin . . . "

"I'm saying, Lambert," interrupted Pearmain, looking at his colleague, "that I don't like coincidences. If four trains crash, and the same ticket collector is on all of them, I begin to wonder."

"Have you talked to Washington?"

Pearmain closed his eyes, enjoying the warmth of the sun on his face. "I believe that we should deal with the problem ourselves, should it become necessary. That's why I wanted to talk to you. You know the fellow. You know what's going on. My feeling is he could become . . . an embarrassment."

Lambert didn't reply immediately. He seemed to be engrossed watching a bee collect pollen from a nearby flower bed.

"Well . . ." said Pearmain.

"I will bear it in mind," agreed Lambert.

"Good."

The decision had been made, the order acknowledged. It was all very gentlemanly.

"Oh, one other thing, Lambert."

"Yes?"

"I believe Miss Norman is coming up for her annual positive vetting."

"Fern? Yes, I believe so."

"I wonder . . ."

Pearmain paused.

"You are perfectly happy with her?"

"Why do you ask?"

"Oh, I have these funny thoughts," shrugged Pearmain. "I wonder if your section shouldn't perhaps dispense with her services. We can always arrange a transfer to something innocuous."

"Could you tell me why?"

The thick set man grunted. "Don't play innocent, Lambert, you know we have a file on Prosser and I don't like her liaison with him. Also, you know she had a relationship with Zarubin."

Lambert's smile was almost triumphant. "Absolutely. That's why we mustn't dispense with her. All her connections are most useful."

Pearmain turned and looked at him. "I never interfere," he said, and Lambert noted how convincingly he lied, "you know that. But I have an inbuilt mistrust of certain people within the department who have such personal relationships. It makes me wonder how reliable Miss Norman really is."

"I wouldn't worry about Fern." Lambert sounded smug.

"But supposing you're wrong. Your section cannot take the risk of its operatives indulging in . . ." he searched for the words, "well, human frailties. Supposing your little Fern turns out to be very human and very frail?"

"In that case, of course, appropriate measures will be taken."

"All right," said Pearmain. "It's your section, your little empire, run it your own way. You do, anyway, don't you? Always have done. I don't even want to know. But, remember, trust only goes so far."

Pearmain walked with him to the garden gate.

"I'm sorry I can't invite you to stay for lunch, but my wife is a little under the weather today. She just can't face guests."

"Oh, I am sorry."

"Don't worry about it," said Pearmain with a dry smile. "It's nothing serious. She'll recover."

Lambert wasn't sure that the vague note of regret he detected was just in his imagination.

"Anyway," added Pearmain, "it's been very useful. Thanks for coming down."

On the train back to London, Lambert reflected that the entire conversation would have taken ten minutes in Pearmain's office in town. But evidently he wanted to make absolutely sure what had been said remained secret between the two of them.

At 7 am the black Ministry Volga called for Salim at the Rossiya.

"Good morning," smiled Yenko, when Salim joined him in the back of the car.

Their destination lay forty miles from Moscow, north east of the city of Kaliningrad. Most of the journey Salim spent looking out of the window, but it was a route designed to leave prying eyes ignorant. Once they passed an airfield, shielded from the traffic by a high fence, and also screened by fir trees, effectively blocking the view of curious people trying to identify the installation.

"All this is closed to foreigners," explained Yenko. It was said so that Salim felt he had VIP rating. He was privileged because he could travel along here. He could stare out at the passing countryside.

They skirted a town, which Yenko obligingly identified as Shelkovo. Then they turned off the highway, and drove along an unmarked road until they came to a guard post. They were expected, and the two sentries just waved them on.

The road continued through a wood, and finally they came to a large clearing, where some anonymous looking buildings fringed the edge of a lake.

The Volga pulled up at the entrance of the main block and a Red Army lieutenant colonel was already waiting for them. Although Yenko and Salim both wore civilian clothes, he gave them a formal military salute.

"Welcome to Friendship Academy."

"Colonel Vladek," introduced Yenko. "The commandant."

"We've been looking forward to your visit," said the colonel. "Please follow me."

So began Salim's tour of the training centre which, to the Liberators, was the West Point of terrorism, the Sandhurst of anarchy, the St Cyr of assassination. Here the hand picked, élite revolutionists of Europe, Africa, the Middle East and Latin America came, eager to learn, impatient to kill.

Each classroom was named after a hero of world revolution. Che Guevara. Giangiacomo Feltrinelli. Mohammed Boudie. Ulrike Meinhof. Andreas Baader. Wadi Haddad. Dead martyrs all, their portraits adorned the walls of the lecture halls.

"Our overseas students spend six months here," Vladek explained to Salim, showing him the dormitories, the cinema, the two canteens, the library and reading room, the gyms. "Their day starts at 5 am with physical training. And it's a long day. We put great emphasis on political education, studying the teachings of Lenin, Marx, Engels, learning the principles of socialism and communism, the struggle against imperialism, analysing the links between Zionism and colonialism, the reactionary nature of so called social democracy, and so on."

As he rattled on like a well drilled rote, Salim wondered who he was trying to impress. After all, no one ever killed a Zionist pig with dialectics.

And as if the colonel had read his thoughts, he added:

"But of course, it's the practical studies which take up most of their time here. Urban guerrilla tactics, the use of incendiary charges and detonators, making bombs, assassination techniques, the handling and maintenance of weapons, grenade throwing, mining bridges and vehicles, booby trapping, the whole art of killing."

That's better, reflected Salim.

"Though, of course, I don't have to teach you, dear comrade, anything about that," concluded the colonel diffidently.

"One always learns," said Salim modestly.

They covered the firing range, and the open air battle course, near the lake, and watched the students, men and women, all wearing brown overalls, going through their paces.

"Why do you still teach them to use the Stechkin pistol?" asked Salim after they had briefly watched a marksmanship class.

"Because it is a first class weapon," replied Vladek, surprised. "A high rate of fire, good muzzle velocity, and it's very light. About two pounds when loaded. An ideal weapon for a woman."

Salim shook his head. "No. It is a bad gun. The recoil and vibration makes one handed operation impossible. The gun takes charge, spits out bullets too fast, and inaccurately. One loses control."

"You're speaking from experience?" suggested Yenko, gently.

"I am," snapped Salim. "Once that gun nearly cost me my life. It is not a professional's weapon."

The colonel didn't appear pleased. "I'll convey your views to the experts," he said, stiffly.

Sharp at 11 am the students assembled in the vast lecture theatre, its walls hung with red banners bearing the slogans of world revolution in Russian, Spanish, Arabic and English. From the platform, Salim studied the rows of attentive young faces. He played a little game, trying to identify nationalities. The Arabs were easy. So, really, were most of the Latins. But the Anglo-Saxons, the North Europeans proved really confusing. Was that group in the third row East German, or Irish? Were those French Bretons. It was harder than he had imagined. Basques. Turks. Greeks. Swedes. Corsicans. The IRA. The Red Faction. The Italian Brigate Rosse. All being trained here. All really so alike.

". . . and we've asked Comrade Salim to say a few words."

There was applause, then they were all looking at him. Slowly Salim stood up, and faced them.

"Comrades," he began. "Fellow fighters. I . . ." He hesitated. What could he tell them? Perhaps something they wouldn't be taught here. All right then. "I want to talk about killing." There was a faint rustle. He didn't see Yenko's thin smile.. "We are all in the business of killing. We all hate our enemies. But let me tell you something. Never kill with hate. If you kill with hate, you kill with emotion. And an emotional assassin is a bad one. To be the perfect executioner, you must be totally detached from the subject you are executing. Ah, you will say, but if I know the victim, if I have met him, if I even like him, personally, how can I be detached about it? *That* is what you have to learn. The ability to switch off emotion. If you look across the barrel of your gun at a beautiful woman, and you are at that moment aware how

191

beautiful she is, your aim may waver. If you have planted a bomb in a bus in which some children will travel, forget that they are children. They are cyphers. They do not matter. Otherwise, you may botch the job."

He paused. There wasn't even a cough in the hall. A blonde girl near the front who had been chewing gum had stopped, and was staring at him fixedly.

"I know what I say is not easy. But we are all chosen people. Only it is we ourselves who have chosen. We are dedicated to achieve what we believe in, we must be ready to stand aside from ordinary people, ordinary feelings, and ordinary trusts. We have chosen never to trust anyone. No one, that is, except ourselves."

There was silence for a moment, then he sat down. They applauded him, but it was a muted applause. They had expected him to talk about his great achievements, the Zionists he had killed, the assassinations he had carried out, the fear he inspired in the enemies of world revolution.

"That was very interesting," whispered Yenko in his ear. "And quite revealing."

"I'm sorry. This kind of thing is not my strong point. I should not have spoken."

"On the contrary," Yenko assured him, "I think we must all take your words to heart. Especially about trusting no one except ourselves. It is a philosophy I adopted at an early age, and you don't often hear someone else preach it. Congratulations, my friend."

They said goodbye to Colonel Vladek.

"A remarkable institution, wouldn't you agree?" commented Yenko in the car.

"Yes, remarkable."

They were back on the motorway when Yenko said:

"Salim, my friend, if we had a mission, a very special mission that required somebody very special, and we all would be eternally grateful to the man who fulfilled it, would you consider taking it on?"

Salim inclined his head. "What kind of mission?"

"To kill somebody of course."

Salim brushed his coat. He seemed to have spotted a minute speck.

"Kill who?" he asked, like a doctor wanting to know the name of the patient.

"An American in London," replied Yenko. "A man called Zarubin."

Salim smiled slightly. Had it just been coincidence that they'd shared the same prison cell?

"Why not?" he murmured. "Subject to agreeing terms . . ."

"You seem quite eager," said Yenko, warily.

Salim's beautiful white teeth flashed.

"Professional pride, Major. It should be an interesting experience, executing Mr Zarubin. And you know how I enjoy interesting experiences."

"Without being emotionally involved . . ."

"Exactly," nodded Salim.

It was not the first death assignment Yenko had handed out, but it was the first time he had no doubt about it being done.

The editor's secretary had adopted her boss's manner of making his summons sound like a casual request. So when she asked Nick Prosser if he could "just drop by his office for a minute," it wasn't a question, more a command.

Those who worked in the Glass Palace had long since recognised the warning signal. An informal invitation "to drop by his office" was sometimes the first hint that they'd be leaving the paper that day with a generous pay cheque but no thanks.

Not that Nick Prosser was worried when he got the command call. He had the confidence of a man with a cast iron contract, and who knows that his byline helped sell the paper. It would cost the absentee peer who owned the organisation a small fortune to get rid of him, and Roberts, the editor, wouldn't be happy anyway. He could swallow most things, except losing circulation pullers.

"Go right in, Nick," smiled the secretary when Prosser reported. He gave a perfunctory knock on the editor's door.

As always, Roberts was in his shirt sleeves. His shirt was always immaculate, even at one o'clock in the morning after a hectic news night. He must keep a stock of freshly laundered shirts in the office, so he can change them two or three times a day, thought Prosser.

Roberts waved to him, although he was only five feet from the massive desk.

"Don't bother to knock, ever," he cried jovially. "Not you. You've got an open door, Nick, an open door. Plonk yourself down."

He looked as youthful as ever, sunburnt, fit, his face hardly lined, more like a man in his thirties than his fifty-one years, twenty of them spent editing mass selling tabloids in Fleet Street, and making a success of each of them.

There were two cabinets in the office; one was a massive television set, and Roberts went over to the other, and opened the doors.

"What would you like?"

"Gin," said Prosser.

"And French. Of course I know." Roberts poured him a drink, and a Perrier for himself. One of the reasons people disliked him in the Street was that he never touched alcohol.

"Cheers." He raised his glass, and smiled at Prosser.

"Well, how are things?"

Roberts had a reputation for directness. Some of his toughest meetings lasted less than five minutes. Prosser braced himself. If Roberts indulged in preliminary fencing, he was leading up to something special.

"All right, I suppose," he replied warily.

"I liked your piece on nuclear madness. All nonsense of course, we'll freeze to death when the oil runs out, but it was well done. You almost convinced me."

He grinned cheerfully.

"Maybe there's hope for you yet," remarked Prosser, arrogantly, but Roberts didn't rise to it.

"Listen, Nick, how would you like to go on a big trip?"

He beamed encouragingly.

"What for?"

Roberts was a good salesman. He knew how to win people over, as he'd proved by talking the paper's board of directors into launching a multi-million pound lottery, or when he'd got them to agree to his dropping its famous cartoonist because his jokes were getting too serious.

"Something really big," he said, persuasively. "I want to send you on a world tour, for a series of features about child prostitution."

"Eh?"

"You don't know what a big story that is," went on Roberts earnestly. "Have you got any idea how much child prostitution goes on? Places like Hong Kong. Naples. Port Said. Mexico. God, I can see it now. Big features." He spread his hands. "Punchy, tough copy, the way you do it. A crusade. With pictures. I'll send a good bloke with you. How d'you like it?"

"Why?" asked Prosser. "Why, all of a sudden?"

Slight irritation clouded the genial face.

"Oh come on, Nick, do I have to spell it out? It's got everything. Sex. Vice. And kids. Everybody will lap it up. I'll arrange for questions in Parliament. I'll get the UN on it. You'll be the crusader fighting for the Innocent Ones."

He was starting to speak in headlines.

"You'll get a TV series out of it, I guarantee it. A book maybe. I Bought A Twelve Year Old Girl. It's sure fire."

He sat back, satisfied with his pitch.

Prosser knew he expected only one answer, and it was wise not to disappoint Roberts. So he said, rather carefully:

"It's got possibilities."

"Possibilities! My God, it's a winner."

"I'll think about it."

Roberts looked at his desk calendar. "I want you to leave next week. Take as long as you like. A couple of months maybe. Go where you like. Expenses no problem. Just bring back the goods."

"I can't. Not that soon."

Roberts' face froze. "Oh, why not?"

"I'm working on something."

"What?"

"I think you'll like it. It's going to shake them. You'll have those questions in Parliament without rigging them. If it works out, it'll be dynamite."

"What is it?" asked Roberts very quietly.

Prosser took a deep breath. "It's going to blow the intelligence people apart. I think I'm on to the biggest exposé

195

since, oh, Philby. There's somebody at the top still working for the Russians. And I think I know who it is. He may even have betrayed Penkovsky."

"Drop it."

"What?"

"Forget about it. I don't want it."

"You can't be serious," cried Prosser, in disbelief. "Do you understand what I'm saying? I can break the story. Expose the traitor nobody's yet caught. All I need is more time. It's going to be a sensation."

"No," declared Roberts, avoiding Prosser's eyes. "I'm bored with Russian moles in Whitehall. It's been played to death."

He didn't sound convincing.

"Well, you're wrong," protested Prosser. "Dead wrong. And I'm going to go on digging until I can hand it to you on a plate. Then you'll need the biggest headlines you've got."

"I won't print it."

Slowly it began to dawn on Prosser, the fearful realisation gradually sinking in. The paper already knew. Roberts already knew. They didn't want him to go on, and it wasn't because they didn't like the story. No, that wasn't the reason they wanted to stop him.

He leaned forward. "They've been at you, haven't they? They've told you to shut me up. They've got hold of his lordship, of you, of everybody and said stop this bloody man digging around. Stop him making waves. Stop him embarrassing us. That's why you want me out of the way. Fucking child prostitution my arse. You just want your bloody knighthood."

Roberts stood up and walked across to the big window, with its panoramic view of the City, and the dome of St Paul's. When he turned round, he looked grave.

"All right, Nick. But it's not what you think. It's not a cover up. The powers that be have hinted that at this moment any speculation about Russian infiltration into our security services will do enormous damage to this country and our special relations with the Yanks. And this paper is not about to do that."

"Even if it's true?"

"They say that it's not. And, if you'll forgive me, you're not exactly known to be a gung ho patriot. You make a business of undermining the establishment. You do a great job screwing authority. We pay you to do it. But there's a line beyond which we won't go. And that's national security."

"Now wait a minute . . ."

"No, you wait," said Roberts harshly. "You are anti NATO. Anti nuclear weapons. Anti American. That's fine. Up to a point. You're going beyond that point."

He went back to his desk, and sat down.

"All right, Nick, when do you leave on the trip?"

But Prosser was already at the door.

"You know what you can do with the trip," he shouted. "I'm on to something, and I'm not letting go. You'll come crawling, wanting the story when I've got it. So fuck you, fuck his lordship and fuck Whitehall."

He slammed the door.

Roberts sighed. He pressed his intercom.

"Phyllis," he said, "I've got something to dictate to you."

It was going to be a short, terse memo.

When Zarubin arrived for his second appearance at Great Marlborough Magistrates Court, he noticed Theo's Rolls-Royce parked on a double yellow line nearby. The empty car hadn't been given a ticket, and he wondered if Theo could fix that too.

Zarubin gave his name to the jailer at the back of the court who told him that because his was a remand case, it wouldn't be called until all the overnight arrests had been heard. He was taken to wait in a big tiled room, which reminded him of a public toilet, and was crowded. People stood around, sat on hard wooden benches, leaned against walls. There were many foreigners, a lot of black people, and a string of street girls. They were the most cheerful; for them a fine was another way of paying income tax.

An hour later a policeman called out Zarubin's name then led him into the dock.

"This is a remand, sir," wheezed the clerk. He seemed to have acquired a bad chest cold since the previous week. "Andrew Zarubin."

As he looked round the court and the anonymous faces in the public gallery Zarubin realised that none of the principal performers was present. There was no sign of Theo or Lambert, and even the blonde vice squad inspector was missing, her place taken by the dapper detective sergeant with the Charlie Chaplin moustache.

"I'm instructed in this case to ask for a further remand," he announced, without glancing at Zarubin.

"Hmmm," grunted the magistrate. "I see that this man got bailed after all."

"That is so, sir."

"What do you need the remand for?"

"We have further enquiries to make."

The magistrate polished his monocle. "He is an American national, isn't he?"

"Yes, sir," said the sergeant, "but we have his passport."

"Very well. Remanded for fourteen days. Bail extended."

It was a formality, and they played it like well rehearsed actors working to a cue.

"You'll have to sign the book," whispered the jailer. "This way."

By the time Zarubin emerged from the court, Theo's Rolls had gone. He crossed the road, and studied some framed posters in Liberty's window. In the glass, he could see a girl walking towards him. She was one of the play-for-pay dolls he had seen in the waiting room of the court.

She came up and stood beside him.

"Hi," she said.

"How much they sting you?" he asked. She had been on the court list for soliciting.

"Fifty quid, the bastard," she grimaced. "And you?"

"They haven't even started on me."

She eyed him speculatively. "Feel like doing something?" It was more a plea than a question.

She was on the way down. Her clothes were showing it.

"Only if you feel like it," she added hopefully. She was shaking slightly, like an addict in need of a fix. She was broke, and Zarubin sensed that the fine had finished her.

She tried to stop herself trembling.

"Here," he said, pressing twenty pounds into her hand.

"Hey, what's this for?" she asked, startled.

"Tax rebate."

She drew herself up. "I don't take charity, mister. I don't beg." She still had some dignity.

"That's why it's only a loan," said Zarubin, and grabbed a cab that had stopped in front of them.

He gave the driver the address of the Steinmetz Gallery, and as the taxi drove off, he saw her out of the back window. She was crying.

Tony Gibson-Greer switched on a forced smile when Zarubin entered.

"Well, hello there," he greeted him nervously.

Zarubin shut the door of the gallery very gently, and slipped down the catch.

Then he went over to the man with the gold earring and hit him. It was a vicious blow, very low, very hard, and would have disqualified Zarubin in any boxing ring in the world.

Gibson-Greer sank to the floor, clutching his groin.

"Get up," said Zarubin pleasantly.

Gibson-Greer's pasty face stared up at him. He tried to stand, but couldn't.

"Get up," repeated Zarubin.

Using the wall for support, Gibson-Greer slowly got to his feet.

Zarubin hit him again. This time, the man gurgled as he slumped to the ground. Then he was sick, spewing the contents of his stomach over the floor. Zarubin stepped aside neatly to avoid being splashed.

Gibson-Greer lay quietly moaning. Zarubin pulled over a chair, and sat in front of him.

"Now," he said gently, "tell me who Steinmetz is."

"You cunt . . ." groaned Gibson-Greer.

"Steinmetz. I haven't got all day."

"I'm sick," Gibson-Greer croaked.

"Not half as sick as you'll be if I have to ask too many questions."

Gibson-Greer clutched his stomach. "I . . . I told you. There's no Steinmetz. It's just . . . just a trade . . . name."

Zarubin sighed. Then he picked up Gibson-Greer by the scruff of his neck with one hand, and slammed his fist into his stomach again with the other.

"Aaaargh." It was half a scream, half a moan. Zarubin let him fall.

"Okay," said Zarubin. "You just nod. If it's the wrong nod, I'll know. And I'll kill you. Clear?"

Gibson-Greer's eyes were glassy. But he nodded.

"Good. Now you tell me if I'm right. Theo is Steinmetz. Right?"

The man nodded.

"It's another front he uses, check? Modern paintings?"

Another nod.

"You sent me a postcard. On Theo's orders."

Another nod.

"To let me know . . . about old times. A reminder . . ."

Gibson-Greer groaned, but again he nodded.

"Theo's the post office, isn't he? He passes it all on. Both ways. Correct?"

"Yes," he moaned in reply.

"Good," said Zarubin. "That's much better. Now I'll help you get up."

He lifted him to his feet. "Can you manage to stand?"

Gibson-Greer leaned against the wall for support.

Zarubin lit a cigarette. "And you. Tell me about yourself. What are you doing in this set up? You're about as professional as a part time milkmaid. How did you get into this?"

"I . . . they . . ."

"They got something on you," Zarubin suggested. "Theo's porn empire is ideal for blackmail. And I suppose it's useful to have a body like you around. Sure, that figures."

Gibson-Greer suddenly clutched his stomach, and doubled up.

"I'm going to be sick," he croaked, turning tail, and disappearing behind the bead curtain into the gallery's back room.

Zarubin wrinkled his nose, the vomit on the floor was starting to smell. He got up and wandered over to the table and began reading the names of those who had signed the open visitor's book. His own entry was on the last page, which he carefully removed, folded, and put in his pocket.

He heard the rustle of the bead curtain, and as he turned

he saw a figure rushing towards him, with a wide eyed, crazy expression on his face, and a long, sharp blade in his hand.

Screaming like a demon out of hell, Tony Gibson-Greer threw himself at Zarubin, the knife aimed straight at his throat.

Simultaneously, Zarubin kicked out, and seized Gibson-Greer's hand that held the knife. Then, with a sudden, vicious twist, he plunged the blade into the man's own body. He put all his weight behind it, burying the knife deep into Gibson-Greer, cutting, severing, destroying.

His eyes flickered for a moment, then blood gushed from his mouth, and he slid to the ground, where he lay sprawled, the knife still sticking out of his body.

It was messy, a growing pool of blood was spreading from Gibson-Greer's body to the vomit.

He hadn't planned to kill him. But he owed the instructor who taught him that particular method of execution a debt.

He looked round. He hadn't touched anything except the door, and he wiped the handle and latch so that they wouldn't find any finger prints.

He slipped out of the gallery. The street was quiet and nobody took any notice of him as he walked towards Ladbroke Grove where he hailed a taxi.

He paid off the cab outside the Ritz Hotel, and he went into a phone box.

The number Zarubin rang put him straight through.

"Yes?" Crawford answered.

"You need a haircut," announced Zarubin. No greeting, no preliminary.

A moment's pause. Then Crawford replied:

"I've just had one."

"It needs tidying up," said Zarubin.

Silence.

"Okay," agreed Crawford at last. "I'll fit it in at three o'clock."

And he hung up. If somebody had tapped the call, they wouldn't have learnt much.

Zarubin wandered into Piccadilly, bought the lunch time edition of the *Standard*, and walked into Green Park. He found an inviting deckchair, and sat down.

It was too soon for there to be anything in the paper about Gibson-Greer, and when they did print something it wouldn't make much of a story anyway. Just a couple of paragraphs maybe. Sudden death wasn't a sensation in Notting Hill any more.

Zarubin tried to work out if Gibson-Greer was number four or number five. That had never happened before. They used to be clearly etched in his memory, each death distinctly defined and listed in his mind. Now he had to think to recall them.

Maybe the same thing happened to surgeons too, after a few patients had died under the knife. A recollection, of course, but the precise details? How long did they go back for?

In his mind's eye, he replayed the scene of Gibson-Greer's end. The blood, the pool of vomit, the ugly angle of the knife protruding from the man's body. But he was relieved that it remained an impersonal picture, like a street accident one had witnessed.

At least that was reassuring. If he started to get involved, it would be fatal.

He closed his eyes, and relaxed. The hum of the traffic in nearby Piccadilly, the laughter of the young couples strolling on the grass, the barking of dogs being walked, it was all reassuring. Here, for a moment, chances were he could shut his eyes. He knew he was safe, because here it was too public for them to try anything. He hoped so, anyway.

Ten minutes switched off was enough to recharge his battery. He hadn't slept, he hadn't even dozed off, but he'd shut out the world for a brief period, and now he was ready.

He stood up, and dropped the paper on the deck chair. The heading "Your Horoscope" caught his eye. Of course he didn't believe in that rubbish. He always sneered at it. How could any rational person believe that stuff. But inwardly, he sometimes wondered if he wasn't so sure after all, and wouldn't admit it to himself. Methinks the man protests too much an inner voice whispered occasionally, and he silenced it angrily.

He picked up the paper again, and looked up his birth sign. It doesn't mean a thing, of course, the inner voice insisted. Of course it doesn't, his mind agreed loyally, but nonetheless he scanned Scorpio.

"Do not be dismayed if you find yourself in conflict with those on whom you rely. Unexpected pressures may cause you problems, and a trusted friend could turn out to be a grave disappointment. Avoid strangers. This will be a trying period, and you shouldn't take risks."

"And fuck you," swore Zarubin under his breath. He crumpled up the paper and tossed it into the trash bin. Then he looked at his watch. It was time.

The zoo wasn't crowded and he reached the reptile house five minutes early. Before he went in, he looked around, but nobody seemed to be following him.

Inside the dim, overheated building, he slowly walked along the glass fronted enclosures. Trust them to think of this place as the contingency rendez-vous. What quirk of Dichter's imagination had selected the home of snakes and reptiles as the emergency location?

Crawford arrived at precisely three o'clock. Zarubin admired the way he timed things. He'd had to get to the zoo, pay his admission, walk to the reptile house, and he'd planned it so well that he'd made it to the second. Traffic snarls never seemed to get in Crawford's way.

Crawford nodded his greeting.

"You sure this is necessary?" he asked.

"Who's going to know? Him?" enquired Zarubin, pointing to a python that hung from a branch in its prison. It had a huge bulge, the only visible remains of a rabbit it was in the process of digesting.

"All right. What's the problem?"

"I want to know about Flexner."

"What about him?" Crawford's voice was flat.

"Who killed him?"

"Hey. Hold your horses. Who said anything about killing?"

"His wife, for one."

"Oh, of course." Crawford sighed. "You know, that's one sad lady. Perhaps she was too much for Cy, too." He stared thoughtfully at the python. "Maybe they should never have made him station chief with her around."

"What the hell does that mean?" demanded Zarubin.

"Come on, man, you know what Nancy is. Slept with anything in pants except her own husband. I don't know how he lived with it." He saw Zarubin's look. "Did she get you in the sack too?"

Zarubin clenched his fist.

"Take it easy," said Crawford, holding up his hands hurriedly. "It's happened to everybody. She made a dive for me, too."

"But, of course, you claimed a previous engagement and departed," suggested Zarubin sarcastically.

"Not at all." Crawford was very cool. "She was a good fuck."

"You're a real son of a bitch, you know that?"

"Strictly in the line of duty," added Crawford. "Dichter's orders."

"What?"

"A field test." He gave a very thin smile. "He wanted to check if it was true what he'd heard."

"Jesus!" cursed Zarubin. "What a bastard thing to do."

Crawford chuckled softly. "Don't tell me you're getting scruples, Andy? Little late for that, isn't it?"

Slowly they walked past the snakes.

"You know, they all still got their poison fangs here," remarked Crawford conversationally. "I don't know how they find guys to look after these beauties. Not for what they pay them. I guess it must take a very special sort of person."

"So, you think that's why Cy killed himself?" insisted Zarubin.

"Sure. He consoled himself with the wrong girl. The British found out, tipped off Langley, then the heavy mob came down on him and he couldn't take it. Cy was a funny guy. He believed in the old way of doing things, including honour before disgrace." Crawford's lips curled. "He was in the wrong outfit at the wrong time."

He looked at his watch.

"Anything else?"

"Yes," said Zarubin. "Theo. Dichter was right. Theo's a connection."

He thought Crawford's reply sounded a little resentful:

204

"Dichter's always right, isn't he?"

Zarubin went on: "And I've had to do a little . . . surgery. You'll hear about it."

"Don't tell me. Just keep us out of it," said Crawford. He paused. "What's it like being on bail?"

"What do you think? I wonder what else Lambert's got in store for me?"

"I wonder what you've got in store for Lambert?" said Crawford. "No, I guess I don't want to know."

Zarubin stopped to watch a snake slowly gliding across some rocks.

Then he said:

"Give the head honcho an update. About everything."

"I already have," said Crawford.

And then they left the reptile house.

Unless you're unfortunate enough to be a well known personality, have an unforgettable face, or certain very distinctive physical features, it is not impossible for a person who has already been deported to return to the United Kingdom, and slip through immigration control. It is done, every year, by scores of Irishmen, for example, and indeed the Dublin-London gateway is much favoured by those who need a hole in the net.

Also, although it is never publicly admitted, because in a sensitive society, dogged by vigilant searchers for symptoms of racism, it would be foolhardy for any government department to do so, it is not always easy for Western immigration personnel to distinguish an undesirable alien amongst certain nationalities. So often certain people all look alike to Western eyes.

Further, Western immigration officers find it difficult to read Arab travel documents, and they occasionally have to depend on the details the traveller obligingly fills in on his landing card. Of course, there are lists of prohibited immigrants, and thick black volumes containing the names and aliases of people who should not be allowed to land, but that presupposes that they play the game by the rules, and use the same names and aliases.

So unless he is especially distinguishable, or has very bad

luck, a man like Salim, backed up by the kind of organisation and facilities that were available to him, equipped with an authentic passport, describing him as Achmet Bin Hussein, a subject of the Hashemite kingdom of Jordan, and which was sufficiently endorsed to convince of its genuineness, didn't have an insurmountable problem returning to the island that once kicked him out. He arrived at Heathrow on an Alitalia flight from Rome, and had grown a pencil thin moustache which did not make him any less handsome, but did alter his appearance slightly. He travelled "clean". He carried nothing illegal, and had with him documents which proved that he was a business man, dealing with British exports to the Middle East, with substantial accounts at two Arab and an English bank in the City of London.

"One month, Mr Hussein," said the immigration officer, and, being a polite man, he added, "Enjoy your stay."

"I'm sure I will," Salim thanked him equally courteously.

Yenko had agreed a good price for the assignment. A cargo of arms for Salim's friends. Crates of Kalashnikov AKM assault rifles, scores of 7.62mm snipers' rifles, dozens of Degtyarev light machine guns, one million rounds of small arms ammunition, 5,000 hand grenades – a treasure trove of an arsenal, to be shipped to the eastern Mediterranean, near Cyprus, where they would be transferred to a tramp steamer for the final stage of their journey. And Yenko had added a personal token of his people's generosity – a money transfer to a Swiss bank in a pseudonym for Salim's exclusive use.

Even if Salim hadn't wanted the mission, he could hardly have refused such rewards.

He didn't make for the green customs control. Instead, he made a point of going through the red channel.

"I've brought some gifts," he explained to the uniformed official, almost apologetically. "A little perfume. For a lady." He flashed his man to man smile.

"Oh, I think that'll be all right," said the customs officer generously, chalking his mark on the case.

Two hours later, he checked into an expensive hotel in Belgravia. The important thing was to avoid his previous haunts. He had to remember not to be seen where he had previously lived, or to frequent restaurants and hotels he had used before he was arrested. It would be stupid to run the risk of being recognised by somebody who remembered him.

On his first evening, Salim took himself out to dinner at the Dorchester grill room. He preferred being on his own at the outset of a job. If, by any chance, somebody was watching him, they would find it a very boring surveillance.

After he'd eaten, he went for a stroll down Park Lane. He was twice propositioned; the first time by a shabby little scrubber, and he rejected her coldly, feeling insulted that a slag like that should approach him. These whores were getting too bold.

But the second girl, near Hyde Park Corner, was something rather more special. She was also evidently successful in her pursuits; the clothes she wore had cost plenty.

"Some other time I would like to very much," he told her, with genuine regret. She gave a delightful smile, he thought.

He had an excellent night's sleep, and after breakfast next morning, he kept the appointed rendez-vous.

Theo had thick, sweet, black Turkish coffee in small cups ready for him – except that Theo called it Greek coffee.

"Are you comfortably settled, Mr Hussein?" he enquired in an unusually respectful tone. Salim's reputation was known to him, and Theo fervently wished for a happy old age.

"Very pleasant," nodded Salim.

"Well, if there is anything while you're in London . . . Please let me know. I am at your disposal."

"Thank you. There is something."

"Please."

"A gun. I need a gun."

Theo didn't conceal his surprise. "I would have imagined . . ."

". . . that I would have one with me? That would hardly have been a good idea, going through airports and customs, would it?"

"No, no, of course not," Theo hastily agreed. He wasn't happy; guns were not in his line. Surely a man like Salim . . . But he left that unsaid.

"I know that I would have no difficulty in acquiring one myself for the right money," added Salim smoothly, "but in a foreign city, like London, I could perhaps make a mistake by going to the wrong source. You understand?"

"My friend, you will have the best."

"Not the best," said Salim, "just a very good one."

"It is as good as done." He eyed Salim warily. "How long will you be staying?"

Salim drained his coffee appreciatively.

"This is very good indeed. You have an excellent blend. Ah yes. How long will I stay? Not long. Only until the job is done."

The name of the man he had come to kill was never mentioned, which showed, thought Salim, what an extremely intelligent man Theo was.

"Yes?" answered Fern warily. "Who is it?"

"Come and get pissed," burped Nick Prosser down the other end of the line. "Hurry up."

He wasn't supposed to ring her at the office. He wasn't even supposed to know her extension.

"What's happened? What's the matter?"

"I told you," he said, his speech slurred. "We're going to get stinking. You and I. Big celebration. Ding dong, the merry bells ring . . ."

"You're drunk." She kept her voice low.

"You haven't seen nothing yet, lady. We got lots to celebrate. I got fired."

"Nick!"

"Damn right. Canned. Chopped. And I've got a great big cheque for £35,000 in my hot little hand."

Mentally, she could see him, swaying in the call booth, grinning inanely, and yet burned up with rage. Waiting to explode. Ready to take the roof off.

"Oh, my God."

"Oh, my God, nothing. I've got them shit scared. They'll do anything to shut me up. They're promising me another £80,000 when I've signed their stinking little piece of paper, promising I'll drop my story."

"Nick," she said urgently, "no more. Not on this line. Please."

He was singing. "What price integrity, what price . . ."

"Nick!" she cried down the receiver.

"All right," he said. "On one condition. You meet me in that pub. In Sloane Square. At six. Otherwise . . ."

"Yes. Yes." Anything to shut him up. "I'll be there. Get yourself a cup of coffee. Sober up. Wait for me. Understand?"

"Yes ma'am. Three bags full. Anything you say, ma'am. See you at six."

And he rang off.

That was the last time she heard his voice.

Prosser was standing at Charing Cross, on the District line platform. The indicator showed that the Inner Circle going west would be the second train into the station.

He was drunk, but Nick Prosser knew how to stay steady on his feet while tight better than most men.

The Hammersmith train came and went and then the indicator changed. Inner Circle next.

There was a distant rumble from the tunnel, and Prosser stepped closer to the edge of the platform. That was his big mistake. As the Inner Circle entered the station, he felt a sharp nudge that was so forceful it pushed him on to the rails, and into the path of the train.

The driver slammed on the emergency brake but too late to prevent the front coach passing over the electrocuted body of Nick Prosser.

He was dead by that time anyway.

Nobody saw what actually happened, it was rush hour, after all. Eye witnesses round about said afterwards that they hadn't noticed anyone particulary amid the thick throng of people on the platform, waiting for the next train.

And the confusion that followed Prosser's fatal accident provided plenty of opportunity for the man who had killed him to get away.

Only one more patient, reflected Wynne, as he went to the corner basin in his surgery and turned on the taps. He felt weary; it had been a busy morning and he'd been up half the previous night waiting for an ambulance to collect a bed-ridden old man who'd suddenly taken a turn for the worse. Perhaps, after lunch, if he was lucky, he'd get a chance to snatch a nap before his afternoon appointments.

He dried his hands, went back to his desk, and pressed the electric buzzer which .signalled to the receptionist in the outer office that he was ready. The names on his note pad were all crossed out, except the last one. He peered at his scrawl. It was a new name. Foreign by the look of it.

After a moment the door opened.

"Sit down, will you," said the doctor. He glanced at the pad again. "I'm sorry, you're Mr . . ." He liked to put his patients at ease, but he couldn't make out this damn name.

"Zarubin." The man started to spell it.

"That's all right," smiled Wynne. "Well, Mr Zarubin, what can I do for you?"

"You can tell me about the Russian," said Zarubin.

The smile faded. "I beg your pardon. What was that you said?"

"I said I'd be very interested to hear about the Russian."

The doctor regarded him for a moment. Then he asked:

"Who are you?"

"Not a patient. I'm sorry doctor, it's not your secretary's fault. But I wanted to see you. Urgently."

"You're American?"

"Correct."

At one time, Wynne trusted his judgment. He made up his mind about people quickly. But after recent events, he wasn't sure any more. Nothing seemed to be what it was.

"Forgive me, but . . . are you from the authorities? Is this official? What is it about?"

Zarubin nodded, like a man who appreciated the reasonable nature of the other fellow's questions.

"Well, I guess the answer is no and again no. Let's just say I'm curious. It seems like a pretty strange story."

"How do you know about it?"

"Doctor, we all got our professional secrets. Can I leave it like that?"

Wynne decided to tread carefully. He still wasn't totally sure of Mr Zarubin.

"You know nobody believes what happened," he said warily.

"Try me."

"The police don't believe it. The Home Office doesn't . . . "

"The Home Office?"

"Yes, a man called Druce came to see me. He more or less said that I'd imagined it all. There's nothing on the record, you see. Nothing to bear it out. Nobody's actually said I made it up, but it's getting that way. Sometimes I start wondering myself." He shook his head sadly. "Can you imagine it, seeing something, and then everybody thinks you're crazy? A doctor at that?"

"Go on."

Wynne frowned. "It's ridiculous, my sitting here, telling you all this. A perfect stranger. But . . . you're the first person who hasn't had that look in his eye when I talk about it."

"What look, doctor?"

He shrugged. "That I need a holiday. That I've been overdoing things."

Zarubin gave him an encouraging smile. "Perhaps you do need a vacation, I wouldn't know. But one thing I can promise you, you're not imagining anything."

"Why are *you* so sure?"

"Because," said Zarubin, "it makes a lot of sense."

Wynne was silent for some seconds, as if he was coming to a decision, and Zarubin didn't rush him.

"Would it also make sense if I told you that I was being followed, that I know I'm being watched?" he asked, at length.

"It would."

"Followed everywhere."

"Yes."

"That my house was broken into and that the only thing that was stolen was a cheap Russian wrist watch which didn't even work?"

Zarubin leaned forward. "How's that?"

"This Russian, he gave me his watch. After I'd reported the whole business to the Home Office, it was stolen. Does that make sense too?"

"Yes, sir."

Wynne regarded him, bewildered.

"Why don't you tell me the whole story. In your own

words," urged Zarubin.

So Wynne told him.

When he had finished Zarubin asked:

"What's your guess, doctor?"

"I believe . . ." began Wynne and paused. He was still uncertain whether Zarubin was taking him seriously. "I think he was some kind of Russian pilot and that he'd escaped from somewhere. He had hurt himself, he had a pretty nasty cut on his hand. I think they were hunting him."

"Who do you think they are?"

The doctor shrugged. "I'm not really sure. The authorities. His guards. How could I know? But I do believe he was trying to get away, to reach London. I think he knew he could get help there. His embassy, maybe, I don't know. Sounds crazy, doesn't it?"

"Not at all."

"He'd got far enough away to consider it safe to get a lift. Then they caught up with him. They didn't want anybody to know." Wynne gave a bitter smile. "I suppose we do things differently. In dictatorships, inconvenient witnesses just disappear. Here, you are simply . . . " He hesitated, searching for the right word.

"Sanitised," suggested Zarubin. "Rendered harmless."

Suddenly the doctor looked at him in a different way.

"My God," he whispered, "you know. You know all about it. You're one of them."

A hint of panic came into his eyes.

"No," Zarubin quickly assured him. "Not the way you think. Believe me."

Wynne stared at him.

"That's really all there is to it," he said at last, in a muted voice. "Not much is it?"

"Enough."

"What do you think has happened to the man?"

"Well . . ." Zarubin sighed. "I guess they got him back. Back where nobody can get at him. Out of sight. Where he doesn't exist."

Wynne relaxed a little. His momentary fear of the man opposite him had passed. Now he was certain that Zarubin *was* different from the others, he had so many questions that

212

needed answering. There was so much he wanted to know. If he could persuade this man to tell him all.

"Mr Zarubin, you're not being absolutely frank, are you? You're not telling me what you really know."

"Such as, doctor?"

"I'm not that much of a fool. Who is this man? Yes, I'm sure he said he was a pilot, but where had he come from? Had he just crashed and, if so, where? Who was he trying to get away from? What's so important about him? Why the lies, the subterfuge? Why this . . . this conspiracy?" Wynne stopped. "I'm sorry. I'm not giving you a chance to get a word in."

He had got quite carried away by having the opportunity of talking to someone who could actually explain all these things that had been puzzling him, eating away at him. Somebody who didn't think him demented.

But he was disappointed. He didn't get his answers.

"Believe me, doctor, I'm doing you a service, a big service if I don't tell you more," Zarubin said. "The less you know, the better for your sake," he added. "I'm sure you understand, after what's already happened to you."

It made Wynne angry. "I'm not a child, damn it. Stop treating me like . . ." He flushed. "I'm sorry, but this whole thing . . . I've just about had enough."

Poor bastard, thought Zarubin. Aloud he said:

"Don't take this the wrong way, doctor."

Wynne was still red faced.

"But perhaps it wouldn't be a bad idea if you took a vacation after all."

The doctor stood up behind his desk, disbelief written all over his face.

"You! You too!"

"Don't get me wrong," said Zarubin. "Not because I don't believe you, you know that. But because I do. I think it might be . . . well, let's say it wouldn't do any harm if you weren't around for a while."

"Why, damn it?"

"Because you've talked to me."

The doctor stared at him incredulously. That's the trouble, reflected Zarubin. People never believe it. How did you make them understand about the invisible empire? The spider's web this man had accidentally got caught up in. The ruthlessness of the people who ran it all. The more you said, the crazier it sounded to them. How could you spell it out to a man who didn't really know what he'd stumbled across that he already knew too much?

"You're threatening me, aren't you?"

"No, doctor," replied Zarubin, a little sadly. "I am not. Truthfully, I'm only trying to give you some helpful advice. You'd really be safer if you went away for a while. Please understand and take my hint. Forget about the whole thing."

The surgery door opened, and Wynne's receptionist stuck her head round.

"Excuse me, doctor," she apologised, "but it's Mrs Bannerman. Her husband's just called to say the baby's started."

Zarubin admired the way Wynne adjusted.

"Yes, of course, tell him I'll be right over."

She closed the door, and Wynne stood up.

"I have to go," he said crisply. Other things had become more important suddenly.

He went to his black bag on the other side of the room, put his stethoscope in it, and checked the contents. Satisfied, he clicked it shut. Zarubin got up.

"If I want to talk to you . . ." He rephrased it. "Where can I get hold of you?"

"Nowhere," Zarubin stated. "Forget you've ever seen me," he went on as he walked to the door. "Forget I've been here. Don't keep my name in your files. Tear up that page of your pad. Forget what we've said. The best thing you can do, doctor, is to give yourself a stiff shot of amnesia. And thanks."

He closed the door and was already out of the building by the time the receptionist reappeared from the back room where she'd changed into her raincoat.

Wynne rushed out of the surgery, clutching his bag.

"I shouldn't be too long," he called out.

"Oh, doctor, about that patient . . ."

But Wynne was out of the door before she'd had a chance to finish the sentence.

She rang the answering service to let them know the doctor was making a house call and that the office would be empty

214

for a while. Then she locked the main door of the surgery and went off to do her shopping.

After Dr Wynne had delivered Mrs Bannerman's fourth child, a seven pound baby boy, he stopped by the Red Lion in the High Street for a sandwich and half a pint of lager. Then he went back to the surgery. His receptionist was still out, and he checked with the answering service to see if there'd been any calls. Thankfully, all had been quiet so he went into his office, closed the door, sat back in his chair, put his feet on the desk and shut his eyes.

A few minutes later he became aware of someone knocking on his door.

"Come in," he called out, thinking it was his receptionist, but a man he'd never seen before walked in.

"I'm sorry," apologised Wynne, hastily getting to his feet. "Surgery hours are . . ."

The man spoke with an effort. "I've got a terrible pain . . . Here," he said, clutching his chest.

Wynne hesitated, then made his decision.

"You'd better sit down," said Wynne, helping him into the chair. "Take your coat off, and unbutton your shirt . . ."

He went to his bag, and took out his stethoscope. When he turned round, the man was still in his jacket, but he was holding a small, snub nosed kind of pistol. There was a soft plop as he fired straight into the doctor's face. Wynne staggered, then collapsed, his eyes glazed.

It wasn't an ordinary gun the stranger was holding and before he'd gone into the surgery, he had swallowed a pill. Now, he took another one; a precaution against inhaling even a wisp of the deadly fumes.

The man left, as unobtrusively as he'd arrived.

When the receptionist returned at 2.45 pm she found the main door unlocked and the answering service disconnected. Obviously the doctor had returned which meant they'd have time to deal with the correspondence before afternoon surgery began at 4 pm. She put away her coat, tidied her hair, gathered up her note book, and knocked on the doctor's door. There was no reply.

"Dr Wynne," called the receptionist, opening his door.

That was when she found his body.

215

He lay on the floor, his blank eyes staring upwards, dead.

The way the local police reconstructed it, Dr Wynne delivered Mrs Bannerman's baby, after which he'd stopped at the Red Lion for lunch. The landlord remembered him leaving at about two twenty and the answering service confirmed receiving his call at two twenty-five.

The attending pathologist's immediate diagnosis was that the cause of death was a heart attack. It was known that the doctor had recently been under some sort of strain. The post mortem which took place the next day only served to confirm that he had died of cardiac arrest.

By then Wynne's blood vessels had relaxed again, so that nothing looked even slightly suspicious. If the autopsy had been performed nearer the time of death, the pathologist might have noticed that the sudden contraction of Wynne's arteries, cutting off the blood supply and so causing the failure of the cardiac system, had been induced.

And it would have taken an expert far beyond the skills of the county pathologist and the local police surgeon to point out that inhalation of prussic acid vapour produces the same symptoms as a heart attack, kills just as swiftly, and leaves absolutely no trace.

It is, of course, an unlikely method of murder and, since as far as anyone knew, Wynne had no enemies nor was there any trace of the patient who had unexpectedly called on him while his receptionist was out shopping, such a possibility was never even considered.

Indeed, since the police were satisfied that Dr Wynne had collapsed and died of natural causes, they made only superficial enquiries. They certainly had no reason to look for any stranger.

It surprised Dr Biffin, his squash partner, that Wynne had suffered from a weak heart. He thought how foolhardy it had been of his friend to exercise so energetically if he had cardiac problems.

But, as the local coroner put it over a glass of port in the Conservative Club, "You know doctors, they're their own worst physicians. Never take care of themselves, always on the go, out and about at all hours, snatch their meals, living on their nerves. Poor old Tom, he should have listened to his

216

friends' advice to take it easy. He'd been under quite a strain, hadn't he?"

He and the Chief Constable decided between them, that since Dr Wynne's death was clearly from natural causes, there was no need to hold an inquest. Heart attacks, unfortunately, were far too common.

It was a shrewd idea to use prussic acid to kill the doctor. After all, although nobody had believed his ridiculous stories about a fugitive Russian, it might just conceivably have aroused some curiosity somewhere if he'd been found murdered. But a heart attack didn't even merit a line in the London papers, although the local weekly gave him a very nice obituary.

Wynne had been a popular local doctor, and the Bannermans' decided to christen their newborn son Thomas in his memory.

They met in Hyde Park, and sauntered slowly across the big open space that led from Marble Arch towards the Serpentine. The choice of location was no accident; here they were in the open, and strangers could be seen from afar. Here no one could follow them without them knowing it.

They didn't kiss, but Zarubin put his arm round her shoulders, and they started walking.

Fern was pale, and it was obvious to him that something had happened, something she didn't want to talk about.

"Well?" she asked, after they'd strolled in silence for some minutes.

"Wynne was the right man," confirmed Zarubin. "He told me everything that happened that night. Thanks."

She nodded. "What will you do now?"

"What has to be done."

"Good."

"It's Prosser, isn't it. That's why you tipped me off," said Zarubin. "After our last time, I thought, well, finish. But now it's different."

She looked straight ahead.

"You know he's dead."

"Sure. I saw it in the paper." He sounded cold, flat. "He had an accident. In the subway." He paused.

"You and he . . . "

"Yes," nodded Fern.

Zarubin shrugged. "Your business."

"Now it's yours."

"Eh?"

"Listen, Andrew, he was on to something. He'd been digging up a story about the past. He was convinced Penkovsky was betrayed at this end, and he believed he'd found the man." She stopped. "The paper told him to drop it. He thought *they'd* got at the owner. But he wouldn't stop. So the accident . . . " She saw his reaction. "You don't believe me, do you?"

He looked up at the sky. "It's going to rain."

"You don't believe a word, do you?" she repeated.

"Let's get a coffee over there," he said.

In the café by the Serpentine, Zarubin didn't speak until they'd been served with their coffee.

"You work for the ministry," he said finally, "and they let you hang out with a guy like Prosser?"

"Maybe they thought there could be a two way traffic. They could use him, through me. It just didn't work out that way."

He lit a cigarette. "Is that why you called me when I first arrived? Because they told you to?"

He wanted her to admit it.

Fern avoided his eyes.

"They thought if we got together," she whispered, her voice trailing off.

". . . they'd have a nice in," finished Zarubin. "That's it, isn't it? Lambert's idea, the whole thing? Find out what I'm really doing."

He didn't sound bitter, just a little weary.

She looked across the little lake, and the rowing boats.

"Well, it didn't work out, did it?" she said.

"But you obeyed orders, lady. I'll say that, you're loyal to the old firm."

Her eyes flashed.

"Don't be so goddamn superior," she snapped. "You're full of shit, you know that? It's my work, and I do as I am told. Just like you. They tell me they're interested in my ex

218

boy friend, and could I see how things stand. Exactly the way you do it, you bastard."

Zarubin pushed away his half full coffee cup. Suddenly it tasted bitter. He wasn't enjoying doing this to her. But he had to press on.

"Now, of course, it doesn't matter. Prosser's death's what's important to you. You believe he was digging around too much, becoming a nuisance, so your own people got rid of him. And now, you've come running to me. Just to get your own back. Is that why you told me what Lambert's been up to?" He shook his head. "Jesus," he said softly, "women shouldn't get involved in this work."

She looked down, and said very quietly, "I thought I'd help you, that's all. I'm glad it's been useful. Shall we leave it at that?"

She bit her lip.

"I'm sorry," he said gently. "You know that, Fern I'm not just saying it." He sighed. "Okay. I believe you. What do you plan to do now?"

"I may quit."

"I don't think they'll let you."

"Why not?"

"Fern," he said. "You *know* why not."

Again she avoided his eyes. "I don't think that'll happen. Anyway, I'll keep in touch."

"You really had something going with him, didn't you?" He sounded sympathetic. "He really meant something to you?"

She nodded, and smiled at him weakly. "The stupid thing is, you're the only one I can turn to."

And just for a moment, he wanted to reach out and hold her. But he didn't.

"Who is the man?" he asked.

"Who do you mean?"

"The man Prosser thought betrayed Penkovsky?"

"Nick didn't tell me. Not right out. But I believe I know. And you do, too."

"Lambert? All those years ago?"

She nodded.

"Okay," said Zarubin, stubbing out his cigarette, "I owe

you. For that. And for Dr Wynne."

Fern shook her head. "Andy . . . You don't owe me a thing. Not as long as you . . ."

"Not as long as I what?"

"Not as long as you do what you came to do."

This time their eyes met.

RAF Thorpehill had once been a war time satellite base for bombers. Now it was an abandoned airfield, overgrown with weeds.

It lay in a remote area, deep in the country, hidden away from prying eyes, it's approaches unmarked by signposts. It was a ghost base, forgotten for forty years, a cluster of deserted buildings, and a long, unused, runway, a phantom relic of long gone war time days.

Eleven miles from the nearest village, and half an hour from the closest motorway, the airfield slumbered on, undisturbed. On a windy day the doors of the empty Nissen huts banged monotonously, but there was no one to hear them.

Barbed wire still surrounded the perimeter, and at what had been the main gate, a weathered wooden sign proclaimed that Thorpehill was "Government Property", as well as "Trespassing Prohibited – By Order".

Yet there were some curious features about the place. The barbed wire was new, its spikes not eroded with rust, and rumour had it that guard dogs patrolled the airfield. Some of the locals thought they had seen lights in the old control tower, but it all remained pub gossip.

Major Ulianov had no idea he was being held in a disused RAF bomber airfield. He'd arrived in darkness, had still been half groggy, and since then he had never seen the place above ground.

In his spacious underground quarters there was plenty of room. They'd given him a comfortable mattress on his bed, and were treating him better than they had in the medieval fortress. The food, too, had vastly improved. Apart from the added luxury of a bathroom, where he was free to shower and bath when he chose, to his surprise they also supplied him with copies of Soviet newspapers. *Izvestia, Trud, Pravda*, five or six days old, true, but what did that matter to a man in his position.

The only hardship was that he could not breathe fresh air, had not seen the sky for days, and therefore never knew if it was day or night. The air he breathed in was filtered; the temperature pleasant, but Ulianov would have given a great deal to feel the wind against his face, or to stand in a field and get drenched by rain. He was a man who loved the country-side. Being stuck in the depths of it without even knowing was a supreme irony.

Nonetheless, Ulianov was in good spirits. He was in good hands, he knew that now. Ever since the note in the cigarette pack. At first he could hardly believe it. He was being held, he had been convinced, by some special agency that had taken over from the military. He believed that these faceless people were going to use special methods to try and break him, and get his secrets out of him.

Then the man in the tweed suit had passed the message telling Ulianov that he was a friend. It was clear that he didn't want the interpreter to know, and that he couldn't say too much, because the place was bugged. But Ulianov remembered his reassuring hand on his shoulder, and the words he'd said in Russian before they'd moved him in here:

"You know you can trust me."

Ulianov had been intrigued by the man's Russian. He spoke it fluently, and at one time he had wondered if he was a fellow Soviet, a man who had infiltrated into the section. But when he'd thought about it, he'd realised he was a foreigner who had learnt the language extremely well. As fluent as he was, he couldn't fool a native Russian.

Ulianov heard the door being unlocked, and, as if he had just thought of the devil, the man entered, alone.

He was carrying a bottle and two glasses, and he smiled like an old friend.

"Are you well?" he asked in Russian, putting the bottle and the glasses on the table. "A little celebration is indicated."

For a moment, Ulianov was suspicious. Had he been mistaken. Was this the enemy after all? Maybe a refined form of interrogator? He had been warned what experts the British were in the more devious kind of brain washing.

"No, my friend," said the man shaking his head, as if he'd

sensed Ulianov's sudden doubt. "Please relax. We can be frank. Here, no one listens."

He poured vodka into the two glasses.

"Don't drink too much," he cautioned, "you will need a clear head."

It was the most reassuring thing he could have said, and Ulianov felt immediately at ease. An enemy would have wanted him to be fuddled; only a friend would warn him to keep his mind sharp.

They clinked glasses, and both drank. Ulianov swallowed hard. It had been so long since he had tasted alcohol.

"Well," said the man, "I know you must have many questions."

"Only one. What is going on?"

"It is quite simple, Major," began the man. "There is an arrangement that intruder pilots on spy missions who are brought down in NATO air space are handed over to the Americans for special interrogation. I have instructions that you are not to be exposed to that."

"Instructions?"

"Instructions," repeated the man.

"I am entitled to know more."

"Instructions from Moscow," said the man in the tweed suit. "You understand?"

"And you? You are . . ."

"Never mind me," stated the man, harshly. "Never mind who I am."

Ulianov shifted uneasily. "What makes me so important?"

The man shrugged. "You know things. Things your superiors do not want them to find out. But that doesn't concern me. Or you."

Ulianov held out his glass. "I'd like some more."

The man only quarter filled his glass. Ulianov drank it in one gulp, his eyes never leaving the man.

"What happens now?" he asked.

"Tell me, Major, do you have any children?"

"Yes." Ulianov was puzzled. "Why?"

"How many?"

"Two."

"Boy or girl?"

"A boy aged seven and a girl of ten." The major frowned. "Why do you ask?"

"I just wondered," replied the man, a little sadly.

He swallowed the rest of his vodka.

"I'm sorry your captivity hasn't been more pleasant," he continued, almost apologetically. "It's been difficult, you understand. Playing a cat and mouse game can be tiresome. But in my position, one has to step softly."

"Of course. You're taking great risks."

The man smiled wanly. "So are you."

"I'm a soldier. It's my job."

"Ah," sighed the man reflectively, "I suppose I am too, in a way. But we don't just do it for pay, do we?"

Ulianov echoed the ideological dogma he'd been taught at the academy. "I do it for the motherland," he declared, solemnly.

"Yes, the motherland," agreed the man, his mind seemingly far away. He roused himself.

"It hasn't been too bad then?" he asked, as if anxious to have any doubt removed. "Under the circumstances?"

Ulianov was slightly bewildered. "No, not under the circumstances. But I do not recommend it as a summer vacation. I find this . . . uncertainty very . . . unpleasant."

"Of course, Major."

He stood up, and almost reluctantly pulled out a .357 Manrhuin magnum.

"I'm sorry, comrade," he said.

Ulianov stared wide eyed at the gun in the man's hand.

"I really am sorry, but this too is for your motherland," he said, firing three times.

The shots reverberated round the room, and left Ulianov sprawled in his chair, the blood spreading across the track suit that had become his uniform; his face a death mask of astonishment.

The man in the tweed suit sighed. He left the room, but returned a few minutes later wearing rubber gloves.

With some effort, he picked up Ulianov's body and carried the dead man along a passage of the subterranean bunker to a bare room with brick walls, illuminated by an unshaded light bulb hanging from the ceiling, in the middle of which stood a forty gallon tank, already filled with liquid.

The man hoisted up Ulianov's body then slowly dropped it into the tank. There was a faint hissing sound as it sank into the sulphuric acid. Within twenty-four hours there would be nothing left of Major Ulianov; no flesh, no hair, no bones.

Then the man in the tweed suit stripped off the rubber gloves, and without a second glance at Ulianov's disintegrating form, he left the room. Although he was in good shape, he was breathing heavily from the exertion; he was unused to such physical effort.

It hadn't been an enjoyable job. He wondered if Central actually realised how unpleasant it was to dissolve a human being in acid.

But he understood the reason. No one knew better than the man in the tweed suit how important it was that Major Ulianov should disappear from the face of the earth.

The coded rapid transmission message took only two seconds to send from the radio room of the Soviet mission in Kensington Palace Gardens to its destination on the outskirts of Moscow. It was an especially speeded up transmission, reducing the despatch to an electronic blur, the sound equivalent of micro dots.

In the Home Counties, it was picked up and recorded by a listening station with the sole task of monitoring certain radio communications between various embassies and Eastern Europe twenty-four hours a day.

Radio monitoring is an art, and the skill lies as much in establishing how messages are sent as in deciphering their content. Station behaviour is given top priority by intelligence analysts, and the volume, speed and timing of transmissions are minutely dissected by both men and machines.

The two second message was carefully appraised by a computer near Cheltenham that had set the British taxpayer back the best part of ten million pounds, and which, in a couple of minutes, could do the work that once would have taken an army of code breakers many weeks.

It managed to slow down the taped transmission, so that the two second signal became a one and a half minute long message. But that was all. It was a special code, and the analysts had only recently become aware of its existence. Transmissions were always limited to very short periods, radioed irregularly, and to no particular schedule. Clearly these messages were so important that the recipients, on the other side of Europe, were on the alert for them continually, instead of just listening out at given periods.

This time again, the eavesdroppers had to give up, and the code remained un-cracked. Even the master computer would need weeks of reprogramming to decipher these complex signals, at which point, of course, the other side would scrap the code, and change over to something new.

In Moscow, the machines decoded the message in three minutes, and the text, in a sealed envelope, was handed to General Maximovich by an armed messenger.

The general read it with satisfaction, and a degree of admiration, which he would be loath to reveal to his subordinates, but in the privacy of his own office, he enjoyed this private thought. They were dedicated people indeed who served the motherland in foreign parts. Admittedly they were secure in the knowledge that everything would be done in Moscow to protect them and even, when finally necessary, to extricate them from the enemy camp. Nevertheless, it took a brave soul to accomplish certain missions. Like this one.

He summoned Yenko, and showed him the message without a word. Maximovich kept his face expressionless, so that Yenko would have to commit himself without knowing how content he was. He liked playing these games; uncertainty was good for the soul, if people like Yenko possessed such a thing.

Yenko read the text, and then handed back the green sheet on which Most Secret messages were always set out.

"Good," he said, simply.

"So far, so far," grunted Maximovich. Never let them get complacent. "The most difficult phase starts now. This is where it could all go wrong."

"It won't."

Maximovich raised his bushy eyebrows. It was not like Yenko to be so smug.

"You seem to have great faith in this operation," he remarked. It was meant as a warning. This was Yenko's brainchild, and he must never forget it. If it aborted, the finger would point . . .

A small red 'ight began to flash on the general's desk, and immediately his manner changed.

"The Chairman."

Konstantin Surov, Chairman of the Committee of State Security, member of the Politburo, heir apparent of the highest in the Kremlin, had many curious habits. One of them was that the second most powerful man in the Soviet Union, the master of the KGB, liked to walk unannounced into the offices of his top executives. When Surov quietly left his office on the third floor, and started prowling the corridors of the building, no one knew exactly his final destination. That was why so many of them had discreetly installed a signal, which a trusted aide in the outer office would hastily flash to warn his boss that *he* was about to appear.

The general and Yenko were already on their feet when Surov entered.

"Am I disturbing you?" he asked mildly, blinking short-sightedly round the room.

Surov's appearance and manner made it hard to believe that he ran the world's biggest army of spies, destroyed the Soviet Union's enemies by the score, and masterminded intelligence operations that stretched from Los Angeles to the Yorkshire moors, from Poland to Tokyo, from Cairo to Buenos Aires. Together with the thick pebble glasses, a high domed forehead with its receding hairline, and his apparent sleepy look, he gave the impression more of an absentminded professor much in need of a good night's rest. His mildness was a famous trade mark; he had never been known to raise his voice.

"Chairman, an honour," breathed Maximovich. He indicated Yenko. "Major Yenko. Special Operations."

"Comrades, please sit down." Surov smiled nervously. "No ceremony, I beg you."

He sat down diffidently, just as he had done in the office of an official who he'd ordered to be executed by a firing squad the same evening.

"I hear that you have some good news," began Surov gently. "About 'Borzoi'."

Maximovich swallowed hard. Borzoi was the code name

of the operation. The signal from London had come straight to him. No one else could have seen it. It was so highly classified that there could be only one copy. And yet Surov already knew all about it. The building with its millions of secrets had no secrets from him.

"Yes, Chairman, it is all going according to plan. We have just heard from England."

Surov peered at him. "I am pleased. Excellent work. Only . . ."

His face clouded a little. Even Yenko tensed.

"Only I am sad about Major Ulianov," went on Surov. "I know it had to be this way, but I mourn every patriotic son of the motherland who has to give his life for his country." He sniffed. "I am told he was a good soldier. Perhaps, one day, his widow could receive a token of his bravery."

"She would be very proud, comrade Chairman."

"You think so, General? Good. And perhaps we can find a place one day for his son at the Frunze academy." He paused, then stood up. "Anyway, I mustn't interfere with your important duties." He blinked at Yenko. "You must be very busy, Major Yenko. Oh, by the way . . ."

Here it comes, thought Yenko. Maximovich was sweating slightly.

"Unofficially, and quite informally, I want you to know that the Central Committee is taking a close interest in this affair. I am sure that will encourage you."

The threat was implicit.

"It is felt that if this daring operation succeeds, it will give us a major advantage over the other side. I thought that would also encourage you, comrades."

In its own way, it was an up to date version of the kind of pep talks Surov had given to the fighting troops in the Great Patriotic War, when he'd been a top political commissar in the Red Army.

Maximovich drew himself up in parade style.

"Assure the Committee that we will not disappoint them," he intoned. "We thank you for the confidence that has been entrusted to us. Is that not so, comrade Yenko?"

"Of course," concurred Yenko. Sometimes he became so weary of these pantomimes. His war was fought in a different way.

"I leave it all in the hands of the experts," said Surov, the pebble lenses peering at both of them. "You have our complete trust."

He gave them a friendly smile, and then closed the door behind him quietly.

The atmosphere relaxed almost visibly. Maximovich sat down behind his desk, once more subservient to no man, his authority unchallenged.

"A great man, Konstantin Fedor," he commented familiarly, as if Surov was a close intimate. "A true leader. A great professional."

You forget, my General, thought Yenko, that I saw you, sweating with apprehension, hanging on to his every word like a rabbit watches a cobra, so save us the charade. You're not impressing anyone. He's not here to hear you, and since your office isn't bugged, nobody will record it.

But aloud, he agreed. "Yes, comrade General."

"Well," said Maximovich, "you heard him. Let's not waste time. Is there anything you want to add?"

"Yes. The decoration for Major Ulianov. There is no question of such an award being made at the present time, I trust? A posthumous medal would . . ."

". . . give the whole game away, I know, I know," interrupted the general, irritated. "What do you take me for? You weren't listening, Yenko. The Chairman talked about a medal 'one day'. 'One day', and who knows when that could be . . ."

He shrugged.

"Anyway, I know your peculiar views. You do not really believe in medals for our kind of work, do you?"

Yenko thought of the six rows of medal ribbons the general had on his uniform. He needed to be tactful.

"Perhaps not for field agents," he replied mildly. "They can be a liability. The enemy finds out about them. And I hope you understand, General, that I show no disrespect for the late Major Ulianov when I suggest that, should any medals be awarded one day, there is one man who is the prime candidate."

The general was reaching for his cigar box. His hand froze in mid air.

"Oh? Who is that?"

"The man who killed him," said Yenko.

By the time the 747 from Heathrow touched down at Dulles International Airport, Washington DC, Nancy Flexner's intake of alcohol would have left most people in an intoxicated haze. But she was a woman who could carry her liquor well, and the driver who had been sent to meet her did not suspect that his passenger had made full use of the first class free drink facilities in the plane's lounge.

They had assured her they would take care of everything and make the necessary arrangements, so after she'd cleared customs she followed the polite young man, who did not wear a chauffeur's uniform, out to the motor pool's unmarked sedan. He helped the porter stow Nancy's baggage, then asked her courteously:

"Shall I take you straight to the hotel, ma'am?"

"Which hotel?" she wanted to know.

"The Hilton, ma'am."

She knew why they had picked it. It was vast, and very anonymous. Twelve hundred guest rooms, surrounded by five acres of grounds. It was the kind of place the organisation liked; one merged into it.

For much of the twenty-seven mile drive to Connecticut Avenue, she sat in the back of the car, her eyes shut. She was not asleep. The driver occasionally glanced at her in his mirror, but not a word was said during the journey.

She was shown to a suite on the tenth floor, given time to unpack, have a bath, and change, then the phone rang. When she answered and heard who it was she said:

"Come on up."

"You must be very tired after the flight," said John Dichter considerately when she opened the door. "I won't keep you long. We'll fix up to meet for a proper chat later."

"No," Nancy assured him. "I'm fine. What would you like to drink?"

He asked for coffee, and she ordered a scotch for herself.

"It's very kind of you to come here," she said. "I appreciate it."

He glanced round the suite.

"Are you sure you're comfortable? If there is anything you want, you know it's yours."

She nodded.

"You're going to try and have a vacation, I understand?"

"Yes," said Nancy. "Spend a few weeks, adjusting. That's what it's called isn't it? Adjusting."

"I don't have to tell you how sad we are about what . . . happened." Dichter spoke gently. "Cy was . . . well, he was one of us. We couldn't believe it."

"Yes," she said flatly.

"And it must have been a terrible shock for you. You're being very brave."

"So people keep telling me."

"I heard from the embassy how well you're taking it. Everybody admires you."

"Do they?"

He regarded her thoughtfully.

"Anything the matter, Nancy?"

"Yes. I want to know who killed Cy."

"Officially . . ."

"Damn officially," she snapped. "You know and I know it was a fake. His gun, sure. The 'Nam gun. But somebody else pulled the trigger."

"It's being investigated, I promise you."

"The way Cy was investigated? Great."

"You're too close to things," Dichter said soothingly. "You're still under pressure. But let me tell you this. When a station chief dies, it doesn't just get filed. Don't worry. We'll keep digging . . ."

She didn't even conceal her disbelief.

"I told Zarubin," she said.

"Zarubin?"

"Your man in London."

"Who told you he was that?" asked Dichter.

"What else can he be?"

"Did Cy tell you?"

"Cy introduced us."

He pursed his lips. "And what did you say to Zarubin?"

"That my husband was murdered. And that I wanted him to do something about it. I told him to get the killer."

230

Dichter put down his coffee cup. "Why Zarubin?"

She reached over, and lit a cigarette, exhaling a cloud of smoke, almost insolently.

"Because he's your executioner, isn't he? That's why you sent him to London. To terminate."

"Cyrus told you that, too?" asked Dichter softly.

"He didn't need to." Her smile had a trace of contempt. "You forget how long I've been a company wife."

"Ah. Of course." He frowned. "Did you know what was going on? Did Cy tell you what he was doing?"

"I know he was looking for a traitor. And that he no longer trusted some of his British . . . colleagues."

She made the word "colleagues" sound like a sneer.

"Did he say who specifically?"

Nancy studied her cigarette. Then she said:

"Is this a debriefing? A duty call on a grieving widow? A social visit? Or an interrogation?"

"I'm sorry, Nancy. How very thoughtless of me, when you've only just got here. But maybe I can assure you that Cy's death won't be forgotten when I tell you a new guy is taking over in London."

"So?"

"The new station chief."

"And who's that?"

"Me."

She sat up.

"Yes," smiled the grey man, "I'm the new station chief."

"But the section . . ."

"We've got trouble in London. Big trouble. Things have got screwed up. Somebody's got to sort them out." He finished his coffee. "So you see, it *will* be investigated."

She wouldn't stay a widow long, he thought to himself. Even after flying half the day across the Atlantic, she managed to look sensuous. When her lips parted, and her eyes flared up, there was something electric about her.

If she noticed the way he was studying her, she ignored it. She did not even pull down her skirt which had slipped just a little over her knee.

Dichter stood up.

"Why don't we have lunch tomorrow? When you've had a

good night's rest and got over the jet lag? Say twelve noon. I'll pick you up here. Then we can have a really good long talk."

She shrugged.

"Fine," said Dichter. "I look forward to it. And you can tell me all about London."

After he had gone, she switched on the TV, but she didn't take in what was happening on the screen. She sat for a long time, staring into space.

Then she reached her decision. No more long talks with Dichter. No more intrigues, conspiracies, lies. She had given too much of herself to that.

She knew them. Whatever Dichter said, Cy's death would end up as unfinished business. So, she was going to put the past behind her and start living for herself.

And when at noon the next day John Dichter arrived to take her out to lunch, the hotel reception desk advised him that Mrs Nancy Flexner had already checked out and had left no forwarding address.

Fern had been home for about ten minutes before she chanced to go into the bedroom.

Immediately she opened the door she saw him reflected in her dressing table mirror. He was sitting right behind her, and she let out a strangled gasp, then turned.

The man got up, and stood in front of her.

Only then did she notice he was holding a gun in his right hand.

"Don't scream, please," instructed Salim very pleasantly. "Why don't you sit over there, on the bed?" he suggested, nonchalantly gesturing with the gun.

She could feel herself panicking, and she knew that was the worst thing she could do. Reason told her that she needed to be cool, not to show fear, to keep control of herself. But the other half of her mind, the part that made the decisions and issued the instructions, knew she wasn't hiding the terror she felt. She had to get a grip on herself; ridiculously, she remembered something she had been told as a child, that animal tamers never let a beast know how scared they feel. They never allowed a wild animal to sense their fear.

"I said, sit down, Miss Norman."

He knew her name, so he wasn't somebody who had just broken in, and whom she'd surprised. He had been waiting for her.

Falteringly, she stepped back, and sat down on the edge of the double bed.

"What do you want?" she asked, her voice hardly above a whisper. She hated herself for betraying her panic. She wished she'd spoken loudly, firmly.

Salim pulled the chair over, and sat down opposite her, close enough for her to be aware of his aromatic aftershave.

"I must apologise for introducing myself like this. I can see it's a shock, but circumstances . . ."

Fern's eyes went over to the telephone by the bed.

"That's something else I'm afraid I must apologise for," went on Salim softly. "I'm afraid I cut the wire. You are temporarily disconnected."

She clenched her hands to stop herself trembling. Maybe the pain of her fingernails digging into the palms of her hands would stop it.

"Who are you?"

That was better. Her voice sounded stronger.

"I am . . . a friend of a friend of yours."

"A friend!" she repeated, incredulously.

"As a matter of fact, that's why I'm here. I'm trying to get hold of him."

Gradually, her fear was replaced by a burning anger, and it was a welcome, warming feeling. How dare this bastard . . .

"I don't know what you're talking about."

Salim flashed his beautiful white teeth. "You will. All I want to know is where I can find Mr Zarubin. I wouldn't have troubled you, but he doesn't seem to be using his flat. You've been seeing him, haven't you, so you can tell me where he is, I'm sure."

She tried to recall if Zarubin had ever mentioned an Arab. Had he ever been involved with one? But, as far as she remembered, he had never said anything.

"Well?" prompted Salim. "Any suggestions, Miss Norman?"

"You've made a mistake. I've never heard of this . . . Mr Zarubin."

Salim stretched his legs languidly. He was toying with the gun.

"One thing you should know about me," he murmured finally. "I never make mistakes. You're a very intelligent woman, and I'm sure you want to be rid of me. I promise you I am in a hurry, so why don't we accommodate each other?"

In her mind, she was trying to link the pieces. If only she could find the connection, maybe she would know how to . . .

"You're also a very attractive lady, you know that," said Salim unexpectedly. "I admire Mr Zarubin's excellent taste. He is a man after my heart."

It was said quite unemotionally. Fern knew what it was like to be looked at by men who stripped her with their eyes, and made no secret of wanting her body. But Salim was quite dispassionate. He spoke like a collector who admired a piece of art in a gallery, but knew it could never belong to him.

Time to pull a bluff, decided Fern.

"I've told you, I don't know a Mr Zarubin so I think you'd better leave now, while you can. I've invited some friends over for a party, and they'll be arriving soon. It's going to be pretty awkward for you when they come, isn't it?"

Salim didn't even pretend to believe her.

"It's a great pity," he sighed. "I thought we could be civilised."

He stood up and looked round the room. "Take your clothes off."

She gaped at him.

"Please," he insisted, pointing with the pistol.

Her expression reflected her thoughts: you're crazy.

"Hurry."

She could not believe this was happening.

"Miss Norman, don't forget I have a gun," Salim reminded her. "No surprises."

She stood, her heart thumping.

"I am waiting," said the hateful, silky voice.

This was insane. She must be dreaming, but she'd better humour this madman. Slowly, she began unbuttoning her blouse.

"I will ask you once more. How can I find Zarubin? How would you get in touch with him? Have you made any arrangements to meet with him?"

"Go to hell!" she cried.

He nodded. This time the gun pointed at her.

"Is that the bathroom?"

"Yes."

He indicated with his gun for her to lead the way. She switched on the light.

"Run the bath," he instructed.

She put the plug in and turned on the taps.

"Not too hot, not too cold," said Salim. "Just the way you like it."

While the water ran, he ordered her back into the bedroom.

"Once again. Tell me what I want to know."

"I don't know anything." She was surprised at her own defiance.

He held the gun straight. "Strip," he ordered.

She stared at him uncomprehending.

"Take your clothes off."

"No."

The motion with the gun spoke for itself.

She was very pale. But she took off her blouse, then unzipped her skirt, and stepped out of it. She stood in front of him dressed only in her slip and tights, a flush on her white cheeks.

"This gives me no particular pleasure," said Salim. "I adore beautiful women, and their bodies are a supreme delight, but I like women to undress themselves for me because they want to. Now, turn off the bath."

He followed her into the bathroom, the gun pointing at her back.

She turned off the taps.

"Now what?" she asked.

"Tell me about Zarubin and we can end this."

His tone was patient, like a teacher explaining a point to a rather dim pupil.

"You've got to believe me, I don't . . ."

"We respect one another too much to lie," Salim cut in.

"Get into the bath."

Now she was terrified. His cold, detatched manner had its own horror. He eyed her body not like a man looking at a desirable woman, but a surgeon about to cut open a corpse.

"Stay in the bath," said Salim. "If you try to get out, I will shoot you."

He stood watching her while she lay in the warm water for what seemed like hours, stiff with panic. They didn't speak, but his eyes never left her. She couldn't begin to imagine what this maniac had in mind – not even when he undid his silk cravat. All she could do was stare fixedly at him, as if mesmerised by the gold medallion hanging from a short, fine chain round his neck.

"Now get out," he ordered.

She stepped out of the tub her wet underwear pasted to her body, and automatically reached for her towelling robe.

"No, don't dry yourself," he said, the gun close to her spine. "Go into the bedroom."

He's a lunatic, she kept telling herself. Humour him, for God's sake. But she wasn't convinced about his madness. He was too organised, too precise, too methodical. This was the first time she realised he was going to kill her.

She stood on the bedroom carpet, the water dripping from her.

"Put your hands behind your back," he commanded, then she felt him tying her wrists with his cravat.

"Lie down," he instructed, the muzzle of the gun propelling her on to the bed.

She lay down, her wet body soaking the cotton counterpane over the bed.

Salim had not been idle while he waited for Fern to return. He had thoroughly searched the place. Then he'd done something unusual: he'd isolated and expertly adjusted the main fuse box's power supply to the bedroom socket.

He walked round the other side of the bed and for the first time she noticed two electric flexes on the floor, the insulation stripped back leaving six naked wires.

He switched on the socket, put his gun on the dressing table, and now he came towards her, the two live cables in his hands. He held them carefully, so that his fingers were

236

nowhere near the exposed wires protruding from each end, and stood, looking down at her on the bed.

"Zarubin," he insisted. "I want to know."

Fern could hardly breathe she was so frightened, her ashen face conveying her raw terror. Her eyes followed the flexes in his hands to where they were connected to the wall socket.

Salim waited a moment. Desperately, she tried to kick out at him. He laughed.

"I'm afraid this is going to be painful," he smiled. "So, why don't you tell me. Where is Zarubin?"

"I don't know! I don't know!" she cried.

Then, like a snake suddenly striking, he touched the damp soles of her feet with the live wires. Her tights melted, and although the shock that shot through her lasted only a second, she screamed.

"You see," he pointed out reproachfully. "Is it worth going through this for him?"

Sobbing, she turned her face away, and an acrid smell of burning hung in the air.

"Please, Miss Norman, tell me where he is. Let's end this."

But deep in her heart, Fern knew, even if she told him, he would kill her. He couldn't afford to let her survive. He was too calculating a murderer to run the risk of leaving alive someone who could identify him. She just prayed that when Zarubin caught up with this sadistic monster, he'd kill him as slowly and as painfully as he was killing her.

Salim sighed, and positioned the cables a hair's breadth from her hips. The exposed wires sizzled as they touched the wet petticoat, and she screamed again, her legs jerking uncontrollably. The force of the electricity passing through her body left her feeling as if she'd been kicked by a stampeding horse.

He bent over her. "Nothing is worth this," Salim whispered.

Fern's eyes remained closed, and slowly Salim snaked the wires towards her breasts.

"Zarubin. Zarubin," he persisted, but she didn't reply.

He touched her breasts with the bare wires. She groaned as the voltage virtually lifted her entire body off the bed, and the pungent smell of burning once again filled the room.

Salim switched off the wall socket, then he went over, and felt Fern's pulse.

"Pity," he murmured in Arabic, and his regret was genuine. Killing such an attractive woman left one with a feeling of terrible waste. But, if what Salim had been told was correct, there was one good thing about her death. Zarubin would be sure to get the message when she was found, and that at least, he reflected, would make the business a little more worthwhile.

He folded the coverlet across Fern's body, so that she lay as if asleep in a cocoon.

Before he left, he searched Fern's handbag. He found her address book which he quickly leafed through. It didn't tell him very much, but he took it with him anyway. But there was something else rather more interesting: a folded photocopy of part of a government Ordnance Survey map. It was only a small section and it covered a part of East Anglia. Someone had drawn a blue pencil circle round an area of land called Thorpehill, which, according to the map, was a disused RAF airfield.

Salim smiled to himself. He had an idea that this abandoned air base might be a convenient place for Andrew Zarubin to meet his death.

The plastic curtain rustled as Zarubin pushed it aside, and entered the porn shop. One obstinate strand attached itself to him, and he brushed it away. The spotty faced greasy haired young man behind the counter didn't even glance up. Customers who came to browse were left in peace. Only certain items could be leafed through anyway, the rest were carefully sealed. If they wanted to buy, they handed the item to the salesman, paid, and left. The price was always marked, and most of the time not a word was exchanged.

The shop was lined with shelves containing colourful arrays of Theo's "soft" publications. These were the magazines which, encased in cellophane, had stood the test of court appearances, and usually escaped conviction.

Zarubin moved over to the counter. The man looked up from the racing form he'd been studying, and glanced disinterestedly at him through his National Health glasses.

"Stronger stuff in the back," he muttered, going back to his horses. Gently, Zarubin pulled the paper away.

"Hey!" exclaimed the youth, getting off his stool. "What's the fucking idea?"

"Theo," said Zarubin. "Where's Theo?"

Spotty face regarded him a little anxiously. He didn't sound like a cop, but he could detect aggro.

"Who wants to know?" he demanded.

Zarubin crushed the racing sheet into a ball, and tossed it on the floor.

"The name's Grange, son."

"Never heard of you, mister."

Zarubin nodded.

"Let's understand each other. You look scared, and I'm kind of edgy. I want to see Theo, and I've got tired of looking for him."

"You tried our other branch in Great Windmill Street, or the shop in Earl's Court?" asked spotty face hopefully. Theo had emporiums all over.

"And Covent Garden, and Hammersmith, and he isn't at any of them."

The hired help smiled weakly. "Well, then he isn't around."

Theo paid him £200 a week to "mind the shop". In return, he was at the receiving end. If Theo's connections let him down, and a shop was raided, he got arrested, and took the can in court. If some ambitious rival merchant wanted to extend his franchise, and smashed up the establishment, he got smashed up too. In return, he could give himself the title of manager, although, in fact, he was nothing more than a minder.

Zarubin stepped behind the counter. He took the spectacles off the minder's nose, broke them in two, and put both halves on the counter.

"What do they call you?" he enquired.

The minder was becoming very nervous. It took an effort to get his name out. "Len," he stuttered.

"Well, Len, it's your nose next, and your jaw after that."

"All right," nodded Len readily. He glanced round the shop as if to make sure that they were alone. "Theo's gone."

"Where?"

"Abroad. For a holiday, I guess." Len licked his dry lips. "Honest. I'm looking after the shop while he's away."

"And who are you?"

"The manager. Each shop has a manager. We take care of things. Ziggy sort of keeps an eye on all of us."

"I bet."

He wasn't quite as young as Zarubin had first thought, now he looked at Len more closely. He reminded him of a pop singer who, at forty, masquerades as its teenage alter ego. It worked, as long as the camera didn't get too close.

"Where's Theo now?" he asked.

"Don't know. Cyprus, I think. Something happened. No idea what. At least, that's the buzz. You know how it is. Nobody knows for sure."

He was so frightened of Zarubin, he'd have told him anything he wanted to know, and he babbled away, all the while eyeing him like a terrified rabbit facing a stoat.

"When do you expect him back?" Zarubin said.

It was a question that didn't really need a reply. He knew that Theo only looked after one person, and that was Theo. Clearly, his little empire was crumbling.

"I don't know," shrugged Len. "Who the hell would bother telling me?"

"Sorry about the glasses," apologised Zarubin, smiling coldly. He sauntered out of the shop.

He had turned into Wardour Street when the unmarked police car pulled up alongside him.

Detective Sergeant Infield got out. "Mr Zarubin?" he enquired, remarkably courteously.

"Yes."

"I wonder if you could spare the time to come to Westminster mortuary with us," said Infield. "Mr Lambert asked us to find you."

That was when he found out about Fern.

Zarubin stared down at her. There was no make-up on her face, and she looked younger, more vulnerable. Her eyes were closed. They hid the torments of her final moments.

He stood stunned. The fury would come later. Now, he felt a sorrow he did not know could exist. It was almost a dull, physical pain.

The man in the white coat slid the container back into the freezer, and Fern disappeared from view for the last time.

"This way, please," he said, and led Zarubin out of the mortuary chamber.

Lambert was waiting in the corridor.

"I'm sorry," he mumbled. "I know it must be a shock."

He was trying to be gentle, sympathetic, and it didn't suit him.

"Why don't we sit down for a moment," he suggested, indicating the bench a little way along the corridor.

Zarubin would have liked to be alone. The numbness was wearing off. Like the shock after a bullet wound, the pain was taking over. She was dead. Fern was dead. It was all over.

"I thought you ought to know. No," he said, correcting himself. "I thought you should know. So I asked the police . . ."

He kept his voice low, confidential, as if he was afraid his words would echo in the shabby corridor of the mortuary.

"Why me?"

"I hope I haven't embarrassed you," said Lambert. "It's no secret, the relationship you two had."

"That was long ago."

Lambert's smile was the model of understanding.

"Of course, but you were still good friends. In fact, I believe the night before last . . ."

He left the sentence uncompleted.

"What about the night before last?"

"I don't want you to misunderstand me," added Lambert, hurriedly. But he had no need to go on. He'd got his point over; he knew that Zarubin had been with her.

"Please don't think that we were snooping. It's just that when something like this happens, every little detail . . . We've had to check things. Security and all that."

Zarubin kept seeing her pale, unmarked, face. It was the face of the young girl she had once been, before even he had known her.

"How did she die, Stuart?"

"She was electrocuted."

"And it was an accident, of course," said Zarubin, mockingly.

"No, of course not. I'm afraid it was no accident."

Such delicacy, thought Zarubin, bitterly. Surely it couldn't be that this prince of deceit considered it insensitive to use the word murder.

"Who did it? Who killed her?"

The man in the white coat and a colleague appeared, pushing a trolley. On it, covered by a white sheet, lay a cadaver, its naked feet sticking out one end, a tag attached to one big toe.

"They're kept busy here," Lambert remarked as they wheeled the trolley into the refrigeration chamber. He turned back to Zarubin.

"We think an Arab."

"What?"

"We're taking the neighbourhood apart. Special Branch is interviewing the whole street, I believe. Two people reported seeing an Arab leave."

"An Arab," repeated Zarubin.

"Yes. Somebody got a good look at him. They said he was smartly dressed and had a gold thing round his neck. The computer's come up trumps," continued Lambert. "You know who we think it might be? Your old cell mate, Salim. Remember him?"

Now isn't that neat, mused Zarubin. And how very convenient. Not only did they have a witness but one who recalled the necklace. Fortuitously, they'd even been able to have their suspicions confirmed by the computer.

"Salim got deported," said Zarubin.

Lambert shrugged. "Sometimes, they sneak back in, and Salim's a slippery customer. It solves one problem, of course. At least we won't have to look for a motive. He's a contract man, isn't he?"

Zarubin remembered the walk in the park, when Fern had told him that Nick Prosser's death had been no accident. That was why she'd started telling him things. Later, he'd gone home with her, and she had told him more. Now she had paid the price.

"No, Andrew," went on Lambert, as if he'd read

242

Zarubin's thoughts. "He wasn't working for us. Anyway, I think he was looking for you. I believe that's why he went to see her. I think he was trying to find out how to get at you, but I don't think she will have told him. She was quite a girl, you know."

Zarubin wanted to hit him. He sounded like Judas paying tribute to Christ. It was as tasteless as Philby praising Churchill.

"Maybe," said Lambert, "you ought to get out of the country. That might be safest all the way round."

And you know, you bastard, that that's the best way to keep me here, thought Zarubin.

He made a pretence of considering it. Then he said:

"I don't know." He glanced down the corridor. "I guess they've always got room for one more here, haven't they?"

Lambert smiled coldly.

"Of course." He nodded. "There's never a shortage of coffins."

He offered Zarubin a ride, and dropped him in Knightsbridge.

Zarubin walked to the north side of the Serpentine and found the tree by the railings where he had last sat with Fern. An empty deckchair was already there, and Zarubin dragged another one over, and placed it beside it, so that they were arranged as they had been the last time, side by side, facing the water.

Suddenly, everything that reminded him of Fern was very precious. Now that she was dead, she seemed much more important to him. It was like that poem. The one about each man killing the thing he loved. Dimly, it came back to him:

> Like two doomed ships that pass in storm
> We had crossed each other's way:
> But we made no sign, we said no word,
> We had no word to say.

Then he glanced at the empty deckchair beside him, the one on the right that she had occupied on this spot, and reality took over. It was vacant and it would remain vacant.

He stared across the water to the lido. It was empty, and

there were few people in the park. He didn't see any of them. His mind was on something else.

Death to Zarubin was not something to get sentimental about. It happened like a power failure. Or it was caused by experts. But, for the first time, he decided there were occasions when death had to be avenged and Fern's murder necessitated an appointment with Salim.

He looked at his watch, and sighed. Time to get on with the present, he reminded himself, and he walked out of the park.

In the cluster of US bases around Bury St Edmund's and Ipswich, Newmarket and Huntingdon, the 807th stayed anonymous and unnoticed, an unpublicised unit occupying an enclave on one of the big installations, keeping its activities to itself.

Colonel Fraser's outfit never asked questions. Its nomenclature was as vague as its mission in life, and 807th Tactical Special Support Squadron gave nothing away. Even the squadron crest, a wasp sporting a silk opera hat at a rakish angle, was hardly informative.

The squadron's operations area was shielded from prying eyes by a tall fence, but those who had access to the flight line were privileged indeed. Strange aircraft, shaped more like missiles than planes, with designations like QT-2, X-36 and YO-3 came in occasionally, and disappeared again. One airman swore that he had seen a MIG 27 touch down, except that the pilot who emerged from the cockpit was a Yank; in the morning the plane had gone.

One remarkable feature of the 807th was that its airmen never misbehaved. Nobody went AWOL, got picked up for speeding, or sold Class VI liquor on the black market. The explanation was simple; you didn't stay in the outfit if you got into trouble.

Spooks were not unfamiliar to Fraser and his men. That was what the special support was for, intelligence operations, curious flights in foreign skies, missions whose flight plans were kept in safes, activities which were never discussed in the officers' club afterwards.

The spooks came and went. Silent men who arrived in

station wagons, usually in civilian clothes, who'd go into a huddle with the commander, and depart again, as quietly as they had come.

Zarubin stood at the window of the colonel's office, staring across the base, feeling distinctly uncomfortable.

"Mr Dichter's ETA is sixteen-o-two," announced Colonel Fraser, checking his watch.

It would be, thought Zarubin. Not sixteen hundred. No, it had to be precisely to the minute. 807th was that sort of outfit, and Fraser that kind of CO. He pitied the executive officer who was thirty seconds late for morning conference. But then, if he was thirty seconds late, he wouldn't be the bird man's exec.

"He's landed at Mildenhall, and they're sending him over by chopper," added the colonel.

You make him sound like a package, reflected Zarubin. One spook chief, by special delivery. Aloud he said, conversationally:

"The U2 used to fly from this place, didn't it?"

"Sir?"

Oh, Christ, the military. He felt like grabbing the colonel by his crisply pressed blouse, and shaking him.

He was going to add, "And now the Blackbird operates from here."

But the colonel was staring out of the window at a dot in the sky. The dot grew bigger, as the helicopter hovered, then put down by the command building.

"There he is," observed the colonel. He glanced at his watch and confirmed with satisfaction, "sixteen-o-two."

Zarubin watched the grey man walk towards the building. He had a raincoat over his arm, and was carrying a briefcase. An officer offered to take his things, but Dichter declined.

"He's coming to clean things up," Crawford had remarked, when he'd informed Zarubin of Dichter's imminent arrival.

Whatever Zarubin had thought, he'd kept to himself.

"Welcome to the 807th," the colonel greeted Dichter as he entered the office. "I was going to meet you out there . . ."

"I didn't want a reception committee."

"No, sir."

"How are you, Andy?" Dichter enquired, with the thin smile Zarubin knew so well.

"Surviving," he replied.

"If you gentlemen would like some refreshment . . ." began the colonel.

"We'd like to talk," said Dichter. "In private. If there's any place that's convenient."

These spooks are all alike, the colonel decided. They don't want anybody around. Unsociable bastards.

"Well, how about right here? Would this suit you?" he offered, waving an expansive hand round his office.

"That's very kind, Colonel. We shan't be long."

"We're at your disposal, Mr Dichter."

He shut the door.

Dichter stretched himself. "After being cooped up all the way across the Atlantic, you don't mind if I stand, do you?"

Zarubin shook his head.

Dichter gave him a long, searching look.

"You look pooped, Andy."

"I'm okay."

"We haven't got much time," announced Dichter, pacing up and down. "We need that Russian."

"Tell me. Just what's so important about this fucking airman?" asked Zarubin.

Dichter blinked.

"What do you mean?"

"What I say. What's so goddamn mighty important about one lost Russian ferret?"

"You don't understand?"

"No."

Dichter took a deep breath. "Okay, the guy was something special. He wasn't just testing NATO's electronics. He was simulating a bomb run, for all we know . . ."

"But John, it happens. Simulated bomb runs are the name of the game. It's nothing new."

Dichter stopped pacing for a moment.

"Not like this one, and we can't take chances. Not when they start penetrating."

Zarubin was getting restless.

"Hell, I know all that."

"No, you don't," Dichter cut in, impatiently. "They're using their apparat in British security to prevent this guy being handed over to us. They've gone to all these lengths to stop us debriefing him. They're even risking their top people, so he's got to be mighty important. More than that even. Vital."

"What about Lambert? You know he's Moscow's man."

"We'll deal with Lambert, don't worry."

You mean you're going to ask me to deal with Lambert, thought Zarubin, lighting a cigarette.

"Our priority is to lift the Russian. Washington's orders. You've got to get him out."

Why me, wondered Zarubin. Why was I picked to do this?

"It's all been fixed with the Air Force," Dichter was saying. "You heist the guy, get him to Mildenhall, the Air Force flies him straight out to the States, and he's in Nevada in twelve hours. Then we can get to work on him."

"Just like that."

Dichter stood in front of him, smiling coldly. "Just like that," he repeated, snapping his fingers.

He stepped closer. "If they're so desperate to keep us away from him, he's the jackpot."

He began walking around again.

"You know where they are keeping him, don't you?"

"No," replied Zarubin.

Dichter studied one of the colonel's pictures on the wall. It was a print of a flight of wartime P-47s. "I thought you might."

"You tell me."

"It's a place called Thorpehill. An abandoned RAF airfield. Hasn't been used since World War Two. Ever heard of it?"

Zarubin tensed.

"One question," he said.

"Yeah?"

"How do you know?"

"Know what?"

"About Thorpehill?"

"Forget what I'm going to tell you. Fort Meade intercepted a message to Central. They cracked the code they're using."

"A message from where?"

"London. Borzoi."

"Who the hell is Borzoi?"

"That," declared Dichter with a triumphant smile, "is the name of the whole bloody operation."

"What happens if I fuck it up?"

"We send somebody else," replied Dichter coolly. He chuckled softly. "Not that you will, Andy. This job is tailored for you."

And that, reflected Zarubin, was probably the truest thing that John Dichter had ever said.

The gym, in the basement of the ministry, was not the place where Yenko would have chosen to discuss the overnight report from London. But the general had been upset by it and had summoned him to his work out.

Athletic prowess was not the huge man's strong point. Too much of his bulk was obesity, and his physical exertions were soon reduced to short bursts in between which he gasped for air. But Maximovich kept up the regime, partly because it was good for his image to be seen for a while every day in the gym. It didn't really matter what he did there.

"This Arab of yours," panted Maximovich, "are you sure he is not crazy?"

He pedalled the fixed bicycle with as much intensity as he could muster, and Yenko leaned against a vaulting horse, watching him, his face expressionless.

"He works in his own way," he shrugged. "His record speaks for itself. How he operates is his business."

Maximovich took a break, rivulets of sweat running down his thick neck.

"Well," he breathed hard, "you picked him. Personally . . ." He dabbed his brow. "Personally, I think Arabs are treacherous."

Yenko recalled the geniality with which the general had embraced Yasser Arafat during his Moscow visit, and the friendly exchanges he had had with Colonel Gadaffi in Tripoli. Protestations of brotherly love, and undying comradeship flowed from his lips. But, of course, Yenko was too tactful to remind him.

"The important thing, comrade General, is that we have a hold on him. He cannot touch the money or collect the arms until the job is done."

The general grunted. He still had another two kilometres to cycle. He began pedalling again, the perspiration making his whole face shine.

"You . . . should . . . take . . . more . . . exercise, Yenko," he puffed. The irony of the remark didn't strike him. Here he was, gross, overweight, lecturing Yenko, lean, slim, without an ounce of fat on his spare frame.

"I'll bear it in mind, General."

Maximovich put extra effort into the final spurt. When the dial showed he had pedalled the required distance, he slumped. Yenko handed him a towel.

"The only reason I mention the Arab is that the death of this woman is . . . well, messy, you understand?"

"Yes General."

"This kind of thing draws attention to itself."

"Yes, comrade General."

Maximovich towelled his hair.

"One of our own people would have done it much better, if it had to be done. Terminations should be clean, classic. Like a Shostakovich symphony."

Yenko raised an eyebrow quizzically. Culture was not the general's forte.

"You understand me, Yenko?"

"Absolutely."

Maximovich grunted. "I'm going to take a shower."

He was recovering from his arduous constitutional, and breathing more easily.

"If the General will allow me one word . . . " Maximovich stopped.

"Yes, Major?"

"I take your point completely, but our Arab friend may have had a very good reason for what he did, and the way he did it. It could have an effect on Zarubin, you see. He might start taking risks. I don't know, but it could just happen . . ."

"Have you read his file?" the general cut in sharply.

"Many times."

"So you know you're talking nonsense, Yenko. Zarubin

doesn't take risks. He only plays certainties. That's why he is still around. If you're thinking that because he once slept with this woman, her death will become a personal issue, forget it. And let me tell you something else ... ."

Yenko waited.

"I wish we had a Zarubin. Yes, I would give a lot to have Mr Zarubin working for us."

Yenko smiled.

Even after he had showered and changed into his uniform, Maximovich was bothered. It still nagged him when he attended a gala performance in honour of the East German minister at the Bolshoi theatre that evening.

Yenko's smile.

During the intermission, Konstantin Fedor Surov honoured him by detaching himself from a group of Kremlin dignitaries and coming over to greet him.

"All is well with you?" asked the Chairman in his gentle, scholarly manner, the pebble glasses peering amiably.

"Everything is well, thank you, comrade Chairman."

The pebble glasses stared at him just a second longer than might have been expected. Then Surov nodded, and wandered off.

Before the curtain fell on the second act, Maximovich decided that, first thing in the morning, he'd go over Yenko's personal file.

Pearmain arrived for the fortnightly meeting of the Eleven Committee by foot, nodded briefly to the commissionaire who screened visitors to the old fashioned office building near Caxton Hall, then took the creaking, wire cage lift to the second floor. Only then did he have to go through the formality of producing his ID card in its chamois wallet.

It was remarkably relaxed security for the meeting place of men who, in their own way, pulled the strings of the realm's secret machinery.

It was called the Eleven Committee because at one time, when they used to hold their meetings in a cavernous citadel in Northumberland Avenue, they had met in Room Eleven. Now the fortnightly game known as Coordination was held in Conference Room B of a different place, but the name had stuck.

Outside the intelligence community, the committee's existence was virtually unknown and, if minutes were taken, not even cabinet ministers got to see them.

The chairmanship of Eleven Committee was organised on a rotating basis, and the seating arrangements on both sides of the baize covered oblong table did not indicate the importance of the individual man, or the organisation he represented.

Pearmain, who spoke for Special Activities, sat two from the end, next to F. F was the initial of the Director of Overseas Control, ascribed to whoever might hold that post at the time. B Division was also there, sitting across from them, a nervous individual with a slight twitch. Section V of MI6 rated its own spokesman, who seldom said a word.

MI11 and room 055 – a section the exact purpose of which remained obscure outside the committee – always sat together, like inseparable lovers. GCHQ doodled, and spoke, when necessary, in terse, clipped terms. He had been stationed in Hong Kong for five years, and missed the place.

There were others. A small balding man from ISLU, whose responsibility, on paper, was inter service liaison, and who, being helpful by nature, wanted to be of assistance to everybody. He was usually ignored. The MI8 man, whose fiat was the radio security service, invariably looked all knowing, and had an irritating habit of smiling quietly to himself at times, giving the impression he knew more than the others.

Y unit was there of course, its representative usually first in his place, a tall studious looking man, a classics scholar who read Aristotle in the original. So was the cold, unsmiling Irish emissary of Section 14, a Civil Service department euphemistically known as Counter Measures, which along with its other activities also kept an eye on the budget allocation each division received from the Service's secret funding.

Many of the departments that formed Eleven Committee were in the shadows, but none more so than Pearmain's outfit.

Until they were called to order, they mostly stood around,

and a soft buzz of conversation filled the room as they discussed trivialities. Golf, the weather, and England's chances in the test match. They bemoaned the unpunctuality of the trains, or the length of the school holidays, but when they got down to business, they were like poker players, polite, even chummy, never giving away anything that really mattered, always keeping their cards well hidden. Even if a foreign intelligence agency such as the CIA or KGB somehow managed to record every word that was said, they wouldn't gather much.

The rules of the Coordination game were basically that brief reports were given about certain matters which they already knew about, and the chairman would then pause briefly to give people a chance to ask questions. It was on the whole considered bad form for one department to be too probing about current activities involving another one.

Goodpaster, one of those described in *Who's Who* as "attached Foreign Office", and who had once disappeared from sight for three years on "special work", took the chair. Coordination was underway.

He ticked off the agenda item by item, and handled the ritual skilfully, thought Pearmain. At this rate they might finish in less than the usual hour.

"ISAD," he called out, looking across at Pearmain. "Nothing from Special Activities, I take it."

Pearmain shook his head.

Goodpaster gave him an understanding smile, and ticked the agenda.

"Question."

Pearmain frowned. Counter Measures seldom asked questions.

The Irishman who headed Section 14 played devious politics, and there was a long standing rivalry with Special Activities, who were, in a way, their competitors.

Goodpaster pursed his lips. He did not approve of inter corridor feuding across the Coordination table. But he had to do his job.

"Yes, Mr Hurley?"

"I'm a little concerned . . ." He corrected himself. "We are a little concerned about the apparent lack of liaison with

Mr Lambert's unit. That comes under your wing, doesn't it, Mr Pearmain?"

The unsmiling Irishman waited expectantly.

"Only overall, Mr Hurley. As you know, Mr Lambert's activities are . . . autonomous." Pearmain paused, deciding to draw him out, and let him play his hand. See what exactly he was after. "Is there a problem?"

"The escape from 010. The Russian who absconded." Hurley stopped.

"Yes?"

"Since then, Mr Lambert's people have . . . kept their own counsel."

"Mr Hurley," intervened Goodpaster mildly. "You know our practice about not discussing specific operational details."

"I'm obliged, Chairman."

Hurley sat back. He had planted the seed.

Pearmain's eyes glinted. These bastards at 14.

"I can always discuss the matter privately, if Mr Hurley likes," he offered. The others round the table sat very straight, and very still.

"All we were wondering was what had happened to the Russian," explained Hurley, glancing at the note pad in front of him. "Major Ulianov, is it not?"

Now he knew. They wanted him to eat crow.

"Chairman," began Pearmain addressing himself to the head of the table, "this is a very sensitive matter. So far, Major Ulianov has not been recaptured. We want no publicity. It is obviously against the national interest that the news should leak out. He was spotted shortly after his escape, but he apparently managed to get a lift from a motorist, and eluded us. I have had a detailed report from Mr Lambert. A full enquiry is being held at 010, and the findings will be forwarded to CSIC control."

The small balding man from ISLU blinked nervously.

"You mean, the Russian is still at large?" he asked.

Again Pearmain spoke direct to Goodpaster.

"Chairman, I don't speculate. I don't know. I have asked Mr Lambert and his department to give this highest priority. May I leave it at that for the moment?"

Goodpaster cleared his throat. This was not what Coordination was about. Nobody was on trial. Nobody had to justify themselves.

"Shall we leave it at that?" he enquired, but it was not a question, it was an instruction.

Hurley made a note on his pad. Pearmain saw it, and decided that Counter Measures, the whole of Section 14, were persona non grata from henceforth.

They briefly discussed a memorandum from the Treasury for the sub rosa accounting of illicit operational funds deposited in foreign banks for covert purposes, then the meeting was declared closed. They pushed their chairs back and stood up, chattering like schoolboys released from class.

Pearmain ambled over to Hurley.

"Sorry I wasn't more helpful," he said amiably.

Hurley was not magnanimous in victory. "Rum business, if you don't mind me saying so."

"Oh I agree, absolutely. Somebody's for the chop at 010. But tell me, why's 14 so interested?"

"It's not every day somebody loses a Russian pilot, is it?" remarked Hurley, snapping shut his briefcase. "And the Americans must be getting curious," he went on, "don't you think? I bet they want to talk to him. Must be embarrassing explaining what's happened, what with the UKUSA agreement, and what not, eh?"

Damn Lambert, thought Pearmain. Aloud he said:

"Not at all." His tone was cold, distant. Hostilities had been declared, so niceties no longer mattered. "Prisoners of war do escape, you know."

But he was uneasy on his way back to the office. He was beginning to wonder if the right hand really did know what the left hand was doing.

In the big hangar on their section of the air base, the crew worked through the night, spraying and painting the Sikorsky Black Hawk.

"Obliterate all identifying insignia," they had been instructed. "Everything."

They didn't know what it was all about, but in the 807th, that wasn't unusual. In the past, they'd done all sorts of curious things to aircraft without being told the reason. After all, that was their mission – Special Support which meant just that.

So, "United States Air Force" disappeared from the side of the helicopter's fuselage, and the five pointed white star markings. The unit code letters were deleted, the squadron emblem erased, the ship's nickname vanished, as did the plane's number, and its service colour.

In the end, what was left brooding behind the hangar doors like a sinister bird, was an anonymous chopper painted black with no markings at all.

After they had finished Colonel Fraser personally inspected the Black Hawk. He walked round it, the master sergeant in charge of the ground crew keeping a respectful distance. When the old man was this silent, you never knew.

The grey civilian with him didn't say a word.

"Thank you, sergeant," said the colonel, nodding approvingly. "She'll do."

He looked at Dichter, who confirmed his agreement.

"Who's going to fly her, sir?" asked the crew chief. Orders were instant readiness.

"I am," stated Colonel Fraser.

If the crew chief wanted to know more, he kept it to himself.

"I want to talk to you, Mr Dichter," said the colonel, as they left the hangar.

In his office, he faced the grey man.

"I hope to hell RAF liaison doesn't get curious."

"No reason why they should ever know, is there, Colonel? The most it's going to take you is forty minutes. Ten minutes to get there, and pick up your passenger. A further fifteen minutes to get to Mildenhall where you drop him, then fifteen minutes later you're back home."

"Passenger?" repeated the colonel, frowning. "Just one passenger?"

"Hopefully, two," said Dichter. "You got the space?"

"I can take seven."

Dichter smiled. "You won't need that much, I promise."

For a moment, the colonel hesitated. Dichter came from Washington, and he had seen his orders, the authorisation, the TWX. But he still had to say it.

"You realise your outfit is asking me to break every regulation in the book?"

"Yes," said Dichter. "I thought that's what the 807th is all about. Special Support."

"Sure. But we still file flight plans. We don't sneak around below radar height. We're in a friendly country. The UK, remember, our allies. We tell them what we're doing, and we don't abuse their air space or their regs. Even on a short hop. We trust each other."

"Do we, Colonel?" enquired Dichter, coolly.

The colonel retreated. The world of spooks was impenetrable.

"What about this old airfield? What's going on there? Who is this man you want us to pick up?"

It was his last try.

"Listen, Colonel," Dichter spelt out, like somebody who understood Fraser's bewilderment. "This is so hot that . . ." He shrugged. "We have to sneak somebody out of England clandestinely. That's all I can tell you. We need your help to do it. The chopper has no markings, so nobody on the ground can identify it. It'll fly beneath the radar ceiling, it'll snatch the man we need, deliver him, and he'll be in the States in eight hours."

"Without the British knowing?"

"Any way we can, Colonel."

He saw the colonel trying to come to terms with it, attempting to put answers to questions he hadn't asked.

"I'll tell you, it's the most classified operation you'll be involved in for a long time," added Dichter. "Can I leave it like that?"

"I guess so," sighed Fraser. He picked up a clip board from his desk and looked at the notes on it. "Civilian clothes only? No uniform?"

"Right."

He frowned. "Side arms?"

"A precaution."

"Are you coming along, Mr Dichter?"

The grey man shook his head. "You won't need me. There's a pretty good man who'll handle it on the spot."

"And he's the second passenger?"

"I sure hope so," replied Dichter, but he didn't sound at all convinced.

The pub where they'd arranged to meet stood by the roadside, the only habitation within sight.

The B-road that passed the door of the Marquis of Granby provided little trade. Those motorists who did occasionally slow down usually changed their minds once they got a closer look at the uninviting exterior, with its single wooden bench, and decided it was worth driving another few miles in the hope of finding something more promising.

So its survival was a mystery, because even on a busy day its customers could be counted on fewer than ten fingers. As a hostelry, the single saloon bar offered only austere amenities. A lone beer pump, a kitchen table with four chairs, a dartboard, and a fly speckled sign that no betting was allowed on the premises.

Herbert, the landlord, and his wife Annie were a taciturn couple. Like two people marooned on a desert island for years, they had long since exhausted each other's conversation.

Instead , the radio played continuously, and Herbert was not a selective listener. He was the sort of person who switches on in the morning, then doesn't move the dial for the rest of the day. The volume wasn't too high, just loud enough to discourage idle chatter. Since the pub was empty much of the time, it really didn't matter.

What a dismal joint to pick, thought Zarubin, as he entered the pub. Whoever the Marquis of Granby had been, he surely deserved something better.

Herbert, his badly fitting trousers hitched up with braces, his shirt sleeves rolled up, regarded him stonily.

"Scotch and soda," ordered Zarubin. He needed a drink, it had been a long drive.

Herbert shifted off his stool behind the bar, carefully measured the drink, and pushed the glass over.

"Ice, please," said Zarubin.

"No ice," grunted Herbert. Maybe he felt that was a bit curt, so he added mysteriously, "Not yet."

"How's that?"

"Not set yet," answered Herbert.

"Oh. Got anything to eat?" Zarubin asked.

"We don't do meals," Herbert informed him, with what he could have sworn was a note of sadistic delight in his voice.

"Sandwich will do. Anything."

Herbert pondered. "I could fix you a ploughman's lunch maybe."

"Fine." Jesus, the names they gave fast food in this country. A piece of cheese and a hunk of bread became a ploughman's lunch, a dish called toad in the hole turned out to be a sausage in a piece of dough.

Herbert yelled through the door:

"Ploughman's lunch."

"Give me more soda," said Zarubin, handing Herbert his glass. He needed a clear head. Soon, every move had to be programmed.

He glanced up at the oak beamed roof.

"Pretty old this place, eh?"

"Yes," said Herbert.

"Seventeenth century?"

"Could be."

Annie appeared. She was a buxom, unsmiling woman with a hairnet. She put a plate in front of Zarubin. A piece of french bread, a pat of butter, some cheddar cheese, and a dollop of sweet pickle.

"Thanks," said Zarubin. She nodded, and disappeared through the door. Herbert handed him his glass.

"I'd like a knife," said Zarubin.

Herbert gave him a reproachful look, but produced a knife.

Zarubin went over to the bare table and ate without enthusiasm. The french bread was a little stale. It was hard work chewing.

"I'll see if the ice is set," volunteered Herbert. He came back with a plastic bucket, containing half a dozen ice cubes, and dropped one in Zarubin's drink.

"You Yanks like ice in your drinks," he said knowingly.

"I guess so."

Herbert turned the radio down a little. He seemed to be in a more chatty mood.

"Tourist?"

Zarubin nodded.

"Not much in these parts," he added, gloomily. "Nothing to see."

A farm labourer came in. He and the landlord knew each other.

"Pint," said the labourer without preliminaries.

Herbert pulled a pint from the single pump.

"How's the missus?" he enquired.

"All right," said the labourer. He took a deep, long draught of the beer.

"Tourist here," said Herbert, indicating Zarubin. The labourer turned and looked at Zarubin as if it was the first time he realised somebody else was in the pub. He nodded.

"The airfield's quite close, isn't it?" remarked Zarubin. They both stared at him.

"The old RAF place, Thorpehill?" said Herbert. "Few miles. You'll have to turn off the road. But it's all waste land. You won't see anything."

"Nothing there now," added the labourer. "Not since the war."

"My old man was stationed there," lied Zarubin. "I want to have a look at it."

"A Yank?" Herbert looked doubtful. "It was RAF."

"No, they had all kinds," the labourer corrected him. He must have been a kid in the war, figured Zarubin. "Yanks, Poles, even Free French. In and out."

A car drew up outside. The door slammed and a man entered.

"Small world, Andrew," grinned Crawford.

The two men at the bar were staring at them.

Zarubin stood up. "Glad you could make it."

"Now, would I let a buddy down in his hour of need?" Crawford enquired, sarcastically.

If he saw the coldness in Zarubin's eyes, he ignored it.

"First, you son of a bitch," he smiled, "why don't you buy me a drink."

He sat down at the table.

Zarubin went to the bar.

"Friend of yours?" asked Herbert.

"Yes," said Zarubin, "friend of mine. Two scotches with lots of soda." He knew Crawford's taste; scotch like himself.

"Where's the man's room?" he asked and immediately realised he wasn't talking the same language. "The toilet?"

"Round the back," said Herbert. "Outside."

Zarubin paid for the drinks and took them to the table.

"Just going to the john." He excused himself lightly.

Parked outside, was Crawford's car. It was a yellow Fiat, and it told Zarubin a lot. Crawford always drove an official car, but on this occasion he had gone to the trouble of renting one.

Zarubin didn't need to see the documents to know that Crawford had leased it under a false name. No one would ever be able to trace the real name of the man who had hired it.

"How are the facilities?" asked Crawford when he returned to the table.

"They smell," said Zarubin.

It was easy to enter the airfield which, as always, lay spread out, deserted, weeds growing, the grass uncut.

It was an airman's equivalent of a Californian gold miner's ghost town. Once hundreds of servicemen had been stationed here, and the place shook with the roar of planes as they took off and landed.

Then they had departed, and the eerie silence took over. Birds built nests in old telephone poles. Doors hanging on one hinge banged and clattered. Pieces of old paper flapped about.

They felt very conspicuous, crossing the flight line, searching among the hangars, and the outbuildings. If anyone was watching them prowling around, he would be ready for them.

Zarubin had hunted men in a steamy Vietnamese jungle, in back alleys in Saigon, he had once played deadly hide and seek in a cemetery in Prague, he had stalked and been stalked. But he had never felt so exposed, so vulnerable as he did on this site in the heart of the peaceful English countryside.

But nothing happened.

"I'll check the hangars and the workshops over there," said Crawford.

"Okay. I'll take the other side."

If the Russian was here, somewhere, they had to find him, get to him, then quickly spirit him away. They didn't have much time. The chopper to pick them up was due to swoop down soon.

They checked their watches, then split up. As they searched, they kept encountering old phantoms. In a derelict dormitory, there were still faded pin ups on the wall. Rita Hayworth. Betty Grable. Long legged ghosts, disintegrating with age.

Zarubin pushed open the door of an old Nissen hut. A wall calendar for the year 1947 flapped as the wind blowing through a broken window caught it.

He raised his walkie talkie:

"Zero, nothing here," he reported.

Back crackled Crawford's voice:

"Okay, Zero. Nothing this end. Alpha, out."

Crawford stumbled across a dog's grave. It had a miniature tombstone. "Bonzo, RIP, Our Mascot, May 12 1943."

The office buildings were falling apart, gaping holes in the roofs, rotted floorboards giving way. One had a map of the Netherlands still on the wall.

Zarubin stared at the blackboard in the briefing room. Incredibly, the last status report was still chalked up. Crew names, plane numbers, the mission roll call. And the target: Hamburg.

"Alpha, you read me?"

"Yes, Zero. Loud and clear."

"Anything your end?" asked Zarubin.

"Nothing so far."

Zarubin paused, frowning. Somebody had to show themselves. If the Russian was being kept here, somebody must be guarding him.

If . . .

Dichter had said they were holding him on this abandoned airfield. RAF Thorpehill. And Fern's last words to him had been that the Russian was being kept on this forgotten base.

But supposing . . .

"The hangars are clear," Crawford's voice confirmed.

Damn.

"Did you read me, Zero?"

"Yes, Alpha. Carry on."

"I'll try the workshops."

"Roger."

Zarubin turned to the control tower building. He decided to search that next.

Crawford checked the old engine sheds, but found nothing. There were two big workshops, and the first one he went in was a ghostly assembly plant, empty and silent.

The second workshop was dark, and littered with abandoned junk that hadn't been worth carting away. He gave a last glance round, and that was when he heard the door creak. It didn't sound like the other doors, idling in the wind; it was a different kind of creak.

"Just turn round very slowly," instructed Salim.

Crawford stiffened.

"Slowly, very slowly," repeated Salim. "I'm sure you understand."

Crawford turned round, and faced him.

Salim had a gun in his right hand with a silencer attached, and he regarded Crawford with frank curiosity.

Crawford still held the walkie talkie.

"Put that down on the ground," ordered Salim.

For a moment, he thought of throwing it straight at the Arab.

"No," said Salim, "I'd still kill you. Just put it down."

Crawford placed it by his foot. He straightened up and Salim motioned with his gun for him to raise his hands.

"Just two of you?" enquired Salim.

"No," said Crawford. "You'll find out."

"Please, I've been watching you since you arrived. There's only two of you. A little over confident, maybe."

He sounded disapproving.

"Never mind, I'm only interested in Zarubin. You don't matter at all."

He squeezed the trigger gently, unhurriedly, and fired only once. It was a beautifully aimed shot. The bullet ploughed straight into Crawford's heart, and he was dead before he hit the ground.

Salim bent down and picked up the walkie talkie. He

pressed the transmit button.

"Hello, Zarubin," he said. "Welcome old friend."

"What took you so long?" asked Zarubin.

But his voice was not distorted by the walkie talkie, and it came from nearby.

Salim dropped the two way radio, whirled round, at the same time firing at where he thought the voice had come from, but there was nobody there.

He straightened up, and listened. There was no sound. Very slowly and deliberately he turned, all the while his eyes searching, his finger on the trigger of his gun.

"You in here?" he called out.

"You got all the odds in your favour," answered Zarubin's voice. "I hate you. I want you to suffer. So I may make a mistake. I'm already making one. I should have killed you without saying a word, then you'd never have known what hit you. But that would be too quick, too simple."

Salim's eyes searched. He thought he saw a shadowy figure at the far end of the workshop, trying to hide in a recess, by an old tool bench.

He fired.

"No," called out Zarubin, his voice coming from somewhere else. "You're nervous. That's bad. Maybe that squares up the odds, eh?"

Salim became aware of a sensation he had never experienced before. It wasn't fear, or at least, he couldn't believe that it could be. But his throat was dry and so was his mouth when he tried to lick his lips. He stepped over Crawford's body and soundlessly walked backwards until he felt the wall. Then he began edging towards the door.

"I'd stay put," suggested Zarubin.

"You're afraid, Zarubin," he shouted, his voice cracking. "You're scared."

"Not half as frightened as you sound, Salim," taunted Zarubin, his voice closer than before. "You'll have to do better than that."

Salim's gun hand was rock still, and he felt reassured. As long as he could keep a steady hand . . .

"How did you know I'd be waiting for you?" he called out, his eyes searching every nook, every cranny.

"Let's say, it was an educated guess," mocked Zarubin.

A shadow moved. That's him, thought Salim, firing once, twice, three times.

He heard an agonised groan and something falling, with a dull thud.

Then silence.

"Zarubin?" ventured Salim. Silence. "Zarubin?" he called again, trying to control the rising exultation that was racing through him.

Silence.

Slowly, warily, Salim moved towards the shadowy corner of the workshop. Now, more distinctly, he could see Zarubin, slumped across a dismantled generator.

He fired again.

Never before had he felt relief at executing a victim. Professional satisfaction, yes. Pride at a job well done, especially if it was tricky. But not until now had he experienced relief at managing to do it. If he'd had time to think, Salim might have admitted to himself that he had been afraid, afraid for his life. Killing Zarubin lifted that fear, and he never wanted to feel it again.

"How did you like the sound effects?" asked Zarubin.

Salim panicked. He gave a shout, as he swung round in a circle, blasting away with his gun, shooting in every direction, until he pressed the trigger and all that came was a click.

Then he knew he was dead. Although nothing had happened to him, he realised he was as good as dead.

"That was very unprofessional," commented Zarubin, emerging from the gloom. He stood a few feet from Salim, unarmed, his hands hanging loosely and surveyed the Arab dispassionately. The hate he had felt was ebbing. Now it was just going to be a mechanical act.

Salim was breathing hard, his eyes wide, his lips parted. He whispered something in Arabic, but whether it was a prayer or a curse Zarubin never knew.

"Zarubin," croaked Salim, all the time registering that Zarubin had no gun. "Why this torture? You and I, we do this work, we have no feelings against our targets, they are like trees that need to be chopped down. We are the tree cutters. Why do you play this game with me?"

Zarubin shrugged. "You know. Fern didn't have to be killed. You liked doing it. The others, they were . . . part of the war, maybe. Even he was a soldier," he indicated Crawford's body where it lay on the floor. "But Fern, she didn't matter. You didn't even have a contract. It was your idea, and you enjoyed it."

"To trap you," said Salim. "To get you."

"Well, here I am," nodded Zarubin.

Salim took a deep breath. "What now?"

Zarubin glanced at his watch.

"It'll take three minutes for you to die, if you're lucky. If you're unlucky, perhaps ten." He sighed. Salim's eyes never left his, beads of perspiration were trickling from his forehead down his face, into his pencil thin moustache. "I hope it won't take as long as that for my sake," went on Zarubin. "It's not the kind of pain I like to watch."

Salim gaped at him, his mouth dry, the salty taste of his own sweat on his lips.

Then, simultaneously, Zarubin moved, something flashed through the air, and Salim felt an agonising stab of pain as a razor sharp blade penetrated his throat, and stuck there. Zarubin had aimed the knife well. With blood gushing like an untapped oil well, Salim staggered, groping for his throat, gurgling as he tried to breathe.

He fell to the ground, his windpipe severed, and threshed the air helplessly with his arms as he suffocated; the ghastly sounds he emitted were those of an animal in its death throes.

Impassively, Zarubin watched the blood soaked body of Salim choke to death. He had been out in his estimate. Although his limbs twitched just a few seconds longer, Salim was dead after two minutes.

That was when Zarubin cursed him, something he had never done to someone he had terminated.

"Go rot in hell, you fucking bastard!" he swore.

Then he remembered that the real job still had to be done.

He didn't at first recognise the man he saw in the distance, but his gradual appearance, as he came up the steps of the airfield's underground bomb arsenal, reminded Zarubin of a mole emerging from its burrow.

From where he was hiding, Zarubin could see he was well

built, and although he wore only an open necked shirt, he had a shoulder holster strapped round him.

Zarubin watched him stretch, then look across the deserted airfield at the cluster of hangars and outbuildings on the other side. He started strolling towards the long runway, now overgrown with weeds and grass.

For Druce, it was pleasant to get out from the subterranean shelter, and to breathe fresh air.

Guarding the Russian bloke was a cock-eyed job, and he'd be glad when his relief showed up. He didn't know what the section was playing at, or why they had picked this old RAF dump.

Druce had safe housed a few of the section's prize catches, but this time he'd drawn the short straw. This fellow got special treatment, which was Lambert's decision, a man who never confided, just decreed. But Druce wished they were using the more congenial surroundings of the house near Wargrave, or the lodge just outside High Wycombe; they were the usual holding places and the amenities were more pleasant for the custodians.

He ambled over to the old guard house and went in.

An ancient copy of *Playboy* lay on a table, and he picked it up. He had read all the magazines in the underground hideout twice over, so it would make a change to look at something else. Keeping watch meant there was not much one could do, apart from sit in the single dilapidated armchair, drinking endless cups of tea. The bloody Russian stayed in his quarters all day, playing chess with himself. Every time Druce went in, he'd look up expectantly, grunt, then go back to checkmating himself, the surly bastard.

Druce sighed, took one last breath of clean fresh air, then once more descended the steps that led into the underground passage. The dank, stuffy atmosphere was unpleasant. It may have been all right as a bomb store forty years ago, but it was a hell of a dump to spend hours at a stretch. No wonder the lousy Russian was morose.

He was turning the corner, when suddenly he was sent staggering by a blow to the back of his head, and collapsed, unconscious.

Zarubin didn't know who he had hit, until he turned him

266

over. After a moment's hesitation, like a computer picking out a file, he recognised him. Druce, the man who worked with Lambert.

Zarubin took the gun out of Druce's shoulder holster, and stuck it in his belt. He went through his trouser pockets, and found the bunch of keys he wanted. Then he lifted one of Druce's eyelids. He'd be out long enough.

He stood very still, listening, waiting for the others, pressing himself into the shadows, so that he'd hear anyone coming down the steps, but they wouldn't see him immediately.

But no one came, and time was running short. Stealthily, he made his way along the oppressive passage, wondering if this was what a sewer was like without the sewage. The brick walls were damp and it smelt musty. He came to a door and stopped. It was locked, but there were three keys on Druce's ring, and he tried them one at a time.

With the gun in his hand, Zarubin unlocked the door, and opened it. A man in a black track suit was sitting at a table, a chess board in front of him. He had short stubbly hair, high cheek bones, and dark, wary eyes, which widened with fear when he saw the gun.

"Who are you?" asked Zarubin, his finger on the trigger.

The man stood up, saying rapidly in Russian, "I warn you. I am a Soviet officer. If you kill me, ten of your men in our hands will be executed. I demand to be treated according to military law."

"Who are you?" repeated Zarubin, this time in Russian.

The man drew himself upright.

"Major Ulianov. Dal'nyaya Aviatsiya. What do you want?" he demanded.

"You," said Zarubin.

The man stared at him. "What do you mean?"

"You are safe. I think they were planning to kill you, comrade, but you are now under the protection of the United States."

Some protection, thought Zarubin wryly. Me. And a gun.

"Where is the other man?" asked the Russian.

"Asleep," replied Zarubin drily.

"But the British . . . their special intelligence . . ."

"Forget the British," said Zarubin, glancing at his watch. "We haven't got much time, we must get upstairs. Now. You first," he ordered, indicating with the gun.

The Russian, bewildered, hesitated, then led the way.

In the passage, Druce moaned and opened his eyes, just in time to see the Russian coming towards him, followed by Zarubin.

"Christ!" he groaned, trying to scramble to his feet.

Zarubin fired, the bullet puncturing Druce's forehead, and he fell back against the wall, his face a scarlet pulpy mess.

The Russian looked at Zarubin, his eyes wide with undisguised horror. Good, thought Zarubin. He's afraid.

"Up the steps," he told him, in Russian.

They emerged from the old arsenal into the open air.

"What is happening?" asked the Russian. He was shaking.

"We wait," answered Zarubin, his eyes roaming over the silent, undisturbed airfield. He checked his watch, and frowned. They should be here.

"I don't understand what is going on," said the Russian.

"I'm saving your fucking life," snarled Zarubin in English. Then he added in Russian, "There is nothing to worry about."

"There is help coming?" enquired the Russian, smiling weakly.

"In a few minutes."

The Russian looked at his wrist watch.

"Good. Anything to get away from here."

"I'm sure," agreed Zarubin softly. "Tell me what happened," he went on, his eyes scanning the sky.

"You must know. One of your planes shot us down. I survived. I was picked up, and British intelligence took over. A special unit. They kept me hidden away. I escaped, but they recaptured me. Since then . . ."

"I know since then," said Zarubin. "Where did they recapture you?"

"I was trying to get to London. It was in a forest. A man gave me a ride but they dragged me out and after that . . ." He shook his head. "I think you are right. They were going to kill me."

268

In the distance, to the east of the airfield, flying low over hedges and fields, a helicopter appeared. Like a huge black bird it came nearer, and circled. Zarubin waved, and the chopper came down fifty feet away, the wind from its rotors whipping the grass.

"That's us, tovarich," said Zarubin. "Start running."

The airman and the helicopter pilot were in civilian dress. Eagerly, Zarubin and the Russian clambered aboard.

"Is that everybody?" yelled Colonel Fraser, who was at the controls.

"Those able to walk it," Zarubin shouted back. "My buddy was killed. I'm going back for his body."

"Sorry, pal, we ain't got the fucking time," howled Colonel Fraser, lifting the helicopter into the air as he spoke.

Blue bereted Air Force police had already cordoned off the area at Mildenhall where the Sikorsky helicopter touched down exactly fourteen minutes and thirty-five seconds later.

Dichter was standing on the landing pad, and the first person his eyes fixed on when the passengers jumped out was the Russian.

Then he greeted Zarubin.

"So that's our boy," he said. "Well done, Andrew."

He glanced round. "Where's Crawford?"

"You want the full body count?" asked Zarubin.

"Who else?"

"One of Lambert's merry men. And Salim."

"Salim?"

"Salim," repeated Zarubin. "My former cell mate."

"Christ!"

"No," said Zarubin. "I didn't kill him."

Dichter wasn't amused.

Two Air Force sedans glided to a halt alongside the parked chopper.

"I'm going back," announced Zarubin. "Even if I have to fly this damn crate myself, I'm going back there."

"What the hell for?"

"To pick up Crawford. We didn't leave our dead, even in the jungle."

The grey man's eyebrows were raised. "A sentimental streak, yet."

"If the boys in blue are too chicken . . ."

"Those were my orders," barked Dichter. "My orders. Lambert will get the message."

Zarubin wanted to punch Dichter in the face, to really hurt him.

"You're a bastard, you know that, sir," he rasped. "A callous son of a bitch."

"Probably," agreed Dichter. "Like you, Zarubin. That's why we get things done."

"You'd have left me there too, to rot, wouldn't you?"

"Oh, don't worry, they'll get buried. Perhaps not in a cemetery, but Lambert will have a hole dug. Probably on the airfield. He doesn't want a pile of bodies around, cops asking questions, he won't leave them lying about."

He took Zarubin's arm and steered him towards Colonel Fraser.

"When does the 707 take off?" he asked him.

"In eighteen minutes."

"Good," said Dichter. He turned to Zarubin. "Tell our Russian friend that in a few hours he will be the guest of Uncle Sam and then he can tell us all he knows."

But what Zarubin said in Russian was:

"They're going to fly you to America for interrogation."

Unexpectedly, the Russian broke into a broad grin, and nodded his head vigorously.

"He seems mighty happy," remarked Zarubin sourly.

"Wouldn't you be?"

"I wonder," muttered Zarubin.

The Russian got into one of the staff cars, looked out of the window, and gave Zarubin a wave as it slowly moved off.

"I'd like to go along with him," said Zarubin.

"Sorry. You haven't finished here yet."

"Somebody ought to escort him."

"The Air Force is looking after that. Leave it to them." Dichter's eyes were following the Russian's car.

"So, who's going to debrief him?"

"Not you," replied Dichter. Then, suddenly, he was genial. "I'm going to buy you a drink, Andrew. You deserve one."

They sat in the corner of the Officers Club, Dichter regarding Zarubin thoughtfully before finally saying:

"You'll be going home soon. After you've tied up one loose end."

"I know," murmured Zarubin. He looked out of the window. "Lambert."

"Lambert must have a lot on his conscience," said Dichter, pointedly. "He's not just a lousy traitor. He didn't just sell out. Who d'you think killed the call girl, Debby?"

"Lambert? Why would he kill her?"

"Maybe to frame you, perhaps to frame Cy, I'm not sure. What I do know is that Cy was getting too close. He had already put the finger on Lambert, so he had to go. And Spiridov, the Russian in the cab. He was going to blow the whistle, so he went. Does that make you feel better?"

"About what?"

"Killing him," replied Dichter simply.

At least it was straight out this time, thought Zarubin. No euphemism. No trade talk. No genteel pirouetting round death.

"I'm not sure," he muttered, taking a long drink. "I'm tired, John. Maybe I've killed one person too many. Maybe I've been doing it for too long." He peered into his glass.

"Everybody gets combat fatigue," murmured Dichter, soothingly.

"Don't bullshit me," Zarubin snarled at him, slamming down his glass. "You know what I mean. Maybe you'd be wise to let me stop."

"What's got at you?" asked Dichter quietly.

Zarubin stared him straight in the eye. "Don't you know?"

"Tell me."

"Oh, forget it."

"Listen," said Dichter. "Lambert's going to panic. When he finds we've lifted the Russian, and he realises the gloves are off. He'll panic and that'll be your chance." He paused. "And don't forget the terrible thing that happened to the girl."

"The girl?" repeated Zarubin thickly.

"Who do you think was behind it? Who put Salim on to her? That's right. Lambert. I don't know how it was between you two again, but I can imagine how you felt when . . ."

"I don't want to talk about it," interrupted Zarubin.

"Of course not, but I want you to know that I'm truly sorry," Dichter added, sympathetically.

"Let's have another drink."

"Sure," nodded Dichter, signalling the barman.

The building vibrated as an Air Force 707 on the flight line became airborne and ascended noisily into the sky.

"There goes Major Ulianov," commented Zarubin.

"Next stop Nevada. The ferrets' nest." Dichter didn't conceal his pleasure. "And we'll start sweating out of him what they were so desperate we shouldn't know. Good work. Blanchard will be pleased." He raised his glass. "Cheers."

"Bully for Blanchard," muttered Zarubin, sourly. Then he raised his glass.

"To treason," he toasted.

Dichter's face froze. "What the hell does that mean?"

"Well," shrugged Zarubin, "where would you and I be without it?"

Dichter chuckled.

"Out of work, buddy."

Sir Leslie Deveaux walked slowly down Burlington Arcade, window shopping. He admired the Georgian silver in one of the jewellers, then sauntered on, stopping in front of a pipe shop. He studied the array of beautiful briars in the window, but the rack of green pipes also on view were not to his taste. Being a man who appreciated life's old fashioned pleasures, smoking a green pipe was unthinkable.

He ambled past the toy shop, then paused outside the pen emporium. That was when he noticed Lambert reflected in the plate glass.

Lambert was looking straight ahead, also apparently studying the display of fountain pens and propelling pencils.

Deveaux glanced at him sideways, then went back to examining the shop window again, and Lambert walked off without a word.

Lambert was waiting by the leather shop, where Deveaux joined him. They stood side by side, seemingly two complete strangers, looking at the same window display. Then, without turning his head, Deveaux said:

"Hello, Stuart."

Lambert gave an imperceptible nod.

Slowly, they made their way towards the Burlington Gardens exit of the arcade. Although they hadn't been in contact for a long while, Deveaux, in the manner that was second nature to him, stopped briefly, and looked back. He was reassured, no one was following them but still they didn't talk until they were in the street.

Lambert was the first to speak.

"I'm sorry," he apologised, as they turned in the direction of Regent Street. "You know I wouldn't have contacted you unless . . ."

". . . you were in trouble."

Deveaux's tone was cold, unwelcoming.

"I don't think I've got much time," went on Lambert.

The old man stopped in front of the tobacconist flanking the entrance to Albany. It gave him a chance to take a good look at Lambert who was mirrored in the window's glass. What he saw was a shock. Lambert, always so cold, so impersonal, clearly was nervous. At a quick glance, he had the appearance of being immaculate, but closer scrutiny revealed a hint of untidiness. The knot in his Harrow tie was not quite tight, his dark suit needed pressing, there was a spot of blood on his chin where he'd nicked himself shaving, and his eyes were bloodshot.

"If you don't mind, I'd like to keep this short," said Deveaux coolly.

"Of course," agreed Lambert, almost obsequiously.

"I presume there's an emergency," murmured Deveaux, stopping to take a closer look at the gift box of Romeo and Juliettas in front of the window.

"I've got to get out."

"I think I'll get myself a present," announced Deveaux, as if he hadn't heard. "Would you excuse me a moment?" And he disappeared inside the shop.

Lambert glanced up and down the street, and even though he saw nothing remotely suspicious, he stayed tense.

Deveaux came out, clutching a parcel.

"I couldn't resist it," he confided, like a conspirator caught in the act. "They're offering them at such good prices, and when you're o.. a fixed income . . ."

They continued along Burlington Gardens, then turned into Sackville Street.

"So it's serious, is it?"

"I've got to get out while I can," insisted Lambert.

"Pearmain?"

"The Americans."

"Really?" Deveaux was surprised. "Which American?"

"Zarubin."

"Ah," nodded Deveaux.

"I'm blown," added Lambert, glancing at Deveaux anxiously.

"Just you?"

"Isn't that enough?" snapped Lambert, angrily.

"Bad," muttered the old man, shaking his head regretfully. "Very bad." He sighed. "You know what Sun Tzu says: 'Subtle and insubstantial, the expert leaves no trace; divinely mysterious, he is inaudible.'"

"I don't need Chinese sayings, I need help," cut in Lambert fiercely. "Now. Today."

The old traitor was filled with contempt. He had stared the ultimate in the face several times, had played the game of double and treble bluff with his life for so long that risk was almost a boon companion. But here was Lambert who, at the first hint of danger, was so panic stricken he was behaving like a frightened rabbit. Deveaux had no time for those who played the Great Game and completely lost their nerve when fate dealt them a bad hand.

"I will inform them," he told Lambert, calmly.

"Leslie . . ."

Lambert's presumptuousness visibly rankled with Deveaux. He had always given the orders, been Lambert's superior, his leader. In the old days, there had been times for familiarity. Now it was different. Over here, he was the eminence, he was law.

"Yes?" he enquired, his voice icy.

"I could be dead this time tomorrow, if they get to me. Now do you understand why they have to lift me?"

Deveaux regarded him disdainfully.

"Stuart, as I've already told you, I will let them know."

"And . . ."

"You will hear."

"When?" Fear had stripped Lambert of his urbane veneer, and revealed a man who to Deveaux was a pitiable sight.

"When it is time," replied Deveaux, patiently. "Get ready," he added, like a lion tamer encouraging an animal with a morsel. "When things move, you'll want to be prepared."

Lambert nodded eagerly. "Do you think I should go over to Paris and wait there?"

After all, that was the way Philby's friends had done it, long ago.

"What!" exclaimed Deveaux, scornfully. "And set all the alarm bells ringing?"

"Oh. Oh, I see."

"Now, I must go. I have a lunch engagement, and you have your instructions. All you have to do is wait until you're contacted."

"Yes, of course."

"One thing," said Deveaux. "You haven't told me what's happened to the Russian."

"The Yanks have him."

For the first time since they'd met, Deveaux was pleased.

"That is good news, Stuart."

"Yes," agreed Lambert dully.

"Don't worry, old friend," Deveaux smiled at him reassuringly. "The British take their time to kill anybody, and the Americans may not find you, if you are clever. Oh, by the way, Stuart," he added, almost as an afterthought. "Don't contact me again." And he walked off in the direction of Bond Street.

Outside Air France's office stood the familiar landmark: the blind match seller.

Deveaux crossed the road, and put a folded five pound note in his tray.

The blind man felt for it, and murmured:

"God bless you, sir."

"Nice day," remarked Deveaux, walking off, but for the

275

sightless war veteran it was his red letter day.

Lambert stood watching Deveaux until he was no longer discernible amongst Piccadilly's lunch time crowd, trying to convince himself that the old traitor's coldness had been nothing other than the aloof, detached manner he had always had, even in the old days, when he'd headed the team, and Lambert had been the tyro.

As he set off for the Westbury Hotel, he reminded himself that, no matter what, Moscow always looked after its own, so they wouldn't default on his insurance policy.

After all, he was one of them, since the first days. He had never let them down.

He stared at his reflection in the mirror above the wash basin of the hotel's gents. He was, wasn't he? He stared harder at himself, wondering why he was frantically trying to reassure himself.

Lambert had often considered how he would feel when the count down came. The moment of no turning back, when he would have to ask them to throw him a life line. Now it was here, he had a curious feeling of anti climax.

So far, or so it appeared at least, he was still secure. No one seemed to be tailing him, there had been nothing to alarm him, even when he'd locked his office door and gone out.

He dried his hands, and threw a fifty pence piece in the attendant's plate as he left.

"Thank you, sir," the attendant acknowledged approvingly. Lambert so typically English, impeccable, correct, epitomised the sort of gentleman he liked to see in the hotel.

He walked towards the bar assuring himself that he would have been summoned into the presence if they'd found the carnage. Not that they had any reason to check the airfield. His clandestine operations were his section's world. Why should anyone want to go there?

Eventually, of course, some clod hopping country bobby probably would stumble across the hastily dug shallow grave and shit himself. Special Branch's nose would start twitching, then Pearmain would get dragged out of his rose garden, and by that time he'd best not be around any more.

Even then, Pearmain, who was more concerned about himself than nailing the last rotten apple, would ponder on what course to take. And the higher it went up the totem pole the more they'd hesitate.

Lambert ordered a sherry, very dry.

And when, finally, the decision was taken to act, it wouldn't be in the way the Americans were playing it, with a killer on the loose, doing their own clearing up and sterilising, the bastards.

No, the ministry wouldn't move fast, he was sure of that. He knew Whitehall too well. They didn't mind treason so much as the waves it caused. That's why Deveaux had never been charged; it was the service's law of life, don't wash your dirty linen in public. Wear it next to your skin, cover up the smell with deodorant, but don't let the outside world know you are wearing soiled underclothes.

All of which gave him just enough time.

So, there were two priorities, he decided. The first, to elude Zarubin. The second to be ready to disappear when Deveaux gave the signal. Two priorities, and they both amounted to the same: save your life.

In the meantime he wanted to reassure himself, he needed reassurance.

Lambert paid for his drink, went to one of the hotel's two phone booths, and dialled the unlisted number of his office.

"Clerk in waiting, please," he requested.

It was the quaint name the service had used since 1909 for the staff duty officer.

"Clerk in waiting," replied the cultured, well educated voice the other end.

"Lambert. Anything for me?"

"One moment, sir."

No change in tone, no sudden hesitation. That was good.

"No, sir, nothing."

"Thank you," he said, then hung up.

The brief conversation had provided the reassurance he'd needed, and Lambert felt better. If there had been a red notice out for him, the SDO would have betrayed it – he wasn't that good an actor, and he would have detected any suspicious pause, or momentary intake of breath, even an apparently casual question like, "Where can we contact you sir?"

Instead, there had been nothing, all appeared perfectly normal.

Lambert straightened his tie. He checked the time. Good. Now the first thing he had to do was drop by the bank, and draw some money. Not too much. Just enough. Money would be taken care of by them, he only had to cover running expenses until they took over.

If the department checked, they'd be reassured that he hadn't taken out a large sum. Reassured. He smiled to himself. That was what everybody wanted – to be reassured. Like so many in the security game, where the stake was insecurity, everybody wanted to be sure they were winning.

After that, he'd go home and pack. He wouldn't take very much, only what he could get into one suitcase.

As for his family, it wouldn't matter to his wife in her Hendon cemetery grave, and as soon as he was safely out of the country he'd write to his son at Cambridge explaining it all. The boy wouldn't believe it, but later he could come and visit. Fortunately, the British never took it out on the family.

Until he actually left the country, he'd better carry a gun just in case Zarubin caught up with him. He was no gentleman, and Lambert wasn't going to give him a chance.

He came out of the bank in Shaftesbury Avenue, and stood for a moment, looking towards Piccadilly Circus. For a second, he felt strangely melancholic. Maybe, he'd never see this view again, perhaps this was the last time he'd breathe the London air, see the red double decker buses, feel the atmosphere. They were not things he really loved, but suddenly he realised he'd miss them in the exile that lay ahead. The club, the streets, the familiar places, the people. All gone for ever.

He pulled himself together.

Bearing in mind how long he'd worked for Central, it was far too late in the day for Lambert to regret his innumerable acts of treason.

Much to his irritation, General Maximovich was still waiting in the Chairman's ante chamber eleven minutes after the time of his appointment.

He had asked for a brief meeting urgently, hinting that the matter concerned a sudden operational development which the Chairman should know about.

"This is urgent, you know," he complained to Surov's aide. "I hope you understand that. I am not used to being kept waiting."

Although he was dressed in civilian clothes, the suave, elegant aide was a lieutenant colonel in the Political Security Service.

"Of course," he agreed sympathetically, "and I'm sure it won't be long now. Only something of supreme state importance would be allowed to delay the meeting."

"Hmm," grunted Maximovich. He sat down and scowled at the rich Oriental carpet covering the polished wood floor.

If Maximovich had known that while he sat cooling his heels, Konstantin Surov, Chairman of the Committee of State Security, far from being busy, was reading a book, he would have been even more disconcerted.

In his office, Surov glanced a couple of times at the eighteenth century carriage clock on his desk, but decided Maximovich could stew a little longer.

Finally, twenty minutes after the scheduled time of the appointment, he pressed the bell.

"The Chairman will see you now," announced the aide.

Maximovich was about to say something, but decided it might be reported back to Surov, and just smiled sourly.

To his surprise, the Chairman rose and greeted him like a welcome visitor, as the aide closed the door.

"Sometimes I think modern communications are a curse, don't you, comrade General? One is always at the end of some wire or another, and completely at the mercy of anyone who wants to talk to one."

Maximovich wasn't quite sure how to take Surov's remark. No one could talk to the Chairman without his consent. Or was it an implied dig at him?

"Please, sit down," invited Surov. He leaned back, and picked up a slim book in front of him. "Have you read this, comrade General? Saul Bellow?"

Maximovich blinked. He felt like a chess player who'd lost his key pieces.

"I regret no, Chairman."

"You should, you know. A Jew, of course, and American, but a very interesting writer. You read English, of course?"

The general cleared his throat. "I prefer the translations."

Maximovich knew he was saying all the wrong things. Surov was toying with him, and it was a bad sign.

"Now," smiled Surov benignly, "what do you wish to confide in me?"

Maximovich considered how to start, and Surov registered the pause.

"Just speak your mind, comrade," he added encouragingly.

"You have seen the signal from London?"

"Yes, and I trust everything is in motion."

"Arrangements are in hand," confirmed Maximovich.

"Good. It should not be difficult to get him out. So what is your problem?"

The pebble glasses stared at him questioningly.

"Chairman, I feel Major Yenko should be transferred to other work."

"Yenko?" he repeated, so softly that Maximovich wasn't quite sure he had heard right.

"In the best interest of operational requirements."

"Why?" asked the Chairman mildly.

"Comrade Chairman, it seems to me that Operation Borzoi is coming apart at the seams. What do we gain if we pull it off, but lose a valuable man like Lambert?"

Surov waited, but Maximovich was silent.

"You haven't explained, General, why this reflects on comrade Yenko?"

Maximovich had long decided he would feel more secure without him. It was a rule of thumb with him to eliminate those under him who were too clever for his own health.

"I do not need to remind you, I know," he confided, and he enjoyed putting in the shaft, "that Yenko is the architect and designer of this whole scheme."

"Is he?" queried Surov, and immediately Maximovich knew he had made a terrible mistake. Instead of making himself more secure, he was suddenly vulnerable.

"I . . ." he faltered, then said, hastily: "Of course, you

know best, comrade Chairman. I see only a small part of the picture. You control the whole. It's just that, as I am sure you understand, comrade Chairman, I have only the efficiency of my department at heart."

"Haven't we all, General," murmured Surov. He stood up, and Maximovich instantly followed suit. "I appreciate you taking the time and trouble to leave your busy desk to tell me all this." So meek, so gentle that Maximovich dismissed the suspicion that it was sarcasm.

"And," continued Surov, "as you will see, comrade, I will act accordingly."

Then he indicated with a slight wave of his hand, and an understanding smile, that the audience was over.

Half an hour later, the aide showed Yenko into Surov's office.

It was a brief meeting.

"I want you to be the first to know that the directorate has decided to make some changes, Major Yenko," declared Surov.

He paused, waiting to see if he could spot a glimmer of apprehension, or a hint of panic in Yenko's response. But Yenko had learnt long ago to hide his reactions.

Surov approved of Yenko's self control.

"You are being promoted, comrade," he went on. "You are to take over some of General Maximovich's responsibilities. The requisite seniority of rank will of course follow automatically. It is the directorate's wish, and my pleasure, to inform you that we are impressed by your outstanding work, and the handling of Operation Borzoi."

He smiled, and Yenko remembered what he had been taught at the officers' school: when congratulated by a high superior, stiffen to attention. He stiffened.

"I don't have to tell you, dear comrade, that because of the nature of our work, this promotion will remain secret, and is not to be promulgated."

"That is the sacrifice we make, comrade Chairman."

Surov walked round his desk, and clasped Yenko's hand, firmly.

"You will always have a friend in me," he asserted. "Even though I myself am leaving here."

"You are leaving, comrade Chairman?" ventured Yenko.

"Yes, I have had the honour of being selected for a higher duty, which means of course that I must leave my life's work here, at Kah Gay Bay. But what greater distinction can our country bestow on a humble worker?"

It was good news, of that there was no question, thought Yenko. He's on his way, streaking ahead like a rocket. A seat in the Kremlin. The Central committee. Following in Andropov's footsteps. Tomorrow . . .

"And you," continued Surov, "you will, I hope, rise like a star too."

Only then did he withdraw his hand.

Yenko clicked his heels.

Surov slowly walked back behind his desk and sat down.

"Any questions?" he asked.

"Yes, comrade Chairman. Two."

Surov nodded.

"Go ahead."

"General Maximovich? What will be his duties?"

"The General," explained Surov, really relishing this part, "is taking over the cadet school in Khiva." He smiled. "Yes, I know, it is rather remote, in fact there isn't even a single taxi. But there is one café, and I am sure he will enjoy it."

I will never trust this man, resolved Yenko.

But Maximovich could be grateful – at least he wasn't going to face a firing squad.

"What is your other point?"

"It doesn't matter, comrade Chairman," replied Yenko.

On second thoughts, Zarubin was a subject he didn't want to bring up. It might spoil the atmosphere.

"Very well." Surov picked up the book on his desk. "I know how fluent you are in English. Perhaps you'd like to read this?"

Yenko looked at it. Then said:

"Very kind of you, Chairman, but I've read all Saul Bellow, including this one."

Yes, decided Surov after Yenko had left, there is a candidate to go high in the KGB.

If he didn't get too clever.

* * *

Lambert decided to treat himself to dinner at Locketts, which was a somewhat arrogant gesture, bearing in mind that Pearmain and the Director sometimes ate there, and he might have bumped into them. But that was the kind of gamble Lambert enjoyed, and nobody from the department showed up. After he'd eaten, he couldn't resist walking past the operations section building in Mersham Street, but again he saw no one.

He had set himself a twenty-four hour deadline, which gave him until the next night and as long as he was out of the country by then, he'd be all right.

As soon as he'd returned from the bank he had packed and the three passports he always had at his disposal were in his desk drawer at home. Not that he'd use them when the time came; experience had long since taught him that truth was often the best cover when one wanted to deceive, and it would amuse him to travel on his real passport, undisguised, using his own name.

He was carrying the standard issue SDECE short barrelled .357 Manrhuin magnum, which he'd acquired through friends in the Direction de Documentation Extérieure et de Contre-Espionnage. He preferred having a foreign weapon which was unregistered at the Home Office, and they had helpfully obtained the French pistol for him.

Obviously, he'd have to get rid of it before finally quitting the country, but until then the gun would be close to him. Just in case Zarubin . . .

He worried much more about Zarubin than the ministry, though, naturally, he was nervous about them too. All day he had been on his guard, checking for any telltale sign indicating he was under surveillance. And now, before going into his flat on the fourth floor of the Victorian mansion block near Westminster City Hall, he walked slowly round, making absolutely sure nobody was loitering, that the few parked cars in front of the building were empty, and that he wasn't being watched from any of the windows on the opposite side of the road.

But there was nobody.

As soon as he closed the front door of his flat, he noticed the envelope in his letter box. Lambert was reassured to see the old man hadn't wasted time, and that communications were as reliable as ever.

There was no stamp on the plain, buff envelope, not even an address, just his name: "Mr S. Lambert MBE".

It was a nice touch, he thought, adding his decoration. The Birthday Honours list never gave a citation when his elevation to the rank of Member of the British Empire had been announced, and he never flaunted his medal. But Central always remembered.

He opened it and pulled out an Austrian Airlines ticket, with a note attached which read simply: "10:30 am Heathrow." The ticket was for the next day's flight No OS452 to Vienna and across the return journey portion someone had written void. It had been bought direct, but then they'd hardly use a travel agency.

So this was the escape hatch they'd opened up for him, and he thought how smoothly it had been organised. He'd be met in Vienna, given a seat on the next Aeroflot departure, and this hour tomorrow night, with luck, he'd be in Moscow.

All he had to do now was get through the night, leave home as usual, around eight-thirty in the morning, so that he was at Heathrow in good time, and farewell England.

If he got through the night. If he got to the airport. If, if . . .

Lambert went into the kitchen and made himself a pot of his favourite Earl Grey tea. Then he took it into the sitting room, turned on the standard reading light which stood to one side of the worn leather armchair, put the gun on the table next to it, sat down and examined the air ticket again, while sipping his cup of tea.

He wished he had a couple of pounds of this particular blend to take with him. It was one of his weaknesses, and although there'd be no shortage of tea where he was going, he doubted GUM would sell Earl Grey.

In his solitary privacy Lambert allowed himself a wry little smile. Who would credit at this moment, on the eve of his final defection, he'd be worrying about his supply of Earl Grey tea?

He closed his eyes and after a time began to doze, but stopped himself from falling asleep. Tomorrow was the big

284

day, and what he needed now was a good night's sleep, not fully dressed, slumped in an armchair, but in bed.

He went into the hall, checked the double lock on the front door, and made sure the chain was in its slot. He didn't bother about the windows; being on the fourth floor meant the front door was the only way into the flat.

As he undressed, he retraced the whole day, and he felt reassured. Perhaps he was even rid of Zarubin. After all, they'd lifted the Russian, and that had been the purpose of Zarubin's mission. But, somehow, although he wouldn't admit it to himself, he knew that was an illusion.

He sat on the edge of his bed, set the alarm for seven, and stared at the white telephone. It hadn't rung once.

Lambert placed the gun next to it, where he could easily reach it, climbed into bed, and switched off the light.

Lying in the dark he considered taking a sleeping pill, but decided against it. Instead, he lay thinking many thoughts, and not long after, he dozed off.

Seven hours later the alarm roused Lambert from a splendid night's sleep, and he awoke with a sense of relief at having got through the dark night. In four hours, he'd be 30,000 feet over the Channel. Beyond reach.

He left a glass of water on the kitchen table for them to find when they finally came, locked up the flat for the last time, then went down in the lift, carrying his single suitcase.

Outside the building he checked to make sure the coast was clear before making his way to the garage.

He had decided to drive himself to the airport. It was a final fail safe measure; if anything went wrong, being in his own car rather than a taxi, meant he'd still be mobile. It wouldn't matter if they finally found the car at Heathrow. It would take time, and by then it would be immaterial if they discovered that was where he'd slipped through the net.

At the garage, he took the lift down to the second level, where he'd parked his car. He didn't see a soul, and that was reassuring too. He unlocked the boot of the Citroën, put his suitcase in, then went round the front, and got into the driver's seat.

"Going places?" asked Zarubin pleasantly from behind.

Lambert wanted to curse. He wanted to curse himself. He

wanted to curse Zarubin. And he wanted to get away. Desperately.

Controlling his panic, he glanced in the rear view mirror, and saw him. Surreptitiously, his hand moved towards his pocket for the gun, but Zarubin froze the movement by saying:

"Don't. Sit very still."

"What do you want?"

"A little conversation," said Zarubin. "A friendly chat."

"No." Lambert felt calmer. "You're going to kill me."

In the driving mirror Lambert could see him shaking his head incredulously. "Kill *you*, Stuart? You know what you're saying?"

"Why don't you get on with it?" asked Lambert a little wearily.

"If I wanted to do that, you'd have been dead the moment you got into that seat. And I sure wouldn't be here."

Lambert half turned and gave Zarubin a puzzled look.

"This heap would have blown to bits . . . *if* I had wanted to kill you," Zarubin continued. "Now, give me your gun. Careful. We don't want to mess up the upholstery."

Mentally, Lambert rehearsed pulling out the Manrhuin, slipping the catch off, turning, firing . . .

"You wouldn't do anything so damn stupid," cautioned Zarubin soothingly, reaching into Lambert's pocket, removing the gun, then emptying its magazine. "There. Can't hurt anybody now."

Zarubin leaned over and unlocked the front passenger door.

"Can't have you getting a crick in your neck, Stuart," he said, swiftly getting out of the back of the car, and sliding into the seat next to Lambert.

Lambert stared at him.

"Come on, you're in a hurry, aren't you? You haven't got much time." He threw the gun on to the back seat. "Carry on."

"You won't get away with this," warned Lambert.

"Get away with what?" asked Zarubin, his expression the picture of innocence. "Helping you?" Lambert was startled. "Yes, Stuart, I'm here to help you get away, so I wouldn't sit here wasting time, if I were you. You may not have much left."

Lambert frowned.

"Come on now," smiled Zarubin. "You don't want to miss the plane, do you?"

"Plane?"

"Sure."

"Who sent you?" asked Lambert softly.

"Why does it matter?"

Lambert regarded Zarubin as if he was seeing him in a new light.

"Who?" he repeated.

"Take a guess," said Zarubin carelessly. He looked at his watch. "I'd hurry though."

Still Lambert didn't move. "No," he insisted. "You tell me."

"That's naughty, Stuart. We don't ask things like that."

"Who gave you orders to help me?"

Zarubin shrugged. "Like I said, guess."

Lambert opened the door and started to get out of the car.

"What are you doing, Stuart?" grinned Zarubin, placing a vicelike grip on Lambert's arm.

"Getting out."

"If you don't get that flight, you're a dead man and you know it," said Zarubin. "Pearmain isn't going to fuck around, so let's go."

Lambert sat rigid, his mind filled with confusion, suspicion, disbelief – and sudden hope.

Then he asked:

"Who *are* you working for?"

Zarubin chuckled.

"There you go again. Have a little faith, Stuart." He glanced at his watch again. "Traffic's heavy at this time of the morning, and you've got to get to Heathrow for check in."

Lambert hesitated. Then, his hand shaking a little, he reached for the ignition key, and started the car.

"That's it," nodded Zarubin approvingly, as the Citröen swung up the levels. "You'll make it all right now."

Lambert turned into the street, and occasionally glancing sideways at Zarubin, headed westwards.

Suddenly he said:

"I'm going to have an accident, aren't I?"

"With me in the car?" retorted Zarubin cheerfully. "My job's to get you on that plane in one piece."

"Your *job*?"

"And I promise you you'll make it."

"Promise!" repeated Lambert sarcastically. "What the devil is our word worth, even to each other?"

He halted at a red light.

"All right," shrugged Zarubin. "But just to put your mind at ease, remember you could have been a dead man any time in the last twenty-four hours. At the hotel in Mayfair, at the bank, in Shaftesbury Avenue. At the restaurant, last night. In Mersham Street afterwards. I was around, Stuart."

Lambert swallowed. The lights changed, and he accelerated.

"God," he said finally. "You!" He seemed to have aged. "Who the hell are you really?"

Sirens from behind were becoming louder, and as the sound came nearer, Lambert looked anxiously into the mirror. Then, out of the traffic emerged an ambulance, weaving its way towards them, then passing them, its emergency lights flashing. Lambert visibly relaxed.

"You got the flight number?" enquired Zarubin.

"Austrian Airlines. OS452."

"That's right," agreed Zarubin. "Vienna."

Christ, thought Lambert, he knows everything.

"You'll get a good lunch," added Zarubin, once again checking his watch. "Well done. You'll make it easily."

Lambert licked his dry lips.

They drove through the airport tunnel into Heathrow, and for the first time Zarubin noticed that Lambert was sweating. Little beads of perspiration stood out along the line of his military moustache.

"Easy," grinned Zarubin, "they'll think you're smuggling two tons of coke."

After he'd parked the car, Lambert turned to Zarubin.

"You won't see me again," he said. "Thanks."

He held out his hand, but Zarubin didn't take it.

"No, Stuart, we're going all the way inside, you and me. I

said I'd see you on the plane, and I meant it."

"There's no need, really," Lambert assured him, but Zarubin cut him short, "That's the deal, friend."

Together they walked into the European airlines building, and Zarubin stood beside him as Lambert checked in his suitcase. Then Zarubin accompanied him to passport control.

"Austrian Airlines now boarding flight OS452 for Vienna at Gate 9," announced the tannoy voice.

"You made it," Zarubin congratulated him.

Lambert, looking pale, glanced about nervously.

"I don't . . . I don't understand you, Zarubin," he said finally. "I was sure you'd . . ."

"You got me all wrong, Stuart."

Lambert shook his head. "No," he said decisively. "I haven't. Not you. But . . ."

"But one never knows, does one?"

They were standing near the news kiosk, and, unexpectedly, Zarubin bought a couple of magazines, and some newspapers, and gave them to Lambert.

"Light reading. And I'm not sure you can get the *New Yorker* in Moscow."

"I . . ."

"Take them," insisted Zarubin firmly, and Lambert tucked them under his arm.

"This is the final call for Austrian Airlines . . ." the tannoy voice reminded the people on the concourse.

"You'd better go," said Zarubin.

He stood and watched Lambert walk up to the passport desk, show the immigration officer his papers, which the man glanced at idly, then nodded him through.

Lambert turned once, and looked back at Zarubin. He had a quizzical expression, the look of a man who is completely puzzled.

Zarubin gave him a wave, but Lambert turned his back and disappeared through the door.

Zarubin walked down the stairs of the departure building, feeling like a man in need of a stiff drink, and needing it quickly.

It was ironical, he thought as he headed towards the bar,

that these well bred, stiff upper lipped pillars of the English establishment had become Moscow's acolytes while he, whose parents had fled from the pogroms of Odessa, was sworn to destroy them. They had all the advantages and comforts of middle class life to nurture their treason. What did they know of the real Russia?

At Vienna Airport Lambert was met by a woman who handed him his Aeroflot ticket. The reception committee in Moscow was a young man who took him to a black staff car which deposited them outside a small block of flats in Gostinichnaya Street. He didn't know the address, and the young man wrote it out on a slip of paper which he suggested Lambert keep on him in case he got lost.

The young man told him to make himself at home. First on the agenda was the debriefing, and afterwards he'd probably like a short vacation. Then he was left on his own.

The flat was impersonal, and austerely furnished. Lambert knew the kind. The ministry had half a dozen like it in London, in the Finchley Road, off Gloucester Road, in Putney, near Victoria Station, for temporary guests of no special importance.

This was not how he'd expected it. It was all so low key.

He received one phone call.

"Hello, old boy," said a very English voice, "just heard you've arrived in town. Welcome to the club. How about a spot of supper? At my place?"

It was Philby. An echo from long ago.

It didn't turn out to be a very comfortable evening. Lambert felt as if he was the new boy, and Philby the house captain, giving him the once over, deciding how he would fit in.

He looked shabby, for a major general in the KGB, reflected Lambert. His sweater had a hole, his corduroy trousers were unpressed, the slippers he had on had seen better days. But then, Kim had never cared. In his time, he was the worst dressed man in Leconfield House.

Is this what I'm going to look like after twenty years here, he wondered. Face lined, eyes watery, wisps of straggly hair hanging untidily, living in a moth eaten flat, papers all over the place. Is this what lies ahead?

"Well, old chap," said Philby, his tone patronising, "what will you do now?"

"They tell me I'm going to be debriefed for the next ten days." Lambert took a sip of the Courvoisier. It made it easier to put up with Philby.

"Yes of course," said Philby irritably. "But after that?"

"I thought you might know."

"Why me?" asked Philby. "They don't consult me about things like that, old boy. It's the old nine to five routine for me, sitting behind a desk, analysing *The Times* leaders for the ministry."

He's still the same fox he used to be back in the old days in Leconfield House, thought Lambert. Sly as hell.

"D'you mind passing that?" requested Philby, nodding at the brandy bottle. He poured a triple measure into his balloon glass. It wasn't his first of the evening.

He caught Lambert's look.

"Ah, yes, I indulge. So will you, Stuart. In due course. Life gets tedious at times." He drank deep. "Wasn't that a song once? 'Life Gets Tedious'? Cole Porter or somebody?"

"I don't know."

"I dare say you'll settle in quite nicely," remarked Philby, sticking a Dunhill into a long cigarette holder, and lighting it. "They'll find something to keep you busy."

"Such as?"

"Who knows? State publishing house. The English service on Radio Moscow. Or maybe . . ."

"Yes?"

Philby's eyes twinkled. "Something more interesting. Once you've got acclimatised."

He was drinking the brandy like mineral water, and poured himself yet another refill.

"Now, tell me about London. Is it as bloody awful as I hear?"

"You wouldn't like it," sighed Lambert. "Not now."

"That bad?"

"Remember Swan and Edgar's, in Piccadilly? Gone."

Philby was shocked. "I didn't know that."

"The London Pavilion's boarded up."

"Good God," gasped Philby. "You know, I had a post box

there. In the gents, in the circle. Such a barn of a place, the Pavilion. Oh dear."

"Stone's Chop House, in Panton Street. You remember?"

"Of course. Don't tell me . . ."

"Yes. Closed down. So has the Talk of the Town, and the snuff shop in the Haymarket. It's all bloody American fast food now. And dirty films."

"Well," said Philby slowly, "thank God I'm not there to see it. Sometimes, one gets a bit nostalgic of course, but the things I've been hearing . . ." Suddenly, for a moment, he was serious. "It makes it easier to live away from it."

He stared into the fire place.

"You'll help me, won't you, Kim?"

Philby slowly raised his eyes.

"Help you, old boy?"

"To get adjusted. To fit in."

"If I can," said Philby, and there was a hint of steel behind the casualness. He drank more brandy. "I wouldn't worry. They always look after people like you."

For Lambert those were the most chilling words he could have said. "People like you", made it clear he was an outsider. Philby may have welcomed him to the club, but only as a guest. As yet, he didn't belong to the group.

"The first year or two isn't easy of course," Philby was saying. "You're not cut off, don't worry. You get all the Fleet Street rags, you can listen to the Beeb, Harrods will send you things. But of course . . ." He shrugged. "It takes some getting used to. But you'll find us very understanding."

There he was again. Rubbing it in. You and us.

The door bell rang.

"And you won't be lacking company, if you need it," he went on, ignoring the interruption. "There are some very attractive girls in Moscow. I know." He chuckled.

The door bell rang again, more firmly.

"Sonya!" shouted Philby. He turned to Lambert, "You must excuse her. She never answers the door. It's a bloody nuisance. Servants are the same the world over. I remember in Beirut . . ."

This time the door bell rang insistently.

"Sonya!" he shouted again, then got up, irritated. "Damn

woman. Excuse me."

He left the studio. Lambert stood up, walked over to the desk, and picked up the Brezhnev photograph with its dedication in Russian.

Philby returned, with two men.

"Mr Lambert?" enquired one formally. "I am Colonel Yenko. Please sit down."

Philby stood by the fire place, watching with a curiously detached look on his face.

"This is Major Patrov. Twelfth Department," continued Yenko. There was no smile on his face, no word of greeting.

Lambert tried to think what the Twelfth Department did. And fear grew. The Twelfth was the Sluzhba. The Service. The investigator of the investigators.

He sat down, feeling very cold.

"Mr Lambert," went on Yenko, "are you being perfectly honest with us?"

"I beg your pardon?"

"Let me put it more plainly. Would it not be best if you told us everything?"

Lambert stared at him in disbelief.

"What are you talking about?"

"I do think you should listen carefully to the colonel, old boy," Philby gently interrupted.

"Major Patrov here," explained Yenko, "has a very suspicious mind. That is his job. He has received certain very interesting information. About you, Mr Lambert."

"I don't understand," said Lambert, keeping his hands folded in his lap, so that they wouldn't tremble.

Patrov's eyes were ugly slits that never left Lambert's face.

"I'm sorry that you are not being cooperative," added Yenko. "You invoked the escape route to get away, correct?"

"Of course."

"You indicated it was a matter of life and death for you." Yenko was relentless. "That time was running out."

"Exactly." Lambert hoped he didn't sound as desperate as he felt.

"A hit man was already on your trail, correct?"

"Correct."

"The American agent, Zarubin?"

Philby was smiling.

"So tell me, Mr Lambert, how is it that you arranged to meet this Zarubin, that he travelled with you to the airport, that he saw you off, waved to you?"

"God almighty, you're not suggesting . . ." Lambert clenched his hands.

"Is it true?" demanded Yenko.

"Mr Lambert," cut in Major Patrov quietly. "Do not deny it. We had someone there. We saw you leave with this man in your car. You were chatting to him. You drove to Heathrow with him. You two got on famously."

"Famously," echoed Lambert, weakly. "That's absurd."

"He even made sure you wouldn't be bored on the flight to Vienna. Like a good friend, a good colleague, he bought some magazines. We know what Zarubin is, Lambert, and he doesn't wave to his enemies."

Philby sat down and crossed his legs.

"It does seem peculiar, doesn't it, Stuart?" he murmured.

"He was going to kill me," insisted Lambert desperately.

"Really?" mocked Yenko. "I think he's working with you. I think, rather stupidly, he came with you to wish you luck. In your new role as double agent over here. I think you're a traitor, Lambert, twice over. You bought your miserable life by agreeing to betray us."

"No." It was a cry of terror.

"Why didn't you report it?" asked the major quietly.

"I . . ." He had worried about it. He had debated it with himself. But who would have believed that Zarubin helped him get away? How could he tell them? Aloud, he said frantically:

"I was waiting . . . until you debrief me."

"That's how people are usually tripped up, old boy, keeping the wrong company," pointed out Philby softly.

Lambert turned to him, appealingly.

"Kim . . . you've known me since . . . since the old days. You don't believe . . ."

Philby tapped out the cigarette holder into an ash tray. "Trouble is, my dear chap, that we simply can't take risks. You can see how it is."

"Get your coat," ordered the major.

Lambert shook his head. "No. No. You can't."

"Don't make a fuss, Stuart," sighed Philby, taking a sip of the brandy.

"Where are you taking me?" Lambert croaked.

"For interrogation," answered the major.

"And then a firing squad," added Yenko. He did enjoy the look of terror on people's faces when he told them their fate.

They took Lambert downstairs, and bundled him into a staff car.

During the short ride to Dzerzhinsky Street, Lambert suddenly realised that, although he wasn't even in Moscow, in the final analysis, Zarubin was going to kill him.

Since two gold prospectors went mad there in the 1880s, it had been known to desert wanderers as Loon Valley, and so it was marked on some large scale maps of the barren territory.

For miles to the south, all the eye could see was desert, white sand waves concealing the immense masses of black lava that thousands of years ago had streamed down from the distant mountains.

The wind blew, but it did little to ease the intense heat. The only vegetation growing in the sterile sand was occasional clumps of dried up, brown shrubs.

Hidden beyond it all was Loon Valley, guarded by a 5,000 foot high mountain range running east and west, walled in by nature on all sides but one.

Strangers didn't get that far. All along the nearest highway, some hundred miles away, the regularly spaced warning signs cautioned:

"US Government. Testing Ground. Keep Out!"

There was nothing to see anyway. Any ancient tracks there might have been were obliterated a long time ago.

Should a pioneering spirit decide to take a chance, turn off the highway, and enter the closed arid wilderness, after driving some twenty or thirty miles, that person would come across further notices which stated firmly:

"US Government. No Entry."

If the explorer persisted, and ignored the final signs which displayed a skull and crossbones and one word, "Danger", eventually, he'd find there was a helicopter, with "US Army" painted on its fuselage, hovering above, observing, taking the licence plate number, then through a loudspeaker peremptorily ordering him to turn back immediately. And the loudspeaker voice would warn any trespasser who hesitated to obey that he was liable to arrest.

It had never happened, but anyone who defied the guardians of the desert would soon discover that they had come to the end of their travels.

So, its remoteness and inaccessibility ensured that the closed zone was seldom bothered by prying eyes on the ground. But once an hour, the Soviet satellite on its regular orbit over Nevada and the western states would take its routine quota of reconnaissance pictures.

The Russian photo interpreters had at first agreed that in the hidden valley lay some kind of research establishment, a small one, just a few one storey buildings and, of all things in the heart of the desert, a swimming pool. Satellite probes had confirmed there was no radiation emanating from this site, so it didn't seem to have a nuclear function. Nor had there been any indication of missile research, or weapon testing.

Perhaps, they figured originally, some bacteriological warfare work was going on here, which explained the choice of such an isolated location. Not that there was any evidence to support such a theory. Very little activity appeared to take place in the valley, and the only link with the outside world seemed to be helicopters. If it had been a more approachable place, an agent might have been sent to take a closer look. As it was, they decided to leave it to the spy satellite to keep an hourly eye on the location. It didn't really seem to be of great importance. Then they found out the truth.

But Loon Valley had a top secret designation, Camp Delta.

The Russian airmen who were held there didn't have a bad life. Much care had been taken to devise an existence which was humane and bearable. The Pentagon psychiatrists who had been consulted about the problems of protracted internment had no idea who the inmates would be, but they came up with useful advice.

These Russians were a special kind. Volunteers, who had

been selected for their particular skills. Radar specialists who fenced with the counter measures they tried to probe over the East Coast, over California, over Alaska, over Scotland. Electronic warfare technicians who, from a height of 60,000 feet, attempted to find the chinks in the electric curtain that protected New York, Los Angeles, London, Chicago, Glasgow. Men who knew they were invading forbidden territory to test the other side's weaknesses.

They were intelligent men, and they had been warned before they set off that if they fell into the enemy's hands, their motherland could not acknowledge it had sent them. Their uniforms would save them from the firing squad, but in times of peace a nation could not admit to sending bombers to another nation's territory to spy.

For their first few weeks in Delta, they were interrogated by teams of Air Force experts. The Office of Special Investigation handled the debriefings and tried to prise out of them every little detail of their unit, their training, their orders, their equipment, what they were specially interested in over San Francisco, or Houston, why they were ferreting over New England, what their instruments were set to record, what electronic game they were playing.

It was a slow, laborious job, and the Russians stonewalled most of the time. Occasionally, they let slip an odd word, a careless fact, and it was added to the machine that digested all intelligence to the computers, and to the analysts' files. But more often than not, they let nothing out.

After that, they would gradually become acclimatised to the daily life of the camp, meet their fellow inmates, and adjust to being phantom men who had vanished.

Each Soviet crewman wore American fatigues, without insignia, and had his own quarters, an air conditioned bungalow. The mess hall served Russian dishes, an excellent library provided Russian books, and Soviet magazines, Russian video tapes were screened on TV, and the cinema showed both Russian and English language films three times a week.

A big gym provided every kind of facility for exercise, there was a well equipped hobby shop for those who wanted to use it, and, as the spy satellite had spotted, a swimming pool.

Congress did not know it had budgeted for any of this, because the funding of the Camp Delta operation was secret, and concealed in Defence estimates.

Within Camp Delta, the Russians enjoyed considerable freedom. They could go for walks, even do some exploring. Escape was no problem. No one had ever managed to climb those craggy mountains, and cross that desert.

Delta's personnel had been hand picked. Colonel Korner, who had developed the programme and was also commandant, had been US military attaché in Moscow, spoke the language like a native. Every member of the camp staff was also a Russian speaker and none was armed. Guns were held only for emergencies.

Although there was only a handful of Russian prisoners, all of them were important. Very important. And they were told the truth. They were the insurance policy for American spy pilots who fell into Soviet hands. They were briefed about the tacit understanding, that nobody said anything, admitted anything. That, on both sides, it was agreed they didn't exist.

And that they would be well treated.

Perhaps, one day, they would be exchanged. So far it hadn't happened. U2 pilots, yes. Secret agents, yes. Not military personnel, invading each other's air on official orders in marked war planes. They didn't get swapped. That was a different game.

Korner encouraged his inmates to believe that they'd see home again one day. After all, every convict knows when his sentence ends, every prisoner of war that he'll be free once peace comes. These men had no idea, and that was his biggest problem.

It needed careful handling. Great understanding. Psychology of a special kind.

There were other problems. The lack of mail. No news from home. From wives, families. But how could there be mail for men who didn't exist? And that was something on which both sides were insistent, because both sides wanted to continue their illegal spy flights, but neither would admit openly that it did, and would carry on doing it.

Women were another problem. The colonel told the Pentagon that it would help a great deal if somehow, now and then, it could be arranged.

Washington was adamant. No way. Unworkable. Undesirable.

So it was a tricky project, Camp Delta. The Russians here hadn't just come down in American air space. Some had been in NATO areas. Over Norway. Ferreting British air defences. Snooping on Holy Loch. Under the UKUSA agreement, Delta was centralised. It was agreed that all Soviet ferrets would be handed over to be held at Camp Delta; too many such installations were risky. Other NATO countries agreed.

Loon Valley had become the ferrets' nest, and the final destination of Major Ulianov.

He was flown, under escort, from Mildenhall in England, had a short stop over at Andrews Air Force base, then a USAF jet flew him to Chandler Air Force base in Arizona, where he was transferred to a helicopter.

He had no idea of the location to which he was going, but he enjoyed flying over the desert, and across the mountains.

The chopper finally touched down in the valley, and he had his first glimpse of Camp Delta.

He found it hard to conceal his excitement. It had been a long journey, but he had finally made it.

"Okay, out you get," said his escort, tapping him on the shoulder.

Ulianov took a deep breath, then, like an actor making his entry, jumped from the helicopter and faced the American colonel standing waiting for him.

"Welcome," the colonel greeted him in Russian.

And to Ulianov's ears those words sounded almost like welcome home.

The Savoy Grill was a convenient meeting place for Roberts, being near Fleet Street, yet handy for those of his guests who came from the opposite direction, and a standing lunch reservation there was one of the perks enjoyed by his lordship's most successful editors. It gave Roberts a particularly piquant satisfaction, because one rainy day many years ago, when he'd still been a struggling reporter, he'd had to interview someone in the Savoy Grill room. In those days he'd been so broke he'd had to walk round with a hole in the sole of one shoe, and he would never forget the embarrassment of being led to the table, his foot squelching every time he took a step.

Although he was now a regular customer, who signed his bills, and received bows from the waiters, he often recalled that awful lunch twenty-five years ago.

Today, however, he had other things on his mind. His once in a while lunch with Pearmain was always an important occasion, and was a mutually beneficial arrangement.

For Pearmain it provided an opportunity to pick up titbits about newspaperland, a world of constant interest to his organisation. It also sometimes offered him the chance to plant a seed which, if it sprouted in a gossip column or a small paragraph on an inner page, could render the ministry a useful service.

For Roberts, contact with The Friends had proven a profitable quid pro quo, especially during his weekend stays with his lordship at his country seat, where he was regularly invited once a month, and when it did no harm to hint mysteriously at his pipeline into the ante chambers of secret intelligence. The idea that his newspaper interests made him privy to the intrigues of state, always fascinated his lordship, and this time Roberts thought he was on to something which would not only make his lordship sit up, but provide the paper with a world scoop. Not confused ravings like Prossers's allegations.

Throughout the meal, Roberts had controlled his excitement, but now, over the coffee, he felt the time had come.

"Have you heard anything about this rumour that's going round?" he asked tentatively. Of course Pearmain would have heard. It was his department, but tact was necessary.

"What rumour?"

Roberts lowered his voice.

"Some suggestion that one of our people has defected."

"Really?" Pearmain wasn't giving anything away. "Where did you hear that?"

"Oh, you know how these things get about."

"No. I don't."

There must be something in it, decided Roberts, otherwise he'd be more inquisitive.

"Story is that it's somebody quite high up. Not in your department, I imagine." He smiled at Pearmain innocently.

"Sounds a load of rubbish," said Pearmain. "Defected where?"

"Moscow, I heard."

"Who's saying that?" demanded Pearmain.

"God knows where it started. I just wondered if you'd come across it?"

"Of course not."

The wine waiter came over. "Any brandies, any liqueurs, gentlemen?"

Roberts glanced over at Pearmain, who shook his head curtly.

"What exactly is the story?" he enquired casually.

"Well, the way I heard it, the Americans have uncovered a mole in Whitehall, and the fellow got so panicky he took the next plane to Moscow."

"Totally untrue," Pearmain retorted, looking Roberts straight in the eye. "Absolute fairy story."

"Really?"

"You know what the trouble is with you people, you so want things to happen, that after a while you believe they really have. That was the trouble with that poor man Prosser, wasn't it? Chasing ghosts. You're twenty, thirty years behind the times. Things have changed since then, you know."

"There's a suggestion that he took an Aeroflot plane from Vienna," continued Roberts relentlessly. "And, you know, I'm beginning to wonder if Prosser really had got it so wrong. I'm almost sorry I agreed to warn him off."

Pearmain's laugh was slightly forced.

"Vienna, did you say? Why not Stockholm? Or Helsinki? Make a change at least. As for Prosser, he saw conspiracies round every corner. That kind of attitude does the country a great deal of harm."

Roberts played his last card.

"Point is, if it's true, and you've covered up another traitor, it could end up very embarrassing to the government.

You don't just want it to slip out by accident, do you? I mean, if it was properly handled, it could . . . well, it could soften the impact."

"You mean," mused Pearmain, after a pause, "that if a friendly paper broke the story, played it down a bit, it wouldn't rock the boat so much."

"Precisely," agreed Roberts eagerly. He was going to get his scoop after all.

"That would be very helpful," nodded Pearmain.

"You've got friends at court, you know," urged Roberts. "Often proved it, too, haven't we? Look at the Cheltenham business. Kept the lid on that for you. We can do it for this one."

"There's only one problem," said Pearmain.

"Oh?"

"It isn't true." He smiled. "Nobody's gone over. Nobody's missing. I know it's a bore, but the story's a phoney."

Roberts said nothing.

"Maybe you could pass the word," added Pearmain. "So it doesn't get spread some more."

"Well, I'm glad to hear it," murmured Roberts, controlling his anger. "You know I always play ball with you, and that's why I told you. I've always been ready to help."

"I know you have. And we appreciate it." He smiled. "And I trust it will go on like that. I'd hate to think that we can't rely on you people."

Roberts drank the last of his lukewarm Perrier. The ice had melted. The coffee was cold. The show was over.

"How do you think these silly rumours get about in the first place?" he asked naively, and Pearmain knew he was being called a liar.

"Disinformation," he replied, coolly. "A favourite Russian trick. They spread some story . . . you know, some scandal, anything . . . they don't really think anybody will believe it, but they hope some of the dirt will stick . . . like this one; you really believed that one of our people had turned up in Moscow, didn't you?" He shook his head regretfully. "You see how easy it is?"

I'll get you one day, resolved Roberts. If this comes out, I'll crucify you.

Aloud he said, "Yes, you can't trust anybody these days, can you?"

Back in his office half an hour later, Pearmain reached for the red phone to call the Director and request that a D-notice be issued forthwith forbidding any information to be published about any member of the British intelligence services who may recently have gone abroad, or to name him.

Then he decided against it. On second thoughts, if there were rumours travelling around, a D-notice would only confirm them.

Much better to play dumb, say nothing, deny everything, plead ignorance. It had worked so well so many times, even during the Falklands business.

So, if anyone wanted to know about a civil servant called Stuart Lambert they would just get a blank look. It saved so much embarrassment.

There were times when Pearmain was deeply grateful he didn't live in America. Thank goodness the service didn't have the Freedom of Information Act to contend with. The British method of dealing with these things was so much more civilised.

There was nothing in the air conditioned room to remind him of the time. No windows, no clock, his wrist watch had for the moment been taken from him and neither of his interviewers wore one. Nor was there anything to interrupt the long process of debriefing – not even a telephone.

The session began slowly, with routine enquiries about his family, his wife, his children, his home town. Gentle stuff that wouldn't alarm him.

At first Ulianov was reluctant to talk, and his interrogators didn't rush him. They were patient men, skilled at their craft, and they knew the secret was to make him feel at ease, to get him relaxed.

It paid off, and, gradually, there came other questions, casual ones, apparently insignificant. Hesitantly, he started to answer them, to laugh at the odd joke, and, as time wore on, to talk more freely.

The interrogators' approach was one of understanding, sometimes flattering him, other times encouraging him and, above all, always listening to him.

Then what Major Ulianov told them in an almost routine way, confirmed to the OSI men that he was a catch all right. An EWO. An electronics warfare expert of the Dal'nyaya Aviatsiya, the long range strike force, the flying rockets. He wasn't ordinary air crew either, that was clear. A graduate of the Lenin Military-Political Academy, he'd spent two years on the staff of General Colonel Reshetnikov, the Deputy Commander of Soviet strategic bombers. He'd been flying special reconnaissance when he was captured.

Here was a man who knew big secrets. Targeting priorities, first strike areas, war plans maybe and the interrogators were hard put to conceal their excitement.

To test that Ulianov was speaking the truth, they asked him questions to which they already had the answers, probed him about things they could confirm.

They played him recordings of Warsaw Pact call signs, and Soviet pilots' codes, picked up by American spy aircraft, and NATO intruders. Tentatively, they asked him about missile guidance wavelengths, and developments in Soviet surveillance radar systems.

Then, gently, tactfully, they started offering him inducements. Planting the idea that if he came up with interesting information, it could conceivably bring him a very pleasant future. That nothing was too good for those who saw their way to being helpful.

They said they were anxious to know more about the latest high power jammer transmitters on Soviet bombers, and the new counter measures to detect weapons-associated radar transmissions. They'd like to know about the reported precision location system which guided counter measures straight into the emissions of NATO radar and, apparently, blacked out the network.

Of course they realised he was a loyal Soviet officer, and they couldn't expect him to tell them things which conflicted with his conscience. Or could they?

He was grateful for their consideration, so the OSI men didn't press it. But they did let it slip that what particularly interested them, of all things, was his work on General Colonel Reshetnikov's staff.

Especially one set of plans. The most valuable folder of all, and which he had seen. The Russian's schedule of priority target locations in the United States. The document that listed the American cities which the Soviets intended to strike first.

For the interrogators, it was the Holy Grail, and the single most important secret.

And when, finally, Major Ulianov agreed that, if they made it worth his while, gave him their word, he'd tell them which American metropolis the Russians had selected as their priority target, he fulfilled their wildest dreams.

The Siamese twins were waiting for Zarubin as he came out of the American Express office in Brompton Road. The stocky one with the Nixon chin closed in on one side, and the lanky one on the other.

"This way, Mr Zarubin," indicated Houghton, while Bowyer took hold of his arm like a helpful guide steering a blind man.

"We've got a car, round the corner," he added, politely.

They strolled, like three close friends, to a grey Ford that had somehow managed to find a parking bay in front of a Spanish shoe shop. As soon as Zarubin saw its official licence plates he knew it came from the Grosvenor Square motor pool.

Bowyer, the hefty one, got in with Zarubin. Houghton slipped into the driver's seat in front.

No point playing dumb, decided Zarubin. But they ought to do it by the book. Even the Office of Security had its etiquette.

"I'd like to see some ID," said Zarubin.

"Sure thing," agreed Bowyer, discreetly pulling out a .38. "This good enough?"

"Can it, Joe. Show the guy your ID," instructed Houghton in the front.

That surprised Zarubin. He had thought the thick set man was the boss. Houghton looked younger, but perhaps it was just his close cropped hair.

"And put that thing away," he ordered. "Mr Zarubin won't cause any problems, will you Mr Zarubin?"

Bowyer holstered the .38 then produced his ID card with

its red diagonal stripe and thumbnail photograph.

"Mind telling me what you fellows want," asked Zarubin mildly. He was pleased. Nearly all the pieces fitted now.

"Somebody wants to see you," Houghton replied, starting the car, and manoeuvring into the mainstream of Knightsbridge traffic.

"They want to make sure you'll show up," added Bowyer.

"You needn't have gone to all this trouble," grinned Zarubin, feeling marvellously in control of events. "A phone call would have done just as well."

The Siamese twins lapsed into silence. But they were sharp. They hadn't even searched him, and Zarubin knew why. They'd been so well briefed they knew he didn't carry a gun, and picking him up outside the American Express had been no accident either. They'd been following him.

"Who sent you fellows?"

Nixon chin stared out of the window, and his questions remained unanswered.

Idly, Zarubin wondered if these two goons bought their clothes together, they were dressed so alike. They both had on the same style suits, corresponding blue button down shirts, and matching striped ties. Houghton probably had an identical .38 and maybe, off duty, they laid the same girl.

At Hyde Park corner, the car swung south and as it turned down Grosvenor Place and continued past Buckingham Palace's garden wall with its anti-intruder spikes, Zarubin began to feel uneasy. The pick up was official which was why they were using a government car, and he'd expected their destination to be the embassy or maybe the Navy place. But this was the wrong direction.

"Where are we going?"

"I told you," replied Houghton. "Somebody wants to see you. I guess you've been a naughty boy."

Bowyer sniggered. It was the first time he had allowed himself the luxury of reacting.

"Were you planning to leave the country, Mr Zarubin?" He grinned.

"Why do you ask that?"

"Just wondered if you were collecting travellers' cheques." And he laughed.

306

"Okay," said Zarubin curtly, "joke's over."

"Maybe." But Bowyer was no longer smiling.

The car crossed the Thames, turned left, and pulled up in front of a modern apartment block.

"Here we are," Houghton told him, opening the car door.

Zarubin got out as well and looked up at a twenty storey building on the Thames embankment, near Lambeth Palace.

Houghton and Bowyer escorted him through the palatial lobby and into the elevator which didn't stop until it reached the top floor.

When they got out there was only one door and Bowyer rang the bell.

The three of them stood silently until the door was opened by a black man in a white jacket.

"Please come in," he invited Zarubin, but the Siamese twins didn't follow, and the black man quietly shut the door.

"This way," said the black man, leading Zarubin across the thickly carpeted open plan sitting room, one wall of which was a scenic window overlooking the river and the Houses of Parliament. From this height the red double decker buses looked like motorised models as they crossed Westminster Bridge.

Zarubin followed the black man along a teak panelled corridor. Somehow the faint sound of a teleprinter in the background didn't fit in with the eighteenth century prints on the walls, and the antique furniture.

The black man stopped at the last door on the right and knocked.

"Come in," called a voice, and he opened the door, then stood aside to let Zarubin enter.

The room had another enormous window, and sitting behind a massive desk facing it was Blanchard, Special Division's Assistant Director.

There was no greeting. It was not Blanchard's style in a crisis.

"I thought it was about time we discussed the last act," he said, without formality. "You know what's going on?"

"I thought so. Until now," replied Zarubin.

"He says you've been working for them ever since

Warsaw. That you deliberately killed the wrong man when you executed Yudkin. He maintains you tipped them off about Spiridov because he was going to identify you, then Flexner became suspicious, so you shot him with his own gun. And when the trap was closed on Lambert, the man you'd been ordered to terminate, you helped him to get away."

Blanchard paused.

"That's what he says," he concluded.

"And do you believe him?" asked Zarubin softly.

Blanchard's chair was in the shadow, so his face was only partially visible, concealing much of his expression.

"Should I?"

"Why not? It all makes sense, doesn't it? Perfect fucking sense."

"No need to swear," reproved Blanchard.

He stood up, walked round to the front of the desk and perched on the edge, so that Zarubin found himself staring at Blanchard's ankle length green silk socks and his hand made crocodile shoes.

"I think you'd better kill him," Blanchard said, almost lazily. "Quietly, inconspicuously, accidentally, if you like. I'm afraid that's the only solution."

"Jesus!"

"That's a curious reaction," remarked Blanchard, glancing at Zarubin questioningly. "What did you expect?"

Zarubin sighed. "I don't know . . ."

"Don't know?" Blanchard snarled. "Don't know what? The due process of justice? Well let me reassure you Zarubin, he's getting the due process of justice."

Then he was suave again, relaxed, softly spoken.

"I imagine you might even get some satisfaction out of it, wouldn't you say?"

"That's why you picked me, isn't it?" muttered Zarubin, feeling slightly sick. "You've known from the beginning, that would be the pay off."

"Never mind how long I've known," interrupted Blanchard. "Suffice it to say that when he selected you for the job, he picked the man I'd already chosen. That's why you were working for me when he thought he was giving the orders.

I've always known you were the only man who could kill him without any publicity, hearings, trial. I knew I could rely on you to get the truth and take on the role of judge, jury, executioner."

Zarubin felt depressed. Dichter had said these very words to him when he'd ordered him to kill Lambert. And now he was hearing them again, the same cold blooded, unemotional words, but this time from the Ivy League witness of congressional committees, the socialite at Washington parties, the collector of antique furniture who had terminated scores of lives.

Blanchard went on. "You need not have any scruples, Zarubin. He set out to destroy his own fellow traitor to protect himself. He knew if you wiped out Lambert's cell here in England, there'd be no one left to put the finger on him. A traitor who betrays his fellow traitors – nice gentlemen, eh?" He paused. "You look uneasy. What's the matter, don't you enjoy it any more, Zarubin?" Blanchard peered at him curiously.

"I guess I'm tired, sir."

"No, that's not it. You're starting to question things, and that's bad. Perhaps when this is all over, you should go to the Farm. Train some of our new people. Teach them the tricks. Get away from field work."

Zarubin didn't care any longer, so he said it:

"Don't you, sir?"

"What?"

"Don't you ever question things?"

"What's there to question?" replied Blanchard, and Zarubin gave up.

"Would you care for a drink?"

"No thanks. Not at the moment."

"Yes," agreed Blanchard, "maybe it is too early." He gave Zarubin an approving smile. "You must be top of the league by now. I suppose it becomes a way of life after a while."

He cleared his throat, as if apologising for the unfortunate turn of phrase. "You know what I mean."

"Yes," nodded Zarubin, "I know what you mean."

That was when he faced the truth. Sure, at this moment he was tired, but he'd go on working for them, the government,

Blanchard, the CIA, whoever, because they gave him the authority and Blanchard was right, fucking right. Yes, he'd continue being their man, executing at their behest. He had to, now that killing had become a way of life.

He was a soldier, like all of them. They didn't wear uniforms, they didn't have badges, but they obeyed orders and, like soldiers, they had to kill. They didn't enjoy killing, that wasn't the object of the exercise, but it was part of the job. They had taken an oath, as Zarubin had, and he believed in loyalty.

"If there's nothing else, sir," he said, standing up.

Blanchard remained seated.

"I don't think so. You go ahead now. I'll arrange with the Air Force to fly you out the moment you're through here."

Zarubin became aware of a prickling sensation at the base of his neck. It was all so well organised – like catching a train.

"Does he know?"

"Who?"

"Dichter."

Blanchard smiled. "Dichter thinks *you* are the one."

Zarubin stared at him.

"The one who's going to be terminated."

He preferred the London station to be based in the Navy complex, because it gave him easy access to CINCNELM's communications and code facilities. As he'd explained, there'd be a lot of classified transmissions between London and Washington, and he didn't want to overload the State Department's signals room.

He also hinted, much to the chagrin of the embassy, that he thought Navy security was tighter.

So, Dichter's new office overlooked the Roosevelt statue in Grosvenor Square gardens, and gave him a good view of the embassy on the other side.

In his role as station chief, John Dichter had become a very busy man. He'd promised himself that the first thing he'd do was some much needed reorganisation. After all, London was one of the agency's most important sections, the crossroad of the entire European network, and he intended to make full use of the confidential information that crossed his desk.

Already there were dozens of files he needed to read himself into, apart from Flexner's own records. In fact, he had so much work to do, he'd had to send out for a tuna fish rye bread sandwich.

Not that he minded working through his lunch hour. It was worth it, as Langley had proven that very morning in their TWX, confirming Major Ulianov's debriefing was turning out to be an invaluable gold mine of defence information, and Dichter knew Ulianov's capture would be counted as one of his section's best achievements.

There was a knock on the door.

"Yes," sang out Dichter, closing the cover of the report he was reading, a long standing habit with classified material.

"Your sandwiches, sir," said the marine who entered.

"Put them over there."

"Yes sir." The marine placed the wrapped pack on a table in the corner.

"Anything else, sir?"

"No thank you," replied Dichter, mentally noting that in future his secretary would have to remain at her desk when he stayed in. He didn't like people walking into his inner office, and she could damn well eat sandwiches too.

"You sure that's all?" pressed the marine.

And for the first time, Dichter actually took in his face.

"Yes," said Zarubin. "Bad news. I'm still alive."

He locked the office door, then bent down and unplugged the telephone.

"What are you doing? Why are you all dressed up," demanded Dichter, his eyes darting about.

"Well, we don't want to be disturbed, do we?"

"What is all this?"

"I'd have thought you could guess."

Like all the marines in the navy building, he was armed, a pistol in his gun holster.

Dichter played it cool.

"Seeing as you're here, Andy, why don't you make yourself at home. I've been wanting to talk to you . . ."

"I'm sure you have," said Zarubin.

Dichter was wary. "Now, tell me, what *is* going on?"

"It's finished," said Zarubin. He walked over to the window and looked out. "Nice view you've got."

"Talk sense," ordered Dichter, sounding slightly irritable.

"Okay, but it isn't easy." Zarubin paused, then looked Dichter straight in the eye. "I mean, John, how do you tell a man that he isn't going to leave this building alive?"

"Who's not?"

"You." Zarubin leaned against the wall. "You're not going to ever get your pension. Not from Uncle Sam. Not from the Kremlin. Tough luck."

Dichter's hand edged towards his desk drawer. His face was impassive.

"Don't bother," warned Zarubin, the .45 in his hand. "You wouldn't make it."

He sat down in the chair opposite, the pistol pointing casually at Dichter, and glanced at his watch.

"Your secretary's due back quite shortly, so that doesn't give me much time."

"Have you gone off your head?"

"No. Just following Blanchard's orders. I've been working for him the whole time."

"You don't make sense, Andy. What is this?"

"It started way back, didn't it John?" sighed Zarubin. "When you were on the Penkovsky team. One of the groups that regularly debriefed him on his London trips. You and Lambert and Leslie Deveaux, right? The Anglo-American ring."

Dichter stared at him, but said nothing.

"Of course today everybody knows that Deveaux was a traitor all along. From the time he was at Oxford, but they never realised Lambert was his acolyte. Lambert, who's risen so high since then, and they never once guessed that you were part of it. That you were the American connection."

The grey man sat very still. Not a muscle moved in his face.

"Other guys have sold out, I guess. In the old OSS days. And in the Agency. We've got our renegades. But you must have started young, John. Right at the beginning of your career, and nobody even sniffed it. That all this time . . ."

"You're raving," muttered Dichter, his eyes not leaving Zarubin.

"Did it start when you were at college? On the campus? In some professor's study? After Korea? Were you one of the Soviet infiltrators in Langley, Bedell Smith warned about in '52? Or Allen Dulles in '63? Never mind. The three of you, your little group, did a good job. Debriefing Penkovsky for the West, and all the while betraying him to Moscow."

"You *are* crazy."

"And it's caught up with you," continued Zarubin relentlessly. "Old ghosts have a nasty habit of rattling in the closet. People dig things up. Spiridov tried to tip off Flexner to buy his passage. Tried to tip him off about an American traitor, not a British traitor. That had to be stopped. Flexner was burrowing, getting nosier. He had to be stopped. Then you had your great idea. Lambert was doing the dirty work to protect all of you. So why not put the finger on him? You told Blanchard that you suspected Lambert was working for Moscow. Got his authority to send in the firm's exterminator. Wipe the lot out, and give yourself a blue chip pedigree."

"You're a lunatic." Dichter was deathly pale. "It doesn't even make goddamn sense. What would be the point of destroying my own people? Why would I betray my own comrades?"

"You would," said Zarubin. "You reasoned that nobody would ever suspect the man who's unmasked the London ring."

Suddenly, Dichter laughed. "You really believe I'm a communist, Andy?" Despite the tension, he was still laughing. "You seriously think that?"

"No. I don't think you're anything any more. I think, John, you're just a traitor, bent on saving his own neck," replied Zarubin, without heat.

"Now I've heard everything!" declared Dichter bitterly.

"Not quite. You've been using me too, John. To help Moscow infiltrate the ferret hideout in Nevada. You sent me to collect their little gift package. Made me snatch the Russian. Getting me to do it, rigging the whole charade, gave it the Good Housekeeping seal of approval, didn't it? Isn't

313

that what you like calling it? It made the whole bag of tricks kosher, eh?"

"I don't know what you're talking about, really I don't," shrugged Dichter. "But I can see you're sick. You need a psychiatrist."

Zarubin shrugged. "Maybe. But, you made a big mistake, John. You shouldn't have told Blanchard that instead of killing Lambert, I helped him escape. How the hell could you have known about the flight from Heathrow, unless Moscow had told you?"

Dichter slumped, like a chess player who'd fought a hard battle, but realised the tournament was lost.

"You got it all wrong, Andy."

"Don't bother. It's finished."

"It hasn't even started," cried Dichter. "You stupid nut, you're messing up the biggest operation we've ever tackled."

"We?"

"Who else? You've got the whole damn shebang screwed up." He lowered his voice. "I'm going to tell you something you should never know, but I'm going to be straight. There's much more to it than you think."

"You can speak out loud," interrupted Zarubin, coldly. "There's only the two of us here."

"You don't understand," muttered Dichter. "I can't give the exact details, not even to you, but the important thing is that I can work with you, and together . . ."

He licked his lips.

"You and I, we've gone through a lot together, right? You're one of the few men I can trust. Okay, you guessed that there's more to it than you've been told. You're smart, that's why I used you. Now listen, and you must never breathe a word of this outside this room, suppose you and I . . ."

"It's over, John."

They faced each other. Dichter looked older, greyer.

"All right," Dichter nodded at last, like a man who knew the talking was over, "but give me two hours. That's all I need. Two hours to get away."

Then he added the difficult word: "Please."

"Save it," cut in Zarubin, shaking his head sadly.

Dichter laughed, desperately, almost hysterically.

"You're not crazy enough to try anything here. They'll . . ."

"As Blanchard said, it's just the due process of justice," Zarubin said stonily.

A few seconds later, those pedestrians in the immediate vicinity of Grosvenor Square, heard the scream of a man as he fell from an upper floor window of the Navy building into the basement area some seventy feet below.

Dichter was dead long before the ambulance arrived.

Suicide was ruled out by the police; they'd found no note in his office, and they could find no reason for Mr Dichter to take his own life. Further investigations proved to their complete satisfaction that Mr Dichter had been looking out of his office window when, tragically, he lost his balance and fell.

Nobody remembered Dichter ordering sandwiches, or had seen the marine who'd delivered them.

The clerk of Marlborough Street Magistrates court called out the name Andrew Zarubin three times. He was supposed to be present at the adjourned hearing in order to answer the outstanding charges brought against him under the Obscene Publications Act.

The magistrate finally concluded that Mr Zarubin had jumped bail.

"He's probably no longer in this country, sir," pointed out the detective sergeant with the Charlie Chaplin moustache.

The magistrate was not amused. He decreed that Mr Zarubin's £20,000 bail be forfeited, and a warrant issued for his arrest should he ever return to the United Kingdom.

The pity of it was that the gentleman who had posted the bail bond had also apparently disappeared abroad.

Greg Sullivan, the FBI agent with the rank of legal attaché at the United States Embassy, listened quietly to the proceedings, but although Zarubin was described as an American citizen he wasn't particularly perturbed by the news that he'd skipped his bail.

It had seemed such a crazy idea when Yenko had first outlined it to him in his office overlooking Dzerzhinsky Square.

315

"We'll substitute you. We'll smuggle you into England, then when the next ferret comes down, you'll switch with him."

"But how?" he'd gasped.

"You'll find out. We've got friends. Friends in the right places."

Yenko had arranged everything: the journey in the submarine, the rubber dinghy that had taken him ashore, the cottage on the moors where he'd been kept under wraps until it was time for the switch. Then he'd become Major Ulianov, and had waited at the deserted airfield. Waited for the Americans to snatch him.

That was Yenko's dream. To infiltrate a phoney ferret into Camp Delta and then, gradually, cautiously, so that it wouldn't look too easy, begin the big operation.

His purpose was to feed misinformation to the Americans that would make them switch their air defences, screw up the plans of the Aerospace Defense Command, lead them to believe that they were defending the wrong priority targets, that the initial strike would be aimed at the wrong cities.

Before he'd been sent, Yenko had rehearsed him, primed him, tested him. Briefed him on what to say, and how to say it.

"You know," Yenko had said with relish the night before his departure, "the Americans are so insecure, so neurotic they may fall for it."

He hadn't been sure then, but that was because he hadn't really known Yenko.

Not that it had been easy for him to agree to go on this mission. Knowing that it meant vanishing from the face of the earth. Perhaps Yekaterina would never find out why his love making had been so frantic that last night, because he hadn't been allowed to tell even her.

Of course they would look after her, no matter how long it took, and he would be awarded his promotions, his rises in pay and allowances in absentia.

Now, in the loneliest part of Nevada, 6,000 miles from Moscow, Major Ulianov stood on the high ridge at the edge of Loon Valley, looking across at the endless expanse of desert, filled with a sense of triumph.

He had managed it, the mission had been accomplished,

and he wished he could share his jubilation with someone. That was going to be the hardest part, existing at Camp Delta, living the routine of their secret hideaways, not being able to gloat, and mock the Americans.

"The homeland is proud of you. You deserve the gratitude of all its citizens," a Russian voice told him.

Ulianov thought he was hearing things, then he saw the speaker, leaning against the rock behind him, arms folded. His face was familiar.

"You've done a remarkable job, Major Ulianov," went on Zarubin. "Except that you're not Major Ulianov."

He stared at Zarubin quizzically, maintaining his composure. After all, he was word perfect in his role.

Then he broke into a welcoming smile.

"My dear friend," he cried, clasping Zarubin and kissing him on both cheeks. "How good to see you again. I owe you my life. If you had not got me out, I'm sure the British would have killed me."

"I don't think so," murmured Zarubin, watching him intently. "They killed Major Ulianov, of course. That is the real Major Ulianov. But they wouldn't have killed you because they were agents working for your people."

"I don't understand," stuttered the Russian. "What are you saying?"

"What *is* your name?" asked Zarubin. Then he shrugged, "No, naturally, you won't tell me. Anyway, it doesn't really matter, I will give you a name. Let me see, what shall I call you? Yuri? Igor? Leonty? Vasili? Pick one."

"But you know my name," he whispered, a hurt look in his eyes.

"I've got to call you something, so I think Vasili sounds good. That okay with you, Vasili?"

The Russian stiffened as Zarubin put his hand in his pocket. But all he pulled out was a packet of cigarettes, Russian cigarettes.

"Smoke?" offered Zarubin. "No? Pity, I thought you enjoyed these."

He lit himself a cigarette.

"You know something else, Vasili? You're not a major at all. In fact, you're not even an Air Force officer. Sure, you give a pretty good performance. Nice. Electronic warfare expert. It must have taken months of practice to become so word perfect. My guess is you're higher. A lieutenant colonel, perhaps, in Department A – Dezinformatsiya. Correct? You slipped up a little," Zarubin continued, chattily. "Like when I rescued you from that airfield, you still had your Russian watch. You didn't know that the real Major Ulianov had given his away. Silly that."

"So?" shrugged the Russian. "I got another watch. What does that prove?"

"Nothing," agreed Zarubin, his smile tigerish. "But then, you see, Vasili, I don't need proof. You've got a department that doesn't either, and so have we. One way and another, we've got a lot in common, you and me."

Zarubin dragged on his cigarette.

"Yes, all we need is to be convinced. Proof is irrelevant. That's why we both have sections that take direct action. You follow me? We can't be bothered with the complicated business of arrests and hearings and enquiries and newspaper talk. We can't be bothered, because there are things that people mustn't know." He threw the cigarette away. "Like how often they are betrayed, for instance. It frightens the public."

Cautiously, the Russian moved nearer to Zarubin.

"Don't think of it," said Zarubin, shaking his head. "Don't even consider it because you'd be dead."

"You're going to kill me anyway," the Russian pointed out gravely. "What does it matter? Perhaps at least I could take you with me."

In the distance, a helicopter buzzed over the desert, and they both looked at it.

"No, Vasili," Zarubin said, "you're wrong. I'm not going to kill you, and you're not going to kill me. You're not even going to see me again. You'll go back to the camp, and you'll rot there, just like the others. None of you exist. You're there for life. Perhaps, one day, you'll get reprieved, when the big boys get together at Geneva or some such place, but until they do, you and your tovariches are stuck here in the desert."

The Russian swallowed, hard.

"I'm not an airman like the others, I deserve special consideration."

The helicopter was coming nearer, hovering over the ridge, then swinging out into the desert again.

"He's just keeping an eye on us," explained Zarubin amiably. "Come, comrade. Let's go back."

The Russian didn't move.

"If you don't go back," pointed out Zarubin, "they'll come and get you."

The man hesitated, then started down the rocky trail that led below, Zarubin following him. Once he stopped, and glanced over his shoulder.

"Relax," said Zarubin.

When they got back to the camp, the Russian turned and faced Zarubin.

"What now?"

"You rot."

They stared at each other for some moments, a look of hatred in the Russian's eyes.

"You see, Vasili," sighed Zarubin, "it's our move now. If something did happen to you, they'd find out sooner or later, and that would make them realise the whole operation had been blown, that we knew you'd been planted to give us a bucketful of misinformation. But this way, we've got all the time in the world and they'll never be sure. Your friends might even believe that we've fallen for it, that we are re-organising our defences, protecting the wrong cities, not guarding the real targets."

"They'll find out, believe me," snarled the Russian.

"Perhaps they will, one day, but you won't be telling them, comrade," Zarubin nodded. "No, if they want to make sure, they're going to have to risk a lot, jeopardise other networks, hazard good agents, just to discover at the end of the day, that we weren't fooled, not one little bit."

He shook his head.

"It's going to be a hell of a waste, Vasili, and we'll take out a lot of their talent."

"I hope . . ." whispered the Russian.

"You hope?"

"I hope that one day we will have you in our hands, my friend."

Slowly, Zarubin walked towards the helicopter pad where the chopper was waiting. He'd had enough of the ferrets' nest.

He called her from a pay phone on East 42nd Street, and she answered after a couple of rings.

"Hi, Sara."

"Who's that?" she asked, puzzled.

"It's me. Remember, Andy Zarubin?"

There was a pause.

"Andy, dear God!" she gasped at last. "It's been so long, I thought you must be dead."

Zarubin laughed softly.

"Oh, no," he chuckled. "I'm still alive and kicking. It's not my turn to die, yet."

But the smile vanished when he hung up.

Andrew Zarubin didn't feel a sense of triumph that, once again, he'd survived.